HIS LIPS BRUSHED HERS LIKE A WHISPER...

Danielle felt the flutter of his mask against her cheek, the throbbing of her heart against his own. He had kissed her! Reverently, she ran her tongue over her lips to savor the moment. Never in all her wildest dreams had she imagined a kiss could be so wonderful. And it had been tender, loving, almost as if . . . as if he cared deeply for her.

Tentatively at first, but then with more determination, she kissed him back, relying purely on instinct to guide her. Her hands clutched his powerful biceps. The sweetness of his kiss sang through her veins, burying deep within her heart, and Danielle was lifted to another dimension where only she and "the Phantom" existed, and nothing else mattered but this moment in time.

* * *

Harper
Monogram

PHANTOM LOVER

MILLIE CRISWELL

HarperPaperbacks
A Division of HarperCollinsPublishers

This is a work of fiction. The characters, incidents, and dialogues are products of the author's imagination and are not to be construed as real. Any resemblance to actual events or persons, living or dead, is entirely coincidental.

HarperPaperbacks   *A Division of* HarperCollins*Publishers*
10 East 53rd Street, New York, N.Y. 10022

Cover illustration by Jean Monti

First printing: May 1993

Printed in the United States of America

HarperPaperbacks, HarperMonogram, and colophon are trademarks of HarperCollins*Publishers*

❖ 10 9 8 7 6 5 4 3 2 1

This book is dedicated to:

My agent, Adele Leone, who recognized a *Scarlet Pimpernel* and knew what to do with it. And who just happens to be one of the nicest, most caring, ladies in this business.

My editor, Karen Solem, who introduced me to the finer points of editing and taught me that although revisions are painful, they are also rewarding.

And as always,

My husband, Larry, whose love and support is a constant in an ever-changing world.

1

January 1781
Off the coast of New York

"Sail ho!"

Heeding the warning cry of the watchkeeper perched high above in the mainmast platform, Captain Andrew Ellsworth of His Majesty's Royal Navy put spyglass to eye and stared anxiously out at the horizon.

The darkened sky was blanketed by a thick layer of fog; he could see nothing—not the whitecaps that slapped lazily against the hull of the ship, nor the sea gull who raucously touted his existence—and his voice registered annoyance when he barked at his first lieutenant standing at his right shoulder.

"Moorman is hallucinating. I see naught but this wretched mist that enshrouds us like a gauzy veil."

Simon Pettigrew took the spyglass thrust at him and surveyed the waters. "Aye, Captain, it would seem Moorman is a touch jumpy. I see nothing resembling a sail. Perhaps our last encounter with that black ship from hell is still fresh on his mind."

The Phantom. Or so the crew had called the ship and its captain after their last encounter a fortnight ago. Ellsworth's mouth slashed thin across his boyish face. The elusive privateer was proving to be the bane of his, and the Royal Navy's, existence.

The Phantom had captured six of His Majesty's finest merchantmen in the last twelve months, stealing valuable cargo to supply the rebellious miscreants who called themselves patriots.

Traitors! The lot of them. And none more so than the Phantom, who had very nearly destroyed Ellsworth's own frigate, *Orion,* during a surprise attack some weeks ago. The fledgling American navy was more of a bother than a threat to Britain's far superior naval forces, but these men who sailed under letters of marque and called themselves privateers were wreaking havoc on supply ships and unsuspecting naval vessels.

"Sail ho! Sail ho!" echoed Moorman's anguished cry, followed by the sharp roar of cannon exploding across the *Orion*'s bow, reverberating over the water, its deadly projectile narrowly missing its mark.

"All hands! All hands!" Captain Ellsworth shouted, grabbing the spyglass once more. But there was no need.

Like a black-winged specter, the sleek schooner was upon them, laying another volley across the *Orion*'s bow before the able-bodied British sailors could effectively man their stations.

"Strike your colors, *Orion.* Or I shall be forced to aim true and destroy you."

The voice rang out against the darkness, but Ellsworth did not need to see from whence it came. 'Twas the voice of the Phantom, ever etched in his memory.

The fog, lifted by a sudden gale of wind, dispersed as quickly as it had come. The large black canvas sails flapped loudly, mockingly in the wind, as if to applaud themselves on such an easy victory.

Silhouetted against them stood a man, his feet braced apart, hands splayed on lean hips. Like his ship, he was covered all in black, from the skintight breeches that housed his muscular legs, pouring into knee-high black leather boots, to the black silk blouson that billowed about the solid walls of his chest and back. He wore a black silk mask that obscured the upper portion of his face. Only his eyes, which were the deepest of blues, and his mouth, which was slanted in a mocking smile, were visible.

"'Tis an apparition!" a frightened sailor murmured as he stared into the darkness, his sentiment chorused by excited comments and whispers.

"What say you, *Orion*? Do you strike your colors and surrender? Or do you wish to be commended for all eternity into the bottom of the sea? The choice is yours."

The acrid smell of sulfur lingered in the air, a humiliating reminder of Andrew Ellsworth's defeat. His aristocratic features hardened. The nostrils of his long aquiline nose flared slightly, while his eyes, as copper-colored as his hair, narrowed menacingly. Balling his fists, he stood rigidly erect, as was expected of a proper British naval officer, and turned to address his first lieutenant.

"Strike the colors. Raise the white flag of surrender." The words, like bile, rose bitter in his throat.

"But, Captain," Simon protested, his face registering surprise, "we shall be dishonored if we don't put up a fight."

Ellsworth looked incredulous. "Would you have me risk the lives of three hundred men to satisfy your honor, Pettigrew? Do as you're ordered and be quick about it. I have no wish to die this day."

The orders were quickly given. The Union Jack was lowered from the masthead and the white flag of surrender raised in its place.

"I commend your good sense, Captain Ellsworth," came the taunting remark from across the water. "How fortunate that we are able to meet again so soon."

Immediately the grappling hooks were affixed and the Phantom's schooner lay abreast of the British frigate. With the surefootedness of catamounts, the men of the black ship, armed with swords and muskets, their heads covered by black silk hoods, dropped gracefully atop the main deck of the enemy ship. Chaos and confusion abounded as the crew of the *Orion* scrambled to heed the commands of the American privateers. Ellsworth and his first lieutenant had already descended the quarterdeck and now stood waiting to be taken prisoner.

Ellsworth eyed the privateer with loathing, studying every detail, committing them to memory. The man's hair was blond and hung down his back in a queue. His blue eyes were cold and fathomless as the depths of the ocean, his chin strongly chiseled. And his lips, which were turned into a mocking semblance of a smile, were full and rounded over even, white teeth.

"Your scrutiny flatters me, Captain. I hope you find me to your liking."

The Phantom's comment produced a chorus of snorts and snickers from his cohorts and brought a crimson stain to the British captain's cheeks. He stiffened and in clipped, nasal tones pronounced, "Nothing about you is to my liking, sir. I demand to know by whose authority you have fired upon my ship and boarded."

With lightning-quick speed, the Phantom pulled his rapier from its sheath, pressing it against the captain's throat. "By this authority, Captain Ellsworth. Perhaps you are unaware, but your country and mine are at war. And there is also the matter of the brigantine *Lady Liberty.*"

The light of recognition entered Ellsworth's eyes, and he paled.

"Oh, so you do remember the *Lady Liberty?* And do you also remember the thirty-six men who died? The men you cast adrift at sea, left to sink to the bottom of the ocean like so much unnecessary ballast. There were no prisoners taken, Captain Ellsworth. You made certain that your victory was complete."

"They were the enemy. I had no idea that storm would materialize out of nowhere."

"Come, come, Captain. You can do better than that. An experienced sailor such as yourself cannot predict a storm?" His voice thickened with hatred. "Your reputation for cruelty precedes you, Ellsworth, and it sickens me. The time for retribution is at hand."

"Your allegiance is twisted, man. You are Englishmen. Even your speech supports that truth."

The blue eyes hardened. "Don't insult me with your pitiful rhetoric that we are all Englishmen. England might have been the country of my birth, but America holds my allegiance now."

"You are all traitors! You'll be hunted down like the criminals you are and hung for your deeds against the crown."

With his sword, the Phantom flicked the top two brass buttons off of Ellsworth's blue uniform jacket, his lips twisting into a sneer. "And who, pray tell, is going to hunt us? Not you, I fear, Ellsworth.

"Ian," the Phantom ordered the first mate who stood behind him, "tell the men to lower the long-boats. I want all of the sailors, save for the good captain here, placed aboard them. You, too, lieutenant," the Phantom added, addressing white-faced Simon Pettigrew, whose thirst for victory had suddenly been quenched by the blade of a sword. "Then make a thorough inspection of the hold. I'm sure we'll find many useful items there."

"It's as good as done, laddie," the older man replied in a thick Scottish accent, turning to give the order.

"If you're meaning to kill me, why not be done with it?" Ellsworth asked.

Slicing the remaining buttons off of the captain's jacket with a flick of his wrist, the Phantom replied, "For a proper man of noble birth like you, Ellsworth, the punishment should be suitable. Killing you is much too easy. I can see by your startled expression you are surprised that I know so much about you. You shouldn't be. I always make it my business to know my enemy."

After the men of the *Orion* were secured in the longboats with orders to row in the opposite direction of shore, the Phantom came within arm's length of Ellsworth, ordering him to strip.

Shock registered on the captain's face. "You must be insane. It's January, the temperature way below freezing. I'll catch my death." Hearing the laughter of the enemy sailors, shock yielded quickly to outrage. "Have you no honor? I demand to be treated with the respect that is accorded my rank."

Throwing his head back, the Phantom laughed derisively before saying, his voice suddenly hard, "You British noblemen are all alike, aren't you, Ellsworth? You speak so freely of honor and duty, as if you were the only ones embodied with it." He took a step closer, grabbing Ellsworth by his uniform jacket. "Perhaps I should put you out of your misery, Captain. The world would be a far better place with one less nobleman to inhabit it."

Suddenly, Ellsworth's hands came up, his fingers curling like claws as he grabbed at his captor's mask.

"Laddie, watch out!" Ian cried, watching in horror as the British captain snatched the mask off the Phantom's face.

His reflexes honed by years of battle, the Phantom swiveled abruptly, refastening the piece of black silk before turning back to address Ellsworth. An intense rage infused the lower half of his face, turning the deeply tanned skin almost purple.

"Withers, Michaels, help the good captain here with his clothing," he ordered the two crewmen who had rushed forward to assist. "Once he's stripped, tie him to the mizzenmast. We don't want any of his countrymen to miss his grand entrance back to naval headquarters."

"Aye, aye, Captain," they responded in unison, saluting smartly before grabbing hold of a now pale Andrew Ellsworth and divesting him of his uniform. Once that was completed, they bound him to the mast with heavy lengths of rope.

"Tsk, tsk," the Phantom said, eyeing the naked body of the British officer with disdain as he focused in on his manly attributes. "You don't look so terribly noble now, Ellsworth. 'Twould seem a man of your exalted stature could unfurl his sail better than that." His ribald remark brought a chorus of jeers and comments from his men.

Rancor darkened the copper-colored eyes, making them appear almost black. His voice shook with suppressed fury when he threatened the Phantom. "I'll kill you for this, you filthy pirate. I know what you look like. I'll hunt you down and kill you if it's the last thing I do. You'd best kill me now, or you'll be forever looking over your shoulder."

The Phantom shook his head. "Your pitiful threats are duly noted, Ellsworth. But you must remember, I've already seen your abilities in battle, and your weapons are less than . . . shall we say . . . menacing." He grinned at the rage on the nobleman's face.

"Set the *Orion* on course for New York Harbor, Ian. We'll follow close behind to make sure the good captain here is delivered safely to his *temporary* home."

There was little danger that Ellsworth would suffer unduly on the short trip back to British naval headquarters. They were only a few miles out, and contrary to Ellsworth's hysterics, there was no frigid bite to the air. Quite the contrary, the temperature was relatively mild for this time of year, the sea calm.

Ellsworth and his men would survive the elements. But there was a distinct possibility that Ellsworth might very well die of humiliation.

Approaching the ship's railing, the Phantom paused, then turned, saying, "It's been a pleasure,

Captain. Enjoy your trip back to headquarters," before bowing deeply and disappearing over the side of the ship.

Ellsworth's face contorted into a hideous mask of hatred. "I'll kill you for this! I swear it on my mother's grave! As God is my witness, I'll kill you."

January 1781
York Town, Virginia

The black-hulled schooner, sporting pristine white sails, snaked smoothly up the York River toward its destination of York Town. Along both shores of the river, beech, oak, and pine trees stood in thick profusion while gnarled vines twisted around their trunks like serpentine fingers.

Standing on the quarterdeck, the captain chatted companionably with his first mate, ignoring the biting wind that gently ruffled his blond hair and billowed the lace at his sleeves.

"'Tis good to be home, Ian. The sight of this harbor never fails to warm my soul."

The little Scotsman smiled, his gold-capped tooth glittering brightly in the early morning sunshine. The glowing orange ball overhead belied the still freezing temperature of winter, and he turned up the collar of his heavy wool pea jacket to ward off the chill.

"Aye, laddie. I canna deny I'm happy tae be home. These bones o'mine are growing more brittle wie each passin' year."

Throwing his arm around the older man's bony shoulders, Phillip Cameron smiled, his blue eyes twinkling. For as long as he could remember, Ian

MacGregor had made the same speech each time they sailed into port after one of their runs.

"'Twas worth a few brittle bones to capture the *Orion*," Phillip replied, thinking of the added bonus they'd found in the ship's hold. Guns, ammunition, blankets, and other supplies intended for British troops headquartered in New York had been discovered and were now in the capable hands of General Washington and the Continental army, who were presently encamped at their winter quarters in Morristown, New Jersey.

Reflecting on General Washington's situation brought a frown to Phillip's lips. The provisions they'd brought had been sorely needed and gratefully received. The half-clad American army looked frozen, their provisions of salt beef and rice hardly enough to sustain them in the bitter cold and deep snow of the north. He had done what he could to alleviate some of the suffering, but it wasn't nearly enough.

Ian's soft chuckle forced Phillip's attention back to the present. "Aye, and enough booty for us tae turn a tidy profit, too," Ian remarked, referring to the additional supplies found deep in the bowels of the British frigate. Besides the munitions, there'd been casks of wine and rum, bolts of fine satins and silks, which would be sold through Phillip's shipping company, the profits split among his crew.

"Profitable indeed, you old sea dog," he concurred with a nod of his head.

"I can see by that smug expression on yer face, laddie, that ye be thinkin' about that Brit captain ye shipped off in disgrace. I wouda given a month's wage to hae seen those proper English bastards when that ship came sailin' into port and he as naked as a willin' French whore."

The grin on Phillip's face deepened, producing two dimples on either side of his cheeks. "'Twas a victory I'll savor for a good long while. I expect poor Captain Ellsworth had a lot of explaining to do. I don't suppose his superiors were too pleased with his performance."

Ian's face suddenly sobered and he clutched Phillip's arm. "He knows wot ye look like, laddie. He's bound tae come lookin' for ye."

"You worry like an old woman, old man. Ellsworth's hundreds of miles away, and he knows not where we've gone."

The graying brows knitted together. "Aye, but I got a feeling in me bones about this one, laddie. The mon be a bad'un. I seen the look in his eyes when we left. It was chillin' I tell ye. We'd best lay low for a while."

"'Tis fine with me. I'm in no rush to set sail again anytime soon. I've neglected my business here in York Town too long as it is." And he knew that if Captain Cameron was looking down from the heavens, he wouldn't be pleased to discover that his shipping enterprise, which had been entrusted to Phillip, was being run aground.

No. The captain had always expected the best of Phillip since taking him aboard his frigate *Falcon*, at the age of six. It was Ian who had rescued the ill-fed, dirty-faced urchin, taking him off the streets of London to be deposited at the feet of merchant sea captain Richard Cameron. But it was Captain Cameron who had seen something salvageable, worthwhile, in the face of the small boy.

Life at sea had been hard on the undisciplined, foulmouthed lad, but the Captain had bestowed patience, wisdom, and most of all love. Like a sponge, Phillip had absorbed all of it and had grown into an able-bodied sailor Richard Cameron had been proud to call son. When Richard died at British hands shortly after the onset of the war, Phillip had been devastated, having lost not only a father, but a true friend.

Captain Cameron's holdings in York Town, his shipping business and his land, had all been bequeathed to Phillip, and Phillip had no intention of letting the captain's faith in him be unfounded.

"Aye, and I've neglected my stomach for too long. I canna wait tae sample another of Mrs. Dunstan's fine meals."

The sound of the anchor being dropped jolted Phillip out of his reverie, and he smiled affectionately at his friend. "Well, then, let's disembark and hie ourselves up the hill. We don't want to keep your stomach waiting any longer than we have to."

The seaport community of York Town was bustling with activity when Phillip made his way down the hill toward the wharves the next morning.

Haggard-looking sailors newly arrived off merchantmen hurried to unload their goods in eager anticipation of the ale that awaited them in the numerous rum shops darting the wharf; and naval officers, splendidly arrayed in dark blue uniforms, waited impatiently while vessels were repaired and their stores replenished.

Several new taverns had opened in his absence, Phillip noted, as well as another ship's chandler, which was sure to provide some needed competition for Thaddeus Taylor's growing concern. Hogsheads of tobacco lined the wharves, as did crates filled with fine china, crystal, and other imported goods.

His own warehouse was filled to bursting, his foreman, Hugh Willis, had complained to him last night; and provision needed to be made to disperse the much-sought-after goods to the other colonies suffering from the war with Great Britain.

At Hugh's request, he had come to inspect the Cameron warehouse and could see upon entering the dimly lit, solid brick building that Hugh's worries were warranted. Row upon row of goods filled the warehouse, and Phillip knew that there was no profit to be made from merchandise that wasn't sold or delivered.

Making his way to the rear of the building, where an office of sorts had been partitioned off in the far right corner, Phillip found Hugh seated at a battered oak desk, his head of curly brown hair bent over a sheaf of papers. He looked up as Phillip approached, relief and concern mingling freely on his face.

"Thank you for coming so quickly, Phillip. As you can see," he indicated the contents of the warehouse with a wave of his hand, "we are inventory rich and profit poor. We need to ship these goods out immediately."

"How many merchantmen do we have in port?" Phillip inquired, realizing the truth of his manager's words.

Hugh shook his head. "None. The *Falcon* left for Boston last week, and Captain Bloodsworth hasn't returned from France yet."

Removing the black tricorn hat from his head and tucking it under his right arm, Phillip brushed impatiently at the unruly lock of hair that had fallen over his brow. "What would you have me do, Hugh? You know my schooner is not equipped to carry such large inventories of merchandise. And besides, she's needed for other, more important duties, at the present time."

"Perhaps your ship could make some short runs while you're home . . . to Savannah or Charleston. At least we could unload some of the more expensive items like the fabric and the—"

Before Hugh could complete his sentence, Ian came running forward, waving a paper frantically over his head, shouting, "Phillip! Phillip!"

Phillip shook his head and smiled. "What is it, old man? You're as red in the face as Fat Annie after she's tumbled a half-dozen sailors."

Ian pulled up short and took a moment to catch his breath, ignoring both men's chuckles. "'Tisna funny and ye willna be laughing when ye see wot I got here, laddie. I was afraid something like this would happen."

Taking the Loyalist newspaper *The Royal Gazette* from Ian's outstretched hands, Phillip quickly perused the pages, his face paling slightly at the notice that appeared on the inside front page. There in black and white was a likeness of himself with the caption in bold letters, "Wanted for Crimes Against His Majesty George III: The Phantom. Reward of Two Hundred Pounds for His Capture, Dead or Alive."

"I see ye ain't smilin' now, laddie."

Hugh rose from the desk and glanced over Phillip's broad shoulder, gasping aloud. He pushed his spectacles, which had slipped slightly, back up onto the bridge of his nose, asking, "What does this mean,

Phillip?"

The loyalist faction in York Town was strong, as it was in nearby Williamsburg. Many did not desire a break with the mother country and had voiced their support for England and King George. Spies were everywhere, and Phillip couldn't take the chance that one of them would see this paper and connect him to the Phantom.

After a moment, he replied, "It means we've outstayed our welcome here in York Town. We'll have to set sail in the morning. I can't afford to have any Tory sympathizers put two and two together and come up with me as the Phantom."

"But where will you go? What will you do?" Hugh queried. "Surely, your likeness will be in other Loyalist newspapers across Virginia."

"Hugh's right," Ian observed. "Yer face will be easily recognized once this missive circulates."

Phillip took a moment to contemplate the situation, then replied, "We'll sail up to Fredericksburg. I'm not well known there. And they don't have a newspaper as yet."

A calculating gleam entered the old Scotsman's eyes. "Aye," he said, nodding in agreement. "Fredericksburg might just be the ticket. 'Tis a thriving seaport town, much like this one. The Rappahannock River will give easy access for the Phantom's secret activities. But we canna take a chance that ye'll be recognized by someone who has already seen this piece of Loyalist trash."

Phillip's voice filled with impatience. "I can hardly stay in hiding, Ian. We've got important work to do."

Ignoring his captain's protest, Ian turned toward Hugh. "Wot kind of clothing do ye have in these crates? I'm in need of fancy gentlemen frocks in satins and brocades. And a wig . . . long . . . white . . . with sausage rolls, I'm thinking."

"Have you gone daft, old man? Here we are discussing our departure for Fredericksburg and you're contemplating a new wardrobe. And a vulgar one by the sounds of it."

Riffling through the crate that Hugh indicated, Ian produced the most garish red brocade waistcoat and matching frock coat that Phillip had ever seen. He screwed up his face in disgust. He much preferred the somber hues of gray and black that his own wardrobe sported than the flamboyant colors many of his peers were so fond of wearing.

"By God, you have gone mad! Who would wear such a hideous outfit?"

Ian chuckled, thrusting the garment into Phillip's hands. "Ye will, laddie. Ye will."

2

February 1781
Fredericksburg, Virginia

"Wench! Bring me another pint of ale and be quick about it."

Danielle Sheridan's eyes narrowed as she recognized the very obese and very drunk form of Thomas Morton, a frequent patron of her father's tavern, the Golden Pineapple.

She had waited on him, and many others just like him, numerous times during the past three years, since she'd turned seventeen and her mother had deemed her of an age to start working the common room.

God, how she hated it! Hated the fetid smells of unwashed bodies and stale tobacco—hated the groping hands when her father's back was turned—the leering looks that said, more plainly than words, what these men thought of her. But she could hardly fault them for that, for no lady of quality or decent reputation ever frequented a tavern, unless circumstances were such that it was totally unavoidable.

And even in a proper tavern, such as theirs, where gentlemen of refinement were served separately in the great room on fine china and crystal, it was still highly improper for a female of any age to be found under its roof.

She might as well have been an indentured servant like her best friend Lottie O'Flynn, for all the good it had done her to be the daughter of tavern keepers. At least after four years, an indentured servant was free to pursue his or her own life. Lottie had only three more months of servitude to Elsie and Luther Sheridan, then she'd be free. Free of eighteen-hour days, of escorting drunks to their pallets, of scrubbing, toting, and all the other endless tasks that were part of a tavern wench's day.

Free. Just the word gave Danielle pause. To be free of her life of drudgery, of her parents' verbal abuse . . .

"Danielle!" Her mother's sharpened tongue lashed out at her, and she caught her angry gaze across the room. "Fetch Mr. Morton his ale, and be quick about it. Have you gone deaf, girl?"

No. But she soon would, if her mother didn't desist in her caterwauling. Her father always said Elsie could wake the dead with her high-pitched shriek. Danielle didn't doubt it for a moment.

Removing the pewter tankard of ale from the caged bar, she presented it to Thomas Morton, stifling the very great urge to pour the cold liquid over his bald pate.

"'Tis about time, wench," the disgruntled customer babbled before taking a swig of the brew and wiping his mouth on the edge of his dirty coat sleeve.

"A man could die of thirst waiting for you to serve him."

If she thought that eventuality might come to pass, she'd be a lot slower the next time, Danielle thought, placing a fresh wheel of cheese and a plate of sliced apples on the table in front of him. She wiped her hands on her apron and turned to leave but was halted in her tracks by the conversation of the two sailors seated at the card table in the corner.

"I hear tell the British got a reward out for that pirate they're calling the Phantom."

Danielle's ears perked up and she edged closer, pretending to tidy up the table next to them.

The dark-haired sailor with the gap-toothed smile nodded. "Two hundred pounds I hear. But they won't catch 'em. He's like the night wind—coming up when you'd least expect it, then fading away like a whisper."

Noting that the common room was starting to thin out a bit, owing to the lateness of the evening, Danielle edged her way toward the door leading to the back hallway. Once there, she grabbed her red woolen cloak off the peg, eased open the heavy oak door, and slipped out the back of the tavern unnoticed.

Taking the narrow, oyster shell-lined path leading down to the river, she paused by the water's edge, perching herself on a fallen log that had become her refuge these past three years. Shivering within the confines of her cloak against the chill of the winter evening, she wrapped her arms tight about her and stared out at the murky water.

There was a full moon tonight, and she loved to watch the gentle current of the river as it glided by on its way to the Chesapeake Bay. It was blessedly quiet near the river, though she could still discern the raucous merrymaking of the sailors who frequented the taverns and rum shops along the wharf, and the creaks and groans of the ships straining against their ropes that were tied up to the dock.

The wind whistled softly, bringing to mind the conversation she had just overheard about the Phantom. He was a true hero in these troubled times, much like Robin Hood or General George Washington. And now there was a price on his head—two hundred pounds—a goodly sum to tempt even the staunchest of patriots. But they would never catch him.

She knew of his bravery and cunning firsthand, for he had risked his life two years ago to save her and her family.

They'd been visiting Aunt Elizabeth, her mother's sister, who resided in Charleston. The trip had been a rare treat, for the Sheridans never ventured far from their establishment in Fredericksburg. But Elizabeth's health was failing, and Elsie Sheridan's constant tears had finally moved her father to relent to the visit.

They'd gone by ship, her father deciding to stock up on supplies while in the seaport community of Charleston, so the trip wouldn't be "a complete waste of time and money," as he so aptly put it on several occasions.

On the return voyage, a short distance off the Carolina coast, their merchantman had been attacked by a British frigate attempting to blockade the Port of Charleston.

Like a black bird of prey, the Phantom had arrived out of nowhere to swoop down on the enemy vessel and dispose of him in short order.

Danielle had caught her first glimpse of the Phantom when he'd boarded their vessel to check on the safety of the passengers. His blond hair had glittered like gold in the morning sunlight; his blue eyes, just barely visible through his black mask, were kind and caring. It had been the briefest of encounters, but one that Danielle would never forget.

She heaved a sigh, hating to admit that her mother was right. For it was Elsie's firm belief that blond hair and blue eyes were the mark of perfection. Of course, her mother hadn't been referring to the Phantom when she'd made her prejudiced statement, but to her sister, Regina, whose golden curls and white porcelain skin were prized by Elsie.

Her mother's opinion of her own tawny complexion and dark hair was not quite as flattering.

"You'll never catch a man, Danielle," her mother had taunted. "Not with that black hair that hangs about your waist like a witch, and those strange violet eyes. Pity you don't possess Regina's attributes. She's by far what gentlemen of consequence are looking for in a wife."

Well, Regina could have all those so-called gentlemen, Danielle thought, tossing a handful of pebbles into the water, watching the swirls they created. She had no use for fops and dandies. She wanted a real man. A man who would sweep her off her feet, rescue her from her life of travail. A man who didn't need to hide behind bright colors and pretty phrases.

A man like the Phantom.

At the moment Danielle was dreaming about the Phantom, he was sequestered aboard his ship, anchored off the town of Port Royal about thirty miles southeast of Fredericksburg, and hiding behind those very bright colors that she absolutely abhorred.

"I tell you, Ian, I am not going to wear these hideous garments." He wrinkled his nose in disgust as he looked at his reflection in the looking glass. The red brocade waistcoat was gaudy enough, but the red satin frock coat was downright ostentatious. "They make me look like some overripe tomato."

"Better tae look like a tomato than tae hang from a gibbet like a side o'beef," Ian countered. "Besides," he added, noting Phillip's fierce frown, "'Tis the fashion of the day."

Throwing the hated red coat on the bed, Phillip removed the waistcoat and cravat until only the white ruffled shirt and his own buff-colored breeches remained. "Your idea is insane. It will never work. Even with the clothes, I still look like me. No one will be fooled for a moment."

Crossing the cabin, Ian pulled open the door, shouting for the cabin boy. A moment later, a lanky blond lad of about thirteen entered, carrying a small leather sea chest.

"Set it there by the bed, Tim, me lad," Ian directed. "And fetch us a bottle o' brandy. I'm thinkin' the captain's going to be needin' a shot of something strong."

Timothy Luck smiled, returning the first mate's broad wink with one of his own before dropping the chest on the floor and departing.

Plopping down on the bunk, Phillip rested his head in his hands, a discouraged look on his face.

"Dinna be lookin' so down in the mouth, laddie. Ian's thought of everything, ye'll see."

Phillip's expression was clearly skeptical as Ian

opened the trunk and reached in, producing a white powdered wig and an ebony cane. He fought the urge to groan.

"These will be complementing your finery, as well as this." He dropped a monocle into Phillip's palm. "All fashionable men wear one, I'm told."

Indignation sparked the blue eyes. "I consider myself to be quite up on fashion, old man, and I don't wear one, nor any of these other repulsive accouterments you've purloined from Hugh."

Undaunted by Phillip's irascible attitude, Ian reached deeper into the trunk, retrieving a wad of cotton batting. "This be the truly brilliant part of my plan, laddie."

Phillip's eyebrows drew together in confusion; he shook his head. "I fail to see what a few pieces of cotton have to do with any of this."

"Stand up, boy, and take down yer breeches."

"I beg your pardon!"

Ian chuckled. "Dinna get missish on me, lad. Just do as I say."

Casting Ian a thoroughly disgusted look, Phillip complied, watching with interest as his first mate proceeded to wrap the cotton batting about his midsection. After he was finished, Ian crossed his arms over his chest and smiled smugly, instructing Phillip to refasten his breeches and walk to the looking glass.

Phillip stared at his reflection with something akin to amazement, then smiled. The cotton batting had added the appearance of extra weight to his stomach, making him look heavier than he actually was. "You're a clever old man. I'll say that for you."

"Once we get that batting sewn into a set of yer

small clothes, it'll be an easy matter for ye tae assume the disguise of an overweight gentleman. No one would think tae connect ye wie the Phantom."

Perhaps Ian's plan did have some merit, but as Phillip sat contemplating the less desirable aspects of it later that night, while sipping thoughtfully on a brandy, he wasn't so sure that he wanted any part of it.

With his booted feet propped up on the mahogany desk in front of him, Phillip watched the lantern, suspended from a hook on the cabin wall, sway gently with the rocking motion of the ship, and was reminded that he would have to find a suitable hiding place for his schooner and crew. Port Royal boasted many fine taverns, so the latter would be no problem. But the ship? 'Twould not be an easy matter to hide a ship of such size and distinction.

Heaving a deep sigh, he took a swallow of the brandy, welcoming the fiery liquid into his belly. How long, he wondered, would he have to perpetrate this ruse? How long would it take him to establish a new identity in the town of Fredericksburg?

They'd already come up with a name for him: James Ashland III. James was his middle name— Ashland, supposedly his noble father's. Bitter bile rose to his throat and he washed it away with the remainder of his brandy.

Pouring himself another, he gazed at the amber liquid and thought of his mother, whose hair closely resembled the color of the liquor. Brandy, the gentlemen had called her when they came to seek their pleasure.

Gentlemen who were hardly gentle. Noblemen who were anything but noble.

Whenever he had doubts or misgivings about his

role in this conflict to free these American colonies from those *noble* bastards, he had only to think of Sarah James, his beautiful mother, castoff of Clinton Ashland, the duke of Southerly, who, upon finding his mistress pregnant, had swept her aside like yesterday's rubbish.

If he closed his eyes, he could still smell the scent of lavender that clung to her dresses, recall the feel of her arms as they hugged him to her bosom, hear her gentle laughter, her words of love and affection.

And so, he would play the role of James Ashland III and the Phantom, if he must. For to free oneself of oppression and tyranny was worth any amount of suffering one might have to endure.

"'Tis a fine day for a meetin', lovey," Lottie O'Flynn declared to Danielle as the two women strolled companionably down Princess Anne Street toward their destination of Saint George's Church. The monthly meeting of the Daughters of Liberty would convene in fifteen minutes and they quickened their steps so as not to be late.

Harriet Coombs, the self-appointed leader of the local charitable organization, frowned on tardiness, and Danielle and Lottie could not afford to incur the older woman's wrath.

The Fredericksburg chapter of the Daughters of Liberty had been Harriet's brainchild. Modeled after the Sons of Liberty, its Boston male counterpart, the group met the first Monday of every month to sew clothing, knit socks, roll bandages, and discuss the events of the current conflict with England.

The role they played in the Revolution was small, but each of them, in their own small way, was aiding America in her fight for freedom.

Sighting the cream-colored, wooden building up ahead, Lottie yanked impatiently on Danielle's hand. "Hurry, Danny, or we'll be late for sure. That old windbag, Coombs, gave us what-for last time we was late."

Danielle sighed, thinking that if her mother hadn't been so stingy with their time off, they wouldn't have reason to be late. But the beds needed stripping and the quilts needed airing, and Elsie Sheridan was not about to let Danielle and Lottie leave until they'd completed the necessary chores.

Of course, if it had been Regina who had needed the time off for one of her frivolous outings, that would have been a different story. Her mother indulged her younger sister, never gainsaying Regina anything, a fact that grew more impossible to deal with as her sister matured. Danielle shuddered to think what a few more years of "indulgence" would do to Regina's character.

At eighteen, Regina was selfish, willful, and horribly preoccupied with herself. She would have given no more thought to participating in rolling bandages for the hospital than she would to laundering her own garments.

Danielle had no more time to ponder her sister's shortcomings, for they had reached the vestibule of the church just as the tall case clock in the corner chimed two.

"Whew!" Lottie exclaimed, pausing to catch her breath. "I'm sweatin' like a pig in a summer's drought." She waved her fingers in front of her face in an attempt to cool off.

Danielle smiled at her friend's antics. Lottie's plump proportions most certainly contributed to her fatigue. But since Lottie's heart was as big as her bottom, Danielle was not about to counsel her friend on her overweight condition.

The meeting had just been brought to order when Danielle and Lottie entered the chapel, seating themselves, as unobtrusively as possible, on one of the wooden benches at the back of the room. Unfortunately, their entrance did not go unnoticed.

"I see you girls have finally managed to make one of our meetings on time for a change," Harriet Coombs remarked sarcastically, causing the rest of the group to turn their heads and stare directly at Danielle and Lottie.

Feeling Lottie stiffen beside her, Danielle caught the young woman's expression of mortification out of the corner of her eye. Her freckled face was turning crimson and very nearly matched the color of her hair. Danielle fought the urge to jump up and tell the buck-toothed spinster just what she thought of her. But common sense prevailed and she merely nodded, patting Lottie's hand in a comforting gesture, while turning her attention back to the discussion of General Washington and his troops.

By the time they left the meeting, the bright sun of the morning had been replaced by heavy gray clouds. Walking briskly to ward off the chill, the girls hurried in the direction of the tavern.

"'Tis a shame, to be sure, about the general and those poor unfortunate lads stuck up there in the snows of New Jersey," Lottie said, a short time later.

"I wish there was more we could do to help them."

Danielle listened to her friend and frowned. She'd thought the same thing when Harriet related the gruesome details of the Continental army's horrendous living conditions.

It was bad enough that they'd had to endure similar circumstances at Valley Forge back in '78, and now history was repeating itself once more in Morristown, New Jersey. As before, food was lacking, shelter was all but nonexistent, clothing bordered on indecent, and their pay was in arrears.

The men were starving; many had already died of hunger or frozen to death in the six-foot snows. And the Congress had done next to nothing to help them. It was a highly deplorable situation.

The wind began to blow harder, and Danielle was certain they'd have some rain or snow before nightfall. Wrapping her cloak tight about her as they walked down Sophia Street, Danielle finally replied, "It's why we need privateers who help bring supplies to those poor unfortunates."

"You're not going to start talking about that Phantom again, are you? I swear you've gone soft-headed on him, Danny. And he, most likely, only a figment of your imagination."

Danielle was not offended by Lottie's lack of belief in the Phantom, for there were few things Lottie believed in anymore. Lottie was a realist. On her own since the age of fifteen, she'd lost her dreams and illusions early on, but she'd managed to retain her good spirits and generous nature. Danielle loved her like a sister.

Patiently, Danielle explained, "He's as real as you or me, Lottie. I've heard tales of his exploits and there's none that can touch him when it comes to bravery or cunning. I know that firsthand. If any man can help the general, it would be the Phantom."

Lottie shook her head. "Danny, are you sure you haven't made this Phantom out to be more than he really is? There's no such thing as a knight in shining armor, girl. That's just fairy tales, like me blessed mother used to tell me when I was a wee girl. There's no one goin' to come rescue you, Danny. A girl's only got herself to look to. Men take, women give. 'Tis the way of things, love."

Danielle's sigh was audible. "Just because Sean O'Toole left you high and dry in Bristol, does not mean that good men don't exist. Someday you'll meet one that will set your heart aflutter. Mark my words."

Lottie could think of no rejoinder for that remark, so they continued the rest of the way in silence, trying to avoid the horse droppings and puddles of muck that dotted Sophia Street.

Lifting the hem of her cloak, Danielle attempted to maneuver around a rooting pig and failed to see the coach and four that had pulled up in front of the tavern.

"Will you look at that!" Lottie remarked, tugging on Danielle's sleeve. "I ain't never seen such a sight in all my born days." Lottie's chuckle turned into a high-pitched giggle.

Danielle glanced up, her eyes widening. Standing before the tavern, dressed in pinkish-purple—a color she'd heard her mother refer to as magenta—satin breeches with matching waistcoat and frock coat was the biggest man she had ever seen. He topped six feet by at least three inches, and his paunch seemed to indicate that he hadn't missed many meals. He had a long white wig fashioned into sausage rolls—which was fitting for someone who looked somewhat like a pig—and carried an ebony walking stick.

"Saints alive! That's by far the ugliest man I ever laid eyes on," Lottie declared. "And I've seen some dandies in my time."

Covering her mouth to suppress the laughter that threatened to spill, Danielle watched as the man stood on the front porch of the tavern and surveyed his surroundings with disdain.

As they drew nearer, she heard him say, "MacGregor, are you certain this establishment is suitable for a man of my standing? I'm quite parched, but I don't wish to mingle with common sorts." He flicked an imaginary speck of dust off his sleeve.

The servant, a short man dressed in black livery, followed the man up the stairs. "Yes, sir, Mr. Ashland. This be a proper tavern. I checked it out myself."

"The short one's kind of cute, don't you think?" Lottie commented, nudging Danielle in the side.

"Ssh! Do you want them to hear us?" Edging toward the side of the porch where they could see but couldn't be seen, Danielle whispered, "I wonder who this Mr. Ashland is. I don't recall having heard the name before."

"Judging by that fine carriage and those matched set of bays, the gentleman's got some wealth."

"Money does not make the man," Danielle stated, watching the two men disappear into the interior of the tavern. Although one would never be able to convince Elsie Sheridan of that fact. She was constantly on the lookout for a suitable gentleman for her precious Regina. It would serve her sister right if she got stuck with the portly Mr. Ashland. That thought brought a smile to Danielle's lips.

"We'd best go in or your mother will flay our hides. It'll be time to serve the evening meal soon."

Realizing the truth of Lottie's words, Danielle made to leave her hiding place but jumped back at the sight of the flamboyant fop and his servant, who were approaching their carriage once again.

"The place isn't fit for dogs, MacGregor. How dare you imply it was suitable for me to take refreshment here! I vow, I've completely lost all interest in libations of any sort."

Danielle watched as the gentleman pressed a lace handkerchief to his nose, as if he couldn't abide the stench of the place. She felt her temper rise at his insulting opinion of her parents' establishment. The Golden Pineapple might not be the nicest, most commodious tavern in Virginia, but it was damned proper!

Turning toward Lottie, Danielle asked, her voice laced with irritation, "Did you hear what that fop said about our tavern? Why, he acted as if it was no better than a horse barn."

Lottie almost laughed at the indignation displayed on Danielle's face, for the gentleman's rude remarks were no worse than many she'd heard Danny utter a thousand times before. Placing a restraining hand on her friend's shoulder, Lottie shook her head. "Bridle your temper, girl. It wouldn't do to accost a gentleman of Mr. Ashland's standing. He be of the gentry."

Danielle smoothed down her cloak, straightened her mobcap, and took a deep, calming breath, trying to get her temper back under control. When she did, she said, "At least we won't be burdened with having to wait hand and foot on the imperious lard bucket."

Lottie grinned, displaying two charming dimples on her chubby cheeks. "Aye. It would take a bit of soap and water to wash the likes of him, I'm thinking."

The thought of Mr. Ashland in a bathing tub brought torrents of laughter bubbling up Danielle's throat. "'Twould be like scrubbing the back of a whale, I vow."

Wiping the tears from her eyes with the edge of her sleeve, Lottie said, "I ain't laughed this hard in years."

"Then we should be grateful and thank Mr. Ashland for providing us with so much amusement. In these trying times, a good laugh is hard to come by."

"Aye. Almost as hard as a good man."

Bursting into another chorus of laughter, the two friends locked arms and climbed up the steps leading to the tavern.

Neither woman noticed the dark blue eyes that glared at them from the rear of the departing carriage.

3

A fresh coating of snow frosted the gray slate roof of the Lewises' Georgian brick mansion and covered the boxwood bushes that lined the carriage drive as Danielle approached the dark green door of the rear entry. Banging the S-shaped knocker twice, she waited, stomping her feet in an attempt to get the blood circulating back into her toes, which now felt like chips of ice. Though the black leather boots she wore were nearly new, they offered little protection from the heavy snow that had fallen during the night.

The morning air was frigid; Danielle could see her own breath as she exhaled into her gloved hands, and she was exceedingly grateful when the door opened and Mrs. Lewis's maid ushered her in.

Thanking the kind woman, who, having noted her distress, had provided her with a foot warmer, Danielle seated herself in one of the green Windsor chairs that lined the wall of the center hall.

Glancing up at the tall case clock, she noted the time; it was nearly ten o'clock. Well, at least she wasn't late. Since beginning her position with the Lewises three weeks ago, she had made it a practice to be on time.

Betty Lewis was wife to Fielding Lewis, a prominent leader of the Fredericksburg community, and sister to General Washington; she frowned on tardiness almost as much as Harriet Coombs, and Danielle had no intention of giving the woman a reason to dismiss her. She needed this job and the three shillings a week that it paid. It was her ticket to a better life, and she was determined to make something of herself.

Like a squirrel storing nuts for the winter, she had hoarded the money, securing it in the floorboard of the room she shared with Lottie, saving every shilling she could get her hands on, knowing that someday she would be free.

Compared to her chores at the tavern, her position as Mrs. Lewis's helper was quite easy. She assisted with the three boys whenever necessary and had been collaborating with Mrs. Lewis's daughter on her wedding, which was scheduled to take place in May.

The fates had smiled upon her that January day when Mrs. Lewis's coachman had posted the notice at the tavern about the helper's position. And though she was only able to give Mrs. Lewis one day a week—her only day off from the tavern—the woman had been most accommodating.

Hearing footsteps on the stairs, Danielle glanced up to see the object of her thoughts descending the stairway. The apple-cheeked woman with the kind brown eyes had a welcoming smile on her face, and Danielle responded in kind, rising to her feet.

"Good morning, dear." Betty Lewis took Danielle's hands and gave them a gentle squeeze. "I'm so glad you were able to come. I thought, perhaps, the snow might make it a tad difficult for you."

"Not at all, Mrs. Lewis. The distance is not that far to travel and I do enjoy spending time with young Betty and the boys."

"Well, I'm afraid you won't find Betty in today. She's traveled west to spend some time with her older brother, John. But the boys are upstairs and eagerly await your presence."

The three boys, Lawrence, Robert, and Howell were well mannered and of an age where they required little supervision. They loved listening to stories, and she spent a good deal of time reading aloud to them. Fortunately, Luther had insisted that both she and Regina learn their letters, so they would one day be capable of operating the tavern. Though he'd been deprived of a son, Luther vowed he wouldn't be deprived of an heir.

"I do hope Mr. Lewis is feeling better today," Danielle offered. But by the worried expression on Mrs. Lewis's face, she could see he was not.

"He's holding his own, dear. I fear being confined to his bed has taken a worse toll on Mr. Lewis's health and disposition than his illness. He's greatly cheered today, however, for an old friend has come by to see him."

Phillip sat in the blue damask-covered wing chair by the hearth, studying the exquisitely carved mantel that the Lewis's had commissioned at great expense.

"I see by that rapt expression on your face that you

are vastly impressed with my wood-carved mantel, Phillip. The same stucco man who molded the plaster ceilings carved the fireplaces. The man is a true genius. George employed him at Mount Vernon, as well."

Gazing up at the ceiling, which depicted each of the four seasons by using plant symbols—palm fronds for spring, grapes for summer, acorns for fall, and mistletoe for winter—Phillip was visibly impressed; it was truly a work of art, the attention to detail extraordinary.

"'Tis most impressive, Fielding," he said, looking down at the withered man propped up against the headboard of the four-poster mahogany bed. The soft rays of the afternoon sun streamed in through the window, illuminating the seriousness of Fielding's condition. "But you must take care to address me as James, not Phillip. Garbed as I am in this hideous disguise, it shouldn't be too difficult for you to remember."

Colonel Lewis smiled. "By your appearance I'd say that your costume is most convincing."

"And by yours, I can tell that your health has not improved a great deal." Phillip was alarmed by Fielding's wan appearance and marked loss of weight, but had done his best to hide his concerns, not wishing to alarm Mrs. Lewis with his opinion that her husband was in permanent decline.

"Nothing more than the ague, I assure you, my boy. Now pull that chair closer and tell me all about your escapades as the Phantom. You've been making quite a reputation for yourself."

Noting the excitement lighting the older man's eyes, Phillip smiled inwardly. Fielding reminded him of a little boy eager for an adventure story. "I shall.

But first you must tell me about the munitions factory. How have things been going here?"

Colonel Lewis had been placed in charge of the manufacturing of arms and ammunition for the Continental army. The shortage of firearms in the colonies was of great concern to the leaders of the Revolution, and John Hancock had taken it upon himself to write to Fielding of the dire need for their production. Colonel Lewis, a devoted supporter of the cause, had jumped into the project headfirst with his usual patriotic zeal.

Apparently things at the Fredericksburg Gunnery plant were not going well, Phillip concluded, for the excitement faded from Fielding's face and a frown had replaced his smile of moments before.

"Charles Dick and I have sunk our personal fortunes into this venture. And though it be for a worthy cause, I don't mind telling you that the cost has proven dear. I'm in debt up to my ears. 'Twas folly of me to build this big, drafty house, though I love it dearly. Between the house, my properties, and the munitions factory, I'm near broke."

"Perhaps if you petitioned Congress—"

"Ha! That's a joke. Poor George is up north without food and ammunition fighting for our freedom from those blasted British—Mrs. Lewis is out of her mind with worry—and the good members of Congress haven't seen fit to alleviate his suffering." Fielding shook his head. "'Tis doubtful that they'd choose to assuage mine."

Having no suitable answer or solution to the dilemma surrounding Fielding's financial situation, Phillip attempted to take his friend's mind off his troubles by relating the Phantom's last encounter with the *Orion*.

Obviously, Fielding didn't find the narrative all that exciting, for when Phillip paused and looked over toward the bed the Colonel was fast asleep.

Rising from his chair, Phillip tiptoed to the door, quietly shutting it behind him. As soon as he entered the dining room, which adjoined the bedchamber, Mrs. Lewis was there to greet him with the promise of strawberry tea and freshly baked gingerbread.

"You must stay and have some tea with me, Phil—Mr. Ashland," Betty said, catching herself just in time. She smiled, giving Phillip a wink. "There's someone I'd like you to meet."

Phillip groaned inwardly. Apparently, Betty was up to her matchmaking efforts again, as she had been every time he had paid her and Fielding a visit. Who, he wondered, would he be subjected to this time? He shuddered, thinking of the horse-faced, buck-toothed woman—Harriet somebody—whom he'd been introduced to the last time he'd come to Fredericksburg.

Following Betty into the drawing room situated at the back of the house, he waited patiently for her to fetch the mystery woman. While he waited, he poured himself a glass of claret from the crystal decanter on the sideboard and studied the twelve black-framed Boydell prints hanging on the pink plastered walls. Though no candles had been lit in the handsomely furnished room, the light from the two double hung windows was adequate enough to see by.

A few minutes later, Betty appeared with her latest "offering" in tow. Phillip turned, expecting to find another pasty-faced creature and was surprised to discover that the woman hovering behind Betty Lewis was neither pasty-faced nor buck-toothed, but an enchanting vision. She wore a dull gray woolen gown, which was partially covered by a white starched apron and neck handkerchief. Traces of ebony hair peeked out from beneath the lace edge of her mobcap.

Remembering his role, he arched a supercilious eyebrow in her direction. "Who do we have here?" he asked in his haughtiest tone of voice. "I say, Mrs. Lewis, are you hiring children these days?" He cast a condescending smile at Danielle, staring intently at her through his monocle.

Recognition came instantly, and Danielle stiffened at the sight of the corpulent fop whom she remembered seeing at the tavern the other day. He was dressed even more garishly today, if that was possible, in a hideous tomato-red outfit. She forced a small smile to her lips as Mrs. Lewis made the introductions.

"This is Danielle Sheridan, Mr. Ashland. She's been assisting me with the children while Fielding is indisposed, and has been a tremendous help."

Danielle smiled gratefully at the brown-haired woman, but her smile soon faded when she heard Mr. Ashland's response.

"Good help is dreadfully hard to find in these provincial towns, Mrs. Lewis." Turning toward Danielle, he said, "How do you do, Miss Sheridan? It's a pleasure to meet you."

He held out his right hand, which Danielle was obliged to take. His grip was much stronger than she had expected. Her eyes traveled up the long length of him, coming to rest on his face; and she found, at closer inspection, he wasn't nearly as unattractive as she'd originally thought.

His chin didn't have the sagging jowls one would come to expect from a man of his size, and his eyes were the most startling shade of blue—a cross between a blue jay's wing and the summer sky—and they seemed to miss nothing as they perused her appearance from head to toe.

Chafing under his scrutiny, Danielle dipped into a curtsy and withdrew her hand as unobtrusively as possible. "The pleasure is mine, I assure you, sir."

Her response was perfunctory and obviously a lie, which didn't surprise him. He had recognized her as the girl he'd seen in front of the tavern the other day, though she and her friend had done their best to hide themselves.

In the business he was in, he couldn't afford to miss much and rarely did. He had overheard their snide remarks and giggles, and at the time, it had irritated the hell out of him. He wasn't used to receiving scorn and ridicule from members of the opposite sex and it rankled.

Even now there was condemnation in the depths of her extraordinary violet eyes, and Phillip could see that the woman was not at all impressed with meeting a member of the gentry. *A point in her favor.* He was, therefore, not at all nonplussed when she said,

"I really should be going, Mrs. Lewis, if you no longer need me for the day."

"Nonsense!" Betty replied, guiding Danielle to one of the mahogany side chairs. "Mr. Ashland is new in town. Perhaps you can entertain him while I check on Mr. Lewis?"

Though her comment was posed as a request, Danielle knew there could be no refusal on her part. She forced another smile and graciously consented.

After Mrs. Lewis departed, Danielle picked up a china cup and leaned toward the intricately carved silver tea urn, which rested on the piecrust table next to her. "Would you care for some tea, Mr. Ashland? I do believe Mrs. Lewis is expecting us to have some."

Phillip seated himself next to Danielle, folding his hands on the bulk of his stomach, as he had seen Captain Cameron do a thousand times.

"Why is it that I detect a sudden chill in the air, Miss Sheridan? I hope I haven't said something to offend you." He stared intently at her, delighting in the roses that filled her cheeks. Even clothed in the plain gray gown and white apron, she was a stunning vision of loveliness. A man would have to be blind not to see past the ordinary trappings to find the curvaceous body hiding beneath. Fortunately, he had excellent eyesight.

Danielle felt her cheeks warm. Her manner had bordered on impertinent, and it wouldn't do for Mrs. Lewis to get wind of it. She might dismiss her for being rude to her guest. Taking a deep breath, she replied in a voice as civil as she could muster, "Not at all, Mr. Ashland. I'm just not accustomed to taking tea with members of the gentry. Unless of course, I'm serving it."

Expecting him to be rebuffed by her remark, Danielle was, therefore, surprised when his mouth tipped up into a smile. She was rendered speechless by the effect it had on her senses. Goodness! The man was almost handsome when he smiled. Too bad he was so fat and his complexion as chalk white as his wig, she thought.

"You work in a tavern, is that correct, Miss Sheridan?"

She smiled sweetly, setting the cup of tea she had poured on the table in front of him. "Yes. In the very one that you found so distasteful the other day."

His right eyebrow arched. "Ahaa . . . the Golden Pineapple. Yes, well . . . perhaps I was a bit hasty in my judgment of it. But it was naughty of you to eavesdrop on my conversation, was it not?"

Her cheeks turned crimson. "'Twas unintentional, I assure you, sir."

Phillip nearly laughed aloud at that. Miss Sheridan's expertise at covert activities would make her a valuable asset to General Washington's staff. Swallowing his smile, he said, "Perhaps I might frequent the tavern again and we could get . . . shall we say . . . better acquainted." He leaned forward, his warm breath fanning her cheek, and there was no mistaking the implication of his words.

Danielle stiffened, balling her hands into fists. How dare the imperious bag of wind suggest that she might be interested in some sordid liaison! She rose to her feet.

"I doubt that will be possible, Mr. Ashland. I don't consort with the customers . . . for any reason. Please convey my apologies to Mrs. Lewis, but I really must be going."

"Pity," he said, following her to the door. "I should think a girl in your situation would welcome the attentions of a man like myself. I'm in a position to be very generous, my dear."

Women were a greedy lot. The ones of his acquaintance wouldn't have batted an eyelash before accepting. Would the lovely Miss Sheridan? His question was answered in the flash of an eye—violet eyes to be exact, which had now darkened to purple in their anger.

"Your kind of generosity sickens me, Mr. Ashland, as does your insulting proposition. We are fighting this war to free ourselves from tyrants like you. Perhaps you should move to England. You may find a friendlier, more accommodating climate there." With those words, Danielle stormed out of the room, missing the spark of admiration in the depths of Phillip James Cameron's eyes.

Pacing across the blue-and-gold Turkish carpet of the study like a caged lion, Phillip swept back his golden mane and cast an incredulous look in Ian's direction.

"Are you crazy, old man? First you talk me into dressing up like some foppish peacock, then we're forced to impose on an old friend's hospitality—I'm sure the Sinclairs will be quite surprised when they return from France to discover that we've been living in their house—and now you expect me to get married. You truly are daft!"

"Now, laddie, calm down. Ye know yerself that John Sinclair has offered his home tae ye a thousand times. He willna be mindin' a bit that we've taken up residence here. Besides, you canna deny that its location on the Rappahannock River is near perfect?"

Phillip sighed. At least Ian was right about the location of the house. The two-story clapboard dwelling on Caroline Street had proved a godsend. How fortunate that Ian had remembered that the house possessed a secret passageway running down to the river—a leftover from John's days as a pirate. Of course, why was he so surprised? Ian had thought of everything, including the ridiculous idea that he, Phillip, should take a wife.

Grinding to a halt before the massive mahogany desk that fronted the fireplace, Phillip poured himself a generous portion of brandy and took a sip before replying, "You've done well up until now, Ian. I'm not denying that. But I'm drawing the line at this marriage business. I've no intention of finding myself a wife." He shuddered. "God's blood! The very idea is enough to send shivers up my spine."

Ian stared thoughtfully at Phillip, who was once again dressed in the familiar clothing of a seafaring man. His nankeen breeches and loose flowing shirt suited him much better than the lace and satin garments he'd been forced to wear. But they were a necessary evil. As necessary as getting married would be. After what he'd just discovered before leaving Port Royal this morning, he knew Phillip needed a wife to make his disguise complete.

"I've been debating about showing this tae ye, laddie. I know ye've had a great burden placed on yer shoulders, but yer stubborn spirit leaves me no choice." Reaching into his leather satchel, Ian retrieved a yellowed piece of parchment, handing it to Phillip. "I found this tacked outside the White Swan Tavern in Port Royal. It willna be any time a'tall before word of it circulates here in Fredericksburg."

"Damn!" Phillip swore, recognizing the likeness of himself once again. He crumpled the paper, tossing it into the flames of the fire. Those bloody British bastards were doing their best to get him. They'd even raised the reward from two hundred to five hundred pounds.

"'Tis even worse than that, laddie. Ellsworth's ship's been spotted in the Chesapeake. He's gettin' a mite too close for comfort."

Phillip's face suffused with anger. "God's blood! All we've worked for will be for naught, Ian, if that scurvy Englishman finds where we've gone."

"I've been thinkin', laddie, that if ye was tae take a wife, 'twould make yer disguise that much better. No one would connect the Phantom tae a properly married gentleman."

Plopping down in the red leather wing chair by the hearth, his face a mask of dejection, Phillip shook his head. "What you're suggesting is impossible, not to mention highly illegal." Giving a woman a name that wasn't even his own seemed the epitome of tastelessness.

Ian chuckled. "You've been doing 'illegal' for the past five years, laddie. And there's nothing that's impossible."

"And just who is it that I'm supposed to marry? The way I'm disguised, I'm not exactly every woman's romantic dream." Far from it, he thought, judging by Danielle Sheridan's reaction.

Ian rubbed his chin and thought for a moment, then smiled, his gold tooth twinkling as brightly as his eyes in the glow of the candlelight.

"There be plenty of ladies in this town who'd be grateful for the companionship a gent like yourself could provide, not tae mention yer money. There's many who would welcome the chance tae marry well withou' a thought tae handsome looks. We'll just have tae find us one o' those ladies."

"You say *we*, but what you're really saying is *me*." He shook his head. "It's too incredulous an idea to consider. I'd rather take my chances with the British than be saddled with some horse-faced spinster." Harriet what's-her-name's face came to mind and he trembled, taking another swallow of the brandy. "I'd rather hang."

"I never thought I'd see the day when the Phantom would act like a coward. 'Tis a sad day in my life, laddie."

"And I never thought I'd see the day when he'd be dressed up like some ugly fat fop that ladies snicker at behind their fans. I used to be considered attractive."

Ian's brown eyes twinkled. "Aha . . . so it's that young girl ye done told me about that's got yer masculinity all in an uproar."

"I made her a proposal any woman of her station would have jumped at. Had it been Phillip Cameron who had made the suggestion, I don't doubt for a minute that she would have gladly accepted it."

A sly smile crossed the old Scot's face. "So, maybe James Ashland should teach the chit a lesson."

Phillip pondered Ian's words and thought of the flashing violet eyes, the creamy ivory skin, and hair as black as midnight, and then he smiled. "'Twould be a fitting punishment for her impudent manner."

"And a bit of a challenge, I warrant."

His grin deepened. No one could ever say that Phillip Cameron wasn't up to a challenge. And bedding Danielle Sheridan would be quite a challenge. His pulse quickened at the thought.

"I fear it's time that we tested the marital waters, Ian." And pray that we don't drown in the process, he added silently.

The news of James Ashland's matrimonial intentions spread through the town of Fredericksburg like an epidemic of measles. No single girl between the ages of sixteen and twenty was safe from the machinations of a well-meaning, husband-hunting mama.

Elsie Sheridan was no exception.

James Ashland had been the topic of conversation at everyone's dinner table. But at the Golden Pineapple, he was discussed from sunup till sundown, making Danielle wish she had never heard the man's name and, after her encounter with him at the Lewises, had never made his acquaintance.

"Mama's positive that Mr. Ashland will offer for me," Regina said, settling herself atop the wooden stool in the kitchen. "She said any man would be foolish not to."

Glancing up from the batch of bread she kneaded, Danielle caught the dreamy expression on her sister's face, and sighed. Obviously, Regina hadn't seen James Ashland or she wouldn't be mooning over him like some lovesick fool.

"Why would you want to marry a man you've never met, Gina? You might find Mr. Ashland not to your liking at all."

"You're just jealous because no man will ever offer for you. Mama says you're too outspoken by far, and you've nearly reached the age of spinsterhood. You're considered 'on the shelf,' and you're going to end up just like Harriet Coombs, taking causes to your breasts instead of babies."

The violet eyes darkened to midnight. "Why you little mealymouthed brat. I'd rather remain a spinster than throw myself at men the way you do. Anyone with two legs and a pair of breeches suits your taste. And I'm not so sure that two legs is a requirement."

Regina gasped.

"Danielle!"

As if on cue, the sound of Elsie Sheridan's voice brought instantaneous tears to Regina's big blue eyes. Danielle watched in astonishment as the girl jumped up from the stool and rushed toward the door just as her mother entered, throwing her arms about Elsie's thick waist.

"Mama, Danielle's being hateful. She's jealous of Mr. Ashland."

"There, there, child. Dry your eyes. You don't want them puffy in case the fine gentleman arrives tonight."

Danielle didn't know whether to retch over Regina's accusation that she was jealous over James Ashland, or the fact that the pompous peacock might put in an appearance at the tavern this evening.

Her worst fears were confirmed a moment later when her mother added, "The short Scotsman came by not ten minutes ago to inform me that Mr. Ashland would be requiring the great room tonight. You'll serve him, Danielle," she said, turning to face her older daughter, "while Regina entertains him on the pianoforte."

A sinking feeling plummeted Danielle's stomach to the floor. "Why not let Regina serve him?" she asked hopefully. "It would give her a chance to converse with the gentleman." A rare treat indeed, and one that her sister was so deserving of, she added silently.

Elsie shook her head. "Regina's too clumsy at handling the dishes. You'll serve." Turning to cup Regina's chin in her palm, a proud smile lighting her face, Elsie added, "Besides, when he hears my sweet angel's voice he'll be swept away to the heavens."

* * *

Hell. He was surely in hell, Phillip thought as he sat listening to the high-pitched squeal of Regina Sheridan's voice. A cat in heat had better tone.

He'd had about all of the simpering smiles and fluttering eyelashes he could take. Not to mention the heated glares, spilt glasses of Madeira, and smug smiles from the other sister.

Danielle Sheridan's impertinence was driving him to distraction. Not to mention the sight of her creamy breasts when she bent over the table to serve him, or the glimmer in her eyes when something he said insulted her.

Damn, but she was a fine-looking wench!

There was no comparison between the two sisters. Danielle was fire—hot and all-consuming, while Regina was the porcelain china doll—cold, reserved and failingly polite.

"Would you care for more wine, sir?"

Did he say hot? The words dripping from Danielle's sweet, kissable mouth were quite the opposite. Funny he'd never noticed the intriguing mole that set just to the left corner of her mouth.

"Sir?"

He looked up and smiled. "I think I should enjoy your company more, my dear," he taunted, pleased by the annoyed expression on her face. The little spitfire was fun to tease, and he'd given her a heavy dose of it these past few days.

Danielle fought to keep her temper in check, though he was making it awfully difficult. With a politeness she didn't feel, she replied, "As I've explained, Mr. Ashland, sir, I do not have the time nor the inclination to sit and converse with you." She smiled sweetly, emphasizing, "I do *not* fraternize with the customers."

He covered his heart in a dramatic gesture. "You wound me to the quick, my dear."

"I'm certain Regina would love to sit and chat with you, Mr. Ashland." Turning toward her sister before he could protest, Danielle called out, "Regina, Mr. Ashland desires your company. Do be a dear and chat with him for a while." Throwing him a vindictive smile, she spun on her heel and quit the room, feeling quite triumphant in her victory over the impossible man.

Danielle's victory was short-lived, however, when the following afternoon she was summoned to the great room to find the members of her family and James Ashland all seated about the oval mahogany table.

It was highly unusual to see her father anywhere but behind the caged bar of the common room, or in his office tending to the business side of his establishment. He never frequented the great room, saying it was "too genteel" for his tastes, much preferring to consort with the commoners than the landed gentry.

Luther Sheridan was a tall man, lean and lanky, with a ready laugh and an even temperament that offset the high-strung nature of his wife. Unfortunately, his preoccupation with his business had allowed Elsie Sheridan free rein to rear her daughters as she saw fit, which had put Danielle at a great disadvantage.

Scanning the rest of the table, Danielle's gaze landed on Regina, who was dressed in a lemon-colored satin frock, her fichu nowhere in sight. She was positively gloating. James Ashland, seated at the far end of the table, looked like the cat who had just swallowed the canary.

So, he had made his choice.

She breathed a sigh of relief and stepped forward, dipping into a curtsy before him, though it galled her to do so.

"'Tis about time you got here, daughter," her father admonished. "You've kept Mr. Ashland waiting a good fifteen minutes."

She smiled contritely. "I'm sorry to be late, but it was necessary to make a trip to the apothecary shop."

Unfolding his wiry frame from the chair, Luther stood, clanking a spoon against the side of a crystal goblet. His hair was dark, though generously sprinkled with gray. And it was easy to see, with her willowy figure and dark complexion, who Danielle took after in appearance.

"Mr. Ashland has asked for an audience with all of us today. I believe it has something to do with his plans to choose a wife."

Elsie and Regina exchanged knowing glances before Regina turned to seek out her sister, smiling spitefully, as if she already knew the outcome of James Ashland's announcement.

Danielle smiled back, but her smile held no malice. Quite the opposite was true, for she was beside herself with glee, knowing that her sister's marriage to James Ashland would kill two birds with one stone: She'd be rid of them both.

Pushing himself out of the chair, James Ashland rose to his feet. The room grew quiet, save for the ticking of the clock on the mantel and the crackling of the flames in the hearth.

"As you all know, I've been in search of a wife these past few days. The stipulation in my father's will, which was read shortly before I arrived here in

Fredericksburg, makes it critical that I find one in all due haste. Though I'm not prone to make rash judgments or hasty arrangements, I have come to this decision rather hurriedly. But I assure you that it is, by no means, a reflection on any of the fine ladies in this room." He smiled at Regina, and Danielle swallowed nervously, wiping her sweating palms on the skirt of her gown, eager to get this whole farcical mess over with.

"I've already discussed with Mr. Sheridan my desire to wed one of his daughters, and he has agreed that my suit would be welcomed by both him and Mrs. Sheridan."

Danielle caught the smug smile on her mother's face and heaved a bitter sigh. *Mama was finally about to see her dream of marrying Regina off to a wealthy man come true.*

"'Twas an extremely difficult decision, I assure you," James Ashland continued, "and one that I spent many an hour pondering; both girls possess such sterling qualities."

Many more than he could ever hope to possess, Danielle thought uncharitably.

"And so, I have come to a decision that I hope will meet with everyone's approval."

Stepping toward Danielle's side of the table, he came up next to her, placing his left hand on her shoulder. Panic assailed her; a lump the size of a watermelon rose to her throat.

Please, God, let it be that he's only trying to console me—to spare my feelings.

"I have decided to enter into matrimonial bliss with Miss Danielle Sheridan."

The room exploded.

Elsie shot up from her chair like a cannonball, nearly upsetting the bottle of Madeira on the table in her haste to comfort poor Regina, who had started to scream, and was at the moment covering her ears as she dashed out of the room in tears. Luther merely shook his head and shrugged.

And Danielle, who was suddenly drenched in sweat, the contents of her stomach roiling about like a tidal wave, made strange choking sounds, clamped her hand over her mouth, swiveled in her seat, and deposited her delight over the satin slippers on James Ashland's feet.

4

"*Tack to windward,*" the Phantom ordered, sighting the British frigate through his spyglass. "As soon as we're close enough, worry her with a blanket of fire."

The ship made a tight arc, slicing through the turbulent waves as it neared the frigate's stern.

"Fire!" he ordered, the cannons' roar deafening as they spewed forth their shot. He shook his head in disgust when the projectile narrowly missed its mark. The snow was falling hard, making visibility all but nonexistent and an accurate hit almost impossible.

The frigate was part of Benedict Arnold's squadron. Phillip had sailed down to Portsmouth for the express purpose of capturing the traitorous bastard, offering to aid French Captain Arnaud de Tilly, who had been unsuccessful in following the British ships up the Elizabeth River.

Phillip's schooner was sleek and small enough to pursue, but in this weather it would be futile to attempt such a daring maneuver. He could be sailing into a trap, with Arnold lying in wait. It would be foolhardy to risk it.

"Bring her about, Ian. We'll not give chase today."

"Aye, aye, Captain," the first mate replied, his teeth chattering so loudly the response was slightly garbled. He blinked several times to prevent his eyelashes from freezing in the paralyzing temperatures.

Phillip, too, felt the cold and stamped his feet several times, blowing into his gloved hands to keep the blood circulating. "Set a course for Port Royal. This weather makes sailing too hazardous. And I've unfinished business to attend to at home."

"Aye, laddie. Now that yer betrothed ye'll be needin' tae make arrangements fer yer weddin'."

Deep lines bracketed Phillip's mouth as he was reminded of Danielle's less than flattering reaction to his announcement. He had made her sick—physically ill—by choosing to wed her.

Damn the chit! She was as hard on a man's ego as a hammer to an anvil. How had he ever let Ian talk him into this? God's blood! Perhaps it would be better to take his chances with the elements. Both the weather and Danielle's disposition were equally as cold.

"I can't marry him! I *won't* marry that pompous, overbearing bore!" Danielle swore, pulling her hairbrush through her hair with vicious strokes. "I don't care how much money he has." She had told her mother as much, though she knew her defiance would get her nowhere.

Elsie and Luther had already concocted grand

plans for the money they would receive upon her marriage to James Ashland. Her protests were in vain, and by the look of pity in Lottie's eyes, she knew it too.

"Mr. Ashland don't seem to be a bad sort, Danny. Perhaps he'll make you a fine husband."

"Are you insane? A fine husband? The man is a degenerate—a satyr with a voracious appetite for young women."

Heaving an impatient sigh, Lottie realized that soothing Danielle's fears was an impossibility. Danielle was stubborn; she hated being backed into a corner, which is just what this marriage proposal had done. If only there'd been more time for the two to have gotten acquainted, then perhaps Danny would have been more accepting of James Ashland.

The marriage proposal was an unusual occurrence, to be sure, but one Lottie thought Danielle would be grateful for, once she took the time to think things through rationally. Unfortunately, rationality wasn't one of Danielle's strong suits. She was prone to impulsive outbursts and headstrong behavior, which was sure to cause her a heap of trouble one day. Placing a comforting arm around her best friend's shoulders, Lottie led Danielle to the bed and took a seat beside her.

"You've let your imagination run wild, Danny," she said, ignoring the mutinous set to her chin. "This be your chance to escape this life that you hate so much. Think, girl. You'll be free."

"I'd be free if I ran away, far away."

Lottie grew alarmed at her friend's rash statement. "Don't talk nonsense. You've not enough money. You'd be hunted down like an escaped bond servant.

You know your mother would not rest until she found you."

Danielle heaved a sigh, knowing the truth of Lottie's words. "But to marry James Ashland would be almost as bad. "I'd just be exchanging one form of bondage for another. At least I know what's expected of me here." She shuddered, thinking back to the lascivious looks and lewd remarks the disgusting man had made.

"Mr. Ashland seems a decent sort. I've never seen him raise a hand to his servant, and he's been generous with his tips."

"Aye, and generous with his pinches and winks, too!"

Lottie smiled knowingly. "So that's it. You not be wanting to slip between the covers with the gent?"

Danielle's eyes widened. "Would you?"

"For a chance at the kind of luxury he'd be providing, I'd bed him in an instant. But then, I'm not quite the dreamer you are, Danny. I learned, early on, to take what I could and make the most of it. There's worse things in life than to be a fine lady in a grand house."

Lottie squeezed Danielle's hand, then pushed herself to her feet. Crossing to the door, she paused with her hand on the brass door latch, a lump of sadness lodged heavily in her chest. "You've got to make the best of things, love. The marriage has been decided, and you are the chosen one. Now you must be strong and face your responsibilities like a woman. There's no white knight who'll come rescue you."

Lottie's words spun around and around Danielle's head long after the young woman departed. Staring into the fire that blazed brightly in the hearth, she watched the blue flames flicker and flash and was reminded of a pair of brilliant blue eyes.

There may not be a white knight, she decided, but there was still the Phantom.

Danielle was surprised, alarmed, and irritated as hell to walk into the common room a few days later and find the object of her misery, James Ashland, enjoying a glass of claret with her father. The word *traitor* came to mind as she stared accusingly at Luther Sheridan's flushed face.

Not one to encourage confrontation, Luther mumbled his excuses and hurried back to the caged bar to tend to his other, less controversial customers.

The room was crowded, smoke filled and noisy, as it usually was at this time of evening. Pewter tankards clanked against wooden tables, and the sound of ribald laughter punctuated the convivial atmosphere.

But laughter was the farthest thing from Danielle's mind as her gaze slid back to her betrothed. Ashland looked completely out of place in his blue satin and lace, sitting amidst the other men, and it made her realize just how totally unsuited they were for each other.

By the size of his paunch and the paleness of his complexion, it didn't look as if he'd done an honest day's work in his life. Though in all fairness, she had to admit that his calves looked quite muscular encased in the white knitted stockings he wore. But then she noted the clocks—the ornamental designs at the ankles that had been embroidered on the material, and the garish jeweled buckles on his shoes—and her disgust at his foppishness overwhelmed her admiration.

It only took a moment for Ashland to notice her arrival. She watched as he pushed himself out of the chair and crossed to the doorway where she stood. He leaned against his ebony walking stick, as if he needed to support his large frame, and the smile on his face made her breath catch in her throat. He really was handsome when he smiled.

"My dear, I'm relieved to find that you're all right. I confess, I'm used to sweeping ladies off their feet, but not at all accustomed to playing nursemaid to them."

She colored fiercely; for in truth, he'd been kind to her, even after she'd vomited all over his shoes. She would never forget how his expression of dismay had quickly turned to one of concern when he'd retrieved his handkerchief and gallantly cleansed her face with it. Moved by the memory, she said, "It was kind of you to assist me, sir. I'm afraid I was overcome by the unexpectedness of your announcement."

"Unexpected? How so?"

"I thought, surely, Mr. Ashland, you would find Regina more to your liking. She's by far what gentlemen of consequence are looking for in a wife." Danielle parroted her mother's sentiments, as if they were second nature.

James's smile produced two dimples and Danielle felt a queer fluttering in the pit of her stomach. *Nerves. Nerves or indigestion. Or both.* The breakfast she had eaten had not settled comfortably, due to the upheaval in her life.

"My dear, Danielle . . . I assume I may call you that since we are affianced." She nodded and he continued. "In a flock of sheep, 'tis always the black one that is the most prized, for it's the most rare." He lifted his hand to touch the shiny black curl that had escaped the confines of her mobcap, noting the blush effusing her cheeks, the soft gasp departing her lips as his hand brushed lightly across her neck.

Gooseflesh sprouted over Danielle's arms and she was grateful for the long sleeves that hid her reaction. Annoyed that she would be so affected by his touch, Danielle replied, "I'm not at all sure that I like the comparison, Mr. Ashland. Sheep confer an image of following blindly. I assure you, I have no intention of doing so. In fact, it would seem this is as good a time as any to discuss this marriage proposal."

James's eyebrows arched so high they almost touched his peruke, and he cast Danielle an incredulous look. Who did this little chit think she was? You'd think by the way she talked, she was something more than just a common serving wench. Why, any woman in her position would be grateful for the opportunity he was offering.

"Perhaps we should adjourn to a more private area for our discussion?" he suggested, quickly canvassing the area, not liking the interest he saw reflected in the eyes of the sailors who occupied the room. He had no intention of becoming the butt of idle gossip and bringing undue notice to himself. He was trying to hide his identity, not make it the center of public debate.

The question hung in the air until Danielle nodded and led the way to the great room—the scene of her most recent humiliation. Everything looked the same as it had just a few short days ago, but things weren't the same and never would be; her life had been altered by Ashland's proposal.

She was relieved to find that there was no one in

sight. Regina had taken refuge in her room shortly after her grievous letdown and hadn't been seen or heard from since. And Elsie, faced with the biggest disappointment of her life in not seeing Regina wed to a rich man, had swallowed her sorrow, along with a bottle of peach brandy, and was, at the moment, attempting to assist the cook with preparations for supper.

Seating themselves on opposite ends of the mahogany table, Danielle waited for James to reply to her last statement. She could tell by the flush that had crossed his cheeks when she'd uttered it, it had annoyed him. Perhaps if she could reason with him, make him see they were ill suited for each other, he would call off this farce of a marriage.

Leaning back in the Chippendale side chair, James crossed his hands over his stomach, his expression moderately interested but not overly concerned. "Just what is it that you would like to discuss, my dear? Your mother and father have already agreed to my suit; your approval is not necessary, as you well know."

"I'm well aware of that, Mr. Ashland. But I thought perhaps if I explained my feelings, my desire not to marry, you might reconsider."

"Am I to understand that you don't wish to marry me?" He took out his quizzing glass and stared at her, as if he couldn't quite comprehend what he was seeing or hearing.

Danielle did her best not to chafe under the scrutiny. The man had a way of totally unsettling her composure. And that damned monocle he wore only magnified the intensity of his bright blue eyes.

"I don't wish to offend you, Mr. Ashland, but that

is correct. I have no desire to marry you. I had hoped, when I entered into marriage, it would be with someone I cared for . . . someone I loved."

"Love?" His tone was mocking, his smile derisive. "How quaint. How very provincial, my dear. But, alas, that sentiment doesn't quite fit in with my plans. I marry for expediency . . . to secure my inheritance. Love is the farthest thing from my mind, though I suppose, I like you well enough."

"But you don't know me, don't know anything about me."

He eyed her appreciatively, making her squirm restlessly in her seat. "I know that I like what I see."

Embarrassment turned quickly to anger. "I don't intend to become some rich man's wife, sitting on my backside all day, issuing orders to maids, who will, most likely, despise me. I have a position here in town with the Lewises, which I have no intention of quitting."

"Really?" He crossed his arms over his chest, taking in the flushed cheeks and sparking, defiant eyes. The woman's audacity aggravated him to the extreme, which was probably her intention in the first place, but he couldn't help but admire her courage. She had a hell of a lot more than that insipid sister of hers.

Mimicking his actions, Danielle crossed her arms over her chest, tilting up her chin defiantly. "Yes, really. And I belong to the Daughters of Liberty, which I also have no intention of quitting." That remark seemed to pique his interest, and she thought she saw a glimmer of admiration in his eyes. But then she realized it was only the reflection of the candles on the table.

"I applaud your independence, my dear, though too much isn't seemly in a woman. I, too, have a very independent nature. And you will find, once we're married, I will be gone a great deal of the time . . . on business." The relief on her face was insulting, and he frowned.

"Just what type of business are you engaged in, Mr. Ashland? You haven't seen fit to reveal anything of your personal endeavors, but yet have no qualms about sticking your nose into mine."

The cravat about Phillip's throat suddenly felt two sizes too small. And he swallowed hard at the innate curiosity he saw gleaming in the bright violet eyes. "I am in the business of supply and demand," he replied evasively. "Though my affairs are really nothing for you to be concerned about. Unlike yours, which I'm afraid, I must take exception to.

"I cannot have you working like some common housemaid once you become Mrs. James Ashland III. It just wouldn't do, my dear. After all, we must maintain our position. As to the other"—he shrugged, asking—"What did you call it, the Daughters of Liberty? We shall see." He examined his fingernails, as if they were far more important than the conversation, buffing them on his coat front.

James Ashland's arrogance infuriated Danielle. Sputtering in indignation, she clenched her hands into fists to keep from slapping the supercilious smile off his aristocratic face, and her eyes narrowed into thin slits before she blurted, "You may have bought yourself a bride, Mr. Ashland, but you didn't purchase a slave. I will do whatever I wish."

He cocked an imperious eyebrow at her. "Really?"

"Yes, really! And if you weren't such a damned

popinjay and more patriotic like—like the Phantom, then perhaps you would understand my hunger for freedom and independence."

Phillip paled slightly at the mention of the Phantom, but hid his dismay behind the anger that was mounting rapidly. Though his words were smooth, the underlying steel in them sent shivers of apprehension down Danielle's spine.

"You should learn to curb your tongue and your temper, my dear, lest you find yourself at the courthouse seated on the ducking stool."

She was so furious she could hardly speak, and when she did it was to say, "You dare to lay a hand on me and I'll—I'll—"

"You'll do nothing," he finished. "For as your husband I will exert complete authority over you." At her heated glare, he added, "We shall see who comes out the victor in this war of wills, my dear. I fear you will learn, one way or the other, who your master is."

At that, Danielle launched to her feet, her hands slamming down on the smooth surface of the table, shouting, "I have no master!"

His only response was a smile.

"God's blood, Ian. I almost fell off the damned chair when she mentioned the Phantom. If she gets wind of my real identity, she'll wreak havoc in my life. Why, she'll probably insist on accompanying me on my missions!" He shook his head, pausing in front of the fireplace to pour himself another drink. He hadn't imbibed so much in years, but the fiery little piece of baggage seemed to bring out the craving for it.

"I should have chosen the other sister. Regina isn't smart enough to cause us any trouble, while Danielle is likely to create nothing but."

"Now, laddie, calm yerself. The lady in question might verra well be clever and a wee bit inquisitive, but it don't mean she'll be able tae figure out yer disguise. 'Tis a damned good one, if I say so meself." Ian eyed the blue satin frock coat appreciatively. "When yer done wie those garments, I may just take 'em. I got me a hankerin' for some fancy duds."

Shrugging out of his coat, Phillip threw it across the room at his first mate; it landed unceremoniously atop Ian's head. "You're more than welcome to it, old man. If not for you, I wouldn't be in this miserable position." Withdrawing his lace handkerchief, he wiped off the white face powder that concealed his tanned skin. Another of Ian's brilliant ideas.

"If not for me, you'd be swinging from the yardarm of the *Orion*," Ian reminded him.

Phillip groaned at the truth of Ian's words, then plopped down in the leather wing chair, kicking off his velvet slippers. Placing his feet on the brass fender, he wiggled his toes and released a contented sigh as the fire brought life back to his frozen extremities. Those damned shoes were too thin to wear in inclement weather. The ground was still covered with snow and his feet were iced from walking the short distance home from the tavern.

It had been a very un-Ashland-like thing to do, he realized, but he needed the stroll to clear his head. Danielle Sheridan, with her demands and impertinent tongue, was going to be a handful.

If only he could take her to bed, make mad passionate love to her, at least there'd be some compensation for his misery. He had thought of little else since feasting his eyes on her voluptuous body, her captivating lips, and the more he thought, the more he realized how much he wanted her. Had to have her.

Phillip thought back to her mention of the Phantom and smiled. She seemed quite taken with the fellow. He hadn't missed the spark of admiration in her eyes, the look of tenderness on her face when she spoke of him. She certainly never looked at James Ashland that way.

Ian's eyes narrowed suspiciously. "Wot ye be concocting, laddie? I dinna like the look of wickedness on yer face."

Phillip flashed Ian a naughty smile that made the first mate cringe. He'd seen that look often enough when Phillip was a wee lad. He be a handful, that one. Oh, the deviltry he could get into. It made his old bones ache jes thinkin' about it.

"Miss Sheridan seems to have an affinity for the Phantom."

"Don't ye be thinkin' what I think yer thinkin'. We canna tamper wie the lady's reputation. She'll be a married woman, after all. 'Tisna proper."

"But she'll be married to me . . . or rather James Ashland. And she's not married to anyone yet."

"What are ye planning, laddie?" Silence, then, "Laddie?"

But like James Ashland, Phillip's only response was a smile.

5

True to her word, Danielle left early the following morning for her position at the Lewises. She had no intention of bowing down to her future husband's edict that she remain a dutiful housewife, but she did have every intention of showing him that her idle threats weren't so idle. No one was going to dictate to her, especially that pompous peacock James Ashland III.

Besides, remaining at the tavern was out of the question. Her mother and sister had cut her like a knife, refusing to speak one word to her, acting as if the marriage proposal had been her nefarious scheme to ruin their lives.

At least in work there was solace . . . and defiance. Snuggling deeper in the confines of her warm woolen cloak, she smiled, hurrying down the muddy street to the accompaniment of barking dogs and a rooster's crow.

The sun was out; the temperature had finally warmed above freezing. But the result was melted snow that had turned the dirt roads to mire. Fortunately, she had donned her pattens before leaving the tavern, else her shoes would have been a sorrowful mess.

Danielle's plans to defy James Ashland did not go quite as she'd planned, for when she arrived at the Lewis mansion, she was kindly informed by Mrs. Lewis, who had smiled most apologetically, that her services wouldn't be needed for a while. She was told to come back in a few weeks' time, in case the situation had altered, and had been advised that possibly Mrs. Lewis's mother, Mary Washington, might be in need of some assistance. She'd then been given a letter of introduction to present to the elderly woman.

Danielle's pace was purposely slow as she trudged the short distance to Mrs. Washington's home on Charles Street. The Lewis and Washington homes were connected by a boxwood-bordered pathway, and Danielle picked at the shiny green leaves that were visible through the remaining snow that frosted the bushes.

Mrs. Washington had a reputation for being difficult. It was said that even her son, General Washington, visited infrequently, preferring to battle the British rather than deal with his cantankerous mother.

She supposed that the old woman had a valid reason for her orneriness. Mrs. Washington had been uprooted from her home in Ferry Farm across the river and had made no secret about her abhorrence of town life. Danielle felt a great deal of empathy for Mrs. Washington's position, for she, herself, was being uprooted from the only life she'd ever known to a world of gentility she knew little about.

Sighting the rambling white clapboard house on the corner, she gathered up her courage and knocked on the door. *How contentious could one old woman be, anyway?*

Not very, Danielle decided, after having been escorted to the front bed-sitting room of the commodious cottage, where Mrs. Washington entertained most of her visitors, and invited to share a pot of tea with the charming matriarch.

The room was attractively furnished with a four-poster walnut bed draped in a coverlet of yellow mustard, a commode chair, washstand, and two green-and-white floral wing back chairs, in which they were seated.

Mrs. Washington's bright blue eyes were as sharp and assessing as the woman herself, and her low, rather deep voice, was pleasant to the ear as she regaled Danielle with stories of life at her former farm.

"I miss it, you know. Fredericksburg is no substitute for Ferry Farm." Her eyes had a faraway look in them, as she remembered happier times. "But George felt it was in my best interest to move to town, and so here I am. He has enough burdens right now; I've no wish to cause him more."

Mrs. Washington rambled on for quite a while, and Danielle was unsure of just how she should approach the subject of her need for gainful employment. She was spared the necessity when the old woman finally said, "It says in this note from my daughter that you seek a position. What is it that you are qualified to do, Miss Sheridan?"

Danielle fidgeted nervously with the folds of her everyday dress, grateful that she had worn one of her better gowns. The lavender wool quilted petticoat with the deep purple overskirt was one of her nicest, and for some reason, she had felt the need to look her best today.

Under Mrs. Washington's searching gaze, Danielle attempted to take a deep, calming breath, but her stays suddenly felt a little too tight and her words came out in a rush. "I know my letters and can read. And I sew a straight seam. My cooking isn't the best, but my bread is fairly tolerable."

The blue eyes twinkled. The young girl was refreshingly honest . . . in some things. But Mary had been made aware, from Betty's missive, that the young woman's betrothed, a Mr. James Ashland, did not desire Danielle to gain employment.

Men. They were all such a bother, ordering women about as if they had no common sense at all. Well, from the brief conversation she'd had with Miss Sheridan, she thought the young woman was perfectly sensible in wanting to occupy her time with meaningful application of her talents. They had already discussed her membership in the Daughters of Liberty, but not the reasons Danielle sought escape from her soon-to-be husband.

"Tell me, dear, why is it that you feel the need to work? Won't your new husband be providing for you?"

Danielle felt the heat creep up her face. Obviously, Mrs. Washington was privy to her marriage plans. It was true, Fredericksburg was a small town of only about two thousand inhabitants, but she didn't expect her personal business to become common knowledge in only one day.

Setting her cup down on the tea table in front of her, Danielle's chin notched ever so slightly. "If you must know, Mrs. Washington, I am not all disposed to this marriage. It was thrust upon me unexpectedly; and though I will do my duty to my parents and comply with their desire that I marry Mr. Ashland, I refuse to be enslaved by another's will. Therefore, I'm seeking employment outside the home, however unorthodox that may seem. I will certainly understand if you do not wish to gainsay my husband's demands."

Mary smiled kindly, noting the defensive posture the young woman had taken, but not at all offended by it. "My dear, you do remind me of myself at your age. I fear you have years of struggle ahead of you. Though our country seeks independence from our oppressors in England, our men here at home can't seem to recognize that they are perpetrating the same injustices to us women that King George has to the colonies. Tyranny is still tyranny, no matter who the executor. And women who display any shred of independence are not held in very high esteem."

Danielle released the breath she didn't know she was holding. "I knew you were a kindred spirit when first I met you, Mrs. Washington. I've heard that you still visit Ferry Farm everyday to procure your drinking water. It's a small bit of defiance, is it not?"

The old woman chuckled. "I am not content to let George have the final say in my life. It's contrary of me, I know, but . . ." The stooped shoulders raised slightly and she added, "If you wish to visit me as a companion and assist me with my sewing, I'll not be opposed. I will not pay you a wage, for you'll not be needing funds with your upcoming marriage. And your husband will be hard-pressed to say that you've been given employment. But still, you'll have a place to escape to when you feel the need. You're welcome here any time, child."

Kneeling before Mrs. Washington, Danielle pressed a kiss to the gentle woman's gnarled hand. "I thank you, dear lady, for your kindness."

"Go, my dear, and return when you will. But remember, though this marriage has been forced upon you, try to make the best of things. I have known many women, myself included, who married for expediency but found true love along the way."

Later that night as Danielle lay in her bed, listening to Lottie's soft snores and the crackling of the logs in the hearth, she pondered the wisdom of Mrs. Washington's words.

She didn't think she would ever have the chance to find the true love Mrs. Washington mentioned. She would be married to a man for whom she had only contempt. She would be living a life for which she was ill-suited. And if she didn't learn to curb her tongue and willful ways, she would be permanently ensconced on the ducking stool.

Suddenly, James Ashland's mocking face materialized out of nowhere, and she pulled the coverlet over her head, attempting to block out his image, but still his countenance filled her head, as he would her bed in a very short time.

Biting her fist to keep her groan of abject misery from waking Lottie, Danielle turned on her side, burying her face in the pillow. She willed back the tears that threatened to spill. She willed sleep to overtake her, for in sleep there was blessed oblivion. But sleep was a long time in coming that night.

"I have no intention of accompanying you on a shopping expedition, and that's final!" If looks could shrink a man down to size, the one that Danielle cast James Ashland would have reduced him considerably; she stood, arms folded across her chest, glaring up at him.

He had turned up early this morning like a bad dream—or was it a nightmare?—insisting that Danielle visit the milliner's with him and refusing to leave until she agreed.

Lottie had even turned against her, stating that she'd be crazy not to let the "good gentleman" purchase her a wardrobe. The two stood together shoulder to shoulder, like some impregnable barrier in the middle of the entry hall, trying to convince Danielle of their wisdom and her stupidity.

"You cannot be married in those servant's clothes you wear. A man in my position can ill afford to be seen with a dowdy woman at my side."

"Dowdy, am I?" Danielle's eyes blazed almost purple and she took a step forward, but Lottie placed her bulk between the two combatants before Danielle did something rash that she might regret, like bashing in the *good gentleman's* head.

"Now, lovey, be reasonable. Mr. Ashland only wants to buy you some pretties. You're to be his wife, after all."

"Don't remind me!"

"Now see here."

Outwardly, James's face was quite the picture of indignation, but inwardly, Phillip was enjoying their confrontation. The little spitfire gave as good as she got. He'd only wanted to purchase her clothes to assuage his guilty conscience at the scheme he was cooking up to seduce her, and she was doing her best to thwart even that. She was a worthy adversary, arousing to the extreme, and he was more determined than ever to bed her.

"Why do I need a new wardrobe?" Danielle continued, impervious to Ashland's offense. "Yours is fancy enough for the both of us." Today he was garbed in a lime green satin frock coat, pink satin breeches, and gold brocade waistcoat. The man looked like a full-blown rainbow, and she made no attempt to hide her distaste.

"I take a great deal of pride in my appearance. I think you should do the same."

He perused her attire, then snickered in an insulting fashion, bringing a bright flush to her cheeks and a groan from Lottie, who noted the resentment on Danielle's face as she gazed down at her outdated gown.

Perhaps the green-and-white checked gown was a trifle worn and threadbare, Danielle thought. And perhaps she did look a fright. But she wasn't expecting company, least of all the Yankee Doodle dandy before her.

At the pleading look Lottie directed at her, and the insistent *tap, tap, tap* of Ashland's walking stick, which was driving her quite mad, Danielle finally relented. "All right, I'll go. But I'll only allow you to purchase the wedding dress, nothing more."

She may as well have been talking to a wall, Danielle thought a short time later, when she found herself within the confines of Mrs. Judith DeBerry's millinery shop on Caroline Street.

The coconspirators, as she now referred to Mr. Ashland and Mrs. DeBerry, had paraded an unending display of materials and patterns before her, not to mention a large ensemble of gowns that were already made up. She'd been shown dozens of pairs of knitted stockings, bonnets of straw and silk, and even sheer white linen shifts, which had made her cheeks burn in embarrassment, especially when she noticed the approving leer of her betrothed.

It had been too much to hope that James Ashland would have hied himself off to Weedon's Tavern and waited like any ordinary gentleman of consequence. But no. He had perched himself like a parrot atop the dainty rose brocade settee, which looked as if it would collapse under his weight, offering his opinion on every piece of material and garment Mrs. DeBerry brought out.

"I think the silk taffeta woven with silver would be just the thing for the wedding, don't you, Mr. Ashland?" The milliner smiled, mentally calculating her good fortune. "Notice the silver lace on the bodice and sleeves. It's quite exquisite."

Though the gown was lovelier than anything she had ever seen before, Danielle couldn't help the frown that marred her features. She abhorred the fact that they were talking about her as if she were part of the furnishings.

Her frown deepened even more when she heard Ashland reply, "'Tis lovely to be sure, Mrs. DeBerry, but a bit too modest for my dear Miss Sheridan. She has such a lovely figure. I think we need to show it off just a bit more."

At that, Danielle jumped down off the stool she was standing upon, unmindful of the pins that were sticking into her ribs from the pinned bodice Mrs. DeBerry was attempting to alter on the lavender satin gown she had on. "I do not intend to be put on display in anything that is not completely modest, sir! I insist on neck handkerchiefs with every gown, Mrs. DeBerry."

"Oh, but Mistress Sheridan," the distraught milliner wailed, holding out her hands in supplication, "surely you do not intend to cover up your bosom for evening wear. It is simply not done."

Ashland's smile was triumphantly annoying. "She's right, my dear. Though you may be very provincial, there's no reason to advertise that fact. Fashion is a very strong indicator of one's social standing. To assume incorrect attire . . . *tsk, tsk, tsk.* Mrs. DeBerry is correct; it just isn't done."

And so it went for several more hours until Danielle thought she would scream. When she was finally redeposited at the tavern with her new assortment of everyday dresses, morning gowns, evening gowns, and an odd array of accessories, like the calash, which she'd just discovered was a bonnet, she felt an inordinate amount of relief.

That is, until her sister discovered her in the lady's retiring room resting from her ordeal.

Regina's eyes narrowed, her face growing red as the stripes in the silk of Danielle's brand new gown as she surveyed her sister's good fortune.

"You stole him from me!" she shouted, advancing on Danielle, who was seated on the small love seat by the window. "Have you no shame, flaunting your ill-gotten gains before me?"

The sun stealing in through the partially opened blinds cast horizontal patterns across the hardwood floor and Regina's pouting face.

Danielle heaved a sigh. After what she'd just been put through, she had no patience with Regina and her tantrums. She was sorry that Regina felt cheated, that she'd been robbed of her chance to marry well, but that wasn't Danielle's fault. She certainly hadn't done anything to encourage James Ashland. Quite the contrary. She had done everything in her power to convey her utter dislike for the man. Was it her fault he'd been too dense to get the message?

"Now, Gina," Danielle began, attempting to placate the childish woman, "quit acting like such a baby. I had nothing to do with Mr. Ashland's announcement, and you know it. Why, I don't even like him. Why would I want to marry him?"

The blue eyes filled with tears and Regina's lower lip quivered. "Because you hate me! You always have. You're jealous of my good looks and . . . and sparkling wit."

Sparkling wit. Danielle almost gagged. Regina's sense of humor was as sparkling as a champagne bottle that had been left uncorked. "You're wrong, Gina. I'm not jealous of you. I love you." And, Danielle realized, staring at her selfish, willful, childlike sister, that she did.

Discounting her sister's avowal, Regina added with a spiteful twist to her words, "Mama says so. And I believe her."

That hurt, and Danielle flinched at the remark. Why did Mama despise her so? She was firstborn; she should have been the cherished one, not Regina. "You and Mama are both wrong, but I won't sit here and debate the topic further. I have to prepare for a wedding."

"And when is the glorious event to occur?"

"Two weeks from Saturday. Mr. Ashland is making all of the arrangements." When he'd told her the date she had almost fainted, but when he had added that he would be gone for most of the following two weeks, she had taken heart in the news. A lot could happen in two week's time. Perhaps he would become drunk and fall off his horse. Or maybe he would have a change of heart, meet another woman.

Of course, there was always the possibility that James already had another woman. That would explain his evasiveness when questioned about his destination; he refused to give her a direct answer, merely saying, "Don't worry your pretty head about it, my dear. You've enough to think about with our wedding." That much was true, she thought; she hadn't been able to think about anything else. But still, foolish though it was, the idea that he might be seeing someone else unsettled her composure, and she pushed the thought to the back of her mind.

"Well, I hope you'll both be very happy." Regina's nasty smirk belied her words. Flipping up her golden curls, she added, "I, for one, couldn't possibly imagine being married to such an overbearing man. Why, he'll probably keep you caged up like a canary."

Danielle tried hard to ignore her sister's malicious smile and comments, which was extremely difficult, considering they mirrored her own thoughts. And it didn't help matters in the least to know that Regina would like nothing better than to be a petted, pampered bird in a gilded cage. After a moment, she replied, "I guess you needn't be concerned then, Gina, since it isn't you who Mr. Ashland has chosen."

With a gasp and a muffled curse, Regina picked up her skirts and quit the room, leaving Danielle feeling somewhat mollified but extremely depressed.

Phillip spread the parchment pages he'd received late last night across the surface of his desk. The courier, a man named Bowers, had arrived well past midnight, and the news he delivered concerning the southern campaign was of the utmost importance.

Rereading the missive, deep lines bracketed Phillip's mouth. Lord Cornwallis, commander of His Majesty's forces now that Clinton had returned to New York, had defeated Nathanael Greene's American army at Guilford Courthouse, North Carolina.

"Damn those bloody British bastards!" Phillip shouted, banging his fist on the desktop so hard the brass candlestick tottered precariously, then righted itself.

Even faced with overwhelming odds, Cornwallis had managed a victory, though at great cost to his army. Small consolation, Phillip thought.

"Ian," he shouted, loud enough to rattle the windows in the study. When the small man appeared a moment later, he ordered, "Tell Mrs. Dunstan to prepare provisions. Have Dunny saddle the horses. We ride for Port Royal at once."

Dunny, who was Mrs. Dunstan's husband and Phillip's sometime valet and sometime seaman, detested the nickname that Phillip had so casually bestowed upon him, and Ian was relieved that the two hundred-fifty pound giant wasn't present to witness the reference.

"Aye, Captain." Ian saluted, forgetting for the moment that he wasn't standing aboard Phillip's ship. "'Twill be good tae put out tae sea. Me bones are itchin' tae feel the spray of salt again."

"Cornwallis has abandoned the Carolinas," Phillip explained. "He is to join the British forces in Virginia. Lafayette has landed at York Town to meet Baron von Steuben and reconnoiter. We will join him there."

Rerolling the parchment, Phillip secured the missive and the maps with a red satin ribbon, tucking them securely under his arm, before retrieving the tricorn hat he'd left on the chair by the door.

"If Cornwallis is in Virginia, then 'tis highly likely that Ellsworth will be wie him." Ian frowned deeply.

"I'm counting on that, old man. I'd like nothing better than to skewer that bastard before he has a chance to kill more Americans."

"I dinna like that rabid look in yer eyes, laddie. Ye must use caution when dealing wie the likes o' Ellsworth. He be a snake that 'un."

"You forget, old man, I've got a wedding to attend in a fortnight. I intend to be extremely cautious." There was a teasing lilt to his voice and a twinkle of mischief in his eyes when he added, "And I'd hate to disappoint Miss Sheridan, knowing how eager she is for this match."

Ian chuckled. "Aye. About as eager as you meetin' up with the good captain of the *Orion.*"

Phillip's lips thinned at the thought of meeting Ellsworth again. He hoped Ellsworth was with Cornwallis, but it was doubtful. Phillip's contacts had placed the British captain in South Carolina and Georgia, riding with Banastre Tarleton's calvary. How fitting, Phillip thought, that Ellsworth should be paired with No Quarter Given Tarleton, as the man was often called. Two ruthless bastards—two men he wanted to kill.

"There's nothing *good* about that bastard, Ian," he finally said. "But you're right about Miss Sheridan. She welcomes my presence into her life about as much as you welcome a case of the smallpox."

"True. But at least you won't leave scars."

The old man chuckled again, but Phillip didn't join in, for he wasn't entirely sure that he wouldn't leave Danielle Sheridan very badly scarred.

6

Standing in the doorway of the Golden Pineapple's largest guest chamber, the Queen Anne suite, named by Elsie for its predominance of Queen Anne-style furniture, Danielle watched guiltily as Lottie stripped the sheets from the tall tester bed.

She had offered to help, but Lottie, parroting Elsie's newest edict that Danielle would not be assisting with the chores anymore, had refused the offer.

Her mother's change of heart had come on the heels of a visit by Mr. Ashland's valet, Herbert Dunstan, who had come at the request of Ashland to deliver the sum of one thousand pounds into Elsie's greedy hands. Her purchase price, Danielle assumed, her eyes narrowing in displeasure. 'Twas a bitter pill to swallow, knowing her parents had sold her as if she were nothing more to them than a slave on an auction block.

"What you be lookin' so fierce about, Danny? You should be smiling and thankin' your lucky stars that you're getting out of this place." Lottie dropped the pile of sheets on the floor, picked up her dusting cloth and jar of beeswax paste and attacked the mahogany highboy with fervor.

"I don't feel right standing idle while you work your fingers to the bone."

"Don't fret, love. I've only got a couple of months left."

Danielle's brows knitted together as she worried over her friend's future plans, or lack of them. Lottie had never made mention of any plans, and the woman had few skills to see her through rough times, save for waiting tables, dusting, and the like.

Except for marriage, there were few opportunities open to a woman. And as Danielle knew firsthand, marriage was far from a solution to one's problems; rather it was the cause for them. Her frown deepening, she asked, "But what will you do? Where will you go?"

The servant shrugged, swiping at the washstand with her cloth. "The good Lord will provide when the time is right."

"But aren't you worried? I would be at my wit's end if I didn't have my future planned."

Lottie grinned at the serious expression on Danielle's face. "Girl, you made fine plans and look where you're ending up—married to a rich man." She ignored the frown that quickly surfaced. "What good did it do, Danny, making all those plans? Life deals out the cards and we play the hand. Besides," Lottie teased, her eyes twinkling as she patted her backside, "I'm sitting on a fortune. My da, bless his departed soul, told me as much." She laughed aloud at Danielle's shocked gasp.

"Charlotte O'Flynn! I've never heard you say such an outrageous thing."

Lottie waved Danielle's words away with a flick of her dusting rag. "Posh! I'm no virgin like you, Danny. Me and Sean spent many an enjoyable afternoon in his da's barn."

A wistful look entered Lottie's eyes, and Danielle wondered at it. Lottie spoke of giving herself to a man as if it was nothing out of the ordinary, as if it was something most pleasurable.

Mama hadn't painted such a rosy picture. In fact, in one of the few times she had ever counseled Danielle on anything, Elsie had instructed, "When the time comes to give yourself to a husband, daughter, merely brace your feet against the footboard, shut your eyes tight against the pain, and wait for his grunt of pleasure, so's you know he's finished." When Danielle, horrified by her mother's words, protested vehemently that she had no intention of doing any such thing, Elsie had taken her by the shoulders, given her a hearty shake, and replied, "It's your duty, girl!"

Mama had made it sound like a dreaded chore, much like emptying the chamber pots. What was really the truth of it?

"Now what?" Lottie pressed, noting the confusion that marred the otherwise perfect features.

Two splotches of color heated Danielle's cheeks to roses as she swallowed her embarrassment, then asked, "What's it like? Being with a man?"

A knowing light entered Lottie's eyes and she smiled kindly. Taking the innocent woman by the hand, she led her to the bed, pulling her down beside her on the mattress.

"It's glorious, love. Like nothing else you've ever experienced. Your heart pounds, your skin gets hot, like you're burning up with fever, and your private parts . . . well, they get to tingling . . . ."

Danielle pressed her hand over Lottie's mouth, preventing the woman from saying more. "Is it always like that?" she asked without thinking, quickly lowering her hand at the muffled reply.

"No. Only when you care deeply for the gent."

Danielle's face fell and Lottie quickly realized her mistake. "Love, don't be frettin' about Mr. Ashland. He looks to be a considerate sort. Didn't he buy you all those splendid gowns?" She fingered the lace on Danielle's lavender silk dress. "I'm sure he'll be giving you your pleasure."

Lottie's words made Danielle's heart beat faster. Could she really find pleasure in James Ashland's bed? It seemed quite unlikely, though she had to admit to wondering, of late, what it would be like to kiss him. To feel his soft lips pressed against her own. The few times he'd kissed her hand torrents of pleasure surged through her, and a strange, breathless feeling had centered in her chest.

Hearing Lottie's snicker, she colored fiercely, objecting a bit too vehemently, "I don't want anything from that pretentious peacock."

"You'll change your mind. 'Tis a woman's curse to seek pleasure where she may. Once you've a taste of the forbidden fruit, you get a powerful hunger."

Danielle jumped to her feet, shaking her head. "That's ridiculous! A strong woman can control her own needs. I won't be a slave to my body, *or* to my husband."

Noting the stubborn set to Danielle's chin, Lottie

decided that there were mules who were easier to reason with than the headstrong woman before her. Once Danielle made her mind up about something, there was no reasoning with her. "You're determined to a fault, Danny. Sometimes you remind me of that sister of yours."

Danielle's eyes rounded in surprise, her mouth dropping open before she said, "What an awful thing to say."

"'Tis, but nonetheless true."

"I'm nothing like Regina. She's spoiled, inconsiderate . . . ."

"Well, she ain't so high and mighty now." The maid smirked at Danielle's questioning gaze, going on to explain, "Not since your mama put her to work."

"Regina's working?" The question in the violet eyes soon turned to disbelief. "Mama's precious is actually soiling her hands doing labor?"

Lottie nodded. "Since this morning. She's taking over all your chores."

"Including the chamber pots?" That was one chore she wouldn't miss doing, not that she'd miss any of the others. But the pots . . . She grimaced.

Lottie couldn't help the giggle that escaped. "Oh, aye. And it did my heart good. Why she actually cried when your mama told her what her new duties were."

Danielle shook her head at the thought of her spoiled sister's fall from her pedestal. Poor Regina. As much as it pleased her to hear that her sister was finally getting her due, she couldn't help but feel sorry for her.

That compassionate feeling was short-lived, for

over the next several days, Regina's cutting remarks, hateful smiles, and multitude of tears made Danielle actually wish that James Ashland would come home, marry her, and take her away from her miserable existence.

What Danielle didn't know was that her betrothed was one hundred miles away, experiencing his own misery.

Though the sky still appeared pitch black in the predawn darkness and he could barely see his hand in front of his face, Phillip knew that dozens of white sails dotted the horizon of the Chesapeake.

British Admiral Arbuthnot's war ships had been sighted yesterday, and a French contingent under Admiral Destouches, with his sixty-four-gun ship *Eveille*, was not far away.

Arbuthnot had come to Portsmouth to reinforce Arnold, whose orders included the destruction of military stores in Virginia, rallying the Tories, and preventing Greene from receiving reinforcements. The British weren't taking any chances, now that the French had entered the war on the American side.

Turning toward his first mate, Phillip eased the tension out of his neck with the back of his hand. The wait was always harder than the work, he thought, about to give the order to set sail when the first cannonade rang out, hitting dangerously close to the bow of his ship.

"Come about, Ian." Phillip shouted to be heard above the thunderous roar of the cannon. "They've got us in their sights."

The men, already at their battle stations, loaded

the four-pounders with shot, their eager faces proclaiming the high anxiety of the moment.

As the sky lightened, Phillip trained his glass on the lone frigate bearing down quickly. A surge of surprise then satisfaction pumped through him at the sight of the *Orion*. At last, Ellsworth had come.

"Fire!" Phillip ordered his gunners, who quickly ignited the four-pounders on the starboard side. Black smoke belched the acrid stench of sulfur as the boom of cannons exploded like thunder, the deadly salvo finding its mark on the *Orion*'s larboard side.

A boisterous cheer went up from the deck of the black schooner as the topmast of the enemy ship, splintered then cracked.

"We've injured 'em, Captain. Shall we go in for the kill?" Ian asked, the smell of burning sulfur a balm to his seaman's soul.

Andrew Ellsworth's face contorted in rage as he surveyed the damage to his ship. Raising a clenched fist toward the heavens, he shouted to his first lieutenant, "Give the order to fire again. I'll blow that filthy pirate out of the water if it's the last thing I do. He won't get the best of me again."

Pettigrew blanched. "But, Captain, we've been hit. If we take another shot, they could sink us where we sit."

"Fire, you spineless bastard!" Ellsworth screamed, his face purpling. "I'll not lose my chance. I've waited too long. The Phantom will die this day."

Before Phillip had time to respond to Ian's question, another volley spewed forth from the *Orion*'s gunports, hitting the schooner's stern, exploding into a fiery ball on impact.

"Get the buckets. Put that fire out!" Phillip shouted. "Tack to windward."

"We're taking in water fast, Captain," gunner's mate Scoggins shouted. "They've blown a hole in the hull. You'd best make a run for it."

The wind filled the sails as the black schooner sliced through the swells, rushing to escape the British frigate, who was hot in pursuit.

"We won't be able to sustain another hit, Ian, and the British bastards are closing in on us," Phillip informed the first mate, his lips thinned into a straight line beneath the silk of his mask.

"Yer no' tae worry, laddie. Ian'll get us o' of this mess."

Truer words were never spoken. For as Ian brought the schooner about to avoid the British frigate's latest attempt to destroy them, the French war ship *Eveille* opened fire with all its sixty-four guns and gave chase to the *Orion*.

Phillip breathed a sigh of relief as he spotted Ellsworth's ship trying to outrun the large French warship.

"Rest easy, men," he bellowed after they were safely out of harm's way. "The enemy has been routed temporarily. Set a course for home, Ian. We've outstayed our welcome this day. I've no wish to attend a funeral, particularly my own."

Soon, the Phantom's ship was out of danger and heading north toward home, and Ian took a moment to address the subject that was uppermost on his mind: that of the Phantom seducing Danielle.

"Ye'll be wantin' tae spruce up a bit 'afore ye approach yer betrothed," Ian advised, eyeing the black costume. "We wouldna want tae give the bonnie lass a fright, now would we?"

Phillip's blue eyes glowed with an inner fire as he stared out at the horizon, now a palette of purples and pinks as the sun rose high in the sky, and was reminded of a pair of violet orbs as lovely as the rarest set of amethysts.

"You're as subtle as a battering ram, Ian, but you'd best keep your opinions to yourself on this matter. The Phantom's next mission involves the lovely Miss Sheridan, and he's not one to fail in his duties."

Noting the stubborn set to the man's chin, Ian's lips puckered in annoyance. "Ye're thinkin' wie wot's between yer legs, laddie, not yer head. For if ye were thinkin' clearly, you'd know that wot yer intendin' tae do is wrong. 'Tis one thing tae enact a necessary charade on the lassie, but tae seduce her . . ." He shook his head. "Mark my words, no good can come o' it."

"She's to be my wife. I'm perfectly within my rights to bed her," Phillip argued.

"Aye. That would be true enough if this be a normal marriage. But ye know it ain't. And ye also know that the Phantom is nae the bridegroom," Ian said and stalked away, shaking his head sadly.

Phillip watched Ian depart, pondering his words, realizing the wisdom of them. But the throbbing ache between his legs was too insistent to ignore, blanketing his conscience and steering his mind on a one-track course.

Be careful what you wish for, you may get it. The adage came to mind as Danielle stared at the note she'd just received from James Ashland.

He was back! And eager for the nuptials to proceed. Good Lord! Had she really wished that he'd come back and take her away? She must have been crazed at the time; she certainly had no such wish now.

Rereading the note, her hands started shaking. In two days' time she would become Mrs. James Ashland III. Tears obscured her vision until the neatly penned missive was only a blur. Padding barefoot across the pine planks of her chamber, the note clenched tightly in her hand, she opened the blinds to stare out at the road below.

The early morning sky was as dark as her mood. Thick black clouds promised a shower before nightfall. A pair of slaves rolling two large hogsheads of tobacco walked toward the wharf; impervious to the cold, they wore no coats or shoes, and Danielle wondered if their feet felt as numb as her entire body did at the moment. Even the sight of tiny buds on the dogwood tree across the road—a hint that spring was not faraway—could not lift her spirits.

"Danny! Danny!" Lottie burst into the room, setting the pot of chocolate she carried down on the wooden table by the hearth.

Scared witless, Danielle spun on her heel, holding her hand over her heart in an attempt to still its beating. "Merciful heavens! You took ten years off my life, Lottie."

"You won't be lookin' so down in the mouth when I tell you what I've just heard." She patted the space next to her on the bed, waiting for Danielle to sit.

But Danielle was in no mood for Lottie's foolishness this morning, and asked harshly as she seated herself on the bed, "Well, what is it?

Lottie bounced up and down, looking like she might burst at any moment. "I've just come from Merriweather's Bake Shop." She thrust the plate of warm scones at Danielle. "I thought these might cheer you up."

Noting the eagerness on her friend's face and the thoughtfulness of her gesture, Danielle grew immediately contrite, knowing she had no right to take her unhappiness out on Lottie and vowing to make up for it later.

"Anyways," Lottie continued, impervious to Danielle's foul mood. "There's word about town that the Phantom's ship has been spotted in the Chesapeake."

"Where?" Danielle's heart started to pound again, but in excitement this time. "Where was it seen?"

"'Twas coming from a southerly direction. But the party involved—a seaman off one of the merchant ships—lost track of it somewheres around York Town."

"Oh," Danielle said, her voice small, her excitement fading as quickly as it had blossomed. It was silly to hope that he'd been spotted near Fredericksburg, she knew, but still . . .

"Cheer up, love," Lottie said, removing one of the scones from the plate and taking a bite of it. "He ain't that far away. There's still a chance that he'll come rescue you from your fate, like you're always praying for."

If only that were true, Danielle thought, wishing she could share Lottie's enthusiasm. But as of late, practicality had won out over fanciful dreams.

"It isn't likely, Lottie. The Phantom isn't even aware of my existence."

"But you met him once."

"It was a long time ago, and I doubt if he'd remember the encounter. I was just one of many passengers on the ship."

Pouring the steaming chocolate into a cup, Lottie handed it to her friend. The delicious smell permeated the room, and Danielle's stomach rumbled in response to it.

"They say once the Phantom meets a beautiful woman, he never forgets her face. He knows where you live, Danny. You told me so yourself that he spoke to your father."

"My father merely thanked him for saving our hides from the British. I doubt it made much of an impression. And besides, what makes you so all-fired impressed with the Phantom? I thought you didn't believe in him."

Lottie shrugged. "I figured if you believed in him that much, there must be something to it. It doesn't hurt to hedge your bets; my da told me that, too."

"Well, you'd best quit gambling on such a long shot, though I thank you for trying to cheer me up. I'm to be married on Saturday, and there's nothing short of a miracle that's going to prevent that from happening. And as you know, dear friend, miracles are in short supply these days."

"Posh! 'Tis a bloomin' miracle that we patriots are still in this war after five years' time. There weren't many who'd have bet on that outcome, especially the Brits. I'd say we fairly shocked them out of their red drawers."

Lottie chuckled, her laughter becoming infectious, and soon Danielle was caught up in it. She was going to miss her cheerful companion when she left to live at Ashland's home, Danielle realized, a lump forming in her throat. But she didn't have time to grow morose again, for Lottie was tugging on her sleeve impatiently.

"Hurry and get dressed. We'll be late for the meeting of the Daughters." A look of mock horror crossed Lottie's face before she added, "And you know what that means?" She wiggled her eyebrows suggestively.

Peals of laughter burst forth from Danielle as she wiped at the tears streaming down her face. "I'm going to miss you, you crazed woman."

"And I you." Lottie sobered. "I've never had a friend like you before, Danny. You've been a real sister to me."

Both women started blubbering loudly.

And that was how James Ashland found them when he opened the door a moment later.

"I say, I hope I'm not interrupting anything."

Both girls quieted, turning to stare toward the door. Danielle shrieked at the sight of her betrothed standing casually in the doorway, staring intently at her through his monocle, and blushed hotly, realizing she was dressed in only a thin shift that left little to the imagination.

And at the moment, Phillip was imagining a great many things, for he hadn't missed the sight of Danielle's pert breasts peeking out through the transparent material; her dusky nipples, like two ripe red cherries, beckoned his attention. He had quite a fondness for cherries.

Feeling himself harden, he shifted his stance, grateful for the red satin three-quarter-length coat he had on. God's blood, but she was beautiful. Her thick ebony hair cascaded around her creamy shoulders and it was all he could do not to run over to the bed and take her in his arms.

The need to make Danielle his own had consumed him like a raging fever. He had thought of little else on the voyage home; and, like a child eager for a new toy, he had awakened early this morning, anxious to see her again.

"Mr. Ashland," Danielle shrieked, quickly covering herself with a blanket. "What is the meaning of this intrusion?"

He stepped farther into the room, tossing his tricorn hat on a chair, nodding perfunctorily at the buxom serving wench who stared openmouthed back at him. "Your mother gave me permission to enter. I had no idea that you'd still be abed."

Her lips slashing into a thin line, Danielle replied caustically, "My dear mother would not gainsay you anything. She has the soul of Judas, and knows which side her bread is buttered on." Danielle was firmly convinced that Elsie would sell her own mother, if there was a profit to be made.

Knowing anger when she saw it, and she saw it on Mr. Ashland's face, though he did his best to hide it, Lottie offered her excuses and made to depart, having no desire to referee another shouting match.

"Now see what you've done," Danielle accused, watching her friend slam out the door. "We were having a pleasant conversation until you showed up."

"My apologies, of course. I merely wanted to give you this." He held out a small package, noting the suspicion and curiosity in the bright violet eyes as she gazed down at the offering.

"There's no need to gift me with anything else, sir. The gowns were quite enough."

Smiling, he stepped toward her, taking a seat on the edge of the bed, which sank down under his weight.

"Sir!" Danielle's eyes widened as she scooted back, doing her best to keep the blanket firmly around her. "You should not be in here. It is most unseemly."

Chuckling, Ashland dropped the box into her lap. "My dear, we're to be wed shortly. No one would think my visit here is the least bit improper under the circumstances. Surely you know, many engaged couples find the necessity to . . . to . . ."

He removed a lace handkerchief from his inside pocket and mopped his forehead. His close proximity to Danielle was making him awfully warm. If he wasn't careful, his sweat would cause his face powder to run all over his face.

"You don't mean to . . ."

The look of abject horror on Danielle's face made him wince. The chit was certainly hard on a man's ego. "Rest assured, my dear, when *that* glorious event occurs, it will be done amidst perfumed satin sheets in a room befitting a man of my station. Not in some squalid, little . . ." He shuddered, smiling inwardly at her outrage before continuing. "I am not some youth in my first bloom of passion, Danielle. I have, what I would modestly say is, a great deal of experience." Leaning over, he patted her cheek. "And you, my dear Danielle, will be the recipient of all that vast knowledge."

Swallowing hard at the picture he created, Danielle pulled back, finally finding her voice. "I don't think we should be discussing such things, sir. And I would appreciate it, if you would leave me to dress."

"But why? Your state of dishabille is most charming, I assure you. As for the other . . ." He shrugged. "Whatever you wish. What shall we discuss?"

Annoyed that Ashland hadn't taken the hint that she didn't desire his *presence* or his *presents*, Danielle searched for a safe topic of conversation far removed from the previous one, settling on one that was closest to her heart. "I understand that the Phantom has been sighted in the Chesapeake Bay."

He stiffened, but only momentarily. "Really? And who is this Phantom of whom you speak?"

Her eyes widened. "You don't know?" Of course, he didn't know! The blank look on his face said it was obvious that he didn't. All James Ashland knew about was stuffing his face and covering his body in frills and furbelows.

Today he had on the most garish red coat. It was embroidered with gold finches, making him look somewhat like a gigantic bird cage. She covered her mouth to keep from laughing out loud, then cleared her throat, saying, "The Phantom is quite the hero. He comes out of nowhere to attack British ships."

"Really?"

She nodded enthusiastically, causing him to remark, "You seem quite taken with the chap."

A wistful smile crossed her face and her eyes got a faraway look in them. "He's wonderful. Strong. Handsome. Muscular. Everything—"

"I am not," he finished, his brow lifting.

"Everything a woman looks for in a man," she corrected, noting the hurt look on his face and feeling sorry she had offended him. She had no idea his feelings were so fragile. He had been generous to her and kind, and she hadn't set out to be purposely cruel. But Ashland couldn't expect her to hold him in as high esteem as she did the Phantom. After all, they were worlds apart in looks and manner.

"I see," was all he said.

"Well, you needn't look so melancholy. Everyone should have a hero—someone to worship and adore from afar. It makes life much more bearable."

"And this Phantom is your hero?"

Her smile was so brilliant it dispelled the gloom of day, lighting up the room, taking his breath away. "Oh, yes!" Enthusiasm sparked her words as she recounted her first meeting with the Phantom, forgetting for the moment whom she was speaking to so freely.

Phillip was shocked at the news that he had once met this lovely creature and hadn't remembered. He must be slipping, he thought. Danielle was very memorable.

"Aren't you going to open your gift?" he prodded, noting how quickly the animation had quit her features. His gut twisted, but he couldn't fathom why.

"I suppose," she said with a sigh, but couldn't prevent the excitement from lighting her eyes as she opened the small box. Her eyes widened at the sight of the exquisite golden heart that lay atop a bed of red satin, and she smiled at him in genuine pleasure. "It's lovely. Thank you."

"It's your wedding gift—a token of my esteem—a symbolic gesture of—" He shut his mouth, realizing he was making a perfect ass out of himself, even as the imperious James Ashland.

A lump of emotion formed in her throat when Danielle realized just what the gift symbolized. *A heart.* He had given her his heart. She was touched, for she'd never received so fine a gift before. "How very thoughtful," she said, closing the lid, not wishing to appear too appreciative, lest he get the wrong idea.

"Well, I suppose if I had been the Phantom, I'd have given you something far more dashing, something far less sentimental. But alas, I am not."

She tried to spare his feelings by saying, "There is only one Phantom, so there's no need to try and compare yourself to him. He's not likely to come between us, so fear not, Mr. Ashland."

Taking her hand in his, James placed a chaste kiss upon it, delighting in the blush that crossed her cheeks. "I'm happy to hear that, my dear, for I fancy having you all to myself."

But Phillip knew there was a distinct possibility—an excellent likelihood—that James Ashland would be sharing Danielle Sheridan with the Phantom. And he fully intended to be very magnanimous about it.

7

Danielle couldn't sleep. Try as she might, the prospect of wedding James Ashland tomorrow filled her mind with nightmarish thoughts.

Peering about the moonlit room, she observed Lottie's sleeping form facing the wall; she snored loud enough to wake the dead, and Danielle doubted if her movements would wake her.

Throwing back the covers, she swung her legs over the side of the bed and stood stock still, sucking in her breath when the floorboard beneath her feet creaked loudly, releasing it a moment later when her roommate did not stir.

Tiptoeing to the door, Danielle yanked her cloak off the peg, covering herself with it. It wouldn't do to be caught wandering down by the river with only her shift on, she thought. Picking up her shoes, which she would don as soon as she was safely out of the tavern, she eased open the door and slipped quietly out of the room.

Her destination was a foregone conclusion. She would go to the river—to her log—and ponder her fate one last time.

The night air was chilly and she hugged herself against the dampness. When she exhaled, she could see her own breath, but didn't need the physical evidence to tell her it was cold out. The gooseflesh on her arms and legs was a much better indicator. March had come in like a lion, hopefully it would go out like a lamb.

The full moon's light guided her progress down the familiar path. The night surrounded her with a cacophony of sound. The wind whistled through the tree branches, an owl hooted, and a dog wailed pitifully for its master to offer admittance into a warm house.

As she drew near the river, the brackish smell of water assaulted her senses, as did the noxious odor from several backyard privies. Covering her nose, she hurried along; upon reaching the water, she plopped down on the log, trailing her fingers over its rough bark in silent farewell.

Tomorrow she would leave behind her childish fantasies. She would come no more to daydream, to escape the harsh reality of her life. Tomorrow there would be no more fanciful thoughts.

But tonight she could still pretend, still wrap her dreams about her one true hero—the Phantom.

She had often dreamed he would come to rescue her. It had been a childish fantasy, but one that had sustained her over these many years. But she knew now that dreams really didn't come true. That Lottie, ever the realist, had been right all along. There was no knight in shining armor who would rescue her. She was doomed to spend her life with a man she didn't love, a man she didn't even like.

Heaving a sigh, she stared morosely out at the river, listening to the soft rush of water as it slapped lazily against the shore.

A few minutes later that sound was replaced by another when Danielle heard footsteps on the path. She twisted about to see if she had been followed, exhaling a sigh of relief when she discovered she was still quite alone. It didn't take her long to realize her vulnerability; she had no weapon—save her sharp tongue—and hoped it would be enough to hold off a drunken sailor, should one happen upon her.

She'd learned to handle her share of amorous patrons over the years. Usually a severe tongue lashing and a slap on the hand was sufficient to cool their ardor.

A strong gust of wind came up suddenly to ruffle the tree limbs overhead, and Danielle had the strangest feeling that she was being watched. It was an eerie, uneasy feeling that made the tiny hairs on the nape of her neck stand straight up on end.

Not one to push her luck, she rose to her feet, deciding to leave. It was folly to be out so late without the security of an occupied tavern. If she were to scream, no one would hear her. Both her parents slept like the dead. Turning, she ran into something solid. Someone, she amended, her heart racing in fear.

"You should be careful out here all alone in the dark, sweeting."

His hands reached out to steady her; his voice was seductively low when he spoke, and she didn't recognize it as someone's she knew.

Taking a step back, her gaze drifted up. She could see by the light of the moon that the man was dressed in black breeches. His firmly muscled legs were molded by the tight material, and as her gaze lifted higher, she could see that they left little to the imagination, bringing flames to her cheeks and making her grateful for the darkness.

The shirt that billowed around his broadly muscled chest was also black, and she wondered at the oddness of his costume, until her eyes landed on the black silk mask that covered the upper portion of his face.

She gasped, blurting, "The Phantom!" then quickly lowered her voice, hoping that no one had heard her.

"You have me at a distinct disadvantage, madam."

Danielle's heart raced so fast, she thought surely she would faint. She blinked several times to dispel the image her mind had conjured up, but when she opened them fully, he was still standing before her, grinning. She noticed how strong his chin was, as if chiseled from a piece of granite, and his lips . . . so soft, so sensual.

She shook herself. "You cannot be real," she said, reaching her hand out to touch him, knowing the vision would disappear if she did. It was always that way in her dreams. Suddenly, a warm hand clamped over hers, and he brought it to his lips for a kiss before placing it over his heart.

"I assure you, sweeting, I am very real and very much alive."

She could see that. Her fingers tingled beneath the wild throbbing of his heart. Or was it her own pulse that beat so fervently? She wasn't sure. He didn't release his hold but stood staring down at her, a bemused expression on his face.

Gathering her wits about her, she realized what a ninnyhammer this man must think her. If he really was the Phantom . . .

"My name is Danielle Sheridan."

"So you're Danielle? I've heard quite a bit about you."

Her brow wrinkled in confusion. "About me? You must be mistaken."

"You belong to the Daughters of Liberty, do you not? And tomorrow you're to be married to that fastidious fop—Ashland, is it?"

She nodded, wide-eyed. "But how . . . ?"

He raised his hand to forestall her question. "I never reveal my sources, or share my knowledge, Danielle. It isn't safe for a man in my position."

She digested that piece of information, asking, "But what are you doing here? Why have you come?"

"I've been wanting to meet you for a long time, sweeting, but duty prevented me from arriving sooner."

"You have?"

"Did you think I would forget our first encounter?"

"But that was two years ago!"

"I never forget a beautiful face."

"Lottie was right," she whispered, not realizing she had spoken aloud.

"Who?"

She waved off the question with a shake of her head.

"Is there a place we can go to get out of this cold?" he asked. "You're shivering; you must be near frozen."

He placed a well-muscled arm around her shoulders, drawing her close to his warmth, and Danielle thought surely she would incinerate right on the spot, so warm had she become.

When Danielle didn't respond to the question, the Phantom prodded, "I wouldn't want to be recognized, Danielle. The British have increased the price on my head to one thousand pounds." He'd become enraged when he'd found out that bit of information upon his return to Port Royal. Ellsworth was persistent, he'd give the bastard that.

The knowledge that he could be arrested seemed to arouse Danielle from her stupor. "There's a small shed beyond the smokehouse. My father stores his liquor there. But it's locked."

"And do you perchance have the key hidden beneath your cloak?" He raked her from head to toe, bringing two crimson stains to her cheeks.

"No! But I know where one is hidden." Motioning for him to follow, Danielle led him back up the path. When they reached the small wooden shed, she bent down to loosen a brick of the foundation, then straightened, clutching a bright brass key in the palm of her hand.

The door creaked on its hinges when the Phantom pushed it open, and Danielle prayed fervently that no one, her father in particular, had heard the noise. Sound sleeper or not, Luther Sheridan was very protective of his liquor.

The small shed smelled dank and reeked of rum and whiskey, but offered, for the most part, shelter from the biting wind. Several clapboards near the roof line were missing, leaving about a three-inch gap, allowing both wind and moonlight to enter.

"Shut the door, Danielle." He grabbed several burlap bags from the pile in the corner. "I'll spread these on the floor to cover the dirt. We can sit here and talk." He lowered himself to the ground, patting the space next to him.

Danielle hesitated briefly until the warmth in his eyes and the seductiveness of his voice drew her forward. Somewhere in the back of her mind a voice was telling her that what she was doing was wrong. That if anyone ever found out, she would be ruined for life. But Danielle was too enraptured in the moment to pay that voice any mind.

"Come, sit with me." He held out his hand, and she took it, noting the strength in the long, deeply tanned fingers. They were callused like any seaman's, but still soft.

"I cannot stay long. I might be missed." Rational thoughts began to resurface, and she rubbed her arm against the sudden chill that swept through her body at the realization that she was alone in an isolated shed, dressed only in a thin shift and cloak, with a man she knew nothing about, save for the tales she had heard.

"Are you still cold?" He didn't wait for her answer but drew her into the shelter of his arms. "Let me warm you, sweeting. Body heat spreads quicker when it's shared by two."

With her head resting against the solid wall of his chest, she knew he wasn't lying about that fact. She felt as hot as a flatiron at the moment, and when his hand began to draw circles over her back, her shivers were replaced by tremors of a different kind.

Danielle felt the cool silk of his shirt beneath her cheek, smelled the musky scent of his skin, and her fears began to subside. Her dreams—her fantasies had come true. The Phantom had come for her. She would leave with him and never have to marry that pompous bag of wind James Ashland. Her heart lightened.

"I knew you would come," she whispered, sighing in contentment as his fingers sifted gently through the silky strands of her hair.

"Did you?" There was a hint of amusement in his voice.

"Oh, yes! I prayed every night that it would be so."

The Phantom set her from him and stared directly into her eyes. He noted the trust, the adulation in them, and for a moment, felt a measure of guilt. But only for a moment. "Your prayers have been answered; I never disappoint a beautiful woman."

His lips brushed over hers like a whisper, and Danielle felt the flutter of his mask against her cheek, the throbbing of her heart against his own. He had kissed her! Reverently, she ran her tongue over her lips, as if to savor the moment. Never in all her wildest dreams had she imagined a kiss could be so wonderful. And it had been tender, loving, almost as if . . . as if he cared deeply for her.

Tentatively at first, but then with more determination, she kissed him back, relying purely on instinct to guide her. She was on her knees facing him, her hands clutching his powerful biceps. The sweetness of his kiss sang through her veins, burying deep within her heart, and she was lifted to another dimension where only she and the Phantom existed, and nothing else mattered but this moment in time.

Phillip was pleased and quite surprised by Danielle's ardent response, but then a woman of her experience had been tutored in the ways of pleasing a man. It was no secret that a tavern wench was a well-seasoned bit of fluff. Any number had warmed his bed on occasion, and he found them to be a most pleasant diversion when he'd visited various ports.

He deepened his kiss, thrusting his tongue into Danielle's mouth, hearing her soft mew of pleasure. Not one to deny a lady, he spread open the folds of her cloak and found to his delight that she was dressed quite suitably for the occasion. Running his hands over the thin lawn of her shift, he could feel the soft pillows of her breasts, the curvature of her buttocks, and felt himself growing harder and hotter by the minute.

Danielle knew she should make him stop. But she couldn't seem to voice the objection. A wonderful lethargy had settled over her; her hands felt weighted and the words of protest she knew she should utter died with each thrust of his tongue. His hands seemed to be everywhere at once, exploring, mapping every unchartered, untutored region of her body.

Phillip eased Danielle down onto the burlap, throwing his leg over her as he continued his explorations, his mouth never leaving hers for a moment. His hands skimmed lightly over her calves and thighs, drawing the shift she wore up, bearing her body to his view.

"You are perfection, sweeting," he whispered, kissing her face, her neck, finally settling his warm lips on the fullness of her breasts, licking at the swollen nipples, sucking until they were rigid with desire.

Danielle felt as if she were on fire. Like molten lava her blood surged through her veins, heating her body to a fevered pitch. She writhed beneath his hands and mouth, spreading her hands under the silk of his shirt until she could feel the warmth of his flesh pressed against her own. Though his chest was rock hard, the soft, curly hair beneath her fingers was soft as down. His large, turgid member pressed into her woman's mound and she arched against it, trying to assuage the persistent throbbing between her thighs.

What magic spell had he cast over her? What madness was this? But what did it matter? For they would soon be wed.

With that reassuring notion, all thoughts of protest quickly fled and Danielle found herself responding as wantonly as a woman of loose virtue. Reaching down, she cupped his swollen member; hearing his gasp of surprise, she smiled into his mouth, feeling the power that only a woman who has pleased her man can know.

The Phantom's fingers slid up her thighs to find the swollen apex of her woman's mound. She was wet and ready for him, and the realization ignited him. Slowly and carefully, he ran his fingers through the soft nest of curls, caressing her, as his tongue, buried deep inside her mouth, plunged and withdrew in replicated rhythmic motion.

Danielle moaned, then bucked toward the pleasure of his hands, her head lolling from side to side as the exquisite torture continued. When his tongue drew a path down her breasts to her stomach, then lower, she stiffened, until the pleasure of its caress against her flesh took all inhibition and conscious thought away.

"Oh, God!" she wailed, as the first wave of pleasure washed over her. She gripped his head, urging him on, spreading her legs wider to give him the access he needed. Just when she thought she would die of the pleasure, he stopped, and she opened her eyes to find him shedding his breeches.

His engorged member jutted forth proudly like a warrior's spear and she knew a moment of fear, until he bent between her legs again to place the tumescent tip against her opening. Slowly he entered, easing himself into her, pushing then pulling, until the sensations increased and she felt every nerve ending in her body on fire. His tempo accelerated, harder and faster, taking her higher and higher until he plunged deeply with one last powerful stroke.

Danielle felt a brief moment of pain; it was registered on her face. But it was nothing to what Phillip felt when he encountered that telltale piece of flesh telling him that Danielle *was* a virgin—*had* been a virgin.

His mind paused briefly on that fact, while his body responded to her increased demands. Cupping her buttocks in both hands, he lifted her, plunging deeply, over and over until they climaxed together.

The look of awe on her face as she floated back down to earth was humbling, and Phillip gathered her close in his arms as he rolled off of her. Her smile was radiant, causing his heart to lurch madly in his chest. Placing a tender kiss upon her lips, Phillip rolled to his feet and began to dress.

Danielle hurried to do the same, embarrassed, now, that he should see her naked.

When they were fully clothed, he helped her to her feet, placing his hands on her shoulders. "You'd best go in, sweeting, else you'll be missed."

"Go in?" Her voice choked, her eyes filling with pain. "But I thought you would take me with you. Isn't that why you came?"

He smiled tenderly, cupping her cheek. "But that I could, love. But there is a war on. Have you forgotten? I cannot take you into battle with me."

She clutched at his waist, disappointment biting into her. "I would be very brave. I could help you . . . help you spy on the British."

The Phantom chuckled. "And I'm sure you would be very good. But I would not risk your life; you mean too much to me."

His admission filled her with joy and she smiled. "I do? Truly?"

"Sweeting, you are to be married tomorrow, but I

don't want you to share what we did here tonight with another man. You are mine. I will not have Ashland pawing over your delicate body."

She looked up at him as if he were crazed. "But I have no choice. He is to be my husband. I cannot deny Ashland his husbandly rights. He would seek an annulment of our marriage, force my parents to return his money, most of which they've already spent. It would create a huge scandal."

"Then you intend to bed him?" Phillip held his breath, waiting for her to answer. After Ian's talk, he had decided that perhaps the old man was right. That maybe it would be unfair to take advantage of Danielle's situation. She had no choice in the marriage; and unlike the Phantom, whom she gave herself to freely, she would be forced to bed James Ashland. He had thought to be chivalrous. But now that he'd been with her, tasted her, now that he knew she would be wife to Ashland in all the ways that mattered, he wasn't so sure.

Uncertainty marred her features. She wanted no man but the Phantom in her bed. But if Ashland should insist, she would have no recourse but to comply. In a voice barely above a whisper, Danielle replied, "I do not wish to share myself with anyone but you. I will do my best to dissuade Ashland. Perhaps he will find me not to his liking."

There was a wealth of hope in her words, and Phillip wanted to smile at her naiveté. How could any man, Ashland included, not want to bed such a glorious creature? It was beyond comprehension. "Then he would be a fool," he replied.

Her eyes filled with tenderness as she placed her fingers to his lips. "You will always be in my heart. I—"

He grabbed her hand, afraid of what she might admit. "I must go."

"But when will I see you again?" The thought that she might not brought tears to her eyes. "You are coming back, aren't you?"

"Of course, love. Do you think any man who has tasted the sweetness of your flesh could stay away? I will be back, but I know not when."

"I will miss you," she confessed, snuggling into him, wanting to delay the moment of his departure.

"And I you. But I won't be so very far away." Not very far away at all, he added silently.

"You will be careful? You won't let the British catch you?" Her fears made her voice tremble as she asked the rhetorical questions.

He grinned, tweaking her nose. "Knowing that you will be waiting, I will be the model of caution."

"May I see your face before you go, so I can remember it always?" She reached up to touch his mask, but he grabbed her wrist.

"No, love." He placed a kiss in the center of her palm. "It would not be safe for you to know my identity."

"But I don't even know your name."

He gave her one more quick kiss and crossed to the door. "You may call me *darling.*" He grinned, winked, then was gone.

She stared at the door, hugging herself, remembering all they had just shared, and her eyes pooled again. "Be safe, darling," she whispered. "Let no harm come to the man I love."

8

Danielle's wedding day arrived, and with it, a small measure of guilt at what she and the Phantom had done the previous night.

Not a large measure, for she really hadn't broken her marital vows; they hadn't been spoken yet.

But soon would be.

James Ashland waited below in the great room, dressed, Lottie had described, in a gold brocade frock coat with matching waistcoat and pantaloons, which just happened, Lottie also noted, to match Danielle's own dress.

Danielle stared into the long cheval mirror her mother had *graciously* provided at the insistence of Ashland, wrinkling her nose in disgust.

Not at the dress—the crisp ivory silk sack-back gown, heavily brocaded with gold gilt in a pattern of flowers and leaves, was stunning, though cut lower than she would have liked, revealing a good deal more of her bosom than she thought seemly. The stomacher, fashioned of gold gilt and sequins and pinned from bodice to waist, formed a decorative triangle. It was truly the most exquisite thing she had ever owned.

"Oh, God," she wailed, using the back of her hand to wipe away the tears that now fell freely down her face. How could she go through with this farce of a wedding? Where was the joy, the ebullience, a bride was to expect on her special day?

You've already had your wedding night. You've already experienced your joy.

At that thought, she finally smiled. Last night had been special—perfect. The Phantom had fulfilled every one of her girlish fantasies. In one fell, powerful stroke, he had taken her from girlhood to womanhood and had given her a gift more precious than any of the monetary possessions Ashland had bestowed upon her; he had given her love.

Hugging herself, she gazed again at her reflection, trying to determine if her loss of innocence could be detected. There was no brand to mark her as a fallen woman. No possible way James Ashland would ever know she had lost her virginity until—she shuddered, refusing to think of the consequence.

Spinning on her heel, she caught sight of Lottie bursting through the door. The young woman looked breathtaking in the rose colored satin gown Ashland had provided for her.

"No attendant in his wedding would dress as a common serving wench," he'd written in the note that accompanied the gown.

Lottie's pleasure in receiving the gift had overridden Danielle's annoyance at the man's high-handedness. And, now, seeing her gowned so beautifully, her smile so radiant, Danielle was grateful for the gesture, self-serving or not.

"You look like a fairy tale princess!" Lottie exclaimed, her eyes filling with tears of joy as she took in Danielle's appearance. "Oh, Danny, I'm so happy for you."

Danielle smiled, returning the compliment, not wishing to put a damper on her friend's enthusiasm, though she could muster up little of her own.

Locking arms, the two women descended the staircase. And with every step she took, Danielle wished that it was Prince Charming who waited for the Fairy Tale Princess. Or at least, his closest counterpart, the Phantom.

"My dear, welcome to your new home," Danielle's bridegroom said as the coach pulled up in front of her new abode. "Of course, it's only temporary, until we can find something more suitable. But until then, I believe it will suffice."

More suitable! The place was a veritable palace compared to what she'd been used to, Danielle thought, standing on the brick walk in front of the charming two-story white clapboard house, noting the large English boxwood, the towering magnolias not yet in bloom, impressed despite herself. "It's a fine house," she admitted, allowing Ashland to latch on to her arm and lead her to the red-painted front door where a plump, round-faced woman waited.

"Mrs. Dunstan, meet your new mistress. This is Danielle Sheridan . . . Ashland, my wife."

There was a moment of awkwardness when the woman, Mrs. Dunstan, cast a reproving look in Ashland's direction. Her eyes were full of censure, causing the usually composed Ashland to shuffle his feet nervously.

"Pleased to meet you, miss," she finally said, easing Danielle's doubts about her welcome. "Come in and warm up. It's still chilly out despite the fact it's March. I have my doubts that spring will be arriving this year." Mrs. Dunstan ushered Danielle into the hallway. "I've prepared a wedding feast of sorts. Thought you might need a bit of sustenance long about now."

Danielle returned the gray-haired woman's smile with one of her own. "Thank you, Mrs. Dunstan. You're very kind."

"'Twas Mr. Ashland's idea." She cast a withering look at her employer, before adding, "He be the one that thought of it." So said, Mrs. Dunstan disappeared, leaving a confused Danielle and an embarrassed Mr. Ashland standing in the hallway.

It was going to be necessary to speak with Mrs. Dunstan, Phillip decided. That was as obvious as her rudeness. He knew she objected to his counterfeit marriage, to his "unscrupulous behavior," as she'd put it, and had already taken him and Ian to task over it. Naturally Ian, ever mindful of his stomach and Mrs. Dunstan's excellent cooking, had blamed the entire idea on Phillip.

Danielle shifted nervously, bringing Phillip's attention back to the present. He immediately assumed Ashland's lofty countenance.

"Hope you didn't mind that I couldn't lift you over the threshold, my dear. It's a charming custom but not one suited to a man with a bad back."

Perhaps if he lost a few pounds, Danielle thought, eyeing the gold-covered paunch. "I assure you, Mr. Ashland, I don't mind at all." She stepped farther into the hall, admiring the expensive red-and-gold Turkish carpet and fine pieces of mahogany furniture.

Removing her fur-lined pelisse—another gift from Ashland—she hung it on the hook of the brass hall tree.

"Have I told you how magnificent you look in that gown, Danielle?"

He eyed the expanse of creamy white flesh that overflowed the bodice of her gown and smiled lasciviously, making Danielle wish she'd had the good sense to don a modesty piece this morning, despite Mrs. DeBerry's admonitions.

"At least ten or twenty times," she responded before turning away from his gaze. Oh, God! How could she go through with this? The man looked hungry, as if she would be his next meal. And she knew what a voracious appetite he possessed. Why, he had practically drooled at the sight of her bosom!

She was saved from his further attentions by the arrival of the Scotsman, previously introduced to her as Ian MacGregor. They were all seated in the parlor, sharing a ceremonial glass of claret, and Danielle wondered how much of the liquor she could imbibe before she would be rendered senseless.

"'Tis good ye hae a hearty taste for the grape, lassie," Ian remarked, his eyes twinkling as he noted Danielle's purposeful efforts to drink herself into oblivion. "I willna trust a woman, or a man for that matter, who doesna enjoy the taste o' spirits now and then."

Danielle smiled warmly at the little man seated next to her on the settee. He seemed kind and not the least bit affected like his employer, who was, at the moment, pinching a portion of snuff from an enameled snuff box and stuffing it up his nostril. Ignoring the offensive sight, Danielle asked, "How long have you been in Mr. Ashland's employ, Mr. MacGregor?"

"It's been a healthy stretch of time, miss. I canna say for sure when the cap—" Ian swallowed his mistake, purposely avoiding looking at Phillip, who he knew hadn't missed the slip. He just prayed like hell that the bonnie lassie had, "fine gentleman hired me on, lassie. I think it be about"—he scratched his head—"twenty years or more."

Danielle's eyebrows arched, for she found it incomprehensible that anyone would want to remain in Ashland's company that long. Perhaps he wasn't as bad as she'd thought. Perhaps she had misjudged him. But gazing at him as he stuffed a handful of walnuts into his mouth, she knew that she hadn't.

"Just what is it that you do for Mr. Ashland, Ian? I thought Mr. Dunstan was his valet."

"Ian's my right-hand man," Ashland interrupted. "He does whatever I ask of him. Sort of a man of all trades. Ain't that right, Ian?"

Ian stiffened at the remark. The lad didn't have to make him sound like some type of lackey in front of the lady, he thought. But he replied, "Whatever ye say, Mr. Ashland, sir!"

Phillip chuckled at Ian's indignation, knowing that his first mate hated being considered anything but an able-bodied seaman. "Why don't you go find Mrs. Dunstan and see what's taking so long with our dinner. I'd like to spend some time alone with my wife."

Noting the ardent expression on Phillip's face, and knowing of his less than honorable intentions, Ian grew instantly alarmed, feeling responsible for the young woman's predicament. Miserable that he had brought the lovely lassie to such an end, Ian attempted to stall by pouring himself another glass of claret.

"Ian?" The question was voiced louder and more insistent this time.

Realizing that his ploy wasn't going to work, Ian patted the young woman's hand in a comforting gesture, rose, and made ready to leave, but not before impaling Phillip with a warning look of his own.

Danielle groaned inwardly at the sight of the Scotsman's departure. For some reason she didn't quite understand, she felt safe in Ian MacGregor's company. Quite the opposite of the way she felt in her husband's.

"Now, my dear," James said, pushing himself out of the Chippendale side chair and onto the settee next to Danielle, the cushion dipping down greatly under his weight, "we can get better acquainted. This is the first time we've had all to ourselves."

She forced a small smile that was full of uncertainty.

"I see you're wearing the necklace I gave you." He picked up the golden heart, resting his hand atop Danielle's bosom as he studied it, and felt the pounding of her heart.

The feel of his hand on her breast sent darts of awareness shooting through Danielle, and she was quite at a loss to understand why. He repulsed her! Why on earth should his touch elicit any response other than revulsion? Unless . . .

Oh, my God! She'd turned into a wanton because of the Phantom. Had she developed those cravings, those hungers, that Lottie had warned her about?

"My dear, is anything wrong? You look positively ashen."

She shook her head and swallowed. "No. Nothing. I'm fine."

"I'm so relieved. I wouldn't want anything to spoil our evening together."

His concerned smile was anything but reassuring, and Danielle felt like a frightened rabbit, wanting to bolt, to run from the attentions of this man who was now her husband. But she knew she could not. For like any form of prey, she'd been firmly ensnared in a trap of her parents' choosing and now must suffer the consequence. She forced a smile and was relieved when his hand finally found its way back into his lap.

"I say, I was quite surprised when your sister didn't bother to attend our wedding ceremony. Was there a problem?" He'd noted Regina's conspicuous absence and been grateful for it. He didn't want anything, especially that spoiled brat sister of Danielle's, to ruin her wedding day. Women put quite a store by such events, counterfeit or not.

"Regina wasn't feeling well, or so Mama said. I think she's upset that you chose me over her. Regina's always been the favored one. She's used to getting her—her own way." She stumbled over her words as his fingers began to play with the hairs at the nape of her neck, creating gooseflesh over her shoulders and arms.

"Regina is too pale and pallid for my taste. I much prefer a buxom, spirited wench. It makes for a better . . . union, shall we say."

Apprehension formed thickly in her throat and Danielle attempted to swallow it. *Union!* Did he mean that in the literal sense, as in *joining*? she wondered.

"Don't you agree?"

She was saved from answering by the appearance of Mrs. Dunstan, who called them in for supper. She had never been so relieved to see anyone in her entire life, save for the Phantom. Why, oh why, didn't he come to rescue her?

As Danielle watched James consume over three

helpings of roast duck and wild rice, a bowl of turnips, two helpings of butternut squash and four pieces of pecan pie, her spirits sank to their lowest ebb; surely his voracious appetite would be carried forth into the bedchamber.

The sun had set several hours ago, and the time was fast approaching when he would expect her to go upstairs and ready herself for bed. How *he* would be able to struggle up to the second floor was beyond her comprehension; surely he had devoured an additional ten pounds of weight at this one sitting. At his contented sigh, Danielle looked up to find his gaze upon her.

"Aren't you hungry, my dear? You haven't eaten enough to fill a thimble." He placed three tarts on his now-empty plate.

"You have eaten enough for the both of us, sir," Danielle couldn't help remarking, her voice filled with disdain. But rather than the annoyed response she sought, Ashland only chuckled.

"I confess, my appetite is enormous. I find that I constantly hunger for things. Don't you?"

He sucked the stickiness off the tips of his fingers, and Danielle found the sight quite erotic. A strange tingling sensation began in her toes, slowly making its way up, causing her to shift nervously in her chair.

"No, no I don't. Actually, I find that to eat sparingly is much better for a body. Dr. Franklin even quotes in *Poor Richard's Almanack* that one should, 'Dine with little, sup with less: Do better still: sleep supperless.'"

Ashland chuckled before saying, "Franklin, a wise man though he be, is one of the biggest lechers I know. The man has a prodigious appetite for things other than food, namely women."

Doubting that Dr. Franklin could be as big a lecher as

James Ashland, Danielle pushed her chair back, rising so quickly she almost knocked over her wineglass. "I'm feeling rather tired, Mr. Ashland. I'd like to retire now."

"Of course, my dear. You go on, I'll be right up. Mrs. Dunstan will show you to your room."

Like a prisoner on the way to the gallows, Danielle's movements were slow and weighted as she trudged up the steps to the second floor. Entering the chamber Mrs. Dunstan indicated as that of the mistress of the house, she breathed a sigh of relief at the sight of the narrow bed that hugged the far wall, until the housekeeper opened the door to the adjoining room and she saw the huge four-poster that practically covered one entire wall.

"This be where Mr. Ashland sleeps, miss. Your room adjoins his."

Danielle's gaze dropped to the brass door latch to discover that there was no lock. "It's lovely," she choked out.

"Shall I help you with your hooks, miss? They look to be a tad difficult."

Nodding, Danielle presented the kind woman her back and waited patiently while Mrs. Dunstan unfastened her gown. Better the housekeeper's fingers touching her flesh than Ashland's.

But you didn't seem to mind his touch a while ago.

"Will that be all, miss?" the housekeeper queried, unable to keep the pity out of her voice as she gazed at the frightened young woman before her.

Absorbed in her misery and unaware of the housekeeper's militant thoughts, Danielle nodded absently and sent her on her way, searching through her trunk for a suitable garment to put on. She soon found that none of her old clothes had been packed, and instead of the comfortable linen shifts she was used to wearing to bed, there were several diaphanous-looking nightgowns in their place.

"Good heavens!" she blurted, holding one up to the light. She could see clean through it. Well, there was no help for it, she thought, placing it over her head; it drifted down about her like a faint whisper. It was either this or sleep naked, and she wasn't about to do that. Absorbed in her dilemma, she didn't hear the door open.

Phillip stared, mouth agape, at the sight that greeted him. Danielle was gowned in the flimsiest piece of nightwear he'd ever seen. He knew he hadn't selected it. God's blood! He wouldn't have done that to himself. But he had a sneaking suspicion Mrs. DeBerry had.

Danielle's firm, ripe breasts were clearly visible through the thin material as was the V of her womanhood, which drew his attention like a magnet. He swallowed, hard, and the sound alerted Danielle to his presence.

She turned to find James Ashland gawking at her from the doorway of his room. His face was even whiter than before, and he was perspiring profusely. She stood motionless, wondering what on earth she was supposed to do now, and praying fervently that his heavy-lidded look wasn't an indication of his ardent desire to bed her.

They stared at each other for several minutes, one in reverence, one in dread, until Ashland removed his handkerchief from his pocket and mopped at his brow.

"You're quite exquisite, my dear. I consider myself a lucky man." His gaze shifted to the two ripe mounds, the dark patch of hair between her legs, and he felt his earlier resolve not to bed her melting away. The Phantom had seen her in the dark, and Phillip wasn't prepared for the sight of such beauty—such sheer perfection.

"Thank you," she said in a small voice that indicated her nervousness.

Approaching the frightened woman, he led her to a small love seat by the hearth. On the table next to it stood a bottle of champagne and two crystal goblets, which Mrs. Dunstan had left at his suggestion. "Sit, my dear. I had Mrs. Dunstan bring us some refreshment. Would you care for a glass of champagne?"

Danielle had already imbibed several glasses of claret, and a glass of wine with dinner, but still she could not refuse the chance to fortify herself for the night ahead.

"Yes, please," she replied, taking the glass he proffered and drinking it down in one gulp, much to his amusement. The chit was bent on getting herself drunk, Phillip thought. Something he could not allow to happen.

Setting the empty glass down on the table, he picked up her hand, which was clammy to the touch, and began drawing circles in her palm, trying to soothe her fears, completely unaware of the havoc whirling within her.

Danielle, confused and alarmed by the heat James's touch created, fought the urge to pull her hand out of his grasp. She tried to check the dizzying current racing through her, tried to ignore the way her heart suddenly pounded in her breast.

"Mr. Ashland. I—I think the champagne has gone straight to my head. I'm feeling a bit dizzy."

He wrapped his arm about her shoulders, pulling her in to the warmth of his chest. "Just relax, my dear. The strange sensations will pass soon enough."

But they didn't. In fact, the strange sensations were becoming more pronounced. What on earth was happening to her? she wondered. "Mr. Ashland—"

"Don't you think it's high time you called me by my given name? After all, we are married. People might think it a bit odd if you continue to refer to me as Mr. Ashland. I wouldn't want anyone to think ours wasn't a love match. A man has his ego to contend with, after all."

And some were bigger than others. And in James Ashland's case, everything about him was big. She quickly glanced down into his lap. Or were they? Her cheeks flamed at the outrageous thought, and she responded in a choked voice, "Of course." Her gaze drifted up to his lips, which were only mere inches from her own, and she wondered again what it would be like if he kissed her.

She didn't have long to wonder; for at that moment, Ashland's head came down to cover her lips with his own. His lips were warm and sweet, his kiss slow and thoughtful; and shivers of desire went racing through her, intensifying when his hand moved to cup her breast, massaging the buds into hardened nubs.

She gave in to the pleasure of his touch, and a low moan of desire slipped through her lips. Alarmed by her reaction, she pulled back, mortified to have responded so. "Please, you mustn't."

What was wrong with her? How could she react so wantonly to a man she professed to dislike? How could she forget so easily what had occurred between her and the Phantom just last night?

His gaze was searching as he studied her face. There was desire hidden in the depths of the violet eyes. And remorse. And they both stabbed into him like a jagged-edged knife.

He fought to get his emotions in check and when he did, asked, "What's wrong, my dear. Am I going too fast for you?"

"Yes!" she blurted. "No! I don't know!"

"There's nothing to be frightened of. I know that you're inexperienced, so I will go slowly." He attempted to kiss her again, but she twisted out of his embrace; pushing herself to her feet, she began to pace the room.

He thought she was inexperienced! He thought she was a virgin! What would he do when he found out differently?

Phillip stared as if mesmerized by the lithe movement of Danielle's body as she strode back and forth across the room. The sheer material of her gown swished softly about her, drawing attention to those places he remembered so well and wanted to touch again. God how he wanted her! But he wouldn't take her by force.

"You seem disturbed, my dear. Do you find the idea of bedding me so repugnant that you cannot stand to be in my embrace?" he asked.

Guilt shot through her for all the times she had thought and said unkind things about his appearance. It was obvious that her body was able to accept what her mind had rebelled against. The hurt look on his face pierced her soul.

"It's not that. I'm just—just not ready. We hardly know each other. Perhaps if we had more time to get acquainted, I wouldn't feel so—so—"

"Embarrassed?" he supplied.

"Yes!" she blurted, grateful for the response he offered. "We didn't exactly get off on the right foot. And well . . . it doesn't seem right consummating our relationship when we've not become friends yet."

He walked to the fireplace, staring into the flames, pondering all she had said. After a moment, he turned toward her. But rather than the anger she expected to find on his face, there was acceptance written there.

"Very well, Danielle. I will accede to your wishes, though it pains me to do so." The stiffened member between his legs lent truth to that statement. "As my wife, you are honor bound to consummate this marriage." He ignored the reddening of her cheeks, which proclaimed her guilt, and the heat rising to his own, which proclaimed his, adding, "I will give you the time you seek. I will not force you to bed me. But when the day comes that you desire to share my bed—and you will, for the passions within you are strong—you must come to me. I bid you good night, my dear. I shall see you in the morning." With that he left, closing the door behind him.

Danielle stared at the closed portal and breathed a sigh of relief. She didn't have to bed James Ashland. She could save herself for the Phantom.

Her smile faded. But how could she?

She was a married woman now. She couldn't break her vows, not and live with herself.

Staring down at the palm her husband had so recently caressed, she recalled the desire she had felt in his arms, recalled the anguish her refusal had caused him.

Oh, God, what have I done? she thought, shaking her head. She couldn't bed the man she loved; she couldn't bed the man she didn't.

What on earth was she going to do now?

9

"*I can't do these ridiculous steps!* Why do I need to learn how to dance anyway?" Danielle stamped her foot in frustration, forcing Ashland's eyebrows to arch so high they almost disappeared into his hairline.

Ashland had been the model of patience during their first week of marriage, and his lack of temper, now, in the face of her current tantrum made Danielle feel like a recalcitrant child.

"I'm sorry to behave like such a shrew, but if you make me attend the Gordon's fete this evening, I'll be humiliated."

"My dear," he began, with only a hint of exasperation touching his words, "to become a proper lady, you must learn the rudiments of appropriate behavior. Dancing is but one of them. Once we conquer this, we shall proceed to the art of the fan." He shook his head and his white curls bounced wildly in riotous indignation. "I'm appalled that your mother was so derelict in her duties."

Biting back the retort that formed on the tip of her tongue, Danielle held out her hand to him as he led her in the intricate steps of the minuet once again.

"That's it," he said, smiling in encouragement as she dipped and swayed in time to the melody of the music box.

How ironic that the student was now the teacher, Phillip thought, gazing at the gentle swell of Danielle's breasts while trying to keep his mind on the steps and the music.

It hadn't been so long ago that Captain Cameron had hired a tutor and dance instructor to teach Phillip all he needed to know before entering the world of polite society. And, Phillip recalled, he'd been about as grateful as Danielle was at the moment.

The blue eyes darkened as Danielle's particularly low dip rendered her breasts, right down to her pink-tipped nipples, clearly visible to his view. He swallowed, lost his step, and landed on her toe.

"Ouch!" she screeched.

He smiled sheepishly. "Sorry."

Damn but the past week had been pure torture. He'd been forced to look but not touch, to feast his eyes but not savor the delicious morsel before him.

During the day he'd been able to occupy his mind by instructing her in dance, parlor games of whist and loo, recitations of poetry, which he abhorred and she seemed to relish, and countless other amusements he'd dredged up from memory.

But at night . . . at night he'd been forced to escort her to their adjoining bedchamber, give her a chaste kiss on the cheek, and retire to his room for an unfulfilled, totally miserable night's sleep.

There had even been two separate occasions when

she'd actually come into his room, dressed in that little bit of nothing she wore to bed, to thank him for all his patience.

Those nights had been the worst yet. Not because he'd had to make a mad dash for his wig and hop beneath the covers, so as not to reveal his disguise; but because after her departure, he'd been forced to sneak down to the river and bathe for a good fifteen minutes in the icy waters of the Rappahannock to cool his ardor.

He couldn't take much more of this torture, he decided, feeling himself harden as Danielle cast a brilliant smile of accomplishment his way.

Fortunately, he wouldn't have to, for he'd just learned that Arnold had sailed down to Hampton Roads, pillaging tobacco and other important crops along the way, and he would be leaving tomorrow to evaluate the situation.

But unfortunately, he would never be able to keep his mind on the enemy in the agitated state he presently found himself in.

It was time for the Phantom to make another appearance. Time for him to partake another sampling of Danielle's ample charms. The thought of taking her again, filling her body with his own, had consumed him until all other thoughts had no room to occupy his mind.

Tonight was the night.

Tonight the Phantom would satisfy the lust in his loins.

And tomorrow he would satisfy his lust for vengeance.

* * *

Many of the guests had already assembled at Thomas and Emily Gordon's spring soiree. The Tayloes had arrived, as had the Burkes. Danielle recognized the acknowledged leaders of Fredericksburg society from her time spent at the Lewises.

She hung back, knowing she would never be accepted as their equal. They were landed gentry, and she was still a tavern keeper's daughter, despite her recent elevation in society as James Ashland's wife.

"Come, come, my dear," James prodded, urging Danielle forward, his hand placed firmly in the small of her back. "You'll do just fine. Don't worry. Just try to remember all that you've learned this past week, and smile. You'll put these other ladies to shame."

That was an understatement, Phillip thought, eyeing the violet satin gown that Danielle wore. She looked every bit as elegant as any of the ladies present. And she was a damned sight more attractive. She wore her hair long in soft curls that hung down her back, and it was all he could do not to tangle his fingers in it.

He despised the current fashion of wearing wigs and had insisted that she not, even though he'd been forced to don the hated powdered peruke himself. Damn if his scalp didn't itch like the very devil, he thought, resisting the urge to scratch.

"They won't accept me," Danielle insisted as he dragged her along into the crowded ballroom. Two enormous crystal chandeliers hung suspended from the gilt ceiling. The soft illumination showered down upon the shimmering satins and silks, making Danielle feel as if she were staring at a rainbow. Tapping her foot against the black-and-white tiled floor, she almost forgot her misery until her husband's next words brought her painfully back to her present situation.

"Nonsense. Of course they will. You're my wife."

But a moment later, he was forced to eat his words when he overheard one of a pair of overweight matrons, her back turned toward them, say quite plainly, "Imagine that serving wench daring to enter polite society! Why, I always said, you can't turn a sow's ear into a silk purse."

Danielle's face flamed in humiliation, but if Ashland noticed, he made no mention of it. Instead, he grabbed on to her hand and pulled her toward the imposing duo.

"Ladies," he said, making a leg and bowing graciously. "This is my wife, Danielle. I've been given to understand that you two ladies are *the* reigning queens of Fredericksburg society."

The first lady—gowned completely in white and looking very much like a ship under full sail—twittered, holding her fan in front of her face as she beamed under the praise, while the second, wearing a heart-shaped patch next to a mouth that looked as wide as a cavern, in Danielle's estimation, replied, "You do flatter us, Mr. Ashland."

She held out her hand for him to kiss and he obliged, though it galled him to do so. He would much prefer to have taken the two old bags and fed them to the sharks as bait. They did resemble whales, Phillip observed, and sharks were very fond of blubber.

Pasting on an affected smile, he replied with just the right amount of condescension, "With good reason, madam. Danielle is in need of guidance and sound advice. She is young and newly married. I'm sure you ladies understand."

They both nodded solemnly, and he wanted to

retch at how easily they'd succumbed to false flattery. But he didn't, for when they turned accepting smiles on his new bride, whose cheeks now flamed in mortification, he knew his efforts had been well rewarded.

Danielle was astounded at the transformation that had just taken place before her eyes. Ashland had charmed the two snooty matrons as easily as a snake charmer did a pair of vipers. She smiled gratefully at him and was rewarded with a wink. At least . . . she thought it was a wink. With the monocle he wore in his right eye, it was difficult to tell.

"I'll leave you ladies to get acquainted." He squeezed Danielle's arm reassuringly. "I shall return when the dancing begins, my dear."

Danielle watched in dismay as her husband strode across the room, but when she turned to face Mrs. Penelope Witherspoon and Mrs. Hortensia Loving and found not only smiles on their lips but kindness in their eyes, her fears quickly evaporated. She spent an enjoyable half hour conversing on a multitude of subjects, of which she had a smattering of knowledge, thanks to Ashland's tutelage.

The evening passed in a whirl of dancing, lavish dining, and pleasant conversation. Danielle had seen her husband in his element tonight. James had proven witty, charming—quite the favorite with the ladies, which had really come as a shock.

Staring at him across the small confines of the carriage as the horses plodded their way back to Caroline Street, she studied his sleeping form and saw him in a different light, or at least an altered one.

She had never noticed how incredibly long his eyelashes were as they rested against his cheeks. Why, they rivaled her own in thickness and length. And his face, as it looked now in repose, had lost the look of dissipation she always associated with him.

He was still somewhat overweight, there was no getting around that. And as imperious as King George himself. But he did possess many redeeming qualities: kindness, patience, and consideration.

"Must you tap those infernal ivory sticks against your knee, Danielle? It's really most annoying," he stated, without so much as batting one of those incredibly long lashes.

Gritting her teeth, Danielle snapped her fan shut and leaned back against the velvet seat cushion to ponder her most recent character evaluation.

Restless for no apparent reason, Danielle padded barefoot across the oriental carpet that covered the floor of her room to stand before the fireplace. She'd been unable to sleep since returning from the Gordons' fete.

Gazing into the dying embers, she rubbed her arms against the chill of the evening and threw another log onto the grate. If she lived to be a hundred, she would never grow used to dressing in such thin garments, she decided, fingering the thin lawn of her nightdress.

Others, apparently, had more liking for such scandalous attire. James for one. She hadn't missed his startled reaction the last time she walked into his room dressed in the revealing gown. He had paled considerably, his forehead and cheeks sweating so profusely she thought perhaps he had come down with the ague.

He wasn't immune to her charms, that was for certain. And she had to admit it was a heady feeling knowing she had the power to excite a man in *that* way. Hadn't she done so with the Phantom?

As if conjured up by her thoughts, Danielle turned to find the object of her deliberation lounging casually against the door frame, a wicked smile hovering about his lips.

A startled cry escaped her before she ran forth to grasp him about the waist. "How did you get in here? When did you get back?"

The Phantom smiled, wrapping his arms about her thinly clad body. "I came through the window. You neglected to lock it." He kissed her then, a soul-wrenching kiss that seemed to go on forever. "Did you miss me?" he asked when he finally raised his head to gaze into her heavy-lidded eyes.

The reality of what they were doing came down upon Danielle's conscience like an anvil. Nodding, she pushed out of his embrace. "Yes. Of course. But you mustn't be here." She crossed her arms over her chest in an attempt to hide her nakedness and cast a quick glance toward the connecting door that led to her husband's room. "Ashland is home. He may hear you and call the authorities." She made no mention of what he'd do to her, should he find a strange man lurking in her bedchamber. She doubted the ducking stool would satisfy; it would be the stocks, the pillory, or worse.

Danielle retreated at the single-mindedness she saw in the Phantom's deep blue eyes as he devoured her body from head to toe, stepping backward until her spine rested flat against the wall.

The Phantom didn't seem the least bit concerned about James being in the next room as he stalked her. He obviously didn't view James as much of a threat. Perhaps he intended to kill him. That thought filled her with alarm. James was her husband; she couldn't let any harm come to him because of her desire for the Phantom.

"Why do you run, sweeting?" the Phantom asked, placing his hands against the wall on either side of her head, effectively blocking her escape. "Don't try to deny that you want me." He reached down to fondle her right breast and smiled at her groan of pleasure. "Your body tells no lies. Even now your nipples are hard with want of me."

"Please," she pleaded, trying to remove his hand from her breast. He was so close, pressing into her, she could smell the spicy scent of his cologne, the musky scent of his need, and was intoxicated by both. She wanted him. God how she wanted him. But she couldn't have him.

"You mustn't. I am a married woman now."

The Phantom's eyes darkened. "Has that bastard touched you? Has he taken by force what you so freely gave to me?"

"No!" Danielle blushed, shaking her head. "We haven't shared a bed, as yet."

"As yet?" His look was incredulous. "You mean you want to sleep with that stuffed shirt?" Now that was a revelation. Perhaps Danielle had changed her mind about bedding James Ashland. It would certainly simplify matters for him if she had.

"James is my husband. And you mustn't speak of him like that. He's really very kind. He's taught me how to dance."

The Phantom threw back his head and laughed, making Danielle not only furious but worried that her husband would hear him. "Ssh!" she said, placing her hand over his mouth. "You're going to wake everyone. You must leave." But rather than comply, he merely licked the palm of her hand with his tongue until her tingling arm fell limply to her side.

"If you wanted to dance, why didn't you say so?"

He pulled her against his chest, twirling her around and around until she thought she would faint. Then slowing his motions, he ground his pelvis into her, pressing his hardened member intimately against her mound.

"This is the dance of desire, sweeting." He covered her lips once again, thrusting his tongue into her mouth, allowing his hands to roam freely over every inch of her body.

The sheer lawn night rail offered no protection against the Phantom's practiced fingers as the material glided over her buttocks, her breasts, making Danielle feel incredibly sensual. In spite of her determination to honor her vows, she found herself responding to his captivating advances as the hot tide of passion surged through them.

Consumed by her need of him, conscious thought receded, and Danielle gave in to the yearning that engulfed her senses. She kissed him back with a hunger that surprised her; she caressed his broad shoulders and back with hands that communicated her love for him.

But when the backs of her legs touched the mattress of the bed, the reality of what she was doing— what she'd been about to do—doused her ardor as effectively as a thundershower. With labored breaths, she pushed out of his embrace, shaking her head in denial. "No! We can't; we mustn't."

Phillip took a step toward her, not really believing what his ears were telling him. *No? . . . No!* The word reverberated around and around his head, until it finally penetrated, bringing him to a screeching halt. "No?" he repeated, noting the pleading look in her eyes, which mirrored his own.

He could force her, he knew. But he wouldn't. She was an innocent; she didn't realize the power she had over men. And God help him when she found out.

Taking several deep breaths to restore his equilibrium, he shrugged, as if to communicate that her decision was of no importance to him. "I'm not in the custom of raping little girls, Danielle," he said, seating himself on the love seat. "But I should warn you, I don't like being teased." The tears filling her eyes tore into his gut like bullets.

"I'm sorry," she said, barely above a whisper. "I was not teasing. I—I—" How could she explain that she wanted him as badly as he wanted her? How could she tell him that she wanted no other man in her bed but him? She couldn't. Not when her husband of a week lay in the next room, a husband who'd shown her nothing but kindness.

"If only you could take me with you," she finally said. "Then I could file for an annulment, and we could be together."

He pushed himself to his feet, his voice harsh with frustration when he spoke. "You know I cannot. What you ask of me is impossible."

Her chin lifted. "And what you ask of me is also impossible."

"So be it. I will leave now, and I know not when I will return."

Her heart grew heavy at the thought that she might never see him again. That he could be injured, or worse. . . . She couldn't let him leave angry and followed him to the window, touching him softly on the arm. "You may not have my body, but you will always have my heart," she whispered.

He stared at her thoughtfully, his eyes filling with an emotion she couldn't fathom. But then, she supposed, his thoughts were as mysterious as he was himself. Finally, he smiled and touched her lips in a farewell kiss.

"I will settle for your heart, but only for now, sweeting. Someday I will claim all again. Very soon, Danielle. Very soon." With that promise, he slipped out the window and into the darkness.

The Phantom's declaration brought a wistful smile to Danielle's lips and renewed hope to her heart. But her faith in him would soon be tested by his prolonged absence.

"But why must you go, James? We've only been married a week. Surely, your business affairs can wait." Danielle stared at her husband across the long expanse of dining room table. His puce satin garments were blinding in the early morning sunshine, and she wondered at her own insanity as she pleaded with him to stay.

She should be overjoyed he was leaving, ecstatic. Or, at the very least, excited. But she wasn't. She had grown used to his company in the short time they had been together. She enjoyed their afternoon walks down by the river, the musicals he had insisted they attend.

"What is so important that you must leave?" she asked pointedly, inhaling the freshly brewed coffee and hot croissants that were on the table before her. But even though she was hungry, they weren't tempting enough to pull her out of her dejected state.

"My dear," he stated, stirring another lump of sugar into his coffee, the third, by her estimation, "I've already explained, I have business to conduct. And," he arched an imposing eyebrow at her, "it isn't your place to question where I go and whom I see."

"But what will I do while you're gone? You've made me quit my position at the Lewises, and the Daughters won't be meeting this month due to Harriet's broken foot."

"What happened?" he asked, slathering butter onto his muffin. "Did she put it in her mouth once too often?"

Danielle smiled despite herself. For all his annoying habits, James did possess a sense of humor. "I didn't know you and Harriet were acquainted."

"My dear, that horse-faced hag has approached me innumerable times about making contributions to the cause. I assure you, it was worth any amount of money I had to pay to escape her presence." His lips twisted into a sneer and he added, "Nasty woman, quite nasty," before finishing his pastry.

"Yes, I quite concur. Harriet's been awfully rude to Lottie. Why—"

"Speaking of your friend Charlotte, Danielle. I almost forgot to mention . . . I've purchased her indenture from your parents. She's no longer employed at the tavern."

Danielle's lower jaw slid to her chest.

"Today she begins her new position . . . as your maid, with a suitable salary, of course."

So overwhelmed by the announcement, Danielle continued to stare openmouthed at James, who was seemingly oblivious to her shock and was indulging in another of Mrs. Dunstan's blueberry muffins.

Then, blinking back tears of joy, she leapt from her chair, plopped down on his lap, and gave him a very heartfelt kiss, startling them both.

Phillip was pleased by Danielle's ardent response. Perhaps his departure would give her time to come to terms with her marriage to James Ashland. Perhaps he needed to give her something else to think about as well. With that in mind, he traced the soft fullness of her lips before thrusting his tongue into her mouth.

The intimacy of James's kiss sent the pit of Danielle's stomach into a wild swirl, and she was shocked at her own eager response to it. She knew she should pull away—she had never meant her kiss to become more than a thank-you—but she couldn't seem to break the delicious contact with James's mouth.

Tentatively, she touched his tongue with her own and his low groan of pleasure sent fire through her veins. When his arms came about to clutch at her waist, she pressed into his chest, feeling the sudden need to get closer. But the feel of his erection beneath her skirts brought her crashing back to reality.

Pulling back, she gazed into his eyes, which were dark with passion, then lowered her lashes and said, "Thank you, James," rising quickly to her feet.

Taking a ragged breath, James replied in an unnaturally high voice, "You're quite welcome, my dear. And thank you for that most pleasurable kiss."

Her cheeks flamed. "I—I was overcome with joy at the news of Lottie's employment. And . . . well, just because we haven't—" Her cheeks grew hotter. "Well, you know. That doesn't mean we can't show affection from time to time. Does it? After all, we are married."

"Of course, my dear. But you must realize that I am a healthy man. And . . . ." What could he say? That he wanted to throw her down on top of the dining room table, amidst the muffins and marmalade, and have his way with her. He mopped his face with his napkin instead.

"Why, James, you're blushing!"

James Ashland was not blushing, Phillip thought, but he was damned near to bursting. Ignoring her observation, he said, "I must be off. Ian will wonder what has detained me."

"Do you really have to go, James?" She saw the indecision in his eyes and it gave her a heady feeling to know she had affected his composure as much as he had hers. "Is there nothing I can do to change your mind about your leaving?" she asked, smiling coquettishly, fingering the buttons on his waistcoat.

A tortured growl came from deep within his chest, then he blurted, "God, no!" and smacked at her hand as if he were swatting a pesky fly.

What on earth had gotten into Danielle? he wondered. Had she suddenly developed an attraction for her husband? Or had the Phantom's visit had an unhealthy effect on her amorous inclinations?

Noting James's reaction, Danielle smiled, pecking him chastely on the cheek. "I'll be here waiting when you return."

Phillip's smile was strained as he fought the urge to groan. Danielle was proving to be more formidable than the enemy and decidedly more dangerous.

God save him from the British. And from himself.

10

June 1781
Fredericksburg, Virginia

Seated in the gazebo at the farthest point of the rear yard, Danielle had an excellent view of the river, though she paid scant attention to the lovely flowering magnolias that bloomed near the river's edge, or the profusion of pink azalea that perfumed the air with their heady, sweet fragrance.

She had come today, as she had come every day for the past month, to wait. To wait and watch for any sign of approaching vessels that might carry word of James or the Phantom.

She was pregnant! At least, she was fairly certain she was. She'd not had her monthly flow the past three months. And unless she was very much mistaken— and the tenderness in her breasts told her otherwise— then what she suspected was true.

She was carrying the Phantom's child. A man who

might never return. A man who wasn't her husband.

Oh, James! she thought, biting her lower lip to keep from crying out the anguish she felt. I'm so sorry.

At the sound of Danielle's sigh, Lottie shook her head, saying, "You're gettin' on my nerves, Danny, staring out at the water like that. What's wrong with you, girl?"

"It's been nearly three months, Lottie," Danielle replied, turning to face her companion, her voice filled with despair. "Surely we should have had some word by now."

Setting down her counted cross-stitch, a newly acquired sewing skill Mrs. Dunstan had insisted she and Danielle learn in their new positions, Lottie reached for her friend's hand. "There, lovey, don't fret. I'm sure there's a good reason for Mr. Ashland's absence. There's a war going on, don't forget. Sometimes it's difficult for regular folks to travel." She patted Danielle's hand in a comforting gesture, adding, "You'll make yourself sick brooding. You've already got smudges beneath your eyes that match their color."

Danielle worried her lower lip as she thought of her husband gone these many weeks. She didn't fear that he'd been hurt; James would never have considered entering the army. It would have been too uncivilized a thing for him to do, and the rations would never have appeased his voracious appetite. No, he was most likely still visiting with his friends downriver in York Town. She'd received several letters from him, assuring her of his well-being.

But she hadn't heard a thing about the Phantom's welfare. Was he still alive? Had he been injured? She'd spent many sleepless nights worrying over those very questions. And he hadn't been as considerate as

James in writing, though she supposed that wouldn't have been feasible, considering who he was, and the fact that she was married.

And even if he had, what could she tell him? That he was going to be a father? That their one night together had resulted in a child? He'd made no avowals of love. And he was definitely not a man to be tied down.

Nervously pleating the folds of her apron, she finally asked, "Do you think they're safe, Lottie? Do you think they'll be returning home soon?" Though she referred to James and the Phantom, Danielle knew Lottie would think she was speaking of Ian and James.

"Ian and Mr. Ashland will be just fine. You'll see. We've just got to keep praying that those we love will return home safe."

"Love?" Danielle's eyes widened as she jumped to her feet, a red flush suffusing her cheeks. "Who said anything about love? Surely, you don't think I've fallen in love with James Ashland?" That thought was ridiculous, preposterous. Then why did the idea of seeing him again bring a queer ache to her breast? And why had she spent many a night reliving their farewell kiss?

"Well you have to admit, Danny, you've been brooding a good deal of the time lately. What else am I to think?"

What else indeed? Danielle couldn't very well confide that she was pregnant by the Phantom. She hadn't told Lottie about her relationship with the privateer, about her love for him; she couldn't bear to face the censure and disapproval she was sure to get from a woman who thought the sun rose and set on James Ashland these days.

The Phantom might be her knight in shining armor, her hero. But for Lottie, it was definitely James.

And with good reason. James had been good to Lottie. To all of them. He was kind, considerate, always sending gifts and doing unexpected things. She had yet to receive a letter where a small token of his affection wasn't included, and he'd purchased Lottie's indenture without being asked. He'd been far more considerate of her than she'd been of him.

What would James say when he found out she was pregnant? It was a question that had plagued her for the past month. They hadn't consummated their marriage; he would know that the child wasn't his. James was proud and rather insecure for all his bluster and braggadocio. It would hurt him deeply to know she had chosen another man over him.

Absently, she patted her stomach, grateful that her trim figure showed no signs of a baby yet. No matter what the future held in store for her, she would never regret having this child. It had been conceived in love— at least on her part—and she would cherish it always.

"Danny, are you all right? You look downright peculiar," Lottie observed.

"I'm fine. Truly," Danielle said hurriedly. "Just a bit distracted . . . about James."

Not entirely convinced, Lottie decided to take matters into her own hands. "'Tis a lovely day. Why don't we stroll down to Mrs. Washington's home and pay the old woman a visit. She's sent several notes, requesting that you come." At Danielle's lack of enthusiasm, Lottie added, "And she may have some news of the war. She is General Washington's mother after all."

And so they went, but Mrs. Washington had no more current information than what they'd already heard. And so, after a glass of lemonade and a slice of gingerbread, they left.

"Now what?" Danielle asked as they strolled down Caroline Street on their way back home. Answering her own question with "I suppose we could go by Harriet's and help roll bandages." But that prospect held little appeal. Harriet had snidely remarked on her marriage to Ashland on the three previous occasions she'd visited, and Danielle didn't think she could put up with another one without smacking the woman across her big mouth.

"I have a much better idea," Lottie suggested, a twinkle lighting her eyes. "Why don't we visit the Golden Pineapple? You haven't been back since you wed. And I'm dying to see how your sister is faring in her new role as tavern wench."

"You're awful," Danielle chided, but a smile lit her face. "It would be delicious to see how things are going. And, I confess, I have missed my family, but don't ask me why."

Her family certainly didn't seem to miss her. There hadn't been one word, one visit, one note, to indicate that they even knew of her existence. And it had hurt. For after everything was said and done, they were still her family, the only one she would ever have, and she loved them, even if they didn't feel the same way about her.

"They've been perfectly dreadful to me, especially after James purchased your indenture," she continued. "Good heavens, they blame me for everything he does. As if I have nothing better to do than sit around all day and hatch ruthless schemes against them." She heaved a sigh.

"Well, you really don't," Lottie reminded Danielle, hoping to lighten her mood. "I haven't had so much

spare time in all my born days. I never thought I'd
say this, but there's something to be said for hard
work. At least it keeps a body busy."

"Perhaps I should inform my mother that you'd
like to go back to work for her." At Lottie's horrified
expression, Danielle burst into laughter. "So you're
not that bored, huh?"

"I'd rather sit in the same room with Harriet
Coombs for twenty-four hours a day than go back to
work for the Sheridans. Does that tell you anything?"

Danielle grinned. "Quite a bit actually."

They entered the tavern just shortly after the noon
meal had been served. Elsie and Regina were bustling
about, looking like a couple of chickens with their
heads cut off as they ran to do their customers' bidding.

And in all honesty, Danielle had to admit, it did
her heart good to see them laboring as she and Lottie
had labored for so many years.

"Hello, Mama," Danielle said when her mother
had finished in the great room and reentered the hallway. "How are you?"

If Elsie was surprised to see her eldest daughter, it
didn't show on her face. But disdain did. "A lot you
care," she said, balancing a tray of dishes on her hip.
"Have you come to gloat, now that you're married to
a rich man? And you, Lottie," she added, turning to
stare at her former servant, "haven't you come up in
the world, putting on airs and the like?" She snorted
contemptuously.

A guilty blush stole over Danielle's cheeks, but it
was soon replaced by the heat of anger. "We came to
pay a visit, nothing more, nothing less. And if my
memory serves me correctly, Mama, it was your idea
that I marry Mr. Ashland. Are you forgetting that

generous sum he settled on you after you sold me off?!"

"So, you've found your tongue after all these years."

Danielle thought she detected a hint of approval in the steely blue eyes, but she couldn't be sure and was soon to reconsider when her mother added, "But you haven't found your manners. 'Tis a good thing I still have my darling Regina, for you certainly don't seem to care a thing about me or your father. Why you haven't seen fit to visit since you've married. And after all we've done for you."

With that Elsie quit the room, leaving Danielle and Lottie to stare openmouthed after her.

About to leave themselves, the two women turned to find Regina coming down the stairs carrying an odorous ceramic container that could only have been a chamber pot.

When Regina spotted her sister, her cheeks turned bright red. "What are you two doing here?" She gazed at the lovely gowns they wore and her eyes glittered angrily. "Showing off, I suppose."

Having had quite enough of both her mother's and sister's "hospitality," Danielle advanced on her sister before the young woman knew what she was about and, to the accompaniment of Lottie's horrified gasp and Regina's cry of outrage, grabbed the chamber pot out of her Regina's hands and unceremoniously dumped the contents over her sister's blond head of curls.

Fortunately for Regina, it was only partially full and didn't do a great deal of damage, though you'd never know it from the bloodcurdling screams emitting from her throat.

"I'll get you for this, Danielle," she shrieked, wip-

ing the smelly liquid from her face with her apron.
"You'll be sorry."

Danielle smiled, feeling better than she had in
days. Looping her arm through Lottie's, she said,
"Come, Miss O'Flynn, I believe we have overstayed
our welcome."

At Regina's less-than-ladylike curse, the two
women stared at each other, grinned, then headed
out the door.

Bending over Phillip's inert form, Ian stared intently
at the bleeding wound and shook his head, his face a
mask of worry. "Yer wound's still bleedin', laddie.
Though the bullet went clean through, I suspect it hit an
artery or something. It'll have tae be stitched." He
unwrapped the soiled, bloodstained bandage from
around Phillip's right thigh. The dried blood stuck to the
gauze in several places, causing Phillip to wince in pain.

"God's blood! That hurts like hell."

"An inch higher and you'd be singing soprano in
the church choir, laddie. Yer lucky ye still got yer leg.
And other, more important, parts."

Phillip's head fell back against the pillow. They
were on his ship, sailing toward home, and he could
think of little else except lying between clean white
sheets and having Danielle wait on him hand and foot.

Timothy Luck entered the cabin a moment later,
carrying a bottle of whiskey, a pot of boiling water,
and clean linens to dress his captain's wound.

"Tim, me lad," Ian directed, smiling at the young
boy as he motioned him forward. "Come, bring me
the whiskey. 'Tis good scotch whiskey, I presume."

When Tim obliged, Ian pulled the cork out with

his teeth and took a large swallow before pouring the rest over the open wound. Phillip paled, biting his lower lip so he wouldn't cry out in front of the lad who stared wide-eyed, looking a bit pale himself.

"Now the water, boy."

Ian cleansed the wound again, patting it dry before reaching for the needle and thread. "Did ye boil these like I told ye, lad?"

The cabin boy nodded, his expression earnest. "Yes, sir, Mr. MacGregor. Just like you said."

"Good, lad." Ian turned to look over his shoulder at his patient. "This is goin' tae hurt a wee bit, laddie, so brace yerself."

"Like the rest of your torture hasn't already?" Phillip would have laughed at the absurdity of the statement if he wasn't in so much pain.

"Och, you canna be too sick if ye still have a sense of humor." Ian winked, then set to his task.

The needle went in and Phillip groaned, gripping the sides of the bunk. He tried to think of other things to take his mind off of Ian's torture. He'd seen some of the canvas sails Ian had mended, and didn't hold much hope that his leg wouldn't resemble a patchwork quilt when the old man got done with it.

He turned his mind toward this evening's events, thinking of the patrol of British regulars he and his men had killed. The British patrol had been part of the raiding party that had landed at Burwell's Landing under Colonel John Simcoe. After driving the local militia out of Williamsburg, the British invaders had rendered swift-moving destruction throughout the Tidewater area.

Phillip and his men had sneaked into their camp under cover of darkness. The red-coated bastards had been drinking, celebrating their murder of American soldiers and civilians. And it hadn't bothered Phillip's conscience one bit to return in kind the same treatment they'd dished out.

It had been worth the ball he'd received in his leg to see those bloody bastards die, especially after having seen the two young girls that had been brutally raped, then left for dead. He groaned at the memory of their lifeless faces.

"Hang on, laddie. 'Twill only be another moment or two."

Phillip squeezed his eyes shut, squeezed the images from his mind, and turned his thoughts toward Danielle's sweet face instead.

He thought of how she had looked that last morning he'd seen her—so happy, so mischievous . . . so desirable. Thoughts of her brought a familiar yearning low in his belly and lower, prompting Ian to comment, "'Twould seem yer in good working order, me lad, despite yer grievous wound." He chuckled. "But I canna offer the kind o' comfort ye'll be needing from here on out."

Phillip's eyes snapped opened to find Ian's grinning face hovering over him, and Tim nowhere to been seen. Red-faced, he deflated like a sail in calm seas. "Wipe that smirk off your face, old man, before I take that needle and thread and sew your lips together."

"I've seen yer manhood rise tae the occasion before, laddie," Ian countered, tying off the bandage, then placing a sheet over Phillip's lower extremities to preserve his newly found modesty. "Hae ye fergotten who took ye tae find yer first whore? Who taught ye wot tae do?"

Smiling at the fond remembrance, Phillip nodded. "Aye. And I also remember that you scared the hell out of me by telling me I was going to catch the pox!"

"I dinna want ye placing yer tool just anywhere, laddie. 'Twas the best way tae teach ye tae be circumspect in who ye took tae yer bed."

"And even now that I'm grown and a man, you're still trying to tell me what to do with my"—his brow lifted—"tool, is it?"

Ian shook his head. "Yer speakin' o' the lovely lass, are ye not? And yes, I'm lookin' out fer her welfare. She's sweet and kind and don't deserve tae be treated in so casual a manner."

"Need I remind you whose idea this whole scheme was?"

Guilt suffused the old man's face. "Nay, and I'm ashamed tae admit 'twas me wot thought it up, but only tae save yer worthless hide."

Heaving a sigh, Phillip closed his eyes, suddenly weary. "So you do love me, old man?"

Ian blinked back his tears, grateful that the lad hadn't noticed his humiliation. "Aye, laddie, like ye was me own son."

"And I . . ." Phillip's words trailed off as he fell into a deep sleep.

But Ian didn't need to hear the words, didn't need the reassurance they would have provided. The lad had a generous and loving heart and wasn't nearly as callous or indifferent as he pretended to be.

There was a lot more of softhearted James Ashland in Phillip than the cynical, bitter Phantom.

One day when the war was over, and he no longer needed to hide behind his disguises, the real Phillip Cameron would emerge, taking the best of both his alter egos.

And it was Ian's determination to keep them both alive until that day arrived.

11

"*He's back, love.*"

At Lottie's words, Danielle glanced up from the book on her lap, her heart leaping into her throat. *He was back! James had returned.* About to jump to her feet, she fell back against the cushion of the sofa, the realization that she had missed James—really missed him—hitting her like a ton of bricks.

"It's Mr. Ashland, love. He seems a bit . . . well, under the weather."

Her excitement quickly turned to concern at Lottie's pained expression. "Is he ill?" Untangling herself from the comfortable sofa in James's study, where she'd been reading one of Mr. Shakespeare's plays, *Romeo and Juliet,* Danielle came to stand before the distraught woman.

Lottie shuffled nervously, staring down at her toes, unsure of how to break the news to Danielle that her husband, who'd been gone for months and who'd been the object of much concern and worry, was drunker than a sailor his first night in port.

"Is it serious?" she pressed.

Heaving a sigh, Lottie confessed, "He's *seriously* drunk, Danny. Mr. MacGregor needed Mr. Dunstan's help to cart him up the stairs. And well, they've put him to bed and none too soon by the looks of 'em. Why he's as pasty white as a . . . ."

"Drunk!" The word reverberated loudly off the paneled walls. She'd been worried sick about him—missed him—and he had returned home drunk.

Danielle's eyes darkened to so deep a purple they appeared almost black, black as her mood, Lottie thought, knowing it didn't bode well for the mister.

"Now calm down, Danny. I'm sure he has a reasonable explanation."

She threw up her hands in disgust. "Explanation!" Her cheeks were bright red, the blue veins in her temples throbbing wildly. "That arrogant jackanapes has been gone for months to who knows where, and you're sure he has a reasonable explanation?" She snorted her disbelief. "Here I've been worrying about his welfare, and he's been whooping it up with his *friends*." Friends, ha! He probably had a mistress tucked away somewhere. Why else would he have been gone so long?

The last word came out so sarcastically, Lottie didn't fail to get the implication. "You don't think . . ." She shook her head. "I can't believe Mr. Ashland would be unfaithful to you. Why, you're the only woman he's interested in. He married you, when he could have had his pick of any."

"Maybe one wife wasn't enough. Maybe he needs a whole harem!"

Lottie gasped. "But that's ridiculous."

Anger made all rational thought fly out the window, and Danielle replied, "Is it? All I know is that the man isn't interested in bedding me."

Another gasp, this time much louder, then Lottie fell down with a plop into the nearest chair; the leather cushion made a swooshing sound as she landed, as if she weren't the only one to have the wind knocked out of her.

"Oh, my!"

It was at that particular moment, with Lottie's mouth hanging open and Danielle's pursed so tight only a crowbar could wedge it open, that Ian stepped into the room.

He had overheard the last of the conversation, and from the angry look on Danielle's face, he knew that Phillip wouldn't be receiving any sympathy or the least bit of attention from his wife.

"Is there a problem?" He smiled at Lottie and was rewarded with a dazzling smile in return. One that made his heart beat just a little bit quicker.

"Hello, Mr. MacGregor," she said, her look so boldly assessing, heat crawled up Ian's neck to land on his cheeks.

"You're looking lovely today, Miss Charlotte."

Noting the exchange between the two, Danielle felt her anger rising again. Had Lottie gone insane, flirting with a man old enough to be her father? And Mr. MacGregor! Well, he was lapping up the attention like a cat with a full bowl of cream.

"Yes, there's a problem, Mr. MacGregor," she snapped. "Possibly two," she added, impaling him with a knowing look that said quite plainly, "Shame on you, you dirty old man!" that produced a crimson stain acrossed his face.

"Danny's upset because Mr. Ashland came home drunk, and she's been wondering and worrying where he's been all this time," Lottie offered by way of explanation, receiving a thankful look from Ian Mac-Gregor but a scathing one from her best friend.

"I can speak for myself, thank you very much."

"Well, you needn't get snippy with me."

Ian held up his hands in supplication. "Lassies, please!" His neck was getting sore from twisting it back and forth between the two quarreling women. "I can explain about Mr. Ashland, if only ye'll let me." He rubbed the back of it to ease out the tension while formulating the story he and Phillip had thought up.

"Mr. Ashland came down wie a wee bit of dysentery while we was conducting some business down in York Town. Naturally, he was too embarrassed tae explain, and no' wantin' tae cause ye any upset, wrote that things were fine."

"Dysentery? Doesn't that have something to do with his"—Danielle's face reddened—"bowels?"

Ian cleared his throat. "Why, yes, miss. Ye've got the right o' it. The liquor is the only thing that dulls his senses, so tae speak, ye ken?"

The flux. He had the bloody flux, Danielle thought, fighting the urge to gag. And not surprising, the way the man ate, as if there were no tomorrow. Overcoming her aversion to a chambermaid's worse nightmare, she said, "I'll go to him at once."

Noting the determination on the young woman's face, Ian stalled for time. Dunny and Mrs. Dunstan were in the midst of changing Phillip's bandages and needed more time to complete their task. "I wouldna, miss," Ian said, "no' just yet. Mr. Dunstan's assisting him wie some . . . personal matters at the moment."

Her flush of embarrassment told him he had made his point.

Ian's gaze drifted from Danielle to Lottie, who winked at him, her dimples burrowing into her cheeks when she smiled, causing his member to stiffen in response and her eyes to widen knowingly as she gazed down at the bulge in his breeches. Sweat broke out on his upper lip and forehead.

"I'd best go up and check on Mr. Ashland," he choked. "He might be needing me long about now." As if the devil himself was on his heels, Ian MacGregor bolted from the room, slamming the door behind him.

Danielle's eyes widened. "What on earth has gotten into Mr. MacGregor, do you suppose? I've never seen him so agitated before." A deep frown bracketed her mouth. "You don't suppose James's condition is more serious than he let on?" Genuine concern for her husband's welfare consumed her, mingling freely with the guilt she felt at the terrible conclusions she had jumped at.

A secretive smile touched Lottie's lips, for she knew what was ailing Ian. "Mr. Ashland will be right as rain in a few days' time. His affliction is only temporary. But Mr. MacGregor's . . . now that could require a bit more attention."

Danielle's brows knitted together. "Mr. MacGregor? Ill?"

"Not ill, love, just a few aches and pains. A man his age is bound to have a bit of stiffening at times. 'Tis only natural. I'll go see to him. Perhaps I can come up with a cure for what ails him." She winked and quit the room, leaving Danielle to stare at her retreating back, feeling more confused than ever.

Lottie seemed pleased that Mr. MacGregor wasn't feeling quite himself. In fact, she was whistling cheerfully as she headed up the stairway. Had the young woman lost her mind? Had *she*?

For in all the confusion about James's return and illness, she hadn't thought to spare a moment to wonder about the Phantom's fate.

And that wasn't like her.

It wasn't like her at all.

Elsie stared at her youngest daughter as she lay atop her bed, unable to squelch the feeling of dread that had consumed her since yesterday's incident between Regina and Danielle.

Regina had not been at all her sweet self. She'd been morose, almost nasty, and Elsie despaired at finding a way to appease her. She'd already offered to redecorate her bedchamber, though the bright yellow gingham coverlet and curtains were practically new.

She had even gone so far as to relieve Regina of her more "irksome" duties, such as the emptying of the chamber pots—that pronouncement had produced a string of shrill epithets—and cleaning the guest chambers, jobs that Danielle and Lottie used to perform with much greater efficiency.

Her sweet girl just wasn't cut out to be a serving wench, she supposed. Approaching the tall tester bed that she'd imported all the way from Paris, France, Elsie bent over to place a kiss on Regina's cheek. "You mustn't fret so, daughter. Your sister and you have quarreled for years. This was but another of Danielle's childish pranks. Why—" Elsie was silenced by her daughter's dark, angry look.

"You don't know what you are talking about, Mama. Danielle hates me; she always has. She took Mr. Ashland away from me, knowing that I wanted to marry him, and now she has humiliated me further. I should have been the one to wear the pretty gowns and travel in the fancy coach. Why even that fat cow Lottie has nicer clothes than I do." She began to wail loudly all over again.

"There, child, stop your crying. You know how it makes your face all puffy."

"What does it matter? No man as wealthy as Mr. Ashland will ever offer for me. I'm doomed to spend the rest of my life living here in this dump."

Elsie was momentarily taken aback by the bitterness of Regina's words. She'd always given Regina everything she ever wanted, sparing no expense, often going without herself. She just didn't understand her daughter, not at all. She said, "But I thought you liked living here. I've given you a lovely room. And your wardrobe is every bit as fine as your sister's."

Regina jumped down off the bed and faced her mother, her voice dripping venom when she said, "You call this lovely, Mama? How ignorant of you to think that." At Elsie's shocked gasp, Regina's smile grew more malicious. "Danielle is living in the lap of luxury, with servants to wait on her hand and foot, and a fabulous house with expensive imported furnishings. That's lovely, Mama. This," she swept out her hand to indicate her room, "is barbaric compared to what Danielle enjoys."

"Your father and I have tried to provide you with the very best, daughter. We can't be blamed if Mr. Ashland chose your sister over you."

The blue of Regina's eyes were like bright flames that glowed in the wake of her anger. "Yes, you can! You accepted his offer. If you hadn't, he would have been forced to marry me. I deserved to be his wife, not Danielle." She crossed to the looking glass, staring at her reflection. "I am the most beautiful. You said so yourself, Mama. No other woman can compare to me."

Fearful of the crazed look in her daughter's eyes, Elsie crossed the room to put her hands about Regina's waist. "Regina, child, you mustn't dwell on what is past. We will find you another husband. One that is just as wealthy as Mr. Ashland. Mark my words. I'll put my attentions to it this day."

Regina laughed, the sound so chilling it sent shivers down Elsie's spine. "You had your chance, Mama. Now I will take matters into my own hands."

Unease settled over Elsie like a damp quilt. "What do you mean?" But by the determined set of her daughter's chin and the avarice in her eyes, she thought she already knew.

"Mr. Ashland will have to be convinced that he married the wrong sister. Once he is, it will be an easy matter for him to throw Danielle over for me."

"But that would create a scandal! Your reputation will be ruined."

"What good is reputation without money? You taught me that, Mama. You should be proud that I'm taking your teachings to heart. You always told me I could have whatever I wanted, that I just had to go after it. Well, I am, Mama. I've decided that I want Mr. Ashland. And if I have to seduce him and get myself with child in order to get him, then I will."

"You'll do no such thing, Regina!" Elsie shouted,

uttering the first harsh words she'd ever thrown at her daughter. "I've worked hard to bring you up to be a proper lady. I'll not have you throwing yourself at some man like a cheap whore."

"Why not, Mama? Isn't that how you ended up marrying a man with property?"

Regina wasn't prepared for the hand that shot out to slap her hard across the face. The force of it rocked her back on her heels.

"You've no idea what you're talking about," Elsie retorted. "So shut your mouth, girl, or I'll take a switch to you."

At her mother's words, Regina threw back her head and laughed, but the laughter soon died, replaced by a look so wicked it sent goose bumps sprouting over Elsie's arms.

"A switch! That's rich, Mama. Why switch me when I tell the truth? I know why you married papa."

"Stop, Regina!" Elsie twisted her fingers nervously in the folds of her apron, fearful of what was to come.

"I saw your indenture papers, Mama. I unlocked the trunk in your room and looked through your things."

Elsie gasped at her daughter's admission, apprehension slithering down her spine like a snake.

"I know you were nothing more than a tavern girl from Bristol who was sold on the auction block to settle your father's gambling debts. Papa bought you, Mama. Just like a slave. But you were smart. You got yourself pregnant, didn't you, Mama? Pregnant with Danielle. That's why you hate her so much, Mama, isn't it?"

Elsie covered her face with her hands, sobbing

into them, shaking her head. "No . . . no. I don't hate Danielle. I love her, just as I love you."

"No, Mama. You always loved me best. I was your favorite. Danielle was a constant reminder of who you were and where you came from. You sold her off, just like your father sold you off, only you got far more from James Ashland."

Elsie's face whitened at the viciousness of her daughter's words. She could hardly believe that this cruel, vindictive woman was the same child she had taken to her breast and comforted, was the same young woman she had cared for and cosseted.

She finally found her voice and tried to explain. "Arranged marriages are not uncommon, Regina. Mr. Ashland's offer was more than acceptable. *You* would have been more than happy to accept it," she accused.

Oblivious to her mother's anguish, Regina picked up the silver-handled hairbrush off the dresser and brushed her long blond tresses. "Do you think Mr. Ashland will like my hair, Mama? Do you think he will want to run his hands through it?" She smiled spitefully at the look of horror on her mother's face.

"Regina, please! You can't mean to go through with this. I've worked too hard to make you into a proper lady. Think of the consequences."

"The Sheridan women have always been whores, Mama. First you, then Danielle, and finally me. It's a fitting legacy, don't you think?"

Knowing to argue further would be useless, Elsie crossed to the door, pausing before it, and shook her head sadly. "Your bitterness has made you twisted, child. I will pray for you."

"Pray for Danielle, Mama. She will need your prayers more than I."

After her mother left, Regina climbed back on the bed and curled up in a tight little ball, rocking back and forth as she contemplated her revenge.

Danielle would be sorry for what she had done, Regina vowed. They would all be sorry. But Danielle would be the sorriest for stealing Mr. Ashland. And for that, she would never be forgiven.

"I don't understand why I cannot see my husband, Mr. MacGregor. It's been two days. Surely he is well enough to see me."

Danielle waited patiently in the hallway in front of James's room for Ian MacGregor to give her a suitable answer. Thus far, the ones she'd received hadn't satisfied her at all. James might be suffering from humiliation, but she was suffering just as much from ignorance.

Ian stepped into the hall, closing the door softly behind him. The light from the chamber stick he held illuminated the gray in his hair and the doubt creasing his face. "'Tis late, lassie, almost nine o'clock. Why no' come back tomorrow? I'm sure Mr. Ashland will feel more like visiting then."

Crossing her arms over her chest, Danielle tapped her foot in agitation, casting him a defiant look. "I'll not leave, Mr. MacGregor, not until I've seen James for myself." When he started to protest, she held up her hand. "You tell me he's fine, that he's resting, but for all I know his condition could be quite serious. I think I have the right to know. Don't force me to pull rank on you, Mr. MacGregor."

Ian smothered his smile at the young woman's vehemence. She was a worthy mate for Phillip, he thought, and as tenacious as a bull terrier. "I'll just be a moment, lass. Let me make sure Mr. Ashland is decent. I wouldna want tae shock yer sensibilities, Miss Danielle, but Mr. Ashland has a habit o' sleeping in the buff."

Danielle's eyes widened at Mr. MacGregor's revelation. How was it that Mr. MacGregor was privy to the fact that Danielle didn't share a bed with her husband? Apparently, James had confided in his servant; the look on Ian MacGregor's face told her he knew exactly what went on, or didn't go on, in the master bedchamber.

She blushed at the thought. "Very well, Mr. Mac-Gregor. I will wait exactly one minute. If you're not out here in that length of time, I will enter this room, naked husband or not."

She was grateful a moment later when Ian reappeared, ushering her into the room. It was dark and took a moment for her eyes to adjust. There was only one candle burning on the nightstand, casting eerie shadows over James's inert form.

"We've had tae keep the light low, miss. It hurts Mr. Ashland's eyes."

Danielle failed to see what Ashland's eyes had to do with his other parts, but she kept silent on the subject and approached the bed. "That will be all, Mr. MacGregor. I'd like to spend a few minutes alone with my husband."

"But, miss—"

"It's quite all right, MacGregor. Danielle is capable of seeing to my comforts." The words were softly spoken, but there was a finality to them that the little Scotsman dared not defy. With a *hmph*, he spun on his heel and quit the room.

"Mr. MacGregor is quite protective of you, James," Danielle informed him, taking a seat on the chair next to the bed. "I had a devil of a time getting in here to see you."

Phillip drank in the sight of her. She was dressed in a simple muslin gown, but the lilac color brought out the violet in her eyes. Her hair was braided in a long plait that hung down over her right breast, shielding the perfect mound from his view, though her body was indelibly etched in his memory.

Danielle shifted nervously, forcing Phillip's attention back to the role he played. "You mustn't blame Mr. MacGregor, my dear. He was only following my instructions."

There was a grayish cast to his skin—a very unhealthy pallor that shocked Danielle when she bent forward to look at him more closely. His eyes were half-closed, the wig he wore slightly askew. "You don't look at all well, James. I think I should call upon Dr. Fortney and bring him here at once."

"I'm fine, my dear." He reached out, grabbing her hand, and his skin felt hot, almost feverish, alarming her. Placing her other hand on his forehead, she gasped. "You're burning up. I'm going for the doctor at once." He pulled her back down when she attempted to rise from the chair.

"I'm fine. And if you continue to exhibit such hysterics, I will be forced to have Mr. MacGregor eject you from this room. You're upsetting me, Danielle. I simply abhor doctors. Now sit quietly and let me enjoy your company."

"But, James!"

"Mr. MacGregor," he called out.

"Very well," she replied, relieved when the door

didn't open at once. "If you want to die, that's up to you. I just hope you'll leave me a wealthy widow."

"I have no intention of leaving you wealthy or otherwise. I found that I missed your charming company while I was gone."

For some reason, his admission pleased her. "Then why were you away so long? I thought surely you'd only be gone a few weeks. But then one month turned into two and. . . . Your letters didn't explain your actions, James." Though if he'd been with another woman, he wasn't likely to write about it.

"My dear," he squeezed her hand before continuing, "where I go, who I see, and how long I'm away, are really none of your concern." She stiffened and he patted her hand soothingly. "I told you before we wed that I value my independence every bit as much as you value yours. Ours is not a love match, Danielle, so my absence shouldn't cause you any unhappiness."

An odd twinge of disappointment flared through her that she didn't quite understand. "One does not have to be in love to be worried about another human being. Forgive me for caring." He brought her hand to his lips for a kiss, and she felt the familiar yearning that his touch always elicited.

"And forgive me for being so callous, my dear. I am not quite myself, as you may have gathered."

He was every bit like himself—rude, pompous, overbearing—which was exactly the problem, but she refrained from saying so. Changing the subject, she asked, "Why do you wear your wig to bed? Surely, it cannot be at all comfortable. Would you like me to help you remove it?" She leaned forward but he sunk back into the pillows.

"No! I mean, no thank you, my dear. I'd be embarrassed to have you see me unadorned. As you are probably aware, it is often necessary to have one's head shaved before purchasing a wig. My hair has not yet grown back from when the peruke maker shaved it. I'm afraid I'm rather bald without it."

"Oh, I see." She waved off his objection with a shake of her head. "But that doesn't really matter. I've seen bald-headed men before. Old Mr. Carruthers down at the cooperage is as bald as your stomach is round. Sorry," she said at his affronted expression. "I assure you, I won't faint."

"But my head gets so chilled when I remove it, you see. It's most uncomfortable."

"You could wear a nightcap. Many men do."

Damn but she was a persistent chit!

"As I'm sure Mr. MacGregor confided to you," he said, pulling the covers up to his chin, "I prefer to sleep in the altogether. Covering my head would defeat the purpose of the freedom I so enjoy. You really should try it sometime, my dear. It's quite a delicious sensation to feel your bare skin against the coolness of the sheets, especially on a night as hot as this one."

A tight smile crossed her lips and she was grateful for the semidarkness that hid her mortification. James had the most annoying propensity for discussing the most absurd, most provocative subjects of any person she'd ever met.

Gazing toward the open window, she welcomed the warm air against her cheeks, listened to the whirring of the cicadas, the croaking of the tree frogs, to get her mind off the persistent images that floated through her mind.

What would it be like to lie naked with James

beneath cool white sheets, with nothing but his hands and the warm evening air to caress her skin?

"My dear, are you all right? You've suddenly grown so quiet. I hope I haven't offended you."

"Not at all," she replied quickly, deciding to give James a taste of his own medicine. "I'm not nearly as prudish as you seem to think, James. I often sleep in the nude," she lied, arching her back, thrusting her chest out, watching how his eyes followed her every movement. If he had been with another woman, then she wanted him to know what he was missing.

"Really," he choked, trying to dispel the torturous image. But as he lay looking up at Danielle, he stripped every inch of her clothing off with his imagination, rendering her as naked as he himself was now. Suddenly the covers tented and he placed his hand over himself to hide the fact he was as stiff as a board.

Danielle hadn't failed to notice where his hand had strayed and it amused her. It was a subtle revenge for his callous treatment of her, she knew. And one that was dreadful to perpetrate against a sick man, but . . .

"As you know, James, I'm quite a follower of Dr. Franklin. And the good doctor always recommends that one should take air baths. He insists that they're instrumental to good health. Perhaps you would care to join me sometime?"

He nodded weakly, then yelled, "Mr. MacGregor!" His voice was surprisingly strong for such a sick man, and Danielle smiled inwardly.

When the door opened, he smiled apologetically at Danielle. "I'm sorry, my dear, but you have quite worn me out. Ian," he said, turning toward the servant who had just entered the room, "Please show

Danielle out. I need to rest."

"May I come back tomorrow and visit, James? Perhaps I can read to you. Or rub your back." She smiled sweetly at the tortured expression he wore.

He groaned and waved his hand at her, as if the decision was too ponderous to make at the moment.

Surprising not only herself but her husband, Danielle bent over the bed and kissed him on the cheek, whispering, "Get well quickly, James. We have much lost time to make up for." There was a wealth of promise in her tone, and she heard him groan again, louder this time, as if he were terribly pained, as she made her way to the door.

"Take care of Mr. Ashland, Mr. MacGregor," she admonished. "I fear his condition is more serious than you led me to believe."

Ian nodded his assurance, shutting the door behind her. But when he viewed the miserable lump who lay before him on the bed moaning in despair, he knew that the lovely lass had the only cure Phillip needed.

And it was the very same one he'd received two days ago from his darling Charlotte.

12

The following day, Danielle entered the hallway to find Lottie sneaking up the staircase, her dress half undone, her red hair flying wildly about her pinkened cheeks.

"Charlotte O'Flynn! Whatever have you been doing?"

The question was purely rhetorical; Danielle didn't need an answer to figure out what her friend, who had pulled up short at the sound of her voice, had been up to, especially when Ian MacGregor stepped out of his room off the hall with the stupidest grin on his face, instantly confirming her worst suspicions.

"Afternoon, lass," he said.

The violet eyes narrowed as she took in his hastily rearranged clothing. The buttons of his waistcoat were lopsided, and his stock, which was usually spotless, was wrinkled and smudged. The evidence was damning.

"Don't you lass me, Mr. MacGregor. You defiler of young women. You—you pervert! Why, Mr. Ashland shall hear about this."

Ian paled as the angry woman stomped up the stairs like an army of one and grabbed on to Lottie's arm, without so much as another glance in his direction, saying, "Come along, Charlotte. We need to talk."

Lottie, who didn't look the least bit perturbed at Danielle's overbearing manner, winked at Ian and blew him a reassuring kiss, before allowing Danielle to drag her the rest of the way up the stairs. Once they reached Lottie's room, Danielle shut the door behind her and whirled about, a look of outrage on her face.

"How could you, Lottie? Why, Ian MacGregor is old enough to be your father for heaven's sake! And in the middle of the day, too!"

Lottie's smile was wistful, and she heaved a contented sigh before replying, "Calm yourself, love. You're starting to purple."

"This isn't time to jest, Lottie. What you have done is serious."

"What Ian and I do is our business, Danny. And don't go looking hurt and offended," she added, noting the fury flaring in Danielle's eyes. "I know what I'm doing."

Danielle doubted that very much. Lottie was far too impetuous to consider the consequences of her actions, and obviously Mr. MacGregor hadn't considered anything else but his own needs. She asked fiercely, "Did that vile man seduce you?"

Lottie burst out laughing. "More like the other way around. Why, I practically had to force Ian to make love to me. He wasn't very cooperative at all . . . at first."

A loud gasp escaped Danielle as she dropped down onto the feather mattress. "You seduced Mr. MacGregor?"

Lottie nodded. "'Twas back in February, shortly after he came."

"February!" Danielle's mouth dropped open in disbelief, then she asked, "Why, for heaven's sake?"

"If you was bedding your husband, you wouldn't be asking me that question," Lottie threw back, looking quite smug as she crossed her arms over her chest.

Danielle stiffened. "This is not about my relationship with James Ashland, which, I might add, you know very little about."

"Well I know that you ain't sleeping together, and that you're probably as untouched as the day you married him."

Heat seared Danielle's cheeks, making them feel as if they were on fire. Placing her palms flat against the burning flesh, she rose to her feet and crossed to the window, refusing to look her friend in the eye. How on earth could she tell Lottie the truth?

Outside on a branch of a blossoming magnolia, a fat robin trilled a happy tune and Danielle's mood soured even more. What on earth did that stupid bird have to be happy about? It was a perfectly miserable day as far as she was concerned.

Despite the fact that the sun shone brightly and the day was warm, despite the fact that James was feeling much better and would probably resume his normal activities tomorrow, and despite the fact that Lottie and Ian seemed to be walking on air, she felt utterly wretched.

"Danny," Lottie called out, trailing Danielle across the room. When she turned around, Danielle's face was as crimson as the bed hangings, confirming Lottie's suspicions and bringing a smile to her lips.

"So, you and Mr. Ashland have been intimate? You're not a virgin anymore." It was a statement not a question, and Danielle's shoulders slumped in response to it. "'Tis nothing to be ashamed of, love. Sean O'Toole did me a big favor when he relieved me of that burden."

Tears welled in Danielle's eyes and her voice was thick with emotion when she replied, "It isn't what you think."

"You're still a virgin?" Lottie's forehead wrinkled in confusion at the shake of Danielle's head. "But you and Mr. Ashland have been intimate, right?" Another shake of the head, this time followed by more tears. "But if you're not a virgin, and you haven't been with Mr. Ashland, then that means"—Lottie stared at her friend with new understanding, her eyes widening— "you've been unfaithful?!"

Still blushing, Danielle wagged her head. "Not since I've been married."

Her response was so low, Lottie had to strain to hear it. When the admission finally sunk in, Lottie grabbed Danielle by the arm and hauled her over to the bed. With her hands on Danielle's shoulders, she pushed the distraught woman down to a sitting position, then seated herself next to her. "We need to talk, girl."

"I wanted to tell you, Lottie, truly I did." She played nervously with the folds of her dress, staring down into her lap. "But I didn't know how. And James has been so good to you. I—I thought surely you'd despise me."

"Now why would I go and do that, love? That would be like the pot calling the kettle black."

Danielle's head shot up. "But you don't know whom I slept with."

"From the color of your cheeks, I doubt you did much sleeping, whoever the gentleman was."

"You're perfectly awful!" But the twitch of her lips belied her anger.

"And unless you tell me it was King George himself or some blimey redcoat, I doubt I'll be too upset."

Danielle took a deep breath. "Even if I tell you it was the Phantom?"

Lottie's mouth dropped open, but noting the anxiety on Danielle's face, she snapped it shut again. "You and the Phantom? So he was real after all?"

"I told you that, Lottie. You just didn't believe me."

Nostrils flaring with fury, Lottie spewed a few choice epithets, before saying, "And how heroic can he be to take an innocent young woman's virginity, tell me that?"

"He didn't take it; I gave it to him," she insisted.

Lottie snorted contemptuously. "If you believe that, girl, you're more naive than I thought."

"But—"

"The man is a practiced seducer, Danny. Like most sailors, he's probably got a girl in every port. An experienced man like the Phantom eats little girls like you for supper, then spits out the leavings when he's through." She placed her hand on Danielle's shoulder, staring intently into her eyes. "Did he leave you with child?"

Tears filled the violet eyes. "Yes!" Danielle blurted, her face reddening in shame.

"God in heaven!" Lottie wailed, slapping her forehead with the palm of her hand. "I knew no good would come of your infatuation."

"But it isn't what you think, Lottie. The Phantom really cares about me; I know he does. And I love him. At least, I think I do." She shook her head. "I don't know what I feel anymore; I'm so confused."

Lottie heaved a frustrated sigh as she stared at the abject misery on Danielle's face. "You're not in love with a man, Danny. You're in love with a fantasy, a larger-than-life legend."

"It was the man I surrendered my virginity to, a man whom I gave my heart to. I'm not a child, Lottie. I know the difference."

"And what of your husband? Have you no feelings for him?"

Lottie's question hung in the air while Danielle searched her heart for the answer. What did she feel for James Ashland? She liked him. For there were many times when he had made her laugh, like this morning, when he related the story of Harriet Coombs's visit.

"There I was sitting in my chair by the window," James had said, "garbed only in my dressing gown, enjoying the warm weather, when who should walk in but that buck-toothed spinster Harriet Coombs.

"Well, I would have given any amount of money to have had a likeness of her face when, in mid sentence, her eyes drifted down to notice that my feet were bare. She shrieked a bloodcurdling scream, then climbed upon a chair, as if she had just seen a mouse.

"Naturally, I thought she had, so I stood up to help her and my robe opened up, exposing my calves. And good Lord, the women fainted, falling smack dab on the floor.

"I tell you, Danielle, after I got over my shock, I couldn't stop laughing; tears were rolling down my cheeks.

"When she came to, roused by my hysterics, no doubt, she started screaming all over again, then bolted from the room.

"I wished you'd been there, my dear."

So had she, Danielle thought, for they'd probably seen the last of Harriet for a while, and what fun it would be to tease her at the next meeting of the Daughters.

Recalling James's face as he recounted the tale, Danielle smiled thoughtfully, finally answering, "I care for James very much. He's been good to me, which is why I have not broken my vows since we've been married." She paused. "And I had the opportunity."

"The Phantom came back?" Lottie's voice was filled with incredulity.

Inclining her head, Danielle explained the events as they'd happened, leaving out only the most intimate details. Engrossed in her recitation, she didn't notice the growing fury on Lottie's face.

"You're a fool, Danny. The Phantom only wants one thing. Now that he's had a taste of it, he'll be back time and time again. You must stop seeing him."

"But I care about him—care what happens to him."

"You've a husband to consider. And if you care about him and that child you're carrying, you won't see the Phantom again."

Her heart grew heavy at the thought, but concern for her unborn child overshadowed all else. "What does the child have to do with seeing him? Once I tell him—"

"Tell him! Have you gone completely mad, girl? You can't tell him. You're married. If anyone found out that the child wasn't James Ashland's, it would be branded a bastard. And you, Danny, you'd be branded a whore."

Danielle's face whitened and she covered her face with her hands. "Oh God! What am I to do? James and I have never consummated this marriage. He'll know it isn't his child."

Lottie wrapped her arm about Danielle's shoulder in a comforting gesture. "If it's any consolation, love, you're not alone in your predicament."

Danielle's head shot up and her eyes rounded. "Oh, Lottie! You mean . . . ?"

Lottie nodded. "Ian didn't shoot any blanks. Like you, I got caught my first time with Ian. I figure I'm almost five months along."

"But that's only a month more than me, and you're so much bigger than I am." She stared down at her stomach, which was still fairly flat.

"You should be thankin' your lucky stars, Danny. My own plump proportions disguise the fact that I'm with child, but you're so thin. . . . Just be grateful you're not stickin' out yet. We don't want Mr. Ashland gettin' suspicious."

"Oh, Lottie," Danielle wailed. "I've made such a mess of everything. I don't know what to do."

"What you've got to do, Danny, is bed your husband."

"Bed James? But how? I mean—that will be terribly awkward. Since my reluctance to bed him on our wedding night, he's never brought the subject up again. I don't think he's interested in bedding me."

Lottie laughed at the absurdity of Danielle's comment. "Girl, with your looks and figure, you won't have a problem seducing your husband to your bed."

Blushing furiously, Danielle stared wide-eyed at her friend. "Seduce! I can't do that." But she would have to, she thought, recalling his words: *"You must come to me."* Suddenly, she had the most nauseating feeling in her stomach that had nothing to do with her baby.

"You've got to do it right away, Danny. The sooner the better, if our plan is going to work."

Danielle shook her head, her forehead wrinkling in confusion. "Our plan? I wasn't aware that we had one. What plan is that?"

"Why, to have your husband fall in love with you."

Furtively, the two men made their way down the York Town wharf, keeping their tricornered hats pulled low to disguise their true identities. It was doubtful anyone would recognize them as British sailors. After all, the colony was full of Englishmen, though they now called themselves Americans.

Andrew Ellsworth sneered, thinking of the stupidity of these misguided traitors. Americans! They were nothing more than rabble who chafed at following the rules of His Majesty's divine providence.

"What's the name of that tavern where we're to meet this Loyalist contact of yours?" Simon asked, not liking the inquisitive stares they'd been receiving from the sailors on the wharf. "Are you certain we won't be recognized, Captain? I feel a bit uneasy about this whole thing."

"Your spine is as flexible as a willow branch, Petti-grew. Had I known you were such a coward, I would never have chosen you to be my second in command."

Pettigrew stiffened. "You're confusing cowardice with prudence, Captain. Your lust for revenge could very well get us killed. We nearly lost our lives during that battle with the French warship. If it hadn't been for that thunderstorm coming up like it did, we'd be dead now."

Ellsworth lowered his voice. "'Tis but one more reason that we need to kill him, Simon. Think back, man. The way he humiliated all of us. I came damn close to losing my commission, and you would have been back working at your father's print shop. Is that what you want? If this man Robbins knows the location of the Phantom, then it's worth the risk we're taking."

The Boar's Head Tavern came into view and Pettigrew was saved from answering. The tavern was smoke-filled and noisy when they entered. Ellsworth spotted his contact sitting alone in the far right corner. "There he is," Ellsworth informed his first lieutenant. "Smile, Simon, we're about to get our hands on that bloody Phantom pirate."

Phillip smiled in relief as the last stitch was pulled out, and Ian, looking very much like the savior of all mankind, pronounced him physically fit.

Having been confined to his room for several days, and still feeling as wobbly as a newborn colt, Phillip was not inclined to agree with his first mate's assessment. "I don't know how you can say that, old man. There's no strength left in my legs and arms. I doubt I could hoist myself up, let alone a sail."

"Exercise is wot ye be needin', laddie. Why no' take that wife of yours fer a stroll. I would consider it a personal favor if ye get the lass out o' me hair fer a while. She watches me and Lottie like a hawk."

Observing the old man's misery, Phillip chuckled. Who would have thought that an old sea dog like Ian would be smitten by a mere lass—and an Irish one at that? Lottie, or Charlotte, as Ian liked to call her, had gotten beneath the old man's skin. He followed the buxom maid around like a faithful puppy, sniffing at her skirts like a randy dog in heat.

Ian had related the confrontation he'd had with Danielle two days ago, and knowing his dear wife's temper, it wasn't difficult for Phillip to understand why Ian wanted her gone.

"I'll take Danielle off your hands and be glad to do it. I relish the idea of spending some time alone with her." If only it didn't have to be in the guise of James Ashland. As ridiculous as it sounded, he was beginning to despise the man with a vengeance, especially now that Danielle seemed to take an inordinate amount of pleasure in torturing him.

"'Twould please me tae no end, laddie. Charlotte and I welcome the time alone together."

But as it turned out, Charlotte and Ian were forced to accompany Phillip and Danielle on their morning constitutional, much to both men's consternation.

Strolling down Caroline Street toward the main part of town where the majority of the shops were located, Ian and Phillip trailed a few steps behind their companions.

"'Tis a fiendish plot against me," Ian whispered to Phillip, who smiled sympathetically in return, not any happier about the recent turn of events than Ian was.

"The woman's got eyes in the back o' her head."

At that moment, Danielle turned and looked over

her shoulder, cocking a questioning eyebrow in the Scot's direction. "Is there a problem, Mr. MacGregor? I forget that you're older than the rest of us. Shall we slow down?"

Ian reddened and Lottie chuckled, returning Danielle's wink. Poor Ian must be in a state, she thought. They hadn't made love in days. But if her and Danielle's plan to bring the little Scotsman to the altar was going to work, she would just have to let him suffer for the time being.

Phillip grinned at Ian's discomfort, prompting the older man to say, "I'd like tae know wot the hell ye've got tae smile about? Ye've been making more trips down tae the river in the dead o' night than me."

At that reminder, the grin dissolved. And if heated stares could burn, Danielle and Lottie would have been seared right down to their stays.

"Look," Lottie remarked a moment later, pointing to the young woman who had just exited Mrs. DeBerry's millinery shop, "isn't that your sister, Danny?"

Danielle groaned inwardly at the sight of Regina making her way toward them. She was dressed very fashionably in an azure blue gown, which was cut shockingly low for daytime wear. It was considered quite improper for a woman to expose her elbows, and here Regina was, flaunting her bosom for all to see. The sweet smile on her lips—so out of character for Regina—could only spell trouble, Danielle thought.

"Why hello, everyone," Regina drawled as she approached, paying particular attention to Ashland, who looked every bit as fashionable as she did in his mauve satin breeches and frock coat. Sidling up next to him, she stood on tiptoe, pressing her bosom into his arm as she grazed his cheek with a kiss. "And how is my handsome brother-in-law today?" she asked.

Preening under the flattery like a proud peacock, Ashland smiled down at the young woman, bringing a frown to Danielle's lips. Men were so easily taken in by false praise, she thought. James certainly seemed to be eating up the sweetness Regina was dishing out this morning. Perhaps she should enlighten her husband on some of the less-than-flattering comments Regina had made about him in the past.

At Lottie's nudge, Danielle stepped forward to come between the two, grabbing her husband's arm. "Don't you have a kiss for me, too, sister dear?" She didn't miss the spark of anger in the blue eyes and smiled sweetly. Apparently Regina's sugary salute wasn't directed at her, but it didn't stop her from saying, "You look charming today, Regina, but I fear you're going to burn that delicate skin by exposing so much of it to the sun. Remember what Mama said about fashionable ladies having milky white skin. And I fear yours is getting terribly splotched."

Regina's small gloved hands went up to cover her cheeks, a genuine look of horror crossing her face. "I forgot my bonnet this morning."

"And your fichu, too, by the looks of those red marks on your bosom," Lottie added, smiling in satisfaction when the girl's hands went from her face to her chest, then back to her face, as if she couldn't quite decide which area to cover up first.

"I must go," Regina announced, and two pairs of eyes silently congratulated each other, while two other pairs held obvious amusement. "But before I do, Mama wanted me to invite you and Mr. Ashland for supper tomorrow evening, Danielle."

"We're busy," Danielle responded without a moment's hesitation and was rewarded with a crestfallen look from her sister.

It soon changed to delight, however, when Ashland announced, "We'd love to come." He cast a disapproving look at his wife, who stared daggers right back at him. "Isn't that right, my dear?"

Unwilling to give her sister the satisfaction of seeing them argue, Danielle was forced to acquiesce. "I suppose we could cancel our other engagement," hastily adding, "but you know that you haven't been feeling well, James. I don't want you to overdo it."

"Nonsense." He bent over to place a kiss on Regina's hand and got quite an eyeful of the small white mounds that were suddenly thrust in his direction. "How can we deny ourselves the pleasure of such lovely"—Danielle's foot came down hard on his instep, making his voice raise an octave—"company."

Smiling smugly at Danielle, Regina picked up her skirts, exposing an unseemly amount of ankle, and turned on her heel, returning the way she had come.

As soon as she was out of earshot, Danielle rounded on her traitorous husband. "How could you, James? After what I told you Regina and Mama said to me." Her eyes blazed with righteous indignation.

"My dear," Ashland said, gazing about to smile apologetically at several interested onlookers, "calm yourself. You're making quite the spectacle." He tried to take hold of her arm but she pulled out of his grasp.

"I haven't even begun."

Ian and Lottie exchanged worried glances.

"Excuse us, won't you?" Ashland said to his companions, latching on to his wife's arm more firmly this time and pulling her down the street until they came to a bench, where he insisted that she sit.

"I realize you're upset with your family, and I'm not denying that you don't have good reason to be. But they're still your flesh and blood, and you must try to make amends. If you had no family, like me, you'd know how painful—"

"But I thought you said you had family in New York."

Phillip quickly realized his blunder, smoothing over it by saying, "My dear, my father's death was what necessitated our marriage, don't you remember? The only family I have left, aside from some obscure cousin whom I haven't seen in years, is you."

Danielle smiled wistfully at that, for she hadn't really considered James her family. And it lessened the loneliness she felt at her own family's defection.

"Do you miss your father?"

The word *father* brought Richard Cameron to mind and he answered honestly, "Yes, very much, which is why I would like you to make amends with your own. Perhaps this invitation has been offered as an olive branch."

"Perhaps," Danielle conceded, mulling over the possibility, adding, "but you certainly seemed to be taken in by that stupid display of affection Regina put on."

The corners of his mouth tipped up into the beginning of a smile. "Do I detect a hint of jealousy?" He arched his eyebrow in that supercilious way that so annoyed her.

"Certainly not! That is the most absurd thing I have yet to hear you say. And believe me, you've said some outrageous things." Though if she were honest with herself, she would have to admit that the sight of Regina fawning over James made her furious.

Picking up her hand, Phillip brought it to his lips. He kissed her wrist, where the bare flesh above her glove was exposed; he kissed her arm, pushing up her sleeve to work his way up to her elbow; then snaked out his tongue and trailed it all the way back down, bringing bright spots of color to Danielle's cheeks and a startled, "Oh!" to her lips.

"Why would I want your sister," he asked, thoroughly amused by her discomfort, "when you are so incredibly delectable and sweet?"

Once the pounding subsided in her breast, and other, lower regions of her body, Danielle gazed into the blue of James's eyes and searched for a suitable answer. When none could be found, she moved to his lips, which were full and looked incredibly kissable. And had the strongest urge to do just that.

As if he could read her mind, Ashland smiled knowingly. "'Tis getting a bit warm out here in the sun, my dear. You appear to be quite flushed. Shall we continue our walk?"

Danielle nodded mutely, furious with herself and James, for she knew that the heat coursing through her veins had nothing to do with the sun and everything to do with the aggravating man standing by her side.

"The dinner was simply superb, madam. Please convey my compliments to your cook."

Danielle stared down at the overcooked chicken and lumpy mashed potatoes that lay on her plate and decided that Ashland was laying it on a bit thick, then glanced at her mother who, she noted, seemed quite pleased by the compliment.

In fact, Elsie was actually smiling, the first smile

she had exhibited all evening. Mama had been unusually quiet throughout most of the meal, not at all her loud, opinionated self, acting as if she had some weighty matter on her mind. And she hadn't paid Regina one effusive compliment, which was curious in the extreme.

But if Regina felt slighted, one would never have known it, for she had chatted animatedly with James all evening, batting her lashes like some femme fatale, and thrusting out her bosom—what there was of it—to display it to best advantage.

Danielle knew Regina was jealous of her marriage to Ashland, but she hadn't expected her to be so blatant in her attempt to gain his interest. Why, the woman was making an absolute fool of herself, preening and posing, as if she were some courtesan from Paris, France.

You'd think someone would say something to Regina. James wouldn't. He was too busy hanging on to her every word. And her father, who normally would have chastised his daughter for her outlandish behavior, had suddenly taken an inordinate amount of interest in his rhubarb pie, which Danielle knew for a fact he absolutely abhorred. The entire situation was strange, very strange.

"How have you been faring, daughter? Has married life agreed with you?"

Danielle glanced up from her pie to stare wide-eyed at her mother. *Mama was actually asking her a question?* She recovered her surprise and smiled. "Quite well, thank you, Mama. I find myself adjusting to the tedium of housewifery with little difficulty."

"She's doing splendid, Mrs. Sheridan," James interjected. "A man couldn't ask for a better mate."

JOIN THE
TIMELESS ROMANCE READER SERVICE
AND GET FOUR OF TODAY'S
MOST EXCITING HISTORICAL
ROMANCES FREE,
WITHOUT OBLIGATION!

Imagine getting today's very best historical romances sent directly to your home – at a total savings of at least $2.00 a month. Now you can be among the first to be swept away by the latest from Candace Camp, Constance O'Banyon, Patricia Hagan, Parris Afton Bonds or Susan Wiggs. You get all that – and that's just the beginning.

PREVIEW AT HOME WITHOUT OBLIGATION AND SAVE.

Each month, you'll receive four new romances to preview without obligation for 10 days. You'll pay the low subscriber price of just $4.00 per title – a total savings of at least $2.00 a month!

Postage and handling is absolutely free and there is no minimum number of books you must buy. You may cancel your subscription at any time with no obligation.

GET YOUR FOUR FREE BOOKS TODAY ($20.49 VALUE)

FILL IN THE ORDER FORM BELOW NOW!

YES! *I want to join the Timeless Romance Reader Service. Please send me my 4 FREE HarperMonogram historical romances. Then each month send me 4 new historical romances to preview without obligation for 10 days. I'll pay the low subscription price of $4.00 for every book I choose to keep — a total savings of at least $2.00 each month — and home delivery is free! I understand that I may return any title within 10 days without obligation and I may cancel this subscription at any time without obligation. There is no minimum number of books to purchase.*

NAME_____

ADDRESS _____

CITY_____STATE____ZIP_____

TELEPHONE_____

SIGNATURE _____

(If under 18 parent or guardian must sign. Program, price, terms, and conditions subject to cancellation and change. Orders subject to acceptance by HarperMonogram.)

GET
4
FREE
BOOKS
(A $20.49
VALUE)

Annoyed by the secretive smiles that passed between the newlyweds, Regina's determination to steal Ashland away from Danielle increased tenfold. "James," she said, licking her lips in what she considered to be a provocative manner, "would you walk outside with me? I find it dreadfully warm in here."

Phillip groaned inwardly at Regina's hopeful smile. Regina Sheridan's spiteful motives were as transparent as glass. But in his role as a gentleman, he knew it would be a flagrant display of rudeness to deny the young woman's request for his company, even with his wife glaring angrily at him from across the table.

"My dear, would you care to join us?" he asked Danielle.

Before Danielle could answer that she certainly would like to join them, her mother said, "Stay and talk with your father and me, Danielle. It's been so long since we've had a chance to chat."

Danielle wanted to remind her mother that the *chat* they'd had the last time they were together had been less than stimulating, but she refrained, nodding instead. "Of course."

As she watched her husband and sister depart through the French doors, a sharp stab of jealousy went straight to her heart, and it was all she could do not to jump from her chair and follow them outside.

When James and Regina stepped out into the garden, the darkness embraced them like a cocoon, and the night air, heavy with moisture, carried the scent of flowering rhododendron and honeysuckle.

"It's a bit chilly out here, don't you agree, James?" Regina asked when they were a goodly distance from the tavern. Chafing her arms to make her point, she admitted, "I should have brought my wrap."

Obviously, Phillip thought. With the amount of flesh she had on display this evening, even a woolly worm would have been chilled. Her breasts were exposed all the way down to her nipples, but oddly enough, the sight of them didn't have the least bit of effect on him, not the way Danielle's did.

"Shall I go back and fetch your wrap?"

She linked her arm through his, pressing her breasts against it. "We can share body warmth; it's so much nicer."

He tried to disengage her fingers, but she clung to him as tenaciously as a hungry leech. The little tart was as appealing as that horrendous dinner he'd just eaten. "That wouldn't be proper, Regina, under the present circumstances."

"Why ever not? You don't really love Danielle. And I could entertain you quite adequately in bed."

Having overheard her sister's comment, Danielle gasped, quickly covering her mouth as she stepped behind a boxwood bush to conceal her presence.

At her mother's insistence, she had brought Regina her shawl and had followed the couple outside, hoping to discover just what had motivated her sister's outlandish behavior this evening; apparently she just had. It seemed Regina was intent on seducing James Ashland.

"Danielle entertains me quite adequately. She is a virtual firebrand in bed. Why, I vow, I've never been so exhausted in my life. I fear it's what has caused my recent affliction."

At Regina's sharp intake of breath, Danielle smiled, her heart swelling at the obvious lie Ashland just told. She knew he had done it to save face, but still she felt indebted to him.

"Kiss me, James. Let me show you how happy I can make you. Let me show you that you married the wrong sister."

Danielle would have laughed if she wasn't so furious at her sister's miserable attempt to seduce Ashland. She watched as Regina wrapped her arms about his neck and attempted to press her body into his. Anger and disgust surged through her at her sister's stupidity. Stepping onto the path, Danielle began to hum a sailor's ditty, allowing the foolish woman enough time to disengage herself before she created an enormous scandal for the entire family.

"There you two are," she said as she approached, smiling at the look of relief on her husband's face when he saw her.

"My dear," he said, rushing to her side, "I'm so glad you changed your mind and could join us."

"Actually, I came to fetch you, James. My father would like to show you his new set of checkers. I think it would please him if you consented to play a game with him." She tossed Regina her shawl. "Mama thought you might need this," she said to her sister as an afterthought.

"Of course," James replied. "I'll go to him directly. Are you coming?"

His look was so pathetically hopeful, it made her heart skip a beat. She wagged her head. "No, I believe I'll remain out here and keep Regina company. I have something I'd like to discuss with my sister."

With a polite bow of his head, James departed, leaving the two sisters alone in the garden.

Crossing her arms over her chest, Danielle presented her sister with the most patronizing smile she could muster. "Really, Gina, you should gain a little more practice before you set out to seduce someone. Your performance this evening was quite pathetic."

Regina's face registered surprise, then satisfaction, before her lips twisted into a malicious smile. "So you saw? I'm glad. You might as well know that your husband desires me above you."

"Really? I find that difficult to believe after what I just observed."

"That little charade was for your benefit, Danielle. I knew you were watching all along. James and I had ample time to exchange kisses before you came out."

"Well I hope you found it enjoyable. I, for one, think James's kisses are a bit wet, his tongue a trifle thick like his waist."

Regina's mouth dropped open as a wave of confusion washed over her. "You're just saying that because you don't want me to have him."

Danielle shrugged. "Perhaps. But maybe there's another reason."

Suspicion lit the bright blue eyes. "Like what? What other reason could there be?"

"Like maybe there's someone else who kisses much better than James. Someone whose body is rock hard, whose tongue burns my mouth with such fire, I feel consumed."

"You've kissed another man?" There was disbelief in her voice when she asked the question. Why would Danielle want another man when she already had the fabulously wealthy James Ashland? And why would anyone else choose to be with Danielle when she, Regina, was obviously the prettier of the two sisters?

Picking a flower off the rhododendron bush, Danielle began to dissect it, noting, with a great deal of satisfaction, Regina's uncertainty. She loved needling her sister, simply adored making her jealous. And after what she had observed tonight, Regina deserved everything she was going to get.

"Maybe. But if I tell you, you have to swear not to breathe it to another soul. It must be our secret." She had no fear Regina would tell; Regina wouldn't want anyone to know she wasn't the most sought-after belle in Virginia, especially if she thought Danielle was.

Her childish curiosity rose to the forefront and Regina couldn't help herself from saying, "I promise. Now tell me who this mystery man is. Is he handsome? Do I know him?"

"Actually, no one knows him . . . his identity anyway."

It took a moment for the enigmatic words to register, then Regina blurted out, "I don't believe you. The Phantom would never come here. Not for someone like you."

"Believe what you want, Gina, but it's true. I kissed him. And it was wonderful."

The rapt expression on Danielle's face was too true to ignore, igniting Regina's temper into a scalding fury. "You can't have them both," she wailed, stomping her foot like a child in the throes of a temper tantrum. "I won't allow it."

Danielle smiled sweetly, and in her most Ashland-like voice of condescension said, "But, my dear, I already do."

13

Seated shoulder to shoulder on the edge of the grassy riverbank, Danielle and Lottie, shoes and stockings removed and dresses hiked up to their knees, dangled their feet in the cooling currents of the Rappahannock.

Overhead, the leafy branches of the towering oaks and maples, shielded their delicate skin from the harsh rays of the afternoon sun but couldn't prevent their dresses from sticking beneath their armpits, or the sweat from trickling down between their breasts.

"Whew!" Lottie exclaimed, fanning herself with the skirt of her dress. "I'm about ready to roast. They can put me on a skewer and cook me up for the fair tomorrow. I'm about that well done."

Danielle smiled, for she felt the same way. She couldn't remember a July so hot or so terribly uncomfortable. The sun was unmerciful in its intensity, the air so heavy with moisture, a body could barely breathe. She dabbed at her face with her linen handkerchief, staring longingly at the murky water.

"I wish I was a fish right now. It would be wonderful to sink down into the water and cool off completely."

Lottie smiled wistfully. "Aye, but Mrs. Dunstan would pitch a fit if we was to forget ourselves and do it. That poor woman is determined to make ladies out of us both."

"I'm sure James had a hand in that endeavor. He's forever correcting my posture and my grammar. I vow, it was much easier being common as dirt."

"Aye. There's something to be said for common folk. Leastways they've got no one to chide them for the error of their ways. Why even Ian took me to task the other day for using the wrong spoon to eat my soup. As if it made a difference! It doesn't make a lick of sense to use the bigger of the two spoons, when the small one is easier to handle. And they both get the job done just the same."

Ignoring Lottie's rationalization, Danielle tossed a handful of pebbles into the water, watching them pit the surface then sink below. She asked, "Has Mr. MacGregor said anything about the two of you getting married?"

The young woman shook her head and the red curls bounced every which way. "No," she said, feeling quite discouraged. Though she'd been dodging Ian's disparaging comments about her increased weight and had let out every one of her dresses, she knew she wouldn't be able to hide her condition much longer.

"And I've got my doubts about this abstinence plan, or whatever you call it. Absence might make the heart grow fonder—as you're so fond of telling me—but abstinence definitely hasn't. It's just made me out of sorts and downright miserable."

Danielle could certainly empathize with that. For though she had made the decision to seduce James, she hadn't done it yet. And other than the chaste kisses he'd given her, or the few times he'd held her hand, she hadn't been touched, and it was the emptiest of feelings, only surpassed by her acute awareness that the Phantom was not coming back.

She sighed deeply, prompting a worried look from Lottie, who asked, "You're thinking about him again, aren't you?"

"Something's happened to him. I know it has. He should have been back by now."

"Love, didn't you stop to think that maybe he ain't coming back because he doesn't want to? Because he got what he came for and has gone on to greener pastures?"

A look of intense grief passed over Danielle's face, making Lottie sorry she had spoken. "I'm sorry, love. But it's time you put the Phantom behind you and get on with your marriage to Mr. Ashland."

Danielle's shoulders slumped in defeat as she kicked out at the water, splashing it up over her legs. "I know you're right, Lottie. You've been right all along. I wore my heart on my sleeve like some silly schoolgirl; I was too trusting and now I'm suffering the consequences."

A sinking feeling churned in the pit of Lottie's stomach as she watched Danielle stare intently at the water, fearing that her impetuous friend would do something rash like jump in and drown herself. It was her fault that Danielle was so depressed, and she had to think of something to pull her out of it.

"I'll not have you thinking bad about yourself, or the fact that you gave yourself to a man you thought you was in love with, Danny. You did what your heart told you to do. What's done is done. I can understand that you still care what happens to the Phantom. He is the father of your child, after all. And it isn't good for you or the baby to be brooding about his welfare."

Lottie rose to her feet, extending her hand. "Come on. We'll go ask Mr. Ashland about the Phantom. He's a smart man. Perhaps he's heard something."

That comment brought Danielle out of her stupor. Her eyes widening in disbelief, she gazed up at Lottie's determined face, replying, "We'll do no such thing! Has the sun melted what little sense you were born with? Ask James about the Phantom? Now that would be a grand irony."

Lottie ignored the insult. "Ian and Mr. Ashland have gone on several trips this past month. Their travels put them in a much better position to hear things; stuck here in town, with no newspaper and only the Daughters' network of gossip to inform us of what's happening, we don't have much chance of learning the latest news."

Pulling on her stockings, Danielle digested everything Lottie said, and the more she thought about it, the easier it went down.

She had discussed the Phantom with James once before. So why not again? Doubtless, it would do little good. James had been woefully ignorant of the subject then. But now, with the new events taking place, perhaps he was a trifle better informed.

Though she doubted it. James might be the foremost authority on garish attire and the finer points of peruke making, but when it came to war, he was definitely out of his element.

She decided to ask him anyway.

* * *

Pacing the confines of his study like a wounded animal, Phillip threw up his hands in disgust as he paused to face his first mate, who was seated in the chair in front of the desk.

"Thank God! Cornwallis has given up his pursuit of Lafayette and has withdrawn to the east toward Williamsburg, Ian. Had he entered Fredericksburg, we wouldn't have had the manpower to route him." Phillip crumpled the missive he'd just received and tossed it into the brass bowl on his desk. With a strike of steel to flint, which he removed from the tinderbox, he set it aflame.

"I feel as useless as a tit on a boar. 'Tis time we got back into the thick of things, instead of whiling away our time like a couple of scared spinsters."

"Calm yerself, laddie. Yer no thinkin' clearly. Washington's asked you tae stay—tae keep him apprised of things at the gunnery plant. Will ye defy yer general?"

Phillip plowed agitated fingers through his hair, forgetting for the moment how he was garbed. When his wig sprung a curl and his fingers got caked with powder, his lips snarled in disgust and a low growl emanated from deep within his chest. "I've got to go before I lose what's left of my sanity, Ian. I'm no saint for chrissake! I've been too long without a woman. I don't know how much longer I can keep up this charade."

Ian frowned. "I feel for ye, lad. Truly I do, for I'm in no better position meself. Perhaps the bonnie lass will come round."

Phillip heaved a frustrated sigh. "That's what I

keep thinking. But I've given her time and she's still reluctant to bed me."

"Perhaps if the Phantom was no longer within her reach . . ."

"But it's the only way I have to get close to her."

"Wot are ye plannin' tae do, laddie?"

Phillip shook his head. "There's nothing that can be done for the present. I just have to wait and—" Phillip paused at the sound of Danielle's voice.

"James? Are you in there?" There was an insistent knock, then louder, "James?"

Quickly, he rebuttoned his waistcoat, readjusting his wig, which was slightly askew, and looked over at Ian for confirmation that his appearance was suitable. When Ian gave it, he replied, "Yes, my dear. Come in. Ian and I were just sharing a glass of port," he said when she entered.

Danielle glanced about, noting that the crystal decanter of port was still full and the two glasses by its side, empty. She then stared at the two men as if they were both deranged and shook her head, too distracted by the heat to pay the obvious lie any mind. "This room is like an inferno, James." Her gaze drifted to the two double-hung windows to find them closed; she frowned. "Whatever can you be thinking, cooping yourself up in here like a hen in a chicken house? Do you want to have a relapse?"

Placing his arm around his wife's slender waist, he led her to the leather sofa, directing Ian to open the windows. "'Twas foolish of me, I must admit, my dear. Thank you for your concern."

Ian's foolish grin signaled to Phillip that Lottie had entered the room. She was carrying a tray laden with lemonade and gingersnaps. "How delightful," he crooned, helping himself to some when she placed the tray before them on the piecrust table. "You certainly do know a way to a man's heart, Charlotte."

Swallowing her disgust at the sight of James grabbing a handful of cookies off the silver tray and stuffing them into his mouth, Danielle chided, "Really, James! You needn't eat so quickly. I'm certain Mrs. Dunstan has more in the kitchen. And remember your promise."

Without even so much as a guilty smile, James ignored her and continued eating, making Danielle wonder what on earth had possessed her to think that he could shed some light on the Phantom's whereabouts. He certainly hadn't been able to shed any weight, though he had promised her on three previous occasions that he would try to be more circumspect in his dining habits.

Lottie tossed Danielle a knowing look, nodding her head, urging Danielle to speak. When she didn't take the hint, Lottie took matters into her own hands, asking,

"Mr. Ashland, sir, I was wondering if I could ask you a question?"

Danielle chewed her lower lip apprehensively, knowing what the question was, praying for the answer she sought.

Ashland smiled benignly between bites of cookie, wiping crumbs from the corners of his mouth with his thumb and index finger. "Of course, Charlotte. How may I be of assistance?"

Tossing Ian a quick glance, she blurted, "Do you have any knowledge of the Phantom's whereabouts?"

Ian paled and Ashland made a choking sound, grabbing for the glass of lemonade that Ian quickly thrust into his hands. Taking a large swallow, he turned his head, belched lightly, then replied, "Excuse me. I must have swallowed too much at once."

"Obviously!" Danielle replied unkindly, tapping her foot as she watched his purple face recede to red, then back to his usual pasty white color. The man needed to get out in the sun; and she would make it a point to tell him so and see that he did. No one could possibly be healthy with that colorless pallor that passed for a complexion.

"The Phantom?" Ashland flashed his wife an irritated look before adding, "I do believe Danielle has mentioned this man to me before. He's a sailor of sorts, am I right?"

Danielle snorted loudly, but before she could say something rude, Lottie corrected, "A privateer. He sails with letters of marque from the American navy."

"I see. Sort of a pirate then?"

Danielle jumped to her feet, her cheeks high with color. "You don't see at all you—you—pretentious . . . . The man risks his life for his country and you call him a pirate! That's outrageous and utterly tasteless. Especially when we consider what *you* have done to aid this fledgling country in its conflict with England. Absolutely nothing!" She crossed her arms over her chest, daring him to deny it.

At the furious flush that suffused Ashland's face, Lottie stared pleadingly at Danielle, hoping she hadn't given herself away by saying too much. The woman was impulsive to a fault! "I'm sure Mr. Ashland has given generously of his time and his money to aid our cause, Danny. He's made sizable donations to the Daughters."

Another snort, then, "Hmph!"

"I'm sorry to be such a disappointment to you, my dear," Ashland said, not bothering to hide his offense. "I do what I can to help. I'm not skilled in weaponry or sailing . . . or fighting, for that matter. But I have donated many bolts of material for the ladies to make uniforms and bandages. And I've called upon several of the plantation owners to provide horses and food-stuffs for the army. Ian and I have distributed the goods ourselves."

Thick black lashes flew up to reveal violet eyes wide with wonder. *James had helped the war effort?* Danielle's voice was full of apology when she said, "I didn't know, James. You've never seen fit to take me into your confidence about these trips you and Mr. MacGregor take. It seems I owe you both an apology."

"No need, lassie. Me and Mr. Ashland are happy tae do our part. There's no finer patriot than Mr. Ashland here."

Danielle wouldn't have gone that far, but by the pleased expression on James's face, she could see he quite concurred with Mr. MacGregor's opinion.

Phillip, noting the pleading look on Ian's face, rose to his feet, stepping forward to take Danielle's hand and place it on his arm. "Why don't we stroll down by the river, my dear? Perhaps we can discuss further this chap you were asking about."

Startled, but pleased by the offer, Danielle smiled, following James out of the room and leaving a very anxious Ian and a very cautious Lottie all alone.

"I think ye been avoidin' me, Charlotte, me love," Ian said. "'Tis been a dreadfully long time since we've been together." He winked suggestively.

"We're together practically everyday, Ian," Lottie

retorted, knowing full well what he meant but unwilling to let him off the hook, even for an instant. She busied herself cleaning up the glassware.

"Hinny," he entreated as he approached from behind, wrapping his arms about her thick waist, "I've been lonely without ye in me bed. Are ye no' comin' back to it?"

Turning within his arms, Lottie observed the ardent expression in Ian's eyes, heard the frustration in his voice, and smiled inwardly. Patting his cheek, she said quite earnestly, "You know I want to, love. It's just that . . . well, a young woman in my position has to look to her future." She pressed her bosom into his face, delighting in the anguished moan that erupted from his lips.

"But ye know that I love ye, hinny. That I canna live wie ou' ye."

Breaking out of his embrace, Lottie reached for the tray on the table, ignoring Ian's confusion. "Well, then, you also know what you can do about it." With that, she spun on her heel and left Ian with an uncomfortable bulge in his pants, his mouth hanging open, and the most terrified expression on his face.

"I'm not sure that I'll be able to shed any light on this Phantom's whereabouts," Ashland said once he and Danielle were seated in the gazebo. "But I'll do my best to answer your questions."

Heaving a disappointed sigh, Danielle patted his hand as if she were talking to a small child. "Never mind, James. It wasn't important. And I doubt you'd know anything anyway."

Phillip did his best not to feel insulted. Danielle

had a way of picking a man's ego apart until there was nothing left but shreds of self-doubt. Not only did Ashland suffer from her abuse, but it seemed now even the Phantom had been rendered unimportant.

"What do you mean, not important? I thought you said this man was your hero. Have you forgotten all about him?" At her probing stare, he added with a note of pomposity, "I'm delighted that I've been able to wipe him completely from your mind," and smiled smugly.

His conceit astounded her. "I told you, the Phantom saved my life once. I was merely concerned for his safety. There's been no word"—She blinked back her tears—"no word at all."

"So you do care about him?"

She stared at him with a look that conveyed how incredibly dense she thought he was. "Of course, I care; we all care. Just as we care about General Washington and those brave men fighting for our freedom." At least she was telling the truth, for the most part.

"Well," he said, playing with the lace-edged ruffle of his sleeve, a look of ennui on his face that conveyed how totally unimportant this whole Phantom business was to him. "I do believe I heard that this Phantom was somewhere in Virginia. Perhaps York Town, or was it Tappahannock? I really can't remember."

"And was he well?" Danielle leaned forward in expectation, unable to contain the excitement in her voice.

"There was no mention of any injury or illness. So I suppose so." Her face fell at that and he wondered at it.

She should have been ecstatic to hear that the Phantom was well, Danielle thought. But her pride suffered so from the news, it was difficult to muster a smile. Lottie was right after all. The Phantom hadn't come because he didn't want to see her. The revelation brought a lump to her throat.

"My dear, whatever is the matter? You look positively ghastly. I would have thought such news would be heartening."

Danielle's stricken expression pierced Phillip's heart like a knife. He wanted to comfort her, to tell her that the Phantom wanted to return. Would return. But he couldn't. He could only watch her suffer in silence and know that it was his own selfishness that had brought her to this end.

Heartening. Didn't he mean heartbreaking? But of course he didn't, for James was ignorant of her feelings for the Phantom. Gazing into his concerned face, she suddenly felt guilty at her unkind thoughts. James was a good person at heart. He might not be a dashing privateer who rescues damsels in distress, but he had taken care of her, taught her how to be a fine lady, and she knew it was time to put the past behind her and look to her future with James. It was time to become his wife in every sense of the word. Tomorrow's fair just might be the perfect opportunity.

With that in mind, she asked, "What do you think we should wear to the fair tomorrow? I thought perhaps it would be fun to match our outfits."

Her question took him completely by surprise, and his mouth dropped open momentarily. Danielle wanting to discuss wardrobe possibilities was the most preposterous thing he'd ever heard. The woman was, by far, the most disinterested, unassuming female when it came to clothing. Dozens of exquisitely crafted gowns hung in her wardrobe, but she preferred the simple unadorned gowns, like the lilac sprigged muslin she had on.

"I really hadn't decided," he admitted truthfully. Fredericksburg's annual fair was the furthest thing from his mind. In fact, he'd much prefer to discuss what he and Danielle weren't going to wear—to bed—at this very moment. That thought brought an instant stiffening to his member, which he hid by folding his hands across his lap.

"You look odd, James. All sweaty and somewhat tense. You're not ill again, are you?"

There was genuine concern in her eyes, which made James feel even more "tense." "Ah, no, my dear. Just a bit flushed. The heat, you know."

"Well, you must promise me that you'll make an attempt to lose some weight, James. It's not healthy carrying around so much extra poundage. I'm sure it puts a burden on your heart, as well."

He had a burden on his heart, all right, Phillip thought. And it didn't have a damned thing to do with his "extra poundage," but with that little saucy wench seated far too close for comfort.

If only he could get back to the war. At least in battle his motives were clear, his feelings directed. But here with Danielle nothing was clear-cut or black and white. Everything—feelings, desires, convictions—was muted into shades of gray, colored into hues of passionate violet.

14

"I vow, the stink of this place is most offensive," James remarked, holding a lace handkerchief over his nose as he viewed the cattle in the pen. "This is a far cry from the fairs I'm used to attending."

Danielle, Lottie, and Ian exchanged amused glances, and continued on with their tour of the livestock pens.

The fair was an annual event where townsfolk and neighbors from outlying areas could come to sell their livestock, goods, and wares.

It was also a time for folks to visit, catch up on local gossip, and eat to their heart's content. An aspect James was presently finding quite enjoyable.

"These sausages are quite good. Care to have one?" he asked Danielle, shoving the link under her nose.

The odor of the spicy pork sent Danielle's stomach into a spin and she turned away quickly to take a breath of fresh air, prompting a look of concern from James, who asked, "Are you all right, my dear? You look as green as my waistcoat."

Danielle didn't think anything could look quite as green as the chartreuse material, but refrained from saying so.

"Danny'll be fine, Mr. Ashland," Lottie piped in, knowing the cause of her friend's illness. She'd had her share of the heaves these last few months. "I fear the eggs she ate this morning were spoiled. I'll speak to Mrs. Dunstan about it."

"Look over there," Ian pointed out, diverting everyone's attention to the bright yellow wagon. "'Tis a gypsy's wagon." The boyish enthusiasm on Ian's face prompted amused looks from his friends, who followed behind him as he headed in the direction of the wagon.

The gypsy's fortune-telling wagon was one of the best parts of the fair, as far as Danielle was concerned. Every year for the price of a shilling, the gypsy would read her fortune. Thus far, none of the old woman's predictions had come true—she'd never foretold of marriage or babies—and Danielle didn't put much stock in her predictions.

Ian and Lottie entered the wagon first, leaving James and Danielle to wait beneath the shade of a blossoming magnolia.

"Is the weather never cool in this miserable place?" James complained, wondering how Danielle always managed to look so cool and fresh, while he felt like a roasting pig. She was garbed in a soft-pink lawn gown, which brought out the color in her cheeks.

Danielle smiled, patting his arm. "Once you've shed a few pounds, you won't notice the heat nearly as much," she reminded him.

He leaned toward her to toy with the pink satin ribbons on the bodice of her dress. "Do you find me unattractive, my dear?" Is that why you haven't bed me? he wanted to ask.

"No! Not at all," she answered quickly, realizing the truth of her words as she gazed into his brilliant blue eyes. Her heart skipped a beat. "You've many things to recommend you, sir. Your face is most pleasing to look at."

He reached up to caress her cheek. "Not as pleasing as yours, my dear. You grow more lovely with every day that passes. There's a glow about you—"

"Oh, look, there's Lottie and Ian," Danielle interrupted, not wishing to discuss her "glow" and where it came from. Lottie had advised her that women carrying babies always seemed to glow like a piece of polished silver.

"So they are," James replied. "Shall we go have our fortunes told as well?"

Danielle smiled, nodding enthusiastically, and followed James into the gypsy's wagon. When they emerged a short time later, Danielle's forehead was creased in consternation.

"I don't know why she thinks I'll be taking a sea voyage," she remarked skeptically. "I'm not partial to the ocean."

Ian and Phillip exchanged worried glances, then Phillip replied, trying to alleviate her concern, "These people make their living by making up tales to tell gullible customers." But he, too, had wondered at the old crone's prophecy that he and Danielle would find danger on the sea. His fortune was true enough. But Danielle's? It left him with an uneasy feeling the rest of the day.

"I never thought I'd see the day when James would be rolling on the ground with a bunch of dirty-faced children," Danielle commented a short time later, smiling in satisfaction at the sight.

She and Lottie were seated on the lawn in front of the courthouse, watching as James and Ian frolicked with several of the local children like a couple of young schoolboys. "He's going to make a wonderful father," Danielle decided, speaking her feelings out loud.

"Ian, too," Lottie proclaimed, her expression softening. "I cannot wait to see him with a wee one of his own."

"Have you told him yet, Lottie? Surely he must suspect something."

The red curls bounced as she shook her head. "Not yet. But I guess I'll have to tell him soon enough. I'm not lean of figure like you. I'm already big, but my weight disguises that fact."

Danielle glanced down at her own stomach, which was barely distended. "I'm still so skinny that I often don't believe I'm with child. But then there are other times, like before, when the smell of certain foods makes me want to vomit."

"Me blessed mother was like you, Danny. When she was carrying my brother Will, she was as skinny as a rail. You'd never know she was with child until the last few months of her term when she popped out as big as a watermelon. I expect that's how you'll be."

" 'Tis fortunate I suppose," Danielle replied absently.

"Have you put our plan into motion yet, Danny? You shouldn't be waitin' too much longer."

Danielle paled at the thought of what she had planned to do this evening. The thought of seducing her husband was exciting but scary as well. What if it didn't work? What if he didn't want her?

"Well?" Lottie prompted.

Danielle nodded, for she knew tonight would be the night.

The sky was velvet black. With the heel of her hand, Danielle wiped at the condensation that formed on the bedroom window and peered out. Outside, the rain pelted down in harsh torrents and she could only make out faint images. The wind bellowed its outrage, banging tree limbs against the glass as lightning streaked across the heavens.

It was the perfect night for seduction, she decided. Tonight she would seduce James to her bed, take him into her body, as she had taken him into her heart.

When had it happened? How? But after today, after the marvelous time she'd shared with James at the fair, she knew her feelings for him had grown beyond friendship.

She loved James Ashland. She smiled and shook her head. Who would have ever believed it could happen? Surely not Danielle. She had done her best to distance herself from him, to keep from growing close. But his kindness and patience had finally won her over.

She wasn't even annoyed by his pomposity anymore, for it was as much a part of him as his horrible wig and tolerable paunch. Yes, she loved James Ashland—monocle, wig, annoying faults, and all. He was a good man, a kind man. And that had never been more apparent than today when she'd watched him romping on all fours with the children. He would make an excellent father for her child.

Discarding her clothing, she lowered herself into the steaming tub of water that Mrs. Dunstan had prepared for her.

The bayberry candles flickered softly, emitting a fragrant scent into the room. It was quiet, save for the howling of the wind and the raindrops that splashed noisily against the glass.

Danielle reclined against the back of the copper tub, feeling no pain. She had imbibed more than half a bottle of wine at dinner, much to her husband's amusement and Lottie's growing displeasure.

"You'll be too foxed to know what you're doing," her friend had chastised.

But Danielle knew exactly what she was doing. For she had carefully plotted her course for the seduction of her husband.

She had needed the wine only as additional courage, to lessen her inhibitions. But as she lay in her tub, naked as a newborn babe, she realized that all those old inhibitions that had once existed no longer did.

Footfalls sounded in the hall, alerting her to James's presence. Her heart pounding in anticipation, she waited until she heard his door open and close, then called out, "James, is that you? Would you be a dear and come in here?"

A moment later the connecting door opened and James stood in the doorway, blue eyes wide and mouth agape, as he feasted on the naked form of his wife. "Excuse me," he said in apology, hurrying to shut the door, but Danielle's words halted him in stride.

"Don't leave, James. I require your assistance."

"Assistance?" Phillip swallowed, wiping his sweating palms on the satin of his coat. It had been a long time since he'd had a woman, a hell of a long time, and he was as randy as a dog in heat. He hadn't been tempted by any of the offers he'd had over the past months. Danielle had spoiled him for any other woman.

The thought of her creamy breasts, lush and full as they were now, bobbing on top of the water, of her long, silky legs, which had wrapped themselves about his waist and his memory, had taken away his desire for anyone else.

A painful bulge formed between his legs, and he turned slightly, so she wouldn't notice it.

But she did. Danielle smiled provocatively, running her tongue over her lips. "I'd like you to scrub my back for me, James." She dangled the washcloth from her fingertips. "It's hard for me to reach."

"Wash your back?" he choked, loosening the stock at his throat, which suddenly felt much too tight, as did his breeches, which were pulled painfully taut against his erection.

"You're beginning to sound like a parrot, James." She smiled, waving the cloth at him until he had no choice but to step forward and take it.

"You'd best remove your coat, unless you want it soaked. And roll up your sleeves. 'Twould be a shame to ruin that lovely silk shirt."

Unable to refuse such an attractive offer, he did as she instructed, then knelt before the tub, feeling like an untried youth in the throes of his first passion. "Are you sure that you want me to do this?" Danielle had been acting strangely toward him all evening, but he'd passed off her amorous inclinations to the amount of wine she had consumed. Even now, with the evidence of her desire written on her face, he couldn't quite believe that she wanted him.

Her smile was blatantly seductive. "Of course. How else would I get my back washed?" she asked, adding, "You look very handsome this evening, James. The blue satin becomes you. It brings out the intensity of your eyes." Which at the moment just happened to be focused on her breasts. She arched her back and sweat broke out over his upper lip and forehead.

"I—I cannot wash your back if you do not bend forward, my dear." He tried to remember who he was, who he was supposed to be. But it was hard. God's blood it was hard!

She smiled, handing him the bar of lavender soap. "Why not start on my front first? It will require the same attention."

A bolt of lightning flashed, followed by the roar of thunder that echoed in his heart. He swallowed at the thought of running his hands over her tempting mounds, of diving them beneath the water to stroke the dark patch of hair between her thighs.

God's blood! She was the very essence of Eve. Now he knew what Adam must have felt.

Taking a deep breath, he soaped the rag he was holding, and gently began to wash her breasts.

"Why not use your hands?" she suggested. "They would be much softer than the rag."

He swallowed hard at the suggestion. "You are so very beautiful, my dear," he whispered, running the soapy palms of his hands over her lush mounds. Her nipples hardened at his touch and he massaged them tenderly until he heard her moan of satisfaction.

Fearing that he would disgrace himself, he pushed himself to his feet, ordering, "Lean forward and I shall attempt to satisfy your wishes by washing your back."

Suddenly she stood, water glistening over her body like diamonds in the candlelight. "You could satisfy more than just my wishes, James. You could satisfy all of me." She stepped out of the tub, coming to stand directly before him, noting the desire in his eyes.

His breathing grew ragged as his blood pumped like liquid fire through his veins. "You want to consummate our marriage?" he choked out, hardly able to believe after all this time that his fondest wish had come true.

Taking his hands in her own, she said softly, "I am your wife, James. I want you to make love to me." She placed his hands over her breasts. "Feel my heart. See how wildly it beats for you. Do you want me, James?" She trailed her hands down his thighs to cup his swollen shaft; it throbbed beneath her palms. "It feels like you do."

A tortured moan escaped his lips before he cried out, "God, yes!" Lifting her into his arms, he carried her into his room.

It was dark, no candles had been left burning. And he knew that the darkness would conceal his identity. His wig would remain, but other than that, he wanted nothing else between their naked flesh.

Depositing Danielle on the bed, he quickly divested himself of his clothing, then grabbed on to her legs and pulled her toward the edge of the mattress to face him.

"What are you doing, James?" she asked, somewhat alarmed by his unconventional method of lovemaking.

But unconventional as it seemed, Phillip knew exactly what he was doing for he'd planned this moment for months, dreamed of it, agonized over it.

"Wrap your legs about my waist, my dear," he instructed, bending over to plant gentle kisses on her face, neck, and breasts. "I am much larger than you. I do not want to put too much of my weight on you." And he didn't want her to feel that his stomach was as rock hard as the Phantom's.

She did as he requested, grateful for the darkness

that hid her embarrassment. Opening to him, she sucked in her breath when his fingers began a gentle, but thorough, exploration of her most private parts, and her breathing quickened.

"Are you a virgin, Danielle? I must ask you this, my dear, so I will not hurt you. I do not intend to pass judgment on what you may have done before we met." Though he already knew the answer, the question was as necessary as his hideous disguise.

The darkness hid her humiliation at the question she'd been dreading. Knowing he would find out anyway, she answered honestly, "No. You are not the first. I am sorry, James."

"Ssh," he replied, kissing her gently as his fingers entered her woman's flesh to ready her for their joining. She was hot and wet, and he wanted her with a mindless passion that frightened him. "I may not have been your first, my dear, but I will be your last."

"Oh, James, I—" the words she wanted to say stuck in her throat and her heart ached, for though she loved him, she was still deceiving him about the baby, "I don't deserve you."

He brought her hands to his hardened shaft. "Touch me, Danielle. Feel the power you have over me."

She did, and it excited her to think that the touch of her hands could bring him pleasure. Gently, she ran her fingers down the velvet length of him, stroking as he stroked her in kind.

When he couldn't stand the torture she was inflicting a moment longer, he removed her hands and placed the tumescent tip of his shaft at her opening; while his hands massaged her breasts, his fingers pulled at the taut nipples. Slowly, he eased into her tightness, reveling in her low moan of pleasure.

"Oh God, James!" she cried out, taking him full within her. Every nerve ending in her body was on fire. Her heart pounded loud in her ears and her blood pulsed in rhythm to his throbbing organ.

The darkness heightened every sensation, every stroke, every kiss, every touch of his hands.

Harder and harder he pumped until Danielle grew taut and her insides expanded. With one final, hard thrust, he took her over the edge of her passion and she exploded into a shattering climax.

When they finally floated back to earth, Danielle clutched James to her bosom, heaved a deep sigh of contentment, and drifted off to sleep, never seeing the look of profound tenderness on her husband's face.

Danielle awoke the next morning to find herself back in her bed; she was quite alone and wondered why. It was apparent that James had not wanted to sleep the night with her. She shook her head. There was still so much about her husband that she didn't understand. But she had the rest of their lives to find out.

Sighing contentedly, she smiled, thinking of the wonderful night they'd shared. James had been a considerate, passionate lover. She'd felt a completeness with him that she'd never felt in the arms of the Phantom.

Thinking of the Phantom brought a lump of sadness to her throat. He was her first love, and would always hold a special place in her heart. But she realized now that she didn't love him. Not like she loved James.

James was her husband, her soul mate. And nothing, or no one, would ever come between them again.

* * *

July 1781
Williamsburg, Virginia

The hanging lantern within the large canvas tent flickered softly, illuminating the nervous droplets of perspiration on Andrew Ellsworth's upper lip and forehead. Fidgeting with the sword at his side, he waited for the commander in chief of the British army, General Charles Cornwallis, to make a decision.

Ellsworth had just suggested a bold plan to the arrogant English earl—one that would enable him to masquerade as a French army colonel, acting as spy for the British in order to ferret out information regarding the gunnery plant in Fredericksburg. Disguised as an officer of one of Lafayette's elite espirit de corps, he would establish himself in the town and gain the trust of the local inhabitants, seeking information that would enable him to locate the Phantom and kill him.

The Loyalist spy Robbins had given him the information he needed. The Phantom's black ship had been spotted on two different occasions. Once in the Potomac River outside of Port Royal, and once plying the waters of the Rappahannock River near Fredericksburg. Now that he had that information, it would only be a matter of time until he could gain his revenge.

Tenting his fingers in front of his face as he studied the man before him, Lord Cornwallis frowned, the deep cleft in his chin growing more pronounced. There was something about Ellsworth that he didn't trust. He wasn't exactly sure what, but at thirty-eight years of age, he had commanded long enough to never discount his intuition.

He prided himself on being a careful man, a tolerant human being, and a courageous soldier. He had no liking for this war, having voted against taxation of the colonies while seated in the House of Lords. But now that he was firmly enmeshed in the fracas, he had no desire to lose, and he wasn't certain Ellsworth was experienced or clever enough to carry off such an ambitious scheme.

His injured eye wandered, as it often did when he grew tired or upset, and he tried to refocus on the man before him. "It would appear, Captain Ellsworth, that you've given this plan of yours quite a bit of thought. However, I still have my reservations as to your capabilities to carry it off. You're naval, Ellsworth, not army, and this is definitely an army maneuver."

Ellsworth hid his animosity behind a polite facade. 'Twas the navy that would eventually win this war, and the arrogant army generals like Cornwallis could go to the very devil when that day came. But for now, he would bite his tongue, bide his time, and play the game.

"Begging your pardon, General, but I feel I am more than qualified to implement this plan. In fact, I am the only man who could do it adequately." He smiled smugly, his eyes glowing with a fervor that Cornwallis thought excessive.

"Come, come, Captain, let's not play word games. If you have additional information that would enable me to make an intelligent decision, then spit it out, man. My time is valuable; yours grows short."

Ellsworth eyed the portly general with contempt. Like all who commanded, Cornwallis was too cautious, too circumspect in his vision. Didn't the fool realize that one had to seize the moment to defeat these rabble-rousers? That unless these Americans were stopped quickly and decisively, there was a chance they could win?

"I know the identity of the pirate known as the Phantom."

Cornwallis sat up straighter, his attention fully directed at Ellsworth's announcement. "You know who this man is?"

"Not his name." Cornwallis snorted derisively, propelling Ellsworth to add quickly, "But I've seen his face. I've unmasked the traitorous bastard."

"And you think you can find this man, if I allow your plan to proceed as you've proposed?"

With an air of assurance he hadn't exhibited up until now, he replied, "I have no doubt. Let me infiltrate the town of Fredericksburg, and I will bring back the pirate known as the Phantom on the end of a rope."

Cornwallis leaned back in his chair, rubbing his chin in contemplation. 'Twould be a feather in his cap to bring the Phantom to justice, there was no denying that. The man had butchered British troops, not to mention the havoc he'd caused the naval department. The capture of the Phantom would be a highly rewarded achievement—the pinnacle of accomplishment in a successful military career.

Withdrawing a sheet of paper from his desk, Cornwallis paused with quill in hand. "I shall write out the necessary orders, instructing my aide-de-camp to procure a French uniform, weapon, and the like, and assist you in crossing over to the enemy side."

Ellsworth smiled in relief. "Thank you, General. I assure you, you won't be disappointed."

"I sincerely hope not, Ellsworth, for if I am, your career will be over. Once you leave here you are on your own. I do not want to see or hear from you again until you have captured this man known as the Phantom."

"But how will I relate information that I happen to stumble upon? Surely, you would want me to write of my discoveries."

"Don't attempt to second-guess me, Captain. General Clinton put me in command with the notion that I knew what I was doing. Please give me the same consideration."

Swallowing, Ellsworth felt the heat creep up his face and nodded. "I apologize, General. I meant no disrespect."

"As I was saying, this capture will take precedence over all else." Scribbling across the piece of parchment, the general sanded the paper to dry the ink, then handed it to Ellsworth. "Your orders, Captain."

Ellsworth saluted smartly, then spun on his heel, about to leave when Cornwallis's voice halted him in his tracks.

"Don't fail, Ellsworth. I'm a tolerant individual, but I can't abide failure of any kind. Remember that. For if you don't, it'll be your neck that's stretched, not the Phantom's."

Ellsworth walked into the darkness, clasping the paper to his breast, cursing the general under his breath as he put distance between himself and the command tent.

How dare that insolent bastard intimate that he might fail! He wouldn't. Not this time.

He clutched the paper in his fist. This time victory lay in the palm of his hand.

15

The bells of St. George's peeled loudly to announce the start of Sunday evening services. The church was crowded, the pews packed with worshipers who'd come to pray for a swift victory to end the war with Great Britain.

Candles flickered softly against the white paneled walls, while the lilies that graced the altar sent forth a haunting fragrance. In the second-to-last pew on the left, Danielle sat next to her husband, who looked resplendent in his bright blue satin coat and breeches with contrasting red brocade waistcoat. Seated next to them, the newly wedded Mr. and Mrs. Ian Mac-Gregor giggled softly in their bliss, in direct contrast to the somberness of the sermon.

"And so we pray, ladies and gentlemen, that this conflict will soon be at an end and our loved ones returned safely to us," the Reverend Blackburn intoned. "Let us . . ."

The reverend droned on but Danielle, lost in her

own silent prayer, paid scant attention. Her thoughts were centered on her husband. There'd been no repeat of their lovemaking—no attempt on James's part to initiate another alliance, though she'd let him know in subtle ways that she would welcome his attentions. Though he'd been solicitous of her, James hadn't attempted more than a chaste kiss on the cheek, and she felt frustrated by his behavior.

Casting a surreptitious glance at her husband, she caught his profile out of the corner of her eye, noting the small bump on the bridge of his nose, the fullness of his lower lip, the strength of his chin.

Had he lost weight? He seemed even handsomer this evening, despite the garishness of his costume and formality of his freshly powdered wig.

Surely his own hair must have grown out by now, she thought, suddenly realizing that she had never seen what color it was. Once, when he was ill, she had caught a glimpse of chest hair before he had yanked the bedcovers up to his chin. It was brownish gold, so she surmised that his hair must be the same.

A hand reached out to cover her own; she glanced up to find kind blue eyes upon her and realized that the benediction had been given, signaling that the service was at an end.

"You were lost in thought, my dear," James whispered, his lips so close to her ear, his breath so warm, jolts of awareness darted through her. She turned her head so quickly, her lips met his for a brief second, brushing lightly over them, before she pulled back, clearly startled by the tremor of desire she felt. If Ashland felt anything at the contact, she couldn't tell; his expression of kind concern remained unchanged.

"Are you ready to leave? I do believe Ian and Charlotte are anxious to return and . . . " His words trailed off as he arched an eyebrow in her direction. But after listening to Lottie's headboard bang against the wall these past three nights, Danielle understood the inference quite well and blushed as crimson as his vest.

The air was warm as they stepped out into the summer evening. Danielle clung to her husband's arm as they made their way to the waiting carriage. A light rain had fallen that morning leaving the streets slippery with mud.

Ian and Lottie sat across, wrapped in the warm glow of their love, impervious to anyone or anything else but themselves.

"'Twould seem we're in for another night of wall banging," James whispered as he settled his bulk alongside his wife's slight form, noting the couple's amorous inclinations.

"Ssh! They'll hear you," Danielle admonished, but her eyes were lit with merriment.

"Good. Then perhaps I'll be able to get a decent night's sleep!"

Danielle's smile was teasing. "Why, James, you sound as if you're jealous.

James's face flushed red and he turned away to stare out the window. Instantly, Danielle regretted having made the comment, reminding herself that James was a gentleman, whose manners had been inbred from birth, and he was far more reserved than she was.

But she couldn't help herself; she craved his touch. It was so cold and lonely in that little bed of hers, and she wanted to share it with James, share the warmth of two bodies pressing against each other. It would be glorious to snuggle against his flesh, feel his arms wrapped around her. She heaved a sigh.

Phillip observed the multitude of emotions flitting across Danielle's face—embarrassment, wistfulness, desire—and wanted to scream his frustration out loud. There was nothing he'd rather do than make mad passionate love to his wife.

But he kept himself in check. For each time they made love, he increased the chances of getting Danielle with child. And with the uncertainty of war, the way he spent his life, he couldn't make the commitment that a child would demand.

But he wanted her desperately, wanted to shout that very thought to the heavens, to bellow as loudly as the church bells, to roar as loudly as—

"Fire!" he shouted, staring at the orange flames that licked the darkened sky. The fire was in the next block of houses, only a short distance from where they were. He gave the order to proceed there in all due haste.

Danielle gasped loudly as she followed his gaze. "It's the Brown's home." She stared, horrified, as the small wooden home of Sam and Sarah Brown went up in flames.

"Pull up, Mr. Lawson," James ordered the driver in a voice used to command, forgetting his role for the moment. "Stay in the carriage and do not leave," he directed the two women. "Mr. Lawson will stay with you; Ian and I will go and see what we can do to help."

"But, James," Danielle protested, latching on to his arm. "You're not up to—"

"Madam, you will do as I say," he barked as he jumped from the conveyance, his tone so harsh Danielle could do nothing else but obey and nod mutely.

This was a side of James she had never seen before, she realized, as she watched the two men enter the burning shack. They were quickly engulfed by thick black smoke and roaring flames that were deafening in their intensity, and she lost sight of them.

In the next moment, a piece of burning timber came crashing to the ground and Danielle cried out, "Oh, God!" covering her mouth, terrified, as she stared at the belching flames and devastation before her. When more timbers collapsed, causing the horses to rear up, there was another brief moment of panic when she thought they would bolt, but the burly driver soon had them under control.

"I don't want to be a widow before I have a proper honeymoon," Lottie wailed, dabbing at her eyes with the edge of her cloak.

"Hush! They'll be perfectly fine, you'll see." But the fear in Danielle's voice belied her self-confident words. Soon the tears in her eyes caused by the smoke and her own terror, made it difficult to see. She swiped at them with the back of her hand, breathing a sigh of relief a moment later when James and Ian emerged from the burning building with two small children clutched in their arms and a grateful Sarah Brown rushing after them.

"Thank God," she whispered. Their faces were blackened by soot, their clothes torn and singed, but as far as she could tell, they were unharmed.

"Thank you, sirs," the black woman said, taking the small babe that James handed to her. "My man has gone to fight with General Washington. No one would stop to help us. We is eternally grateful, sir."

James spent a few more minutes discussing Mrs. Brown's plans to stay with her sister-in-law's family, then deposited a small purse of money into her hands. "Use this to get resettled."

Wide-eyed, the woman stared at the generous gift.

"But I can't pay you back, sir, and I can't accept charity from strangers. Me and Sam is free blacks. We earns our keep and pays our own way." She tried to hand it back, but James closed her fingers around it.

"Then consider this wages for your husband's aid to Washington. I doubt he's been paid for some time. The Congress's treasury is as dry as these house timbers that caught fire."

He stared at the blackened rubble that was once a home and shook his head, wondering if America's bid for freedom would soon go up in smoke as well.

An hour later, Phillip lay on his bed, naked as the day he was born, hands folded behind his head, staring up at the ceiling, too exhausted to move. His eyes still burned from the smoke, but other than that minor discomfort, he and Ian had come through the fire unscathed.

Closing his eyes, he inhaled deeply as he willed his tired body to sleep, but a soft knock at the connecting door brought him wide awake.

"James, can I come in? I can't sleep; I thought, perhaps, we could talk."

He sighed wearily at the sound of Danielle's voice. "Can't it wait until tomorrow, my dear? I'm dreadfully tired. I fear I've overdone it a bit."

"Please?" she insisted. "I won't stay long; I promise."

Another sigh, deeper this time, then, "Very well. Wait just a moment." The room was dark, which was just as well, under the circumstances, he thought, climbing down off the bed to search for his chest in the dark.

"Ouch! God's blood!" he cursed as his toe came into direct contact with said chest. Pulling open the drawer, he found a nightshirt that Ian had procured for "emergencies." Well, he guessed this was one of them.

Putting it on, he hurried back to the bed, reached under the pillow for his wig, then drew the covers up to his chin. "Come in, my dear."

Danielle opened the door and a small shaft of light from her room spilled into his. "Shall I light a candle, James? It's quite dark in here."

"I like it this way. My eyes still burn from the smoke. The light bothers them."

She padded across the room to the bed and could barely discern the large lump that lay beneath the covers. "I can't even make out your face, James. How can we converse in the dark?"

He smiled to himself. "I wasn't aware that one needed to see in order to speak."

Ignoring his sarcasm, she climbed on top of the bed, much to his consternation. "Whatever are you doing, my dear?"

"I've decided that it's silly for us to sleep apart like strangers. We've been married almost five months, and we've yet to sleep in the same bed together."

Knowing what a headstrong individual his wife could be when she set her mind to it, which was far too often in his estimation, he set about to nip Danielle's idea in the bud. He'd experienced enough torture the last few months sleeping separately, and couldn't begin to imagine what hell he'd be in for if they began sleeping together in one bed. He'd never be able to keep his hands off of her, never be able to refrain from making love to her all night. And there was also the problem of the late-night couriers who often brought messages to the house.

"I prefer to sleep alone, my dear. I'm often restless and

find myself reading late into the night. I wouldn't want to disturb you. You work hard and need your rest."

"I want to lie beside you, James. It's so cold in my room, and you've this big bed."

Cold! God's blood, it was July! "I could have Mr. Dunstan build a fire in your room if you like," he offered. "Or perhaps Mrs. Dunstan could run the bed warmer over the sheets a few times."

She ignored his suggestions and pulled back on the covers, which he held in his fingers with a death grip. "Let go, James." She giggled at his defeated moan and slid beneath the sheet as he released them. "There, isn't that better?" she asked, settling herself next to him.

Phillip lay on his back, stiff as a board, not daring to move, not daring to breathe.

"James," she said, reaching across the mattress. She encountered his arm, patting it soothingly. "Please don't worry that you'll disturb me. I'm a heavy sleeper. Your restlessness won't bother me a bit."

He rejected her logic, rejected her silky voice that poured over him, making him crazed with desire. "I'm not sure that this is such a good idea, my dear."

Danielle thought it was the best idea she'd had in a long time. There'd be no way James could avoid intimacy with her if they were sleeping in the same bed. And she intended to be very intimate. "Turn on your side," she directed, yanking on his arm. "That's right," she said when he finally complied.

She pressed her rear end into his stomach, which Phillip was forcibly distending, through no small effort on his part. His stomach might still feel soft, but there were other parts of his anatomy that were definitely hard!

"I think you've lost some weight, James. You don't feel nearly as fat as you used to."

He cursed himself inwardly for not putting on his padded smallclothes. His nightshirt had no padding. "Yes, well, I've been trying."

Phillip bit his lower lip to keep from crying out in frustration at the feel of Danielle's firm buttocks pressing into his stomach and lower regions. She had on some type of satiny gown, different from the ones she usually wore. He supposed he should be grateful that she wasn't wearing that damn transparent negligee. At least there was some substance to this garment. She wiggled her rear, and he yelped like a wounded dog.

"Isn't this much better? I feel so snug and safe now."

"Words escape me," he choked out, trying to put distance between his front and her back.

"Quit fidgeting and wrap your arms about me, James. It's late. Tomorrow's your birthday, in case you've forgotten. It's going to be a busy day, and we need to get some sleep."

Fat chance of that, he thought, gathering her into his arms, unsure of where to place his hands. When she settled them on her waist, he breathed a sigh of relief, saying, "In all the excitement, I'd nearly forgotten about my birthday." *Damn Ian for his big mouth!*

"Well, I haven't forgotten. I've already invited my parents to dine with us. And Lottie and Ian are looking forward to the festivities like a couple of small children," Danielle replied, smiling contentedly at the feel of James's arms around her. Feeling safe and blessedly warm, she soon drifted off to sleep.

Danielle didn't know what awakened her a short time later, but when she opened her eyes, darkness still enveloped the room and James's soft snores crooned in her ear.

She felt a hard object pressing against her rear end, and realized, with no small amount of satisfaction, that it was James's erection.

He wanted her!

His hands had moved up from her waist to cover her breasts with tantalizing possessiveness, his fingers plying her nipples until they formed two stiff peaks.

She tingled in all the right places and closed her eyes to enjoy the sensations he aroused. Soon a dull throbbing began between her legs, and she bit her lip to get herself under control. Oh, Lord! she moaned silently, feeling the familiar wetness flood her thighs.

Turning to face him, she reached out her hand, intending to touch him, but he merely let out a loud snore and rolled over onto his other side.

Good Lord! He was asleep. Even in sleep the man had the power to arouse her. Surely she must be turning into a wanton.

As quietly as she could, so as not to wake him, she moved toward the edge of the bed, putting a safe distance between her and James's nocturnal, instinctive behavior.

Heaving a frustrated sigh, she shut her eyes and in a few moments drifted off to sleep, unaware of the secret smile that curved her husband's lips.

"Your birthday dinner is turning out to be a disaster, James," Danielle wailed, surveying the beautiful dining table she'd spent hours to prepare.

The crystal water goblets and wineglasses sparkled brilliantly under the glow of the brass chandelier overhead, and the lovely rose-patterned Canton chinaware enhanced the cream-colored crocheted table-cloth beneath, while repeating the design in the paper-covered walls of the dining room. In the center of the table, a pineapple cone centerpiece—the symbol of hospitality in Virginia—welcomed guests to the table.

"My first real dinner party, and it's ruined. First, Mrs. Washington sends her regrets, and now three more cancellations have arrived. I told you I wouldn't be accepted into society."

Clutching her elbow, he led her into the parlor. "Nonsense! Have you bothered to look out the window, my dear? We are in the midst of a terrible thunderstorm. The rain is coming down in torrents, with no letup in sight. You can hardly blame those who didn't want to venture out in it. Besides," he added, smiling, "the fewer guests that come, the more delectables you'll have for me." After filling two glasses with champagne punch, he handed her one.

Danielle sipped thoughtfully as she gazed at the man before her. James had a way of making her feel good about the most dreadful situations, she realized. He had his faults—overindulgence for one—but he had a kind and generous heart. She would never forget what he'd done for the Browns last night. He had risked his life to save others—blacks, no less, a class of people for which most men would not have lifted a finger to help.

Watching as James poured himself another glass of punch, she reconsidered her previous opinion that he'd lost weight. In fact, in the light of day, he looked the epitome of dissipation. His eyes were bleary and red, as if he'd consumed a quart of brandy by himself, and his face looked puffy.

She'd have thought he would have gotten a glorious night's sleep, as she had, but from the look of him, she doubted that he'd slept at all.

He'd made no mention of what had occurred between them last night, and had been conspicuously absent from his bed when she awoke this morning.

She sighed deeply, not knowing quite what to make of his behavior. At times he seemed to want her desperately; but then he would do a complete turnaround and try his best to avoid her. Perhaps he just didn't desire her as much as she desired him.

But when her gaze slid down to his crotch and she noticed the definite bulge in those tight breeches he wore, she knew that he did. There were some things a man couldn't hide, and that was one of them! Her cheeks suddenly flared to match the color of her red batiste gown when her eyes lifted to his, and she saw for a brief moment that he was remembering last night, but then they shuttered closed and she couldn't tell what else, if anything, he was thinking.

There was no more time for her to pursue her outrageous and improper thoughts, for Ian and Lottie had entered the room.

"Good day, Danny . . . happy birthday, Mr. Ashland."

Lottie was garbed in a bright green cotton gown that contrasted nicely with the red of her hair, and Danielle couldn't remember a time when Charlotte O'Flynn MacGregor appeared lovelier. A look of total contentment and joy, which nearly matched that of her husband's, suffused her face, and Danielle felt grateful to Ian for putting it there. She smiled at the little man and was rewarded with a grin so wide, his gold-capped tooth nearly blinded her.

"Come in, come in," Ashland directed. "Let me pour you both some of Mrs. Dunstan's famous champagne punch. 'Tis an old family recipe, or so she tells me." He winked at Danielle, then handed his guests their refreshments.

Phillip needed desperately to keep busy—to keep his mind on anything but what had occurred in that big bed last night. It had been pure hell and pure heaven to lie with Danielle in his arms, feel her soft curves pressed against his body, touch her in the most intimate of places, and hear her soft mews of pleasure while she slept.

It had been the most exquisite torture, and one he was reluctant to admit he wanted, nay needed.

"Ye both look splendid in yer finery this fine day," Ian remarked. "But a wee bit tired. Was ye up late last eve wie all the excitement?"

Violet eyes locked with blue, and something strange and wonderful passed between Danielle and her husband, then was gone in a flash when Ashland blustered, "There was nothing remarkable about last night that I can recall, save for that incident at the Browns'. Other than that, it was the same as all other nights."

Danielle's heart plummeted to her toes, and she turned away quickly to stare out the window before anyone could notice her disappointment.

The wind howled mournfully, whipping the leaves against the tree branches. A pair of pink-nosed brown bunnies hopped quickly, scurrying to find shelter from the storm.

They seek shelter, as she had sought shelter in James's arms last night, she thought, heaving a sigh of despair as she recalled James's words; they had hurt. It was obvious that he didn't love her. Possibly never would. To him this was purely a marriage of convenience. She was foolish to think it could be otherwise.

She was saved from her disturbing thoughts by the arrival of a carriage. Danielle breathed a sigh of relief, until she saw who it was that emerged from the vehicle.

"And I thought things couldn't get any worse," she lamented loud enough for the others to hear.

James stepped up behind her, placing his hands on her shoulders, and caught sight of Regina hurrying up the walk. He groaned softly, but couldn't be sure if his response was directed at the unwelcome arrival of Danielle's sister or at the scent of lavender that wafted up to tease his senses when Danielle turned in his embrace.

She was so close he only had to bend his head to capture her soft, kissable lips, but he set her away from him, knowing he could not. And at that very moment, he hated this war, Andrew Ellsworth, his hideous disguise, and everything else that prevented him from being with the woman he . . .

Loved!

The realization hit him like a ton of bricks. God's blood! He was in love with his wife. A wife who wasn't really his, a woman who didn't even share his true name and identity.

He loved everything about her: the way her cheeks dimpled when she smiled, the way her nose wrinkled up when she pondered something difficult, the way she indulged him.

His mind drifted back to this morning, when Danielle had presented him with his birthday gift. He had been vastly amused and touched by her gift of imported chocolates.

"I realize you shouldn't have these, James," she had said, "but I know how much you adore sweets."

He adored sweets all right, he thought. Especially ones with big violet eyes and honeyed lips.

"Obviously Mama and Papa are not coming, but

how fortunate that my dear sister has managed to conquer the storm."

Danielle's voice brought him back to the present. He heard the sarcasm in her words, noted her bellicose expression, and hoped he'd be able to reason her out of a confrontation with her sister. As much as he dreaded having Regina in his home, he had no desire to see the two women at each other's throats.

"'Tis my birthday, Danielle. Let's put aside our differences and welcome Regina with open arms."

He was to do just that a moment later when Regina burst through the doorway and fairly flew into Ashland's arms like a long lost lover. "James, my darling, how wonderful it is to see you again."

Danielle caught her husband's eye above Regina's head and screwed up her face in disgust, mimicking silently, "James, my darling . . . " She wasn't at all pleased by his amused response.

Extricating himself from his sister-in-law's embrace, Ashland said, "Danielle has been waiting anxiously for your arrival, Regina. Aren't your parents coming?"

Removing her cloak in a queenly fashion, she dropped it into her sister's hands as if Danielle were no more than a servant. "Alas, no. Poor Mama was stricken with some type of stomach ailment." Possibly from the spoiled meat she'd been fed, Regina added silently, knowing that her parents would never have allowed her to proceed with her planned seduction of James Ashland.

Her animosity masked by worry, Danielle handed the cloak to Lottie. "Is Mama going to be all right? Should we fetch the doctor?"

Sweeping passed Danielle, Regina followed Ashland into the parlor and seated herself beside him on the love seat.

"You know very well that Mama would never allow a doctor to treat her," she said once everyone had assembled. "I procured an emetic from the apothecary and she gave up most of what she ate. Father is tending to her needs; she should be fit in a few days."

And knowing her sister as well as she did, Danielle wasn't the least bit surprised that Regina hadn't stayed to tend the ailing woman, not when she might miss the chance to practice her wiles on James once again.

Poor James. He looked quite ill at ease. Regina was pressing her thigh into his as she whispered something in his ear that made him blush, and Danielle didn't need much of an imagination to guess what she'd said.

"Why don't you come out to the kitchen and help me check on dinner, Regina? Ian and James would probably like to relax with a pipe and discuss the events of the day."

The blue eyes widened in dismay. "And soil my new dress?" Regina twisted this way and that, making sure James had an adequate view of her bosom, which was generously displayed. "You don't wish me to leave, do you, James?"

Phillip wanted nothing more than to kick Regina out of his house on her sweet, conniving rear, but that would appear hypocritical in light of his advice to Danielle, who was now staring at him with an "I told you so, and you deserve everything you get" look on her face. Tactfully he suggested, "If Danielle needs your help, it would be gracious of you to assist her, Regina."

She stuck her chin in the air and crossed her arms under her breasts, pushing them up until they were dangerously close to spilling out of the confines of her blue gown.

Noting the fury on Danielle's face, Ian tried to alleviate the tension by offering, "Lottie and I will assist Danielle. There's no need for you to bother yourself, miss."

Regina smiled triumphantly, not so Danielle and Lottie, whose mouths dropped open in disbelief before they hurled angry looks at Ian and marched out of the room. The old man, clearly perplexed, scratched his head as he followed them out to the kitchen.

"That wasn't very kind of you, Regina. Usually it is customary for guests to offer assistance to their hostess, especially when asked."

Placing her hand on his thigh, she leaned into him and he could smell the cloying fragrance of her cologne; it reminded him of dead gardenias. "I'd be happy to assist you, James." Her hand inched higher, but before she could reach her intended destination, he grabbed onto it, squeezing it none too gently.

"Playing the whore doesn't become you, Regina. I thought I'd made myself perfectly clear last time we met. Danielle is all the woman I need or want."

Her eyes narrowing in anger, she yanked her hand from his and spat out her response. "Well, you're not the only man she needs. She told me herself that your kisses repulse her, that she'd much rather be kissed by the Phantom."

Phillip whitened, but only at the knowledge that his wife had discussed the Phantom with this scheming, gossipy little bitch. But to Regina, it seemed that she had struck a nerve and so continued.

"She told me that your tongue was too thick . . . and your waist as wide as a tree trunk."

Rising to stand, James pulled Regina to her feet. She thought he was going to kiss her when he pressed his nose next to hers, and was therefore startled when he replied in a voice as frigid as the weather,

"My wife lied to spare your feelings. We're very happily married. With Danielle in my bed, I have not the strength nor the desire to bed anyone else, including you, Regina. I am completely, totally satisfied."

Regina gasped, holding her cheeks in mortification. "You vile man! How dare you!" She ran for the door, but James was a step ahead, handing Regina her cloak.

"You and my sister deserve each other," she said, ripping it out of his hands. "You're both wicked! And I will make you both sorry that you have treated me in such a despicable fashion."

The front door was pulled open, emitting a welcome blast of fresh air as Regina stalked out, slamming shut just as Danielle and the others walked into the room.

Glancing about the room for her sister and finding her gone, Danielle's forehead creased in confusion. "Is there something wrong? Why has Regina left?"

"Nothing to worry yourself about, my dear. I fear Regina was suddenly overcome with too much *passion* of the moment. She took ill and left."

"And will she be returning?"

He caught Ian's knowing smile, returning it with one of his own. "Not for quite a while, my dear. Not for quite a while."

16

On a bright summer's day in August a stranger arrived in Fredericksburg, a stranger who wore the uniform of a French army colonel and rode a large chestnut mare.

The man, a mustache and beard disguising the lower half of his face, was resplendent in his dark blue uniform jacket with gold epaulets, which distinguished him as a commissioned officer, as did the long red sash at his waist. He nodded politely at the curious onlookers who lined the main thoroughfare to welcome his arrival, smiling as they waved and cheered, doffing his cockaded hat to reveal a short, white-powdered wig while urging his horse down Sophia Street toward the tavern where he had chosen to reside.

Directing his mount toward the rear of the Golden Pineapple, he dismounted and called out, wiping the sweat from his face and neck while he waited. The air was as hot as his temper.

A freckle-faced, brown-haired lad appeared to take the reins. "Good day to you, sir."

"*Bon jour, mon ami,*" the man said with a distinctive French accent. "Do you know if this establishment has a room to let? I will require board for my horse, as well."

"Yes, sir," Billy Small, the stableboy, replied eagerly, doffing his knit cap as a measure of respect, while admiring the impressive blue-and-white uniform. "There's always room for those who fight them scurvy British bastards." He smiled to reveal two missing front teeth.

Andrew Ellsworth clenched the silver hilt of the small sword at his side, wishing he could deprive the miserable little urchin of the rest of his teeth by knocking them down his throat, but he needed a room and a place to rest.

With the British army's usual incompetence, his departure had been delayed. He'd ridden hard these past weeks, trying to make up for lost time, preferring to keep the element of surprise on his side by traveling overland rather than by ship. He was in need of a bath, bed, and a decent hot meal, and not necessarily in that order, and would go to any length to obtain them. Even if it meant humoring rebel sympathizers.

Having spied several taverns upon entering the thriving seaport community of Fredericksburg, he had chosen this one for its location on the riverfront. Sailors frequented these type of taverns, and he was in need of information.

Even if his efforts to find the Phantom failed, there was still the munitions plant to consider. Fredericksburg contained a gunnery factory used to supply the rebel forces with arms and ammunition, and he intended to find out what he could and use that information to destroy it. 'Twould be a feather in his cap, almost as prestigious a feat as capturing the Phantom.

Noting the adulation in the young boy's eyes, Ellsworth congratulated himself silently for choosing to portray a Frenchman. As the son of a British nobleman, he'd been well versed in the language and customs of France, having been sent abroad to study at the age of twenty. Upon completion of his grand tour, he had acquired a commission in the British navy and had gone on to distinguish himself as a capable officer, that is, until his confrontation with the American pirate.

The ploy to impersonate a French artillery officer had been a brilliant one on his part. The French were held in high esteem for aiding the Americans in their fight against the British king. He'd been wined, dined, and treated quite splendidly.

For all their affectations, these Americans were an uncivilized, boorish lot of traitors, as evidenced by the filthy scamp before him. The sooner he could accomplish his task, the sooner he could get out of this loathsome country and back where he belonged.

"Will you be needin' anything else, sir?"

"Non," he replied, tossing the boy a coin. "Take good care of my horse; he's valuable to me."

"That I will, sir. And God bless you, sir."

Ellsworth fought the urge to sneer and bowed instead, hoping that others in a position to help him would be as easily duped as the boy.

Rolling the wide strip of linen into a bandage,

Danielle placed the finished product next to the pile she'd already done. Lottie sat next to her, as did several of the Daughters who had come to her house to assist in the necessary chore.

It was a mindless task to occupy her time while she waited for James to return. She'd just received word that he'd be home before the month's end. Lord, how many bandages would she have rolled by then? she wondered, staring at the growing pile.

Still, if not for their efforts, the wounded soldiers in the field might not have adequate supplies to aid them. As always, foodstuffs were in short supply, and the harshness of last winter had only added to the problem of supply and demand, or so James had written in his letter.

The shadows of the afternoon lengthened and Danielle instructed Mrs. Dunstan to light more candles. She felt guilty at times for requesting her to do so; they were such a dear commodity, expensive to purchase and time-consuming to make, and she knew that many of the other women at her dining room table were not as fortunate as she to be married to a man of such wealth as James Ashland.

"Are you and Mr. Ashland planning on having babies, Danielle?" plump Mrs. Euphemia Waxworth asked, cupping her ear so as not to miss a tasty morsel of gossip she might be able to pass along. Mrs. Waxworth's penchant for gossip was only second to her penchant for sweets, as evidenced by the multitude of chins hanging from her face.

Startled by the question, Danielle caught Lottie's worried glance out of the corner of her eye before responding, "Why you know that's God's will, Euphemia. We can't predict when such an event might occur." She smiled politely, hoping her answer would be adequate to satisfy the woman's curiosity. It wasn't.

"But you've been married several months, my dear. Surely there must be some problem. A young girl like you should have quickened by now."

Danielle's cheeks pinkened, prompting Lottie to respond, "There's a war on, Mrs. Waxworth, in case you ain't noticed. Some women are more affected by nerves . . . high-strung, so to speak. Now me blessed mother, God rest her soul, used to say that a nervous wife was the same as a nervous cow, neither one was goin' to produce milk fit to drink."

Euphemia gasped, turning a bright red, then directed her attention back to her bandages.

When the ladies left a short time later, Danielle and Lottie situated themselves on the love seat in the parlor to share a pitcher of lemonade and shrewsbury cakes. The windows were open and a soft breeze floated in, ruffling the drapery.

"This is rather like a picnic, don't you agree, Lottie?" Danielle asked, forcing a smile to her lips as she filled two pewter cups with the cold liquid.

"You don't fool me, Danny. You let that old bag get to you today. We no sooner got rid of old horse face and now we've got that porker Euphemia to reckon with. I'm not sure which one's worse."

Danielle smiled at the remembrance of what had eliminated Harriet Coombs from their lives. Harriet's visits had been infrequent and blessedly businesslike, thanks to James and his hairy legs.

Thinking of James brought Euphemia's question to mind, and a frown to her lips. She still had not told James about the child. And soon, despite the fullness of her gowns, there'd be no hiding the fact of her pregnancy. Her breasts had grown fuller, her belly softly rounded. 'Twas only the infrequent intimacy with her husband that kept James from knowing the truth. Absently, her hands went to her stomach and she covered it protectively.

"I can see your mind's working overtime again. You're thinkin' about the wee one, am I right?"

Swallowing the lump in her throat, Danielle nodded. "I feel so dishonest, Lottie, not telling James about the baby."

"Love," Lottie answered, grabbing on to Danielle's hand, "you mustn't worry so. It isn't good for the babe. Mr. Ashland is a good man. He'll be happy when he finds out about the babe. Things have a way of working out, you'll see."

"But what if he doesn't want it?" Her eyes filled with tears, a frequent occurence of late. "He's never even told me that he loves me."

Lottie shook her head. "Girl, are you blind? I've seen the way his eyes follow you. I say the man's crazy in love."

Danielle wished she possessed Lottie's confidence, but she didn't and decided to change the depressing subject. "Are you planning to tell Ian about the baby, Lottie? I would have thought you'd have written him by now."

Lottie's generous proportions made it difficult to tell that she was pregnant. But by the time Ian returned with James, it wasn't going to be an easy fact to hide, especially when Ian noticed that glow in her cheeks.

Lottie sighed, setting the cookie she was about to bite back down on the plate. "The stubborn fool thinks he's too old to become a father. We've discussed it before, which is why I'm hesitant to tell him now. He might not be happy about the fact that I'm breedin'."

"Posh!" Danielle threw Lottie's words right back at her and smiled. "Ian worships the ground you walk on. He'll be ecstatic to learn he's to become a father."

"I hope you're right. We're still so newly married; I don't want nothin' to spoil our happiness."

"A baby will only add to it."

"Then take your own advice, love, and tell Mr. Ashland about the babe."

Lottie's words drummed through Danielle's head that day, and for many more days to come.

Ellsworth ogled the pretty blond serving wench with a practiced eye. She was a trifle sparse for his tastes; he liked a woman with big, fleshy breasts, but he supposed hers would do in a pinch.

Taking a sip of his bordeaux, he smiled inwardly at her obvious intent to impress him as she bent low over the table to refill his glass, giving him an eyeful of small, pert breasts and rock-hard nipples.

'Twould be a pity to disappoint such an eager creature, he thought. It had been a good while since he'd buried himself between the thighs of a willing woman. And from the seductive smile on the chit's face, she was more than willing.

"*Merci, mademoiselle,*" he said, smiling kindly at her. "Would you permit me to purchase you a refreshment? I am newly arrived and would welcome the companionship of someone as lovely as you."

Regina preened under the compliment, curtsying

prettily. "My mother does not allow me to socialize with the customers, sir."

"And do you always do what your mama tells you, *chérie?*"

His softly spoken accent sent curls of desire all the way down to Regina's toes. She blushed like a schoolgirl in the throes of her first crush. "Not always. But I must be careful. I would not want to ruin my reputation. It is spotless, I'll have you know."

His eyebrow arched at that. A serving wench with a spotless reputation. Ha! That was as likely as a dog without fleas. Her attempt at deception amused him. "I meant no disrespect, *chérie*. I assure you, my intentions are of the highest sort."

She smiled; her cheeks dimpling. "You are a flatterer, sir. But I am used to that. Many men have vied for my favors, but, as yet, I have given them to no one."

Reaching for her hand, he placed a tender kiss in her palm and felt her tremble. "We French are an impatient breed, *chérie*. I do not know how long I shall remain in your charming establishment. Perhaps you would permit me to get to know you better?"

Regina had heard that French men were excellent lovers, and after the touch of this one's lips on her skin, she was sure of it. And he was quite handsome, though she would insist that he shave off his scratchy beard, if she decided to take him to her bed.

As yet, she had allowed no man to touch her. She foolishly thought she would remain pure and unsullied, in the event James Ashland wanted to marry her.

Her eyes narrowed. Well that vile dandy had made it abundantly clear how he felt about her. Let him have Danielle; he didn't deserve her anyway. The

Frenchman was probably just as wealthy; of course, she would have to find that out. And he was far handsomer than Ashland. Yes, he just might be her ticket out of here.

She leaned forward, the front of her gown gaping open to give him an unencumbered view of her breasts, pleased by the spark of passion in his copper-colored eyes. "Perhaps I will allow that, Colonel. But you must promise that you will behave as a proper gentleman."

He reached for her hand, brushing across her breast as he did, and heard her sharp intake of breath. "*Chérie*, you have my word that I will behave as this uniform dictates. I am an officer, am I not?"

She smiled and so did he, but his did not quite reach his eyes.

"They're coming!" Danielle remarked, letting the drapery fall back into place. With excitement lighting her eyes, she turned to stare at Lottie. "Now promise me that you'll tell Ian about the baby as soon as they're settled. No more secrets; secrets are poison to a happy marriage." She had decided to tell James about the baby, as soon as the right moment presented itself.

"Oh, all right. He'll probably guess when he sees how fat I am anyway."

A moment later the two men entered. Ian and Lottie exchanged warm hugs and kisses. Almost shyly, Danielle walked up to James, who was hanging his hat on the hall tree, and wrapped her arms about his neck, kissing him full on the lips. Disappointed when there was no response, she pulled back, whispering,

"I've missed you, James," startled a moment later when he pulled her hard against his chest and ravished her mouth with a kiss that said more plainly than words that he had missed her too.

"God, Danielle, I—" remembering his role, he quickly amended—"my dear, it's wonderful to see you. I've missed your charming company."

Warmed to the very tips of her toes, Danielle spun on her heel and joined Lottie and Ian in the parlor, feeling happier than she'd felt in weeks. James had missed her!

Ashland led her to the love seat and pulled her down beside him. "What news is there? Has everything run smoothly while I've been gone?"

"Yes, quite smoothly, though there is one bit of news you haven't yet heard." Actually two, but she wasn't prepared to go into the other one right now.

Lottie tossed her a panicked look, but Danielle merely nodded her head in encouragement. The young woman turned various shades of red, her cheeks glowing so crimson Danielle thought she would incinerate on the spot.

"Well?" Danielle prompted.

Taking a deep breath, Lottie grabbed hold of Ian's hand, made the sign of the cross in front of her face, and in a high-pitched voice blurted, "I'm going to have a baby!"

Ian's mouth dropped open as he stared first at his wife, then Danielle, and finally at Phillip; he teetered before he fell to the floor in a faint.

"Oh, my God!" Lottie shrieked, kneeling down beside him. "I've killed him. He's had a heart seizure. He's dead!"

But a moment later when Ian opened his eyes, he

had a smile on his face as wide as the York River. "A bairn, ye say? We're goin' tae have us a bairn?" He pushed himself to his feet, grabbing Lottie around the waist, and kissed her soundly on the lips. "'Tis glad I am tae hear it, lass. I thought ye were jes gettin' fat."

"Well, I guess Ian isn't upset at the news," Danielle remarked, smiling at the happy couple's antics.

Ashland stared at her quizzically. "Should he be? Most men would be delighted to have a child."

Her gaze was searching. "Would you?"

The question hung in the air, but Ashland was saved from answering when Ian erupted with a loud Highland yell and Lottie said laughingly, "Saints be praised, the man's lost his mind."

Danielle studied her husband beneath lowered lashes. He seemed genuinely happy at the news of Lottie's pregnancy. Perhaps, as Lottie had suggested, James would welcome the news of his own child. But it wasn't his child, and therein lay the rub.

Phillip didn't like the way Danielle was looking at him. He knew as soon as Lottie had made her announcement he was in trouble. Pregnancy spread like the wrath of God once it started. What if Danielle desired a child? What if she pressed him to have one?

God's blood! What a horrible mess his life had become.

When no answers were forthcoming, he did the only thing a reasonable man could do under the circumstances. He grabbed the bottle of whiskey off the table, proposed a toast, then proceeded to get himself blessedly drunk.

17

Tap . . . tap . . . tap. The soft rapping on the glass pane brought Danielle instantly awake. Her heart jumped in her chest. Climbing out of bed, she made her way to the window and unfastened the latch, lifting up on the sash to peer out into the darkness, wondering why Mrs. Dunstan had shut it in the first place; the evening was quite warm.

There was nothing. Only a clear, starlit sky and a moon nearly full.

Relief washed over her and she turned back toward the bed, clutching herself to fend off the sudden chill of unease that coursed through her body. It was silly to think the Phantom had come back. It had been too long. And too much had happened for her to welcome him with open arms. Still, she couldn't help the anxiety she felt for his safety. He was the father of her child, after all.

Tap . . . tap . . . tap. There it was again. She spun around, her eyes rounding at the sight of the black-clad figure climbing in through the window; her heart pounded with trepidation and relief. He was still alive!

She stared unable to believe that her eyes weren't deceiving her. He looked the same as he always did—tall, tan, muscular—and her heart gave a queer little lurch. But as handsome as he was, his profound good looks didn't have the same effect on her as they once had. She was in love, and James's portly countenance looked better to her with each passing day.

"You're back," she whispered, her words swallowed up by the whirring of locusts outside her window.

"Thank God you unlocked the bloody thing," the Phantom said, brushing off his breeches. "I've been waiting outside, tapping on your window for over thirty minutes. You sleep rather soundly."

At his cavalier words, the excitement faded from her eyes, replaced by a bitterness that surprised her, a feeling of disenchantment that overwhelmed her.

Who did this man think he was, coming in and out of her life when he damned well pleased? She had agonized over his welfare for months, cried until she had no more tears to give. And now she was supposed to welcome him back with open arms, as if the last few months hadn't existed? Hurt and resentment welled up inside of her. And concern for a husband who cherished her.

She turned to stare toward the door that connected her room to James's and felt comforted that he lay on the other side of it. He was a constant—stability in a world turned upside down.

"You'd better pray that my husband also sleeps soundly," she said. "Your timing is poor; he's just arrived home today."

He grinned, crossing his arms over his chest as he

stepped farther into the room to lean casually against the door frame, as if coming into her room in the middle of the night was an everyday occurrence.

"I doubt old blubber guts could hear a thing above his snores. I've just spent the past thirty minutes listening to him. Unfortunately, it was his window that was open, not yours, sweeting."

Her eyes sparked angrily. "I've asked you not to speak unkindly of James; he's a good man."

"So I recall. And has this paragon of virtue given you lessons in things other than dance? Lovemaking perhaps?"

His probing stare unsettled her, and she felt heat creep up her neck to land on her cheeks in two red blotches. "That is none of your affair. James is my husband."

"Oh, but it is, sweeting," he said, determination lighting his eyes as he stepped toward her, chuckling softly as she backed toward the fireplace. "I told you long ago, you are mine." He reached for her, but she darted away. "Let's not play coy, sweeting."

"I'm not playing coy," she insisted, taking refuge behind the wing-backed chair, as if it could actually protect her from this man. "I think you'd better go."

He grinned. "We both know that's not what you want."

She took a deep breath and her voice filled with determination. "But it is. Please, you must go."

"But I've missed you; dreamed of seeing you again, like you are now, warm and soft, and so utterly desirable."

She swallowed. "Don't say such things. What was once between us is no longer."

"You care about me; I know you do."

The Phantom's words pierced her heart because

they were true. She did care about him, which was going to make what she had to do doubly difficult. She had to say good-bye.

"There is something I must tell you. Much has happened since you've been gone." There was the baby, but she couldn't tell him that. He must never know that she carried his child. She walked to the bed and reached for her wrapper, putting it on to cover her near nakedness. Her action seemed to amuse him, for he chuckled.

"I already know what you want to tell me."

Her eyes widened, and unconsciously, her hand went to her abdomen, her heart pounding in fear. "You do?"

The Phantom's smile was full of self-assurance. "You want to tell me that you love me. Well I—"

She breathed a sigh of relief. "No! That's not it." At his shocked look, she stared down at her bare toes, playing nervously with the ties of her robe.

"You don't?"

She looked up to find the confusion on his face. "I care for you very much. At one time I thought I was in love with you, but I realize now that it was only a girlish infatuation."

"Infatuation? But we made love. You gave yourself to me, wanted to run away with me."

"Yes, I know. But that was before."

"Before?" he prodded, combing his fingers through his long hair, which he'd left unbound.

"Before I married James Ashland," she explained. "I'm in love with my husband." Like a ship whose sails had been rendered windless, the Phantom seemed to deflate before her eyes, as he dropped openmouthed to sit on the bed.

"I'm sorry. I shouldn't have blurted it out like that."

Phillip stared, unable to believe what Danielle had just admitted. She loved James Ashland? That fat, pasty-faced piece of blubber! Did the Lord have no mercy? Was the woman addled? When he could think of no suitable response, he merely replied, "I see." But he didn't, not by a long shot.

"I realize this sounds rather odd to you. You're so handsome and women must throw themselves at your feet."

Not lately they hadn't.

"But James has only me." She tried to spare his feelings. "He's so . . . well . . . James is not what one would call devastatingly handsome, and he is a trifle overweight. And bald under his wig; he told me so himself."

"He sounds utterly charming. Every woman's dream."

She smiled softly. "You are every woman's dream, but James is my reality. He cares for me in his own way. He can give me what you cannot—security, honesty, commitment."

"But can he make your heart sing when he kisses you? Can he make the blood boil in your veins?" He rose to his feet and stepped toward her, drawing her into his embrace. "You cannot deny that what we have between us is special. It's something few married people share. Call it passion, call it desire, call it lust. But whatever you want to call it, it's between us, Danielle."

She backed away, unwilling to be lured into his web of desire. He was right. There was attraction and passion between them, but it wasn't enough to build a lifetime on. And he had never offered a lifetime.

"'Tis true, we shared something special; but James and I also share something special. We have formed a bond between us. We are man and wife. And"—she blushed—"James is a very good lover. We share a mutual attraction, a passion, for each other."

His eyes shuttered closed to hide his pleasure at her words. And when the full realization of what she'd just admitted hit him, his heart soared. She loved him. Or at least she loved James Ashland.

"I will hold dear all the memories we have made together. But what has been between us is over. I must let go if I'm to have a successful marriage with my husband. I can no longer let you come between us."

An ironic choice of words, Phillip thought as he studied her face, which was now etched with tears, making his heart ache. If only he could tell her how much he loved her. But he couldn't, for the Phantom wasn't any more real than James Ashland. Only Phillip Cameron was real, and he didn't seem to exist anymore.

He took her hand. "I will honor your wishes, though it grieves me to do so."

"You will always be in my heart, and I will pray to the Almighty God that your life will be spared in this war and that one day you will find great happiness."

"I will carry your memory with me always," he said softly, "for you have already given me great happiness."

She swallowed the lump in her throat. *And I will carry your child and care for it always.*

He tipped up her chin. "May I kiss you good-bye? For luck," he added at her hesitation.

She nodded and was soon enveloped in his embrace. Strong arms encircled her, hot lips branded her, and she wondered why his kiss still had the power to affect her. She loved James with all her heart. And yet, there was still this underlying chemistry between her and the Phantom that she didn't understand.

When they finally parted, he gazed into her eyes and smiled sadly. "I will miss you, sweeting."

As quickly as he had entered her life, he was gone, melting into the night. She blinked back the tears that burned behind her lids, swallowing her sadness as she stared out the window.

The Phantom had been her will-o'-the-wisp, her elusive goal. But now she had another: to seduce James Ashland back into her bed. And she meant to get started on it at once.

James's room was pitch black when Danielle entered it a short time later. She sucked in her breath, tiptoeing across the floor to his bed. James snored loud enough to wake the dead, and she smiled at the futility of her efforts to be quiet.

She realized it had been wrong for her to acquiesce to James's wish that he be allowed to sleep alone. He hadn't seen fit to touch her, to make love to her again, since that first time when she'd seduced him to her bed. And if she had to do so again to make love to her husband, then she would.

Pretending to be asleep, Phillip lay still beneath his covers. He'd heard the door open, heard Danielle's footsteps, knew she was staring down at him, plotting her next move, and he prayed fervently that she wouldn't act on her impulse to try and sleep with him again.

The last time had been pure torture, and he wasn't sure his resolve was strong enough to resist her. A man could only take so much, and Danielle had pushed him to the very limits of his endurance. And dammit, he loved her! Which made it doubly *hard*—a painfully accurate term—to shun her advances.

"James," she whispered, pulling back the covers to slide in next to him.

He groaned silently, thanking the Almighty that he knew his wife well enough and had donned his wig upon his return to the house, although he hadn't bothered with the rest of his disguise and was totally naked. And much more vulnerable. He rolled over, presenting her with his back, hoping she'd take the hint and leave him alone. But she didn't.

Scooting toward him, Danielle pressed her naked breasts into James's back. She waited, breathlessly, hoping for some sign of a response. *Nothing.*

Bringing her thighs into contact with the backs of his, she wiggled provocatively, rubbing herself against him. *Still no response.* Starting to get annoyed, she reached down to feel the bare flesh of his thigh and felt a quiver. She smiled; James always slept in the nude. She'd been counting on that eccentricity to aid her efforts.

With the tip of her right index finger, she toyed with the whorls of his ear while her left hand insinuated itself between his legs. She heard him groan and smiled. *Finally, she was making progress.*

Moving her hand to slide between the crevice, she cupped his member and squeezed gently. It was rock hard and pulsing beneath her hand. Another groan, this time louder.

"James," she whispered again, stroking the long length of him. He was quite large. But why was she so surprised? Everything about James was big. Smiling to herself, she continued stroking him.

Phillip bit his lip until he tasted blood. He forced

himself to take deep, even breaths, issuing a loud snore every now and then to complete the deception of his slumber.

God's blood! If she didn't stop soon, he would disgrace himself. He tried to think of awful things: the war, Ellsworth, death and destruction. But those thoughts were muddled by the throbbing ache, the glorious sensations Danielle was creating with her hands.

James's loud snores were starting to get insulting. Here she was doing her best to give him pleasure, and all the ungrateful wretch could do was snore in response. Well, not quite all. But that was most likely involuntary.

Realizing that her assault from the rear was not at all effective, she slipped from beneath the covers, deciding to take a different approach.

Phillip breathed a sigh of relief when he felt the bed bounce and knew Danielle had left it. He rolled over on his back, about to utter a thankful prayer, when he felt the covers being jerked off of him. A second later, Danielle mounted him, as if he were a docile stud, lying full length atop his body.

Bloody Christ! he swore silently, willing himself to remain motionless, though there was nothing he could do about the stiff shaft that jutted forth like a flagpole from his loins. He feared she would notice the absence of a paunch, and purposely pushed his stomach out to simulate one. The stubborn female was going to be the death of him yet.

Danielle rested her hands atop James's chest and propelled herself forward until her mouth rested against his lips. She kissed him lightly, so as not to alarm him, then proceeded to lick his lips with her tongue, using quick, butterfly strokes.

Was that brandy she tasted? Sliding her tongue over his mouth once again, she tried to insinuate it between his lips to gain entry, but they were sealed as tight as a miser's purse.

"James, wake up," she said impatiently, shaking him a bit. *No response.* It was then she noticed the empty bottle of brandy on the nightstand; she frowned fiercely. It was obvious from James's loud snores and lack of response he had imbibed a great deal this evening and was in his cups. "Dead to the world and feeling no pain," as her father was fond of saying. Just her luck, she thought.

Of course, men were usually more amorous when they were drunk, she reconsidered. At least that had been the case with several of the male customers at the tavern who had tried many times to push their unwanted attentions off on her.

If she could just break through his stupor, she was sure she could get a response out of him. Climbing a little higher so her belly rested against his chest, she straddled him, pressing her nipples against his lips. They grew pebble hard as she trailed them over his mouth, causing her to moan aloud.

"Darling, open your mouth," she coaxed, waiting, knowing she would not be able to continue this assault much longer. He might not be the least bit affected, but she was ready to explode like a firework.

Her thighs and sensitive mound abrading against him tingled and tortured, making her crazed with yearning. She pushed a little more insistently, breathing a frustrated sigh of relief a second later when his mouth opened to draw her nipple in.

Suddenly, she found herself flipped on her back. James was on top of her, positioning himself at her opening and she splayed her legs to receive him. Currents of desire charged through every nerve ending in her body as he sucked furiously at her breast. Instinctively, she ground her pelvis into him with slow, circular motions. He sucked harder, first one nipple, then the other, generating fire in the very center of her being, and her motions grew quicker, more frenzied, as she felt the tension build within her.

Phillip was mindless with desire. Danielle had driven him to the brink, and whatever the consequences, there'd be no going back now. He slid his turgid member into her welcoming, wet warmth, sliding in and out, matching her frenzied movements. Harder and harder he pumped, thrusting deeper and deeper.

"Oh, God! Oh, God!" Danielle cried out as the tension between her thighs built. Every sensation in her body seemed to be centered there—throbbing, pulsing—until at last she reached the zenith of her passion and exploded.

Taking deep breaths to stem her erratic heartbeat, she stared up at James's face, but it was too dark to see the expression there. She caressed his cheek, unable to hold back the words that filled her heart. "I love you, James," she whispered, hearing his sharp intake of breath before his lips came down on hers to steal whatever else she was going to say.

He rolled off of her then, but no avowals of love escaped from his lips and his silence wounded. "I know that you don't love me, James. But I have enough love for both of us, and I want us to have a true marriage."

The words he wanted to say were on the tip of Phillip's tongue, but he couldn't utter them. How could he profess his love to a woman he had deceived, was still deceiving? She would hate him if she knew that he'd only married her to perpetrate his disguise. She was in love with James Ashland, and James Ashland didn't exist.

"My dear," he finally said, "I care for you a great deal. I'm quite content with our life as it is."

"But I am not, James. I want to have children. I want to have a normal life, like Lottie and Ian. I love you."

She started crying then, heart-wrenching sobs that tore into Phillip's gut like bullets. She wanted children. And after tonight, despite all his past good intentions, she might just get her wish.

"I'm not quite sure that I'm ready to become a father, Danielle. It's a huge responsibility. And with the war and all . . ."

Her heart sank at his words. *Tell him,* her mind screamed. Tell him that it's too late, that he's already going to become a father. But she couldn't. Her pride would not allow her to beg for something he did not want. And he didn't love her. That was the cruelest thing of all.

"I understand," she said, easing off the mattress. "I'm sorry I brought in up. It was foolish of me."

"Danielle," he called out, feeling utterly helpless as he watched her pad across the room and out the door, into her own room. But there was no response.

"God's blood!" he cursed, ripping off the hated wig and throwing it across the room. He couldn't take much more of this deception. He would either have to leave or confess all. For he couldn't stand to hurt Danielle. And he feared he had hurt her very much.

"Dammit, Regina! It's been weeks and still you offer me only chaste kisses. Come, *chérie,* let me make love to you. You know you want me to."

The Frenchman attempted to kiss her breasts again, but Regina pushed him away, tugging the edges of her bodice together, grateful for the trees and shrubbery that hid their presence. They had found a secluded spot down by the river; surrounded by thick foliage, it had become the perfect trysting place for lovers, and they'd come many times since André had ridden into town.

But lovers they had not yet become, for Regina was no fool in giving herself to a man unless she was assured of getting something in return. And as yet, that something she coveted—a wedding ring—was still out of reach.

Smiling coyly, Regina patted the Frenchman's cheek. "You must learn to control yourself, André," she counseled, lowering her hand to stroke the hardened ridge in his pants, delighting in the fire that blazed bright in his eyes. "You are much too impatient. We have only known each other a few weeks. I told you, I am a virgin. When I give myself to a man, I must be sure of that man's intentions."

He grabbed her hand, squeezing it until she cried out. "I am not some callow youth you can tease and torment, *chérie*. I have only so much patience, and I am nearing the end of it with you."

Quite the understatement! Ellsworth thought, resisting the urge to squeeze her neck as fiercely as he did her hand. The woman's inane chatter had driven him to the brink of madness. Her teasing manner, designed to be provocative, inflamed his anger more than his desire. He would find another cave to mine, one that wasn't accompanied by a scheming tongue.

"You're hurting me, André!" She pulled her hand

out of his grasp, rubbing her wrist where he'd chafed it, trying to think of an explanation that would placate him for the time being.

He wanted her; she knew that. It would only be a matter of time until she allowed him to take her maidenhead, but first, he must propose marriage. He was a man of noble birth, he had told her as much. He could offer her what she wanted, provide the comforts of life that were her due, that had been viciously taken from her by Danielle.

Tears formed in her eyes, her voice quavering slightly when she said, "I was engaged to be married. My sister stole my betrothed away from me by luring him to her bed." She sobbed into her hands. "I am sorry if you think me too cautious, André, but I don't wish to be hurt again."

Ellsworth sighed, feeling quite empathetic with her former betrothed, whoever he might be. He detested weeping women, and Regina was dripping like a faucet. Handing her his handkerchief, he said to shut her off, "You are a lovely woman, *chérie*. I'm sure you will receive many offers of marriage."

"Perhaps. But I was desperately in love with James Ashland, and he threw me aside so he could rut with my slut of a sister. More fool he. Danielle confided that she's taken a lover. Of course, I didn't believe her. What would the Phantom want with a—"

His voice rose in surprise as he grasped her shoulders, turning her about to face him. "Who did you say?"

"Oh, I'm sure you've heard of him. He's supposed to be some hero for the patriotic cause. They call him the Phantom because he's constantly making fools out of those silly British sailors."

His lips thinned before he asked, "And you say that this man is your sister's lover?"

"Well, nearly. Danielle claims to have kissed him, but I didn't believe her for a second."

He released the breath he didn't know he was holding. "When? When did she claim to have done this?"

Regina shrugged. "I think sometime last spring. I'm not really sure. Why?"

Suddenly the inquisitor assumed a calculating, sympathetic smile. "Your betrothed was a very foolish man to have let you go, *chérie*." He trailed his finger up her arm, across the fullness of her breast. "If you were to be my wife, I would never think to let you go for another."

At Regina's joyous expression, he smiled inwardly, gathering her into his arms, kissing her passionately, until he felt her resistance ebb. Perhaps she was an innocent, he thought; she certainly kissed with the expertise of a wet fish.

Regina wore a dazed expression when he released her. Her eyes had darkened with passion, her face had softened at the French words of endearment he had whispered in her ear. He could probably take her now and she wouldn't say a word.

But he wouldn't.

He had more than just a tumble in mind for the marriage-minded chit. She was going to be the instrument of his revenge. And he was going to play her as expertly as any musician ever plied his craft.

18

Phillip paused before the pillared portico of the Lewises' mansion and thought of the message he'd just received from Fielding, requesting his immediate presence.

The sun had not yet reached its zenith; it was early and hardly an appropriate time for a social call. And with Lewis's health so precarious, Phillip knew that the colonel had more on his mind than congenial chitchat.

No doubt Lewis had heard the news of Cornwallis's takeover of the British army in Virginia. Replacing Tarleton, Lord Cornwallis now commanded a combined force of over seven thousand men. The American forces didn't come anywhere near that number, which created genuine concern for all who served, Lewis included.

A few minutes later, Betty Lewis ushered him into Fielding's bedchamber. A cool, early morning breeze drifted in through the open window, ruffling the curtains and lessening the odor of death and decay that permeated the room.

Phillip did his best to hide his alarm at the sight of the withered man lying before him. Fielding Lewis was dying, and it saddened him to think that this once strapping, energetic man would soon be gone.

Stepping closer to the bed, Phillip shook the sleeping man gently, whispering, "Fielding, it's Phillip. I came as soon as I got your message." The eyes that opened slowly to stare at him were clouded with pain.

"Thank you, Phillip," he replied in a hoarse whisper, attempting a smile. "Or should I call you James? I see you're still in disguise." With Phillip's help, he propped himself against the pillows.

"Whatever pleases you, my friend. I find that I don't know myself who I am most of the time. 'Tis an awkward situation."

"Married life can oftentimes make great demands on a man."

If only you knew, Fielding, Phillip thought, pulling up a side chair to seat himself. "Your note hinted at some urgency. Is there a problem at the gunnery plant?"

The man nodded weakly. "Not a problem as such. Unless you count that seven thousand pounds I have yet to recoup from Virginia's treasury. I wrote back in February, asking for repayment of the monies I'd loaned, but they have not yet seen fit to pay me, and the taxes are now in arrears on my properties."

Noting the distress covering the man's pasty cheeks, Phillip reached for his hand, patting it comfortingly. "You're not to worry yourself over trifling matters, especially debts. I have money to lend if you need it. I'll not let Betty and the children fall prey to the tax collector's gavel. On that you have my word."

The dark eyes watered. "Bless you, Phillip. You've been a good friend, which is why I wanted to confide my suspicions to you."

"Your suspicions?" Phillip's forehead wrinkled in confusion. "What is it you suspect? I have not been apprised by my contacts of anything that would cause immediate concern."

"I've received reports from the gunnery plant that a military officer has been snooping around, asking a lot of questions."

"One of the Continentals?" As far as he knew, Washington's troops were still in the New Jersey–New York area.

The colonel shook his head. "This man was dressed as a French army colonel; he's not familiar to any of my men."

"One of Lafayette's troops?"

"Perhaps, but it doesn't seem likely that he would need to ask questions pertaining to the operation of our plant and the disposition of our munitions. Lafayette is privy to such information; I'm certain his officers would have been taken into his confidence.

"Lafayette is presently headquartered in Williamsburg. Perhaps it would be politic to send someone to inquire as to this stranger's identity."

"You're probably right. I'll see to it at once."

"It may be nothing more than an old man's intuition, but I have a funny feeling about this Frenchman. I think his movements bear scrutiny."

Phillip nodded, hoping to put the old man's fears to rest. "You're not to concern yourself about this matter a moment longer, Fielding. Concentrate on getting well, and leave this matter to me. I assure you, if this man is a spy, he won't be long for this world."

The gnarled fingers wrapped around Phillip's strong ones. "I knew I could count on you, my friend. But promise me that you'll be careful. The price on your head grows with every day that passes; the British may have eyes and ears planted that we know nothing about."

"'Tis not always money that spurs a man to turn colors," Phillip remarked.

Distaste twisted the old man's lips into a sneer, and he shook his head. "Except in Arnold's case, I fear." His eyes filled with sadness. "Washington was devastated at the betrayal. He'd treated the boy like his own son; he didn't deserve such deception."

"We all must keep our eyes open in these trying times, Colonel, and remain on our guard. Men we trust can easily turn traitor, and those we love can wound us with a smile as painful as any musket ball."

"Why are you looking so depressed, Danny? You've hardly cracked a smile all week," Lottie pressed, observing Danielle from the parlor doorway. She waddled into the room, setting the pitcher of milk and plate of oatmeal cookies she carried down on the tea table in front the sofa.

Danielle pushed her needlepoint aside and rose from the love seat to pace the floor. "There's nothing wrong. I'm just—" Suddenly she burst into tears and Lottie rushed forward to comfort her.

"What is it, Danny? What's troublin' you?"

Wiping her eyes on her apron, Danielle felt foolish. She had never been one to give in to tears, and it seemed all she ever did lately was cry. "James doesn't love me, Lottie. I was going to tell him about the baby, but he's made it clear that he doesn't want any children."

Lottie led Danielle back to the sofa. "Love, just because a man says he doesn't want a child, doesn't mean anything. Remember what Ian told me, about being too old to become a father. And look at the old fool now. Why you'd think he was the Creator himself, the way he struts around like a bloody rooster." Lottie shook her head. "Men don't know what they want. That's why they got wives to tell 'em."

A small smile touched Danielle's lips as she gazed at the earnest expression on her friend's face. It was awfully hard being depressed with someone like Lottie around. She squeezed her friend's hand. "I don't know what I'd do without you, Lottie. You've been a good friend to me."

"Oh, quit gettin' all sentimental or you're going to make me cry. You're not the only one who's pregnant." A disgusted look crossed Lottie's face. "I even cried yesterday when Mrs. Dunstan ripped the head off the chicken she was preparin' for supper. The woman looked at me like I had lost my mind."

"So you think once James gets used to the idea of having a child, he'll come around?"

"Girl, men are always caught up in the notion that a child will carry on their name and bring them immortality. 'Tis all Ian ever talks about. He's going to be awfully depressed when he finds out that we're going to have a girl."

Danielle's eyes widened. "But how do you know that? Not even Dr. Fortney knows how to tell whether it will be a boy or a girl."

"Ha! Dr. Fortney don't know nothin' about women having babies. He's a man, for heaven's sake.

Only women are capable of knowing such things. And I can tell you that my ma was rarely ever wrong when it came to predictin' whether a babe would be boy or girl."

Danielle's expression was clearly skeptical and Lottie awkwardly pushed herself to her feet to make her point. Turning sideways, she pointed at her stomach. "See how low I'm carryin' this babe. My ma always said that when a woman carried a babe low, it was sure to be a girl."

Danielle glanced down at her own protruding mound and frowned. Though Lottie's baby was only a month ahead of hers, you'd never know it by comparing the two women. Lottie was huge. Mrs. Dunstan had even commented that she might be carrying twins. Whereas Danielle looked only slightly heavier than normal. A fact that caused her considerable concern, though Lottie had assured her that everything would turn out as it should come November.

"What's wrong, lovey? You look a million miles away."

Danielle shook her head and smiled. "Can you tell what mine's going to be?"

"Stand up straight. Here," she said, grabbing hold of Danielle's skirts, "pull your skirts taut across your belly, so I can get a good look at you."

Danielle did and Lottie frowned. "What's wrong?" Danielle asked, worried about the confused look on her friend's face.

"'Tis the strangest thing; but I can't tell a bloody thing. You're carryin' that babe as much in the back as in the front." It was at that moment that the baby let go with a sharp kick, hitting Danielle right under the ribs.

"Well, if its contrariness means anything," she

said, "it'll probably be a boy. Men always cause the most discomfort."

Lottie giggled. "Aye. And they always have the most discomfort. At least Ian always complains that his "tool"— that's what he calls his *what's-it*—gets harder than the mizzenmast of his ship when he gets into bed with me."

Danielle's face flamed, and she said, "Charlotte MacGregor!" before she burst out laughing.

Both women began to laugh until tears rolled down their cheeks, and they had to clutch their sides to keep them from hurting, which was how Ian and James found them when they strolled into the room a few moments later.

"Hinny, hinny," Ian said, rushing forward, his eyes immediately traveling to Lottie's belly. "Wot's wrong? Has the bairn arrived?"

Lottie and Danielle paused in their merriment to look up at Ian's concerned face, then burst out laughing all over again.

"'Tis not the babe, lovey," Lottie finally managed when she'd gotten herself under control. "'Twill not be born for months yet."

Ian breathed a sigh of relief and scratched his head, while James peered at the duo through his monocle, and said, "It would appear that our wives are engaged in a bit of frivolity." And he'd been worried about Danielle's morose behavior. Worse than worried. He'd felt responsible because of what had occurred the other night. Women! Who could ever figure them out?

Danielle smiled and held out her hand to her husband. "Good afternoon, James. How are you this fine summer day?"

"I've been gone less than two hours, my dear. My health has not failed since I saw you last."

"But you were gone so long," she parried, stepping forward to play with the watch fob on his vest. "I missed you." She pressed a kiss to his cheek, delighting in his embarrassment.

Phillip stared at his wife's behavior, clearly baffled. She'd hardly spoken to him all week, and now she couldn't keep her hands off of him. "I told you Ian and I were to pay a visit to the gunnery plant. I promised Fielding I would check on things, since he's indisposed and unable to do so himself."

Danielle sobered instantly. "Has there been any improvement in the colonel's health? Last time I visited with Mrs. Lewis she was beside herself with worry."

James shook his head, sadness touching his eyes. "I'm afraid not. But I was able to set his mind at rest about the plant."

Though it had put Fielding's mind at ease, Phillip was still concerned. Ellsworth was still out there somewhere. An enemy who lay in wait was by far the most dangerous kind, and he knew deep down inside that Ellsworth would never rest until he had his revenge.

Regina stared at the sleeping man at her side, smiling happily. It had finally happened. André had proposed, and she had surrendered all to him. The place between her thighs still ached, but the pain had been well worth it. What was a few minutes of pain, when she would gain a lifetime of pleasure from it?

"André," she whispered, leaning over to place a kiss upon his cheek. "Wake up. My parents will return from the market square soon. It wouldn't do to have them find me in your bed."

The dark lashes raised and the copper-colored eyes landed on the blond woman's porcelain features. Ellsworth sighed deeply. Asking Regina to marry him, then taking her to bed, was a big sacrifice to make for his career, especially when one considered how totally inept the stupid chit had been at making love.

A virgin! Who would have thought it? Well, there was no help for it now. The distasteful deed was done; he just hoped his seed did not take root. He wanted no by-blows from this foolish woman.

He smiled to hide his contempt. "*Chérie*, you were wonderful. Did I make you happy?" He kissed her before she had a chance to answer, then extricated himself from her embrace. "I need to dress," he said as a way of explanation, then proceeded to do so.

"I'm very happy, André. When will the wedding be? I can't wait to tell my mother."

Pulling on his pants and boots, Ellsworth turned back to face her, a deep frown creasing his lips. "You can tell no one of our affair, Regina. It would spoil my plans."

Her forehead wrinkled in confusion. "Your plans? I don't understand." Fear lit her eyes and a note of accusation entered her voice. "I thought you said we would be married. I thought you said you loved me."

"I do, *chérie*," he said, sitting down next to her on the bed. "But I am on a secret mission and it is important that no one discovers my whereabouts or my identity."

Surprise then annoyance crossed Regina's face. She wanted to tell her mother, and most especially she wanted to tell Danielle about her marriage to André.

Her sister would be green with envy when she found out Regina was marrying a titled French nobleman.

"Did you hear what I said, Regina?" Andrew repeated, wondering how anyone could be so obtuse.

"Of course I heard you, André. I'm not deaf. You're here on a secret mission. Does that mean you're a spy?"

"Of sorts."

"Well, what is this mission that is so important I can't tell anyone about our marriage. And it had better be good."

"I am here to arrest the Phantom."

Her mouth dropped open before she launched herself out of the bed, wrapping a sheet around herself. Her face was as white as the bed linen that surrounded her. "The Phantom?! But why do you wish to capture him? I thought you were both on the same side of this war."

"It's true, *chérie*; we are on the same side. But I am not so patriotic that I wouldn't turn him in to the British for the reward they're offering for his capture. It is a sizeable sum and would make me even richer."

Ever the opportunist, Regina's expression of surprise turned quickly to one of curiosity. "I really have no interest in this war, André. I was perfectly happy living under British rule. And if capturing the Phantom will bring us great wealth, then I will do whatever I can to help you."

"I was hoping you'd say that, Regina," he said, coming to stand before her. "I am of noble blood. My estates rich, my holdings varied. You would want for nothing once we are married, *chérie*." He used the endearment she was so fond of and saw her face soften. Regina might have been a virgin, but she was definitely a whore at heart.

"And once we capture this Phantom, we will be rich?"

"The reward has been raised to two thousand pounds sterling. Is that rich enough?" It hadn't been difficult to convince the Admiralty to increase the price on the Phantom's head, not after the recent loss of the frigates *Mars* and *Minerva*.

Regina's blue eyes glowed with the fervor of her greed. "Tell me what I must do to help you."

Leading her back to the bed, he instructed her to sit, occupying the space next to her. "I want you to tell me everything you know about your sister's relationship with the Phantom."

"You want to know about Danielle?"

He nodded. "Tell me everything and leave nothing out. Even the smallest detail might help us in capturing him."

Regina was only too happy to discuss her sister's marriage to James Ashland and her alliance with the Phantom, what little she knew of it anyway. She didn't embellish this time, only told the facts as she knew them. She wanted nothing to come between her and that reward money. Two thousand pounds. 'Twas a fortune.

But the best part of the scheme wouldn't be the money, she decided; it would be bringing disgrace down upon Ashland's head, depriving Danielle of the man she'd set her heart on.

Regina smiled widely as she thought of her sister's total ruination. Revenge was going to be sweet.

19

"*Laddie! Laddie!*" *Ian rushed* into the study, slamming the door loudly behind him. Panting, his face gleaming with sweat, he gasped, "I seen him. I seen the British captain."

Phillip spun on his heel, the book he held falling to the floor as he stepped forward to assist his first mate. "Calm yourself, old man. You're going to have a seizure," he said, helping Ian to sit down on the leather sofa before handing him a glass of water. "Now take some deep breaths and tell me what's wrong."

Ian calmed himself as best he could, then blurted, "I seen the British bastard. Ellsworth! I know 'tis him. I couldna be mistakin' abou' such a thing."

Phillip masked his alarm, saying, "Tell me."

"I was down tae the docks, watching some sailors load their cargo. Ou' of the corner of me eye I caught a glimpse of a mon. He was standing verra straight, hands behind his back, watching. He had a wig and a beard and mustache too. But I tell ye, laddie, I'd recognize that cocky stance anywhere. 'Tis him, I tell ye."

Pacing back and forth across the confines of the study, Phillip finally drew to a halt before the window and looked out. Dark clouds clung to the horizon; there'd been rain before nightfall. Fitting, he thought, turning back to face Ian.

"I'm not saying you're not correct, Ian. But my contacts place Ellsworth farther south with Cornwallis. It's doubtful he would know of my whereabouts." But still, the possibility existed, and he would have to use extreme caution from here on out.

"I tell ye it's him, lad," Ian insisted, pouring something other than water into his glass and gulping it down. Good Scotch whiskey! Nothin' better to calm a man down, Ian thought.

"Then maybe it's time we faced him, Ian. Time that we brought this whole miserable farce to an end."

"Don't be sayin' such nonsense, boy!" Ian quickly crossed himself. "Ye'll bring bad luck upon yerself. Ellsworth wants tae kill ye. He's raised the price on yer head to two thousand pounds, laddie. The mon wants ye badly, he does."

Phillip's fist pounded the desk so hard the brass candlestick toppled over, spilling wax over the desktop and floor. "That bastard is at the root of all my trouble. If not for him, I wouldn't be playing this miserable charade."

"If no' for him, ye wouldna hae met and married Danielle, and I wouldna hae met me darlin' Charlotte. There's good that's come o' it."

"But what good is it, Ian, when I can't even tell Danielle that I care deeply for her, want to marry her? I love her! Goddammit!" He held his head in his hands, staring at the decanter of whiskey on his desk and wondered how long it would take to drink himself to death and put an end to his misery.

"Well, ye needn't look so happy abou' it," Ian remarked, grinning. "I've seen happier men on their way tae the gallows."

"'Tis where I wish I was going."

Ian shook his head, concern glittering brightly in his eyes. He'd never seen the lad in such a state. But then, the lad had never been in love before.

"Things'll work ou', lad. I'm sure o' it."

Phillip wasn't nearly as confident as his first mate professed to be. Eager to change the subject, he was grateful for the knock that sounded at the door. Mrs. Dunstan stuck her head through the doorway.

"A messenger's come," she said, reaching into her apron pocket to produce a sealed piece of parchment, handing it to her employer.

Phillip recognized Lafayette's wax seal immediately and frowned. Something was amiss; he could feel it in his bones. "Thank you, Mrs. Dunstan. Have Danielle and Charlotte returned from their meeting yet?"

"No, sir. But I expect them momentarily."

"Send my wife in when she returns. If this message is what I think it is, I'll be needing to speak to her directly."

After Mrs. Dunstan departed, Phillip tore open the missive, his frown deepening as he read it.

"Cornwallis has evacuated Williamsburg. He's crossed the James River and has encamped in York Town." He read further and his face brightened. "Finally some good news. Baron von Steuben has united his force with Lafayette's. The marquis now commands over four thousand Continentals and militia. They're planning to move against Cornwallis."

"From that smile on yer face, laddie, I would say that yer thinking abou' joining 'em."

Phillip nodded. "Aye. The Phantom may be able to create a little havoc for the British navy. Now that they've evacuated Georgetown, South Carolina, they'll be heading north, and I'll be there to greet them upon their arrival."

The excitement of adventure lit Phillip's eyes, but Ian's face clouded with unease. "'Twill be dangerous, laddie." He picked up the porcelain figurine off the mantel, fidgeting nervously with it. "I'm torn between your welfare and Charlotte's," he admitted.

Phillip crossed the room, draping his arm about the older man's shoulders. "You've got responsibilities now, Ian. I'm full grown, but your new babe will need a father. I want you to stay with your wife and Danielle, keep an eye on things for me here at home. If Ellsworth is truly here, I'll feel better knowing that you'll be here to protect our women."

Ian's chest puffed out but deflated a moment later when Phillip added, grinning, "Besides, you'd be as useless as a frigid whore, worrying about Charlotte and the babe."

Ian smiled, a sigh of relief escaping his lips. "Thank ye, laddie. I guess I'm getting soft in me old age."

A rueful smile crossed Phillip's lips. "I think we both are. I never thought to admit it, but there's nothing I'd like better than to settle down and raise a family of my own. I'm tired of war, of deception, of having my life blown about every which way. 'Tis time I planted these feet somewhere besides the deck of a ship."

"The war will be over soon, laddie."

"Aye," Phillip said, nodding. But would he be alive to see its end?

In the midst of applying a fresh coat of beeswax to the furniture in the parlor, Danielle looked up as the door knocker sounded. Knowing that Mrs. Dunstan and Charlotte were occupied with the laundry chores out back, she wiped her hands on her apron, adjusted her mobcap, and proceeded to answer the impatient caller's summons.

Opening the door, she was stunned to discover her sister standing on the porch. Regina was garbed in a blue dimity gown over a white lace petticoat, looking every inch the porcelain doll her mother had always thought her to be. Gowned in serviceable gray cotton, Danielle felt as dowdy as an aging matron in comparison.

"Regina, what brings you here?"

Tears filled Regina's eyes, alarming Danielle that her mother might be sick again. "Is mama ill?"

The young woman shook her head. "Mama is fine; 'tis I who am troubled."

Ushering Regina into the parlor, Danielle indicated that she should sit, staring at her quizzically. Regina had a flair for the dramatic. Most likely, her clothing allowance had dwindled or she hadn't been receiving the required amount of attention she desired. For her expensively gowned sister certainly didn't look as if she suffered unduly.

"Would you like some lemonade or perhaps some iced tea?" Danielle offered, going through the motions of polite behavior, though it galled her to do so. Her memory wasn't so short that she had forgotten Regina's last visit and her reprehensible behavior.

Removing her handkerchief from her reticule,

Regina dabbed at the corners of her eyes, further igniting Danielle's curiosity. "What's wrong, Regina? Have you and Mama had a tiff?"

"I've come to make amends with you, Danielle. I realize how utterly selfish and awful I've been to you."

The violet eyes rounded as Danielle plopped down in her seat. Of all the things she'd expected her sister to say, an apology wasn't one of them. "I don't understand why you've come now, Gina. James and I have been married almost seven months. In all that time you haven't seen fit to grace us with your presence, except for the occasions when you attempted to throw yourself at him."

Regina reddened in anger. She wanted to tell Danielle exactly why she had come—that André had insisted that she ingratiate herself to her sister to find out what she could about the Phantom. Though she hated debasing herself so, there was a great deal of money at stake, so she sobbed into her handkerchief, saying instead, "I want to beg for your forgiveness, sister."

Regina sounded so anguished, so contrite, Danielle was actually beginning to think that perhaps her sister was sorry for what she had done. But a kernel of doubt still existed.

"I know I've been dreadful, Danielle. Mama has chastised me for it several times."

That brought another startled look from Danielle. *Mama had chastised her precious? Would wonders never cease?* "Why has your conscience started to bother you now, Gina, after all this time? We've never been, what one would call, close; I fail to see what you hope to gain by this reconciliation."

Dropping to her knees, Regina knelt before Danielle, placing her head in her lap. "I've grown up,

Danielle. Truly I have." She looked up, tears spiking her lashes. "I can no longer live with a guilty conscience. I had to purge myself and beg your forgiveness. I know we've never gotten along all that well, but that was my fault. I've always been jealous of you."

"You've been jealous of me?" Danielle laughed, her voice thick with uncertainty. "You, who had all the fine clothes, the lovely room? You, who didn't need to lift a finger to help at the tavern? Come Regina, do you really expect me to believe that?"

Though her vanity was sorely wounded, and she nearly choked on the words, Regina swallowed her contempt, saying, "You're by far the prettier one, Danielle. I know Mama always doted on me, praised me for my looks, but I saw the way men looked at you."

Staring down at her sister's guileless face, Danielle saw only repentance in the depths of the watery blue eyes. Was Regina telling the truth? she wondered, knowing firsthand what guilt could do to a soul. Perhaps her little sister had finally grown up. Perhaps it was time that she let bygones be bygones and forgive her. James had counseled her in the past to make amends with her family; now might be the perfect opportunity.

"Get up off your knees, Gina, and sit here beside me." Danielle indicated the space next to her on the settee. "I confess I am quite taken aback by your heartfelt apology." She took her sister's hands in hers. "I have always loved you, Gina, though I know there were times when I didn't act like it, and you didn't think so. I want nothing more than for us to be friends. I accept your apology."

Regina embraced her sister, hugging her to her breast. "I'm so relieved," she said. And truer words had never been spoken.

But Danielle was unable to see the malice in her sister's eyes, or the sinister smile that twisted the young girl's lips.

James had left once again to solicit merchandise from the Richmond merchants to supply Lafayette's growing army. As proud as she was at his endeavors to assist the war effort, Danielle missed him dreadfully and was grateful she'd been able to occupy her time sharing her sister's company. It had made her husband's absence so much easier to endure.

Regina was a frequent visitor to the house on Caroline Street. Lottie had even grown used to her company, grudgingly, though she wasn't buying this new and improved version of Regina.

"A leopard doesn't change its spots," Lottie had advised after one of Regina's visits. "Your sister is up to something. I can smell a rat from fifty yards, and my nose itches like the very devil when Regina comes to call."

Danielle stared as her sister preened and posed before the mirror in Mrs. DeBerry's dress shop, trying on one hat after another, and thought again of Lottie's words.

She bit her lower lip indecisively. Perhaps Lottie was a bit jealous of Regina. After all, Danielle and Lottie had grown very close since her marriage to James. Perhaps her newfound friendship with Regina posed somewhat of a threat to her, especially now that she was pregnant. "Pregnant women were known for their irascible moods," or so Ian had remarked on many an occasion.

Danielle could certainly agree with that, for her mood of late had not been all that pleasant. She'd finally had to let out some of her gowns in the waist and bust to accommodate her growing proportions, and only because she wore such voluminous skirts was her pregnancy hidden from view.

At least she hadn't had to contend with her sister's surly moods. Regina had been the devoted sister of late. She'd come over several times to assist with the baking, though Mrs. Dunstan had likened her bread to granite and implored Danielle to keep Regina out of the kitchen. She'd offered to help Lottie with the laundry, an offer which Lottie had not so very graciously declined.

But the most startling offer came the day she'd attended her first meeting of the Daughters of Liberty. Up until that day, Regina's social conscience had been solely confined to Regina's needs and wants. It had been an eye-opening experience to watch her sister roll bandages and prepare foodstuffs for the soldiers.

This new side of her sister was astonishing, and she couldn't wait for James to come home so she could discuss all the latest happenings with him.

One more week. One more week and he'd be home and she could tell him about the baby.

James had been more affectionate to her of late, and she was more determined than ever to see that their marriage succeeded. She could see now that Lottie had been right. Once James knew of the child, he would be ecstatic about it. Hadn't he been pleased when Lottie announced her pregnancy? All he needed was a little nudge in the right direction, Danielle thought, smiling. And she knew just where she was going to nudge him.

"What do you think of this one, Danielle? I can't decide between the black satin with ostrich feathers or the straw with grosgrain ribbons. They're both so darling."

Directing her attention toward the bonnets, Danielle

considered both, but found it difficult to muster enthusiasm for either one. They were dreadful, but she didn't want to hurt Regina's feelings and offered graciously, "Why not take both? It will be my treat."

The blue eyes sparkled with delight, the bow-shaped lips turning up into a smile. "Truly? Oh, thank you, Danielle. Wrap these up for me, Mrs. DeBerry," Regina ordered the milliner, "and these fans, as well. You don't mind, do you, Danielle?"

Danielle hesitated only briefly, wondering how she was going to explain all these additional purchases to James. Regina's shopping excursions had already cost her a pretty coin. "No, of course not," she finally replied.

"You're so good to me, Danielle," Regina remarked once they were back out on the cobblestone street. "Come back to the tavern with me. I want to show Mama my purchases."

Danielle consented, and a few minutes later they were entering the retiring room of the tavern, where they found Elsie seated with her feet propped up on the footstool before her. She looked tired and wan, and Danielle worried that her mother had taken too much upon herself.

It was obvious that Regina wasn't doing much, if anything, to help her. And she made a mental note to speak to her sister about it when they were alone.

"It's good to see you again, Mama," Danielle said, leaning over to kiss her mother's cheek. She noted the pleased smile that crossed Elsie's lips and wondered at it. Elsie had never been given to demonstrative displays of affection, except with Regina. In the past when Danielle had tried to kiss or hug her mother, she'd been brushed off with a terse comment or worse, laughed at.

"Sit down, daughter, it's been so long since we've had

a chance to talk. I'm sorry that I missed your husband's birthday celebration. I was indisposed." She shot Regina a pointed look, making the young girl blush.

"I'd better go put these things away," Regina said hurriedly, bundling up her purchases. She made to leave, but Danielle's comment halted her before she could make good her escape.

"I thought you wanted to show Mama what we bought, Regina."

"I've—I've changed my mind. I'll show her some other time. I'll see you soon, Danielle," she said, then turned and quit the room.

Danielle shook her head at her sister's flighty behavior. It definitely wasn't in Regina's nature not to want to show off, especially when it came to new frills and furbelows. She asked her mother, "What's gotten into Regina? She seems as skittish as a mare in heat."

"Perhaps she is," Elsie remarked, clearly annoyed. "Your sister is quite taken with one of the gentleman boarders, a Frenchie, no less."

The violet eyes widened. "Regina has a beau? But she's never even mentioned it." How odd that she hadn't confided in her, especially since they'd grown so close over the past few weeks. Regina certainly had no reticence in asking Danielle all sorts of personal questions about her relationship with James. Some had been so direct and intimate, they had brought a crimson stain to her cheeks on several occasions.

"She's never mentioned it to me either, daughter, but I'm not quite as dull-witted as the girl seems to think."

"Regina is seeing this man behind your back?" No wonder Mama was so upset. She had such high hopes for Regina; a sordid affair was definitely not part of her grand plan.

Elsie nodded. "Aye, and I don't mind telling you that I don't like it. If she thinks he'll marry her after she beds him, she'll be in for a rude awakening. I've washed my hands of the whole situation."

"Regina is still your daughter, Mama. You shouldn't give up on her. Perhaps she's in love. Love often makes a sane person do foolish things."

Elsie smiled kindly at her daughter. "I sense that you've fallen in love with your Mr. Ashland, am I right, child?

Heat stole into Danielle's face. "Yes, I do love James. He's been good to me, Mama."

"'Tis no more than you deserve, daughter."

"You shouldn't be too hard on Regina, Mama. She was vastly disappointed when James chose me over her. Perhaps this Frenchman has restored her self-esteem. She certainly seems a changed person of late."

Deep lines bracketed Elsie's mouth. "You're too kind, Danielle. It was always your greatest fault and your greatest asset." Tenderly, she caressed her daughter's cheek. "I may not have always been the best mother to you, daughter. But know this, I do love you."

Tears misted Danielle's eyes, and she swallowed the lump in her throat. This was the first time her mother had ever admitted such a sentiment and the revelation was a balm to her soul. "I love you, too, Mama, as I'm sure Regina does."

Elsie scowled. "Your sister loves only herself, Danielle. Always remember that. I was a fool for not realizing it sooner." She leaned forward in a conspiratorial fashion, her voice hushed. "Be careful, Danielle. Don't be too trusting. Things aren't always what they seem."

Danielle's dark brows drew together in confusion. "I don't understand what you're trying to tell me, Mama."

"I can say no more. Just heed my words and use caution. These are troubled times."

Walking back to her house a short time later, Danielle pondered her mother's enigmatic words, but still they made no sense to her. Why would Mama warn her to be careful? Why had she suddenly turned against Regina?

Something was dreadfully wrong, and she aimed to get to the bottom of it. She was somewhat to blame for her sister's rash behavior with this mysterious Frenchman. Not directly, for she hadn't set out to win James away from Regina; but still, the end result had been the same. Regina had been forced to look elsewhere for her rich husband. And Danielle had no doubt in her mind that this Frenchman was wealthy. It wouldn't be Regina's style for him to be anything else.

Yes, she thought, lifting her skirts to avoid the animal droppings in the path. She would have a heart-to-heart talk with Regina, get her to confide in her. Then perhaps she'd be able to rectify Regina's relationship with their mother.

'Twas a bitter irony that she should be the one to help patch things up between Regina and Mama, Danielle thought. Perhaps Regina wasn't the only one who had grown up.

20

A few days later, Danielle invited her sister over for lemonade and cookies to discuss Regina's supposed affair with the Frenchman.

But Regina wasn't at all anxious to discuss the mysterious André, and as Danielle sipped thoughtfully on her cold drink, she realized that she was getting no closer to breaching the rift between Regina and their mother.

A warm breeze ruffled the lace edges of her mobcap as Danielle bent forward to refill her sister's glass. They were seated in the gazebo, but even the shade of the towering oaks and magnolias and the proximity of the river, couldn't lessen the discomfort of the hot afternoon.

August had melted into September, and Danielle feared she would melt right along with it.

"I don't know why you insisted on taking our refreshment out here, Danielle. It's so hot I can hardly draw a breath," Regina complained, fanning herself with quick, irritated strokes that threatened to break the ivory sticks she held.

Danielle fought to keep her temper in check. Regina's never-ending complaints were starting to get on her nerves. Lottie was right; Regina hadn't changed completely. There was still much of the temperamental, spoiled child within her that Danielle remembered only too well.

"I can understand Lottie wanting to lie down inside in the middle of the afternoon—her baby's due in a few week's time, and she's nothing short of miserable—but you're young, Regina, and much thinner. You should be able to tolerate the heat better than you do."

"I don't see your husband out here, sweating with the rest of us. Is he taking a nap as well?"

Danielle paused, not wanting to tell Regina the real reason James had left the house as soon as he heard Regina was coming to visit; she didn't think Regina would appreciate being compared to the plague.

"James has gone to visit his friend, Mr. Lewis. He has so little time to socialize since he's away on business so much of the time. We've been married seven months, and in that time, he's only been home a few weeks, total."

"But that makes it easier for you to socialize while he's gone, doesn't it?"

Danielle shrugged. "I suppose. I have been able to visit with Mrs. Washington and Mrs. Lewis more frequently. And, of course, there's my obligation to the Daughters. That takes up quite a bit of my time."

Regina did her best to hide her disgust at the mention of the patriotic organization. How beneath her it had been to sit and roll bandages with a bunch of old crones. She'd given André an earful about it too. Of course, he'd been able to soothe her feelings with a gift of a new fur-lined cloak.

"I wasn't referring to your socializing with women, Danielle, more about the men you meet upon occasion."

Tiny fingers of apprehension tingled Danielle's spine. Why had she been so stupid to have mentioned the Phantom to Regina so long ago? She could see by the determined glitter in her sister's eyes that Regina had no intention of letting her sidestep the question. She tried anyway.

"I really don't know what you mean, Regina. I'm married, and it would hardly be proper for me to associate with gentlemen other than my husband."

"Not even the Phantom?" At Danielle's silence, Regina's tone grew mocking. "I knew you had made all that up. I should have known a man like the Phantom wouldn't be interested in you." She smiled spitefully.

"I didn't make it up!" Danielle snapped, not realizing what she'd just admitted.

"Then it's true? You and the Phantom are lovers?"

Cautiously, Danielle replied, "I didn't say that. But we are friends."

"Friends see each other, do they not? And I haven't heard you mention that the Phantom had visited again."

"My relationship with the Phantom is personal, Regina. And I would rather not discuss it."

Her sister's voice grew tearful. "Here I'd hoped we were getting close, and you've been keeping secrets from me. I'm terribly hurt, Danielle." She sniffled, and Danielle sighed.

"We are close, dear, but you can't expect me to

discuss such personal details of my life with you. 'Twouldn't be proper."

"How does he contact you?" There was a calculating glimmer in the depths of the blue eyes.

Danielle grew instantly suspicious of Regina's probing questions. Obviously, Danielle's offhand remark about kissing the Phantom had nettled Regina's composure; she hated being bested by anyone. But Danielle had no intention of revealing more than she already had. The woman was a notorious gossip. "I told you, Regina, I will not discuss the Phantom."

Regina continued as if Danielle had never spoken. "When will you see him again? Soon I hope." André's impatience was driving her to distraction, and she wanted to get this whole, miserable affair over with as quickly as possible.

A sad smile touched Danielle's lips for she knew she would not. Then her voice grew harsh. "Really, Regina, leave off. I don't wish to discuss the Phantom further. As I told you, we're just friends." At the disbelief registered on her sister's face, it was apparent that Regina wasn't buying her story; Danielle changed tactics.

"Why, may I ask, are you so interested in the Phantom? You want to know everything about my relationships, yet you tell me nothing about your André. Fair's fair, Regina."

The white porcelain cheeks tinted pink. "I see mother's been filling your head with nonsense, Danielle. I've told you before I've no wish to discuss André. Besides," she added, "I'm old enough to have a beau."

"Of course you are; just be sure to use caution with this man. If you give too freely, you may end up with nothing."

Danielle's opinion hit too close to home, and Regina, not wanting to face her own fears that she had, indeed, given too freely, merely pasted on a gloating smile and said, "Andre loves me; we're to be married."

Danielle's face brightened instantly and she smiled. "But that's wonderful, Gina. When's the wedding to be? Mama never mentioned it."

"Mama doesn't know, and you must say nothing." André would kill her if he knew she'd told; he had threatened as much. At Danielle's questioning gaze, she added quickly, "We're going to surprise Mama, that's why we haven't told her. André is waiting for . . . for his funds to reach him from France. He's very proud and doesn't want to appear penniless in front of Mama and Papa."

Danielle listened intently to Regina's explanation, and though it sounded plausible, something about it did not quite ring true, though she couldn't put her finger on it.

Regina quickly changed the subject to fashion, and Danielle let the matter drop . . . for the time being.

"She wouldn't tell me anything, André. I couldn't get Danielle to admit that the Phantom was meeting with her." Regina wrung her hands nervously, noting the anger on her betrothed's face.

Andrew's lips thinned in displeasure. He should have known better than to send the stupid chit to ferret out information. Her mind was as cavernous as her mouth. And equally as empty. But what other choice did he have? Regina was the only one capable of infiltrating her sister's household. And there was always the chance that she would stumble upon a useful piece of information, or even some correspondence. He took a deep breath, plowing impatient fingers through his hair.

"You must continue to try to find these details out, *chérie*. Without them, we will not be able to capture this pirate. And that means, we will not be able to get our hands on that two thousand pounds."

Regina wrapped her arms about the Frenchman's waist. "You still love me, don't you, André? Even though I wasn't able to find out anything." There was uncertainty in the depths of the big blue eyes.

Kissing her forehead, he replied, "But of course, *ma chérie*. That will never change. But if you succeed it will only add to our fortune, make our relationship that much stronger. *N'est-ce pas?*"

Regina nodded, smiling, thinking that her life couldn't be more perfect. She had André, soon she would have the money, and Danielle would be left with only her memory of the Phantom.

The house was as quiet as a cemetery at midnight. Holding a brass chamber stick, Danielle tiptoed down the stairs on her way to the kitchen to fetch a glass of buttermilk—one of the many odd cravings she'd been having of late—but pulled up short at the sight of her husband deep in conversation with a man she'd never seen before.

They were standing in the hallway, whispering, and though she strained to hear, she couldn't make out what they were saying.

James was wearing a red satin robe. His feet were bare, as were his legs, and Danielle felt a queer flutter in the pit of her belly at the sight of them. Of course, it could have been the babe. But she didn't think so. She thought it had more to do with the fact that James was probably naked under his robe.

Staring in frozen tableau, she saw the stranger hand James a thick sheaf of papers. Odd, she thought, that one of James's business contacts would be calling so late at night. Wondering if there might be a problem with one of his mysterious suppliers—he'd never seen fit to elaborate on them, though she'd asked him numerous times—she cleared her throat and proceeded the rest of the way down the staircase.

James's conflicting emotions were clearly visible as he turned to look at her. First he appeared shocked, then guilty, then nervous as a cat on an icy fence rail. His demeanor was extremely curious.

Before she could introduce herself to the stranger, James shoved the man out the door and slammed it shut behind him. Turning to address her, he said, "My dear, whatever are you doing up at this hour? I thought you'd be asleep."

Danielle held the candle higher, trying to see what was written on the pages James held, but he thrust them behind his back before she could decipher the script. "Is something wrong, James? You're acting most peculiar."

Phillip thought quickly. What bad luck that his contact had chosen this particular night to deliver General Washington's missive. "Nothing to concern yourself with, my dear. Just a small problem with some blankets we had hoped to ship south to Nathanael Greene's army. The supplier we ordered them from has now refused delivery."

"How awful!" she replied, not believing a word of what he said. No one would be *that* nervous about a few blankets. "Isn't it rather late to be conducting business?" She watched closely for his reaction, but other than the slight flush to his cheeks, which could have been a trick of the dim light, he seemed quite composed.

Damn Danielle for her unending curiosity, Phillip thought. She'd grilled him like a staff sergeant every time he'd left on one of his missions. She was too smart for her own good, and he'd have to throw her off track. There was no way anyone could learn that Washington had moved his army of Continentals south.

Stepping toward her, he removed the chamber stick from her hand and set it on the gateleg table, and at the same time, shoved the documents into the drawer, intending to retrieve them later.

"War has no set hours, my dear. Now," he added, grabbing on to her elbow, "where may I escort you? It isn't safe to be wandering about in the dark by yourself. You're not ill, are you? I can fetch Mrs. Dunstan. She's quite proficient at doctoring."

"No!" Danielle replied a little too quickly. Mrs. Dunstan had been casting her suspicious looks of late. She had no intention of letting the astute housekeeper get a really close look at her.

"I merely had a few aches and pains . . . in my back." She quickly manufactured the lie, placing her hands on her hips, arching her back for effect. "Lottie and I were scrubbing the laundry today, and I fear I overdid it. I came down to fetch a glass of warm milk. I thought it might ease my discomfort. 'Tis nothing serious." She paused, then impaled him with a probing look. "But I'm still rather curious to know who that man was that called upon you so late this evening."

Phillip could barely tear his eyes away from the

luscious mounds that were being thrust in his direction as Danielle stood rubbing her back. She looked quite desirable in her state of dishabille. Though the cotton nightgown and wrapper she wore were concealing, he only had to close his eyes to remember what was hid beneath the thin material. But at her words, he did and knew that there was only one way to dull Danielle's thinking. If he couldn't satisfy her curiosity, he could damn well satisfy something else.

Leading her toward the stairs, he said, "Allow me to assist you, my dear. I'm quite proficient at relieving muscle spasms." His hand dropped from her elbow to her waist and he palmed the small of her back. "Let's go up to my room and I'll rub your back for you."

Danielle's heart caught in her throat and excitement lit her eyes. This was the first overture James had made toward her without being prompted. Perhaps he was softening toward her; perhaps he cared after all. She smiled up at him. "That would be wonderful."

Before she knew what was happening, James swept her up in his arms. "I wouldn't want you to strain yourself further, my dear."

She gasped in surprise. "But, James, what of your back?"

"My back?"

"Yes. On our wedding day you said you couldn't lift me over the threshold because you had a bad back. Won't this create too much of a strain for you?"

Phillip thought that it was much more of a strain on his front than his back, but he retorted, "My back hasn't bothered me in months, Danielle. I think the warm weather has had a salubrious effect on it." How could he have been so stupid to have forgotten such a thing? he wondered.

"That's wonderful, James. Perhaps the fact that you've lost some weight has helped. You don't seem nearly as chubby as you used to." She snuggled into his chest and Phillip groaned, realizing that he'd donned nothing but his wig and robe in his haste to meet Bowers.

"I've taken your advice, my dear, and cut down drastically on my eating. I actually think I've lost weight."

There was such pride in his voice, Danielle had to smile. She patted his cheek. "I'm so proud of you."

Embarrassed, Phillip didn't have a proper rejoinder for her praise and was relieved when his bedroom door came into view. Pushing it open with his foot, he deposited Danielle on the bed.

Only one candle burned on the nightstand, and it cast eerie images across the walls and ceiling. The dimness lent a cloistered feel to the room, as if she and James were cocooned in a world all their own. The windows were open and the night sounds drifted in to add to the enchantment.

"Would you care for a glass of sherry before we proceed, my dear?" He could certainly use some fortification at this point. Danielle's nearness was making him crazed with desire. Perhaps the liquor would take the edge off of it, he thought.

She nodded and he filled two glasses with the golden liquid, handing her one. "This will help to relax you," he said, taking a seat next to her on the bed.

She sipped thoughtfully, studying him. He looked so handsome this evening. In the darkness of the room, his complexion looked more natural, not so pasty. She could see the light furring of hairs on his chest where his robe gaped open, and she longed to run her fingers through them. A strange tightening centered in her loins, and she gulped down the remainder of her sherry.

"You look quite beautiful tonight, Danielle." He reached out and touched her hair. "I like your hair this way. It's like a black velvet mantle. You should always wear it down." He sifted the silken strands between his fingers, then caressed his cheek with them, and Danielle couldn't swallow past the lump in her throat.

"Thank you," she finally managed.

His hands went to her waist and he began to untie the sash of her wrapper. "Let's get you out of this robe, so we can begin your massage."

Massage. That word had such wicked connotations, she thought, but hurried to assist him in his endeavors. With her wrapper removed, all that remained was her thin cotton shift. Though it was more substantial than many of the other nightgowns she owned, she still felt naked beneath his scorching gaze.

"Your breasts are perfection, my dear. So full, so adequate. See how they fill my hands?" He demonstrated by placing his palms over her lush mounds, massaging them tenderly. Slowly, his fingers moved up to untie the ribbons that held her gown closed. "I should like to get a closer look, my dear."

Danielle sat perfectly still as James untied her gown and pushed it down around her waist. He stared at her reverently, as if she were an exquisite piece of artwork, and it made her feel utterly desirable.

"Ah," he whispered, moving his hands up her waist, his thumbs making small circles over her nipples. At her moan, he smiled. "Do you like that, my dear?" Without waiting for her reply, he lowered his head and said, "Then surely you will like this," taking the erect nipples into his mouth and suckling them.

Danielle thought she would explode. He hadn't done anything but touch her breasts, and already she was ill with desire. "Please," she whispered.

He heard the plea in her voice and knew what she wanted, for her need matched his own. "Roll onto your stomach. Though I hate to let go of such delicious morsels, we must attend to your back."

While Danielle followed his instructions, Phillip took several deep breaths, trying to get himself under control. His shaft was so hard, his robe was tenting straight out, and he felt as if he would erupt at any moment, so great was his need for her.

He eased her nightgown down passed her hips until her body was completely bared to his gaze, then, with gentle hands began massaging her back with slow, circular motions.

"Hmmm," Danielle moaned. "That feels wonderful."

Phillip smiled. "Yes, it does. I can't begin to describe how it feels," he replied as his hands moved down to cup her buttocks, squeezing the soft pillows of flesh. He rubbed the backs of her thighs, her calves, massaging her feet with aching tenderness.

Heat surged through every nerve ending of Danielle's body as he began to plant soft, butterfly kisses where his hands had so recently massaged. "Oh, God," she whispered. What was he doing to her?

With gentle exploration, he made sure she was wet and ready for him, then positioned himself at her opening. "I want you, Danielle. I want you so much it hurts."

"Then take me and make me yours. For I love you."

Her words inflamed him and he slid into her welcoming warmth. "You're so tight. So perfect," he said, thrusting into her.

Soon they were caught up in the age-old rhythm as their bodies met stroke for stroke. Their breathing grew shallow, their motions more frenzied, until at last, reaching the pinnacle of their desire, they convulsed in an earth-shattering climax that left them both shaken.

When her breathing had subsided and she felt him leave her, Danielle rolled over, feeling more content and happy than she had ever felt in her life. "That was wonderful," she said on a sigh.

"You were wonderful," he said, drawing her into the circle of his arms. But though his words were tender, there was a pained look in his eyes that Danielle didn't understand and he couldn't disguise.

"What is it, James? Didn't I make you happy?" Doubt infused her, making her wonder at her adequacy. She had never made love in such a manner as they had tonight. Maybe she had done something wrong. Maybe he hadn't achieved such total satisfaction as she.

He sat up, pulling his robe up to cover himself. "Of course you made me happy. I've never felt more content."

"Then what is it? What's wrong?"

"I should have pulled out. I shouldn't have spilled my seed into you. Now there is even more of a possibility that you will get pregnant."

His words stabbed into her heart like a double-edged sword, piercing her newfound happiness and shattering her composure. With tears in her eyes, she sat up and faced him. Drawing a deep breath, she looked him straight in the eye and said, "I am already pregnant."

21

"Pregnant!" Phillip bolted upright, dragging Danielle right along with him. He shrugged into his robe, tying it securely about his waist. Searching the nightstand, he found his tinderbox and attempted to light the oil lamp there; but his hands were shaking so bad, it took him several tries and several choice epithets before the lamp finally burst into flame.

Immediately the room was bathed in a soft golden glow, illuminating the shock in Phillip's eyes and Danielle's tear-stained face. He stared at her, pulling the curls away from his right ear, as if they somehow hindered his hearing.

"I don't think I heard you correctly, my dear. I thought I heard you say that you were pregnant."

Wiping her face with the sleeve of his robe, then blowing her nose on it, Danielle replied haltingly, "I—I did. We are going to have a baby." She smiled tentatively.

He stared briefly at his sleeve, wrinkling his nose in

distaste, then more intently, and not the least bit distastefully, at the pair of ripe breasts that were displayed to his view. They *were* larger, as was her abdomen, which was definitely rounded, giving evidence to the truth of her words. He swallowed, forcing his attention back to Danielle's face and the problem at hand.

"How could this have happened? We've only made love on two occasions that I can remember?" Three, he amended, counting the first time. But he couldn't admit to that.

She folded her arms across her chest, her voice brimming with frustration. "It only takes one time, James. Perhaps you are just more virile than you thought." At his look of astonishment, she bit her lower lip, hating herself for having to lie to him. But she had no choice. She loved James, and she loved her unborn child, and she would do what she must to keep them both.

Fear gnawed at Phillip's composure for the first time in a very long time. Danielle was pregnant. And by the looks of her, by the Phantom, no doubt. God's blood! How had he let this happen? She wasn't legally his wife; the child she bore would be branded a bastard.

"I was hoping that you would be happy about the baby, James. After all, most men like the idea of having their name perpetuated, their lineage carried forth."

But it isn't my name! he wanted to shout. But seeing the hurt look on her face, he merely replied, "My dear, under different circumstances, I would have been delighted. I always hoped to have a child one day—a son. But the war has made those plans difficult. I could be killed tomorrow or next week. Then you would be left a widow with a small child."

Blinking back her tears, she said, "You don't want this child because you don't love me. Isn't that the real reason, James? It has nothing to do with this war. Be honest. You married me to fulfill a stipulation in your father's will. Ours was a marriage of convenience, not a love match, as you were fond of telling me long ago."

She took a deep breath. "Well I was foolish enough to fall in love with you, James. I was foolish enough to think that in time I could make you fall in love with me." She laughed a mocking, self-deprecating laugh that sent chills careening down Phillip's spine.

He reached out to her, but she backed away, reaching for her wrapper that lay on the bed and put it on. "Please, James, don't touch me. I can't bear to have you make me feel all those wonderful things I feel when I'm in your arms."

Her words lashed out at him, tearing away at his composure. "Danielle, please don't say such things. I—I—I care a great deal for you."

Disappointment washed over her. "But you don't love me. Admit it, James. Say it. It will make things so much easier."

"There are things that you don't understand. Things that prevent me from speaking what is on my mind." If only he could admit the truth. If only he could tell her who he really was.

"I don't care what's on your mind. I want to know what's in your heart. I love you, James Ashland, so I'm going to give you one more chance to tell me that you love me and want to have this child I carry."

Phillip paled as white as the bed sheet. How could he admit what she wanted without compromising his disguise? How could he reveal that there was no

James Ashland, the man she was madly in love with? He'd sooner commit suicide; it would have the same result.

"Well . . . ?"

A lump the size of a watermelon formed in his throat. He tried to swallow it, saying, "I—I—"

A knock sounded at the door and he felt a huge measure of relief as Ian's agitated voice floated into the room.

"Wake up! Wake up! Lottie is goin' tae hae her bairn!"

Phillip's sigh of relief was audible, but Danielle's face registered alarm.

"She can't have her baby. It's too early. The baby's not due for more than a month yet," Danielle said, her face paling.

Phillip was so relieved to have been spared the ordeal of explaining things to Danielle, Lottie's predicament didn't quite register. "Too early?" He shook his head in confusion.

She sighed in exasperation. "I need to get dressed. Lottie needs me. I'll deal with you later." Turning on her heel, she hurried out of his room and into her own to dress.

The banging on the door continued and Phillip rushed to open it. Ian stood there, red-faced from the exertion of his bellows. "Are ye deaf, mon? My wife's abou' tae hae her bairn. How can ye sleep at a time like this?"

Ian's concern finally penetrated and Phillip frowned deeply. He'd never seen the old man so riled. What an army of British regulars couldn't do, one pregnant woman could. "I'll be right there, old man, as will Danielle. Go fetch Mrs. Dunstan; she'll know what to do."

"Are ye sure, laddie? I dinna want nothin' bad to be happening to me Charlotte." Tears filled his eyes.

Phillip wrapped his arm about Ian's shoulders. "Charlotte and the babe will be just fine. I give you my word, old man. Just go," he said, pushing Ian out the door then shutting it behind him.

This has been one hell of a night, he thought. And it wasn't over yet. But when it was, and the glow of the newborn babe had worn off, there'd be hell to pay. Danielle would see to it.

A resigned expression crossed his face as he stared at the connecting door to Danielle's room. It was time to do some soul-searching, time to make a decision.

Grace Mary-Margaret MacGregor entered the world at exactly eight o'clock the following Sunday morning. Hence the child's name. She was as red-haired as her mother, but possessed Ian's soft brown eyes. She was a tiny, little thing; but Mrs. Dunstan had assured them that the babe would grow big and strong in no time.

"She's perfect, Lottie," Danielle said, trailing her finger over the baby's soft cheek. She had never seen a more beautiful child than the one she now held in her arms. "And so good. Why she's practically slept this whole day through with hardly a whimper."

Reclining against the bed pillows, Lottie smiled proudly. "You'll probably be changing your opinion about that tonight, love. I hear tell most babies like to make themselves heard in the middle of the night. Me mother used to say it was God's way of punishing those who enjoyed the carnal side of marriage too much. If that's the case, I'd say we're in for a bit of howling."

Danielle smiled, placing the child in the crook of her mother's arms and stared wistfully down at the duo. "I'm so anxious to have my baby be born." She patted her growing mound. "If only . . ." The thought was left unsaid.

Sighing, she crossed to the open window and stared out. It was cloudy; the wind had picked up, rustling the leaves on the tree branches outside. Most likely they'd have a thundershower before long to cool things off; though September, it was still unbearably hot and humid.

In the distance, down by the river's edge, stood James and Ian; they appeared to be engaged in a heated discussion. "It would appear that our husbands are having a bit of a disagreement," she told Lottie.

"That's probably my fault. You see, I asked Ian to speak to Mr. Ashland about the baby."

Danielle spun on her heel, her cheeks burning in mortification. "You didn't! Oh, Lottie, how could you? I feel so humiliated."

"Now, Danny, I only did what I thought best. Ian was quite sympathetic to your plight. And I didn't let on that the babe wasn't Mr. Ashland's."

Danielle's voice filled with resignation. "It won't do any good. James doesn't want the child, even though he thinks it's his. I've decided that I have no alternative but to leave here." At Lottie's gasp of surprise, she went on to explain what had occurred the previous night.

"Oh, Danny, I'm so sorry. I feel guilty that I'm happy when you're so miserable."

"Don't be. I have no one to blame but myself for the way things have turned out. This is God's way of punishing me for my relationship with the Phantom."

"Posh! I don't believe that for a moment. Now you're starting to sound like me mother. Anyway, I have every confidence that Ian will be able to talk some sense into that husband of yours."

But he couldn't. At least not about the subject they were arguing so vehemently about. After hours of soul-searching, Phillip had made the decision to reveal his true identity to Danielle. He would not risk losing her, or the baby, even if it meant endangering his life. His decision did not set well with his first mate.

"Yer daft, mon! I'll no allow it, ye ken? No' after spending the better part of a year protecting yer identity. Hae ye forgotten that Ellsworth is still searching for ye? That he wants tae kill ye?"

"I don't care about that anymore, Ian. I can't risk losing Danielle over this. And now there's the baby to consider. I've thought it out completely. I'm going to tell Danielle everything. Then I will remove this hated disguise once and for all and reveal my true identity to my wife."

"But Danielle is no' yer wife, laddie. Hae ye given any thought as tae wot she's goin' tae say when she finds out she's be livin' in sin wie a mon who is no' her husband?"

Phillip paled slightly, for he had thought of that very thing. But he had every confidence that once he explained his reasons, once he assured Danielle that they would remarry quickly and privately, that all would be well. "I have to take my chances, Ian, and believe that Danielle loves me enough to forgive me."

"Yer a fool to think it, lad. Women who hae been

duped are no' the forgivin' kind. And yer pickin' the worst possible time to make a clean breast o' things. Washington is marching down tae York Town as we speak. We'll be needin' tae leave tae join French Admiral De Grasse and his naval forces. There's still a war on, laddie. And we're right in the thick o' it. The Phantom canna hang up his mask just yet."

Everything Ian said was true. Admiral De Grasse's French fleet of ships had already engaged Admiral Graves's fleet outside the Virginia Capes, forcing the British admiral to return to New York, thus closing off one avenue of escape for Cornwallis's forces.

The combined American and French army would be arriving in Williamsburg any day, following close on the heels of their commanders, General Washington and the comte de Rochambeau, who were scheduled to confer with De Grasse aboard his flagship *Ville de Paris*. The outcome of that meeting could very well affect the entire denouement of the war.

But as serious as all that was, it paled in comparison to the very urgent problem facing Phillip at the moment: revealing his identity to Danielle. He'd almost rather face a British firing squad than his lovely, little wife.

"I've made up my mind, Ian. I'm going to tell Danielle everything and pray that she forgives me."

The old man shook his head. "I still say yer mad, mon."

"True," Phillip said, a soft smile ruffling his mouth. "But I'm mad about Danielle."

The object of Phillip's consideration was at that very moment in her husband's bedchamber awaiting his decision about the baby.

Danielle paced nervously from one end of the room to the other, making tracks in the colorful Turkish carpet, wondering if she truly had the courage to go through with her threat to leave.

Hopefully, Ian would be successful in convincing James of the benefits of fatherhood and she wouldn't have to, she thought. If he accepted the baby, then she was sure in time he would grow to love her. She loved James with all her heart. And the thought of not being married to him, not being able to see him ever again, brought a dull ache to her breast.

Pausing before the window, she pulled back on the heavy drapery and looked out to find James still engaged in conversation with Ian. She sighed, knowing it would be a while before he came back up to change for supper.

Well, she would just have to occupy her time until his return. She had no intention of letting him avoid the topic that she was adamant about pursuing, and meant to confront him as soon as he stepped through the door. She would have her answer, one way or the other.

But in the meantime, she would straighten up her husband's room. It was a mess. With hands on hips and a frown on her lips, she surveyed the area. Ceramic wig curlers were scattered everywhere, as were traces of flour and cornstarch, which he used to powder the blasted thing. His clothing—expensive silks, satins, and brocades—was strewn about carelessly, with no thought whatsoever to their cost.

Shaking her head in disgust, she rolled up her sleeves and walked back to the window to pull the drapery apart. It was a wonder the man could see to dress, he kept his room so dark. And with the absence of the sun today, it made it even gloomier; she crossed to the nightstand to light the taper.

After fluffing the feather mattress and airing out the linens, she remade the bed, then began to retrieve the various items of clothing off the floor. One by one, she picked them up—waistcoats, stocks, ruffled shirts—depositing them in a heap upon the bed until she could fold them neatly and return them to their proper place in the wardrobe.

Picking up his robe, which lay across a battered chest at the foot of the bed, she brought it to her nose and inhaled. The scents of wig powder and the bay rum cologne James always wore brought a queer ache to her chest.

The sound of Grace's high-pitched screams split the air, scaring Danielle out of her wits. Her hands flew up to cover her heart, which pounded rapidly beneath her fingers, and she dropped the robe to the floor.

Realizing what had frightened her, she took a deep breath, smiling in relief. 'Twould take a while to get used to having a baby in the house, she thought. Bending over, she made to retrieve the garment when a piece of black silk sticking out of the corner of the chest caught her eye.

Shaking her head at her husband's slovenly ways, she attempted to open the chest so she could refold the garment properly, but it wouldn't budge. Odd, she thought, that James would keep such an old, battered-looking trunk.

As fastidious as he was about his possessions—about acquiring them anyway, not necessarily about taking care of them—she couldn't fathom why he would keep such an ugly thing.

Dropping to her knees, she tried once more to open it and discovered, upon closer inspection, a carving of a ship's anchor engraved on it. *This definitely did not look like something James would own.*

Confusion etched deep lines into her forehead and niggling doubts began to surface in the far reaches of her mind. Why would James have a sea chest? she wondered. As far as she knew, the man had never been to sea. *Or had he?*

Questions and doubts began to batter her composure, wrestling with her common sense that told her what she suspected was wrong, nigh onto impossible. With suspicion darkening her eyes to purple and a premonition of dread gnawing at her serenity, she removed one of the pins from her hair and picked at the tarnished brass lock. After a few tries, the lock sprang open.

With her heart pounding loud in her ears, she removed it, pushing up on the heavy lid. Her eyes widened in disbelief, the color draining from her face.

There, lying atop a pile of unfamiliar clothing, was the black silk mask of the Phantom.

22

She stared, mouth agape, unable to believe the implication of what she'd just discovered. James Ashland was the Phantom?!

It was impossible, inconceivable, downright ridiculous! But it was true. And here was the proof.

Fingering the soft silk, she held it to her face and inhaled, recognizing the musky scent that clung to the material. The Phantom's scent!

It couldn't be true. She would have known. Surely she would have known.

She should have known.

Like pieces of a puzzle, all the scattered doubts and suspicions began to fit together. All those late-night visits from the Phantom. All of James's mysterious trips to who knew where. His reticence in making love to her. His fears about getting her with child. The evidence had all been before her, but she'd been too blinded by love to see it clearly. It had been masked behind his clever deception and her own stupidity.

James. James Ashland, her pretentious, arrogant husband, was in reality the Phantom.

Replacing the garment, she relocked the chest, rising to her feet. She had to think. Had to sort out this startling disclosure. She began to pace.

If James was the Phantom, then she was married to the Phantom. That revelation was not at all displeasing. In fact, other than feeling deceived, she could almost be happy about it.

Almost. But then, she didn't like deception, had anguished over her own betrayal of James, cried over how she had deceived him, only to find out he had perpetrated the biggest ruse ever imagined: She was married to a lie.

"My God!" The implication of what he had done washed over her in waves of resentment and fear that their marriage might not be legal in the eyes of the church. She might be branded a whore, an outcast from society. And worse, her child would be branded a bastard.

Her pace quickened, as did her anger. How thoroughly she had been duped. "Stupid, girl!" she chided herself, shaking her head, her fists railing at the heavens. "Stupid, stupid, girl!"

But after a few more minutes of pacing and castigating herself, the positives began to outweigh the negatives, and possibilities started to surface, making Danielle feel immeasurably better.

She was married to the man she loved—both men, in fact. And other than feeling like the biggest fool of the year, she was beside herself with joy. She loved James Ashland; she loved the Phantom. And her baby would have a father—his real father. Her life would be complete.

But first she would make them both pay for the misery they had caused her. She smiled in satisfaction, and the thought of getting even brought a mischievous sparkle to her eyes. In fact, they glowed with determination.

Two can play this game, my darling husband, Danielle thought. And who the better teacher than the Phantom?

It was all Danielle could do not to jump out of her chair, launch herself across the dining room table, and wrap her hands about James Ashland's deceitful throat.

There he sat in all his brocaded glory, eating his supper, stuffing his face with baked ham and corn on the cob, paying an inordinate amount of attention to his food and very little to her.

In fact, he'd hardly spoken a word since they'd entered the dining room. Obviously, he had a lot on his mind, like conjuring up other ways to deceive her. If he suffered from a guilty conscience, it certainly hadn't affected his appetite. And he'd said he'd cut down on his portions. Ha! That was rich. He ate as much as he ever had.

She stared as he devoured another of Mrs. Dunstan's flaky biscuits, and wondered again why she hadn't noticed the similarities between James and the Phantom. The startling blue of his eyes should have given James away immediately. And there was the very undisguisable fact that he was exactly the same height as the Phantom. There were very few men as tall as James or the Phantom, save for General Washington or Thomas Jefferson.

Love was definitely blind, she decided, shaking her head.

"Is there a problem, my dear?" James asked between bites of his biscuit. "You've hardly touched your supper this evening. You're not ill, I hope."

She fumed inwardly at the innocent expression of concern on his face, wanting desperately to dump the gooey bowl of mashed potatoes atop his powdered peruke. But she didn't. Instead, Danielle forced a smile to her lips and replied, "I am feeling a bit poorly, James. We were up awfully late last night." She thrust him a pointed look, pleased by the red flush now masking his face.

Masking. An apt word. What did he really look like beneath his mask of deception?

She said, "I'm afraid we'll have to postpone our discussion until tomorrow. I'm going to retire early." His relief was obvious and annoying. She might be the one feigning illness, but he'd be the one receiving a taste of his own medicine.

Phillip stared intently into the depths of his wineglass, as if it were a crystal ball that could foretell the outcome of his decision.

Would Danielle forgive him? Would she still love him after he told her the truth? Or would she, like Ian had predicted, smack him across the face and pack her bags and leave?

"God's blood!" he cursed at the very idea, downing the bordeaux in one gulp. He could never let that happen.

Removing his watch from the pocket of his waistcoat, he flipped it open: nine-thirty. He would give her some time to ready herself for bed. Then he would go to her and confess all.

His hand began to shake as he poured himself another glass of wine, and he smiled ruefully. He was the Phantom. Fearless. Determined. Unconquerable. Or so the British thought. Too bad they didn't have Danielle on their side. She had vanquished him without lifting a finger.

Danielle hurried to her room. By the time she arrived she was furious with James. There was nothing she could do or say that would be too horrible, too perverse.

Crossing to the commode, she poured a generous amount of water into the porcelain bowl, splashing it over her face and neck. It felt wonderfully cool. Just the remedy she needed to lower her overheated temper.

Stripping off every inch of her clothing until she was deliciously naked, she brushed the long length of ebony hair until it shone, letting it fall loose about her waist, then went to her trunk and pulled out a nightgown she had never worn before.

It was as red as the flames of her desire and as transparent as James's ruse. She smiled, pulling it on, letting it drift down over her body.

Padding to the cheval mirror, she gazed critically at her reflection and smiled. This was exactly the effect she was looking for: provocative yet innocent.

Spying the vial of perfume on the dresser, she retrieved it, splashing a bit between her breasts and on her wrists. James liked this particular scent of lavender. And the way she was dressed, she didn't think it would take much to torture him over the edge.

She heard him enter his room and decided to allow him a few more minutes to undress, then she would put her little plan of revenge into action.

Phillip stood at the connecting door, his hand poised on the latch, ready to enter Danielle's room and confess all, when suddenly the door was yanked open and there she stood, wearing little more than a smile.

Hiding her surprise that he was fully armored in his disguise she said, "Why, James, what a coincidence. I was just coming in to see you." But she knew it would be no protection from the assault she'd planned. Her motive gave her strength, her weapons, age-old and all too powerful for a mere man, the advantage. Smug in her knowledge, she brushed passed him and entered his room, knowing he would follow.

Like a bull who'd had a red flag waved in front of it, Phillip, nostrils flaring, stared at the diaphanous red gown and swallowed, hard. "You were?"

"Why, yes, we must talk. There's something I must tell you."

He groaned inwardly; he knew what was coming. But he didn't want to get into that right now, not before he had a chance to explain himself. "I thought you said that our discussion could wait until tomorrow."

"I haven't come to talk about your feelings for me, James."

Relief washed over him as he stepped toward her. "I'm glad, Danielle." He reached for her, smiling tentatively, taking her into his arms. "You see, there is something I must—" Before he had a chance to explain, Danielle burst into tears, pressing her face into his chest.

"I'm so sorry, James."

He shook his head. "Sorry? Sorry for what?"

She stared down at her toes. "I've betrayed you with another man."

"Betrayed me? I don't understand."

She explained in agonizing detail. "I've been meeting another man. I have lain with another man. Made love to another man."

At her admission, a sharp pain speared Phillip's heart. His blood pounded loud in his ears, his grip tightening on her arms. "What do you mean, you've lain with another man? Who? Who is this man?"

At the lethal look in his eyes, her voice wavered, but she took a deep breath and plunged ahead, recklessly, purposely. "I have been unfaithful to you. The child I carry is not yours." She watched the color rise in his cheeks and felt an inordinate amount of satisfaction.

Clenching his fists, Phillip tried to tamp down the overwhelming rage that coursed through his body. Flames of jealous anger clouded his eyes and his judgment. He heard nothing, thought nothing, but of the fact that Danielle had been with another man.

"I'll kill him! I'll kill you both!" he shouted, banging his fist against the bedpost, causing it to crack in two, much to Danielle's consternation.

She watched wide-eyed as he gripped at the odious wig covering his head and yanked it off, revealing a mass of sun-streaked blond hair. He was just about to throw an expensive Meissen vase at the wall, when

Danielle couldn't contain herself any longer and burst out laughing. She laughed so hard tears rolled down her cheeks, and she had to hug her sides to keep them from stitching.

The sound of her laughter brought Phillip crashing back to reality. He stared at Danielle, his face turning crimson when he realized that he'd just been played for a fool. "You know?" His voice went from disbelief to disconcertion to disgrace. "You know!" He stepped toward her with menacing steps.

Still laughing, Danielle nodded, wiping the tears from her eyes, backing toward the bed. "Yes, and I've never seen anyone jealous of themselves before. It's—it's really quite amusing."

"Amusing? I'll show you what's amusing." With a purposeful gleam in his eyes that rocked Danielle back on her heels, he ripped off his remaining garments, tossing them onto the floor, wiping at the powder covering his face with the edge of his expensive silk shirt.

She stared openmouthed at the transformation, as layer upon layer came off to reveal a completely different man. Though he had the body of the Phantom, he didn't have the Phantom's face, for she had never seen his face before.

This man standing totally naked before her was a stranger to her. He was massively built, blond and beautiful, like some ancient Greek statue that had been carved from granite. There wasn't an ounce of Ashland's fat on him, and the spear that jutted forth from his loins was huge.

A sudden, inexplicable shyness came over her, and she backed away from him. But there would be no escape this night.

With the grace of a panther, he reached out in one swift motion to lift her body in his arms, tossing her over his shoulder as he stalked toward the bed.

His high-handedness angered her and she finally found her voice. "Put me down you—you imposter," she cried, pounding at his back with her fists.

He laughed, and quite unceremoniously, lowered her onto the bed, covering her body with his own. "We have unfinished business to conduct, sweeting. And a great deal of time to make up for."

His words excited and irritated at the same time. "How dare you presume to make love to me when we don't even know each other!"

He stared strangely at her. "Are you insane, woman? Not know each other? Why, we've lain together, made love together. I know every exquisite inch of your body, and I'd venture a guess that you know almost as much of mine. I'm not quite as sound a sleeper as you think."

"Oooh!" she shouted, her face flaming in humiliation. "You're detestable!"

Holding her face between his hands, he kissed her, then said, smiling, "Yes, I am, aren't I?"

The first crack of lightning split the sky, the roar of thunder punctuating his words.

"You're vile!" But her voice didn't hold quite as much conviction.

He kissed her again, this time plunging his tongue between her lips. "Thoroughly reprehensible," he conceded.

She was breathing hard now and had difficulty formulating her insults. The thunder continued to bellow, but she couldn't be sure it wasn't her heart that was roaring so loud in her ears. "And . . . and a disreputable rogue," she added. "Ahh . . ." She screamed as his tongue trailed down to lick at her swollen nipples.

"And you are delectable," he countered, laving at the protruding buds, moving lower to caress her stomach and beyond. "And utterly delicious." He ignored her moans of protest. "And I can't seem to ever get enough of your sweet, sweet body."

He continued his delicious torment until Danielle was mindless with longing; she screamed out as Phillip brought her over the crest of her desire. Her screams were swallowed up by another flash of lightning and clap of thunder, and when the rain burst forth from the heavens, Phillip did too, plunging into her, impaling her with his need, stroking her flames of desire, consuming her completely until they crested the pinnacle of their passion and became one with the other.

"I love you, Danielle," he whispered. "I've always loved you."

She breathed a deep sigh of contentment. "And I love you, James."

He smiled, kissing her nose. "It's Phillip; James is my middle name. But we'll talk more about that tomorrow. Now, I want to make love to my wife again."

Her love shone brightly, making her eyes sparkle as prettily as amethysts. "Am I truly your wife, Phillip?" She tested the name on her lips and found she liked it.

"You are my wife of hearts, now and forever. Never doubt it. No matter what."

"And the baby? Are you happy about the baby?"

He kissed her passionately, communicating just

how great his happiness was at the news he was to become a father.

"I have so many questions."

"And I promise you that they'll all be answered. But not now. Now I want to make love to you. Is that all right?"

"Oh yes!" she said, smiling widely. "It's quite all right."

23

"*Do you know* what must be done, *chérie*?" Regina's eyes filled with the passion of the moment as André's fingers teased her sensitive, swollen nipple.

"Yes," she answered breathlessly, unable to stand the torment he inflicted. "I . . . I know the plan." André was making her crazed. Teasing and tormenting her body with his hands and mouth, bringing her to the edge of desire, then stopping abruptly, until she couldn't form rational thoughts anymore.

The small tavern room was airless, and a faint sheen of perspiration covered her naked body. She was hot, so very hot. "Please, André," she begged, "I need to feel you inside me."

His smile was unkind as he trailed his hand up her thigh until it rested near the apex. "Wasn't it you who told me not to be impatient, *chérie*? Good things come to those who wait."

She arched against his hand but he withdrew it. "Patience, Regina," he counseled. "We must be patient. Soon everything will be ours for the taking."

Tomorrow the plan to capture the Phantom would be set into motion. Though he counseled patience, he knew time was running out. The American general Washington was marching on York Town, and the Phantom would be leaving to meet his commander there.

Danielle Ashland was the key to the Phantom's capture. She would be used to draw the pirate out of hiding, then he would kill him. He might even dally a bit with the lovely Mrs. Ashland. He'd seen her a time or two at the tavern; her lush breasts and pouty lips were not something a man could forget easily.

Just the thought of what he would do to the Phantom's whore made him hard, and he lowered himself over Regina.

"Genius is nothing but a greater aptitude for patience," he thought, remembering something the French naturalist Buffon had said as he smiled into his mistress's trusting face.

"Let me reward your patience, *chérie*," he said, spreading her legs wide and ramming his cock into her.

"Oh, André," Regina cried out, "that feels so good."

His smile was sinister and filled with satisfaction. "Victory always does, *chérie*."

Not far away another pair of lovers held each other closely, basking in the contentment of their lovemaking. The late morning sun shone in, reflecting off their sweat-glistened bodies, while a gentle breeze wafted through the open window, cooling off their heated flesh.

"Oh, Phillip, I'm so happy and yet so sad," Danielle whispered, caressing his cheek. "I can't bear the fact that you must leave again."

He kissed her sweetly on the lips, brushing the dampened strands of ebony hair away from her face. "I told you last night, sweeting, that it is time for me to go. As much as I'd prefer to lie here in this bed all day and make mad, passionate love to you, I must join the forces in York Town."

"But we've only just found each other. It's only been two days. I can't bear for you to leave me." *And what if something were to happen to him?* She pushed that terrible thought to the back of her mind.

"And in that two days we've spent just about every waking moment in this bed making love. If I don't leave now, I won't have the strength to fight the British. Ian and Lottie must think we've expired."

"They're so wrapped up in little Grace, and their own farewells, I doubt they've even noticed our absence. Besides, we're on our honeymoon. We never really had one, in case you've forgotten."

He tweaked her nose. "You weren't the only one to walk around unfulfilled, sweeting. There's been no woman but you for me and never will be."

Her eyes lit with pleasure. "Truly, Phillip? You've bedded no one else since that time in my father's storeroom?"

"I existed in a perpetual state of arousal, sweeting. Why do you think it was necessary for me to absent myself from your charming, but disturbing, company? You put me through hell, Danielle."

"Good, for it was no more than you deserved." She grinned at his look of mock indignation. "I did my best to seduce you. 'Twas not I who played hard to get." She trailed her finger down his chest, toying with the hairs matted there.

He clasped on to her hand when she made to go lower. "I should take you with me, sweeting. Your methods of torture are far more effective than any the army could think of to use against the British."

She stretched her arm back, thrusting an impudent nipple dangerously close to his mouth and asked innocently, "Do you really think so, Phillip? I've never considered myself an instrument of war before."

Staring at the blatant invitation in her eyes, he groaned, feeling himself harden in response to it. There'd be no leaving this day if he didn't get out of this bed. But when he looked at Danielle's seductive smile, at the pink-tipped nipples waiting for his tongue, he could only shake his head in resignation. *The bloody war could wait.*

Reaching for her, he lifted her, positioning her to sit atop his body. "I seem to remember a time when you had a strong desire to mount me," he said, grinning wickedly at her blush. "Let's see how well you ride, madam."

Needing no further encouragement, Danielle eased herself onto the hardened shaft, taking Phillip deep within her. With his hands fondling her breasts, and hers on her thighs, she leaned back and rode him with a rocking pelvic motion, reveling in the intense pleasure she saw on his face and felt within her own throbbing body.

"You're killing me, sweeting," he cried out, his voice hoarse with passion, sweat, once again, dotting his upper lip.

But his words inflamed rather than subdued

Danielle and she moved faster and harder until her breathing grew as ragged as his, and the pulsing center of her being cried out for release at the same time his exploded within her.

"God's blood, woman!" Phillip exclaimed when she finally fell in an exhausted heap against him. "You've drained every bit of strength out of me."

She nibbled his lower lip, smiling confidently. "Care to place a bet on that?"

His only response was a groan.

Phillip left the following morning, taking Ian and a very large part of Danielle's heart with him.

She was miserable and made no effort to conceal the fact. Seated at the long mahogany table, she stared down at the opposite end where her husband usually sat and frowned dejectedly, feeling more lonely than she'd ever felt in her life. She loved Phillip with an intensity that frightened her, and the thought that he might not return left her terrified.

Lottie, who was seated in the chair next to her, nursing little Grace, caught Danielle's dejected look and sought to lift her spirits. "'Tis no wonder you're so tired and wan-looking, Danny. The way you and Mr. Ashland—I mean Mr. Cameron—have been holed up in your bedroom like a couple of ruttin' rabbits. Why you haven't seen the sunshine nor smelled the fresh air of autumn. I vow, 'tis my favorite season of all."

Danielle blushed, turning her head to stare out the window at the leaves of red and gold, hoping to avoid Lottie's knowing gaze. She had no intention of discussing what she and Phillip had been doing "holed up" in their bedroom. In fact just thinking of the joy she'd experienced made her all the more depressed.

Even the sight of the colorful leaves couldn't bring pleasure. Normally, she would have enjoyed the spectacle immensely. Autumn was always a welcome relief from the harsh days of summer, and it signaled the coming of the Christmas season, which was always a great favorite of hers. But her mind was too preoccupied with Phillip's safety to take pleasure in either one.

She couldn't shake the feeling that something ominous was about to happen, couldn't help feeling that Phillip was somehow in danger. What if something were to happen to him? She wouldn't be able to go on living.

"I'm so afraid something might happen to Phillip," she confided to Lottie. "What if he doesn't come back?"

"You're not the only one suffering on that account, Danny," her friend advised, leveling a disappointed look at her. She hoisted Grace to a more comfortable position. "I've got a babe to think of, and if Ian . . ." Her voice grew thick. "If Ian shouldn't happen to survive, well, my little Grace will be fatherless."

Danielle blushed guiltily at the fear she heard in Lottie's voice, at the worry in her eyes as she stared down at the babe in her arms. "I'm sorry, Lottie. I've been thoughtless as usual, only thinking about myself. Can you ever forgive me?"

"Posh! There's nothing to forgive, love. I've got no doubts that both Ian and your Phantom will be comin' home safe and sound. 'Twould be a cruel hoax if they didn't, and I doubt the Lord would be that mean."

Danielle prayed silently that Lottie was right. She

needed to believe that Phillip would be coming home to her, needed to believe that this wretched war would soon be over, as he had promised.

Please, God, let it be so, she prayed.

Eyeing the lopsided baby's blanket with disappointment, Danielle heaved a frustrated sigh. Despite all of Mrs. Dunstan's patience in trying to teach her to crochet, Danielle knew that this was one skill she was not going to master anytime soon.

The door knocker sounded and she set her sewing aside, pushing herself to her feet. Which was no easy feat, considering how much the baby had grown in the last few weeks. She patted the growing mound and was thankful she'd had the good sense to alter several more of her dresses. Though Phillip had insisted she purchase more, Danielle thought it impractical when the gowns in her wardrobe could serve just as well.

Stopping to gaze at her reflection in the hall mirror, she smiled in satisfaction. Despite the fact that the baby was nearing term, the full skirts of her gowns hid that fact. Her breasts were considerably larger and her face a bit puffy, but only a practiced eye could discern those changes.

Of course, Mrs. Dunstan had recognized the truth quite easily. The older woman had been like a brooding mother hen with her chick, Danielle thought. No wonder she felt like a cow; she'd drank enough milk in the past few weeks to qualify as one.

The knocker pounded again and Danielle hurried to open the door. She was surprised to find her sister waiting on the porch.

Regina was an infrequent visitor at best these days, which was just as well, considering that Regina had reverted to her former obnoxious self. Her need to repent had somehow been usurped by her Frenchman's marriage proposal. Danielle had yet to meet this paragon of manhood, and, if it hadn't been for Elsie's assurances that he did indeed exist, she would have thought him to be a figment of her sister's imagination.

"Why, Gina, what brings you here today?" Danielle asked, ushering the elegantly gowned woman in. Apparently, Regina had found her rich man, judging by the lavishness of the blue taffeta gown she had on.

Regina's eyes darted about nervously. "I need to talk to you, Danielle. It's very important."

"Come in to the parlor and sit down. I was just about to have a cup of chocolate. Would you care for some?"

Seating herself on the love seat, Regina gave Danielle an appraising examination and shook her head. "Perhaps you shouldn't have any, either, Danielle. I think you've gained a few pounds. Why, I've never seen your face so fat before." She couldn't help the gloating smile that crossed her lips.

Danielle continued to pour the chocolate, resisting the urge to dump the hot liquid over her sister's head. "What is it you wish to discuss, Gina?" she asked, ignoring her sister's rudeness.

Regina bit her lower lip, trying to remember everything André had coached her to say. "It's about my marriage to André. We've—we've decided to elope."

Danielle's eyes widened and she set down her cup. "Elope? But why? I thought you were waiting for funds to arrive, so you could be married here."

"André's mother is ill. He needs to sail back to France to be with her. I'm going with him. We will be married by the captain aboard the ship; André is a good friend of his."

A feeling of misgiving overtook Danielle, for she knew her mother would be devastated by the news. "Do Mama and Papa know of your plans?"

Regina shook her head. "No! And you must promise not to tell them, Danielle. You know how possessive Mama is. She would never allow me to go if she knew."

"But, Regina, Mama will be so hurt. You know you were her favorite. She'll be crushed when she learns that you've eloped. Mama has always wanted to give you a big wedding."

Tears filled Regina's eyes and her voice grew pleading. "Please, Danielle, you must help me. I love André so much. I couldn't bear to be parted from him."

Danielle was surprised by the conviction in her sister's voice. She hadn't thought Regina capable of loving anyone more than herself. "This André must be very special, for you to care so deeply for him."

Regina's face brightened. "He is, Danielle. He's handsome. And has the most delicious French accent. And he's fabulously wealthy."

Regina would never change, Danielle thought sadly. She would always be impressed by wealth and looks, never giving a thought to the man beneath the fancy trappings.

Her voice full of resignation, she asked, "What is it you would like me to do, Regina? I don't like being a party to your subterfuge, knowing how much it's going to hurt Mama."

"Our ship leaves tomorrow. Mama would get suspicious if I were to leave the tavern carrying my portmanteau. If you could bring it to the tavern's stable tomorrow night, I would be forever beholden to you."

Danielle gave a quick survey of the room but saw no traveling bag, and her forehead creased in confusion. "Where is your bag? Did you bring it with you?"

Her cheeks pinkened and Regina nodded. "I left it on the front porch. I didn't want you to know until I could be certain you would help me."

Hurt filled the violet eyes. "You would have left without saying good-bye?"

"Of course not!" Regina assured her, rushing over to hug Danielle. "I was planning to write you a note."

She sighed again. "Tell me your plan, and what I must do. Though I know I'm being unwise to help you, you are my sister and I love you. I want you to be happy."

Regina smiled widely. "I knew I could count on you, Danielle. I knew you would help me."

Forcing a small smile to her lips, Danielle couldn't help but think she was being foolish. Very foolish indeed.

24

October 1781
York Town, Virginia

The black sharp-hulled privateer sliced swiftly through the turquoise-blue waters of the Chesapeake as it made its way toward York Town and the siege already under way. Clouds of white canvas flapped wildly in the wind, like wings of gulls anxious to reach their destination.

Phillip's blond hair caught the breeze, much like the sails above his head, flying out behind him, free and unencumbered. He stood the morning watch on quarterdeck, observing the sun inching its way slowly above the horizon as he scanned the area. The darkness lightened to gray and then purple, finally giving way to azure blue as the sun rose into the sky.

He loved this early time of morning when he could be alone with his thoughts. And he had much to think about of late. Since shedding his Ashland disguise, a great burden had been lifted from his shoulders. He had confided to Danielle about his childhood, his life at sea, about his mother and the burning hatred he felt for British nobility. And she had listened. Asked questions. And understood.

Danielle returned the love that he so freely gave, and that knowledge had him thinking of settling down, preparing for fatherhood, and spending the rest of his life making love to his wife.

Up till now, the sea had been his only mistress. He loved the way the deck swayed beneath his feet, the way the brisk salt air whipped across his face, but he would have no trouble giving it up for the woman he loved.

Soon this war would be over and he could return to make Danielle his proper wife. There would be no more lies between them, only love and unbridled joy.

He had wanted to tell her about Andrew Ellsworth before leaving; it was the only secret he still harbored. But there had never been an appropriate time, and he hadn't wanted to frighten her, to burden her mind, which was full of his departure.

And Ellsworth could already be dead. Though he doubted it. Men like Ellsworth didn't die; they just slithered about from one place to the next, advancing their goals and careers at the expense of anyone who got in their way. Benedict Arnold had done it for greed. Andrew Ellsworth for revenge. And soon both men would pay for their treachery.

Lifting his spyglass, he spotted a large flotilla of ships in the distance—French ships—De Grasse's ships—bottling up the entrance to the bay, preventing Cornwallis's escape.

The British earl was trapped by his own stupidity

and his superior's, Clinton's, egocentricity that the American rabble would be easily defeated.

He knew from a communiqué he'd just received that Washington and Rochambeau had already arrived. The Franco-American contingent in the immediate area outnumbered the British troops two to one. 'Twas about time the advantage had fallen to the patriot side, Phillip thought.

Washington's decision to march his army over four hundred miles from New York to Williamsburg, then on to York Town in the space of thirty-three days had been a daring maneuver. The general, having given the British the impression that he was about to mount an attack on New York, had outwitted Clinton, and now Cornwallis and his seven thousand troops were at Washington's mercy.

Victory was close at hand, and it felt good. Damn good!

"Ye must be thinkin' about the bonnie lass, else why would you hae such a stupid grin on yer face."

Lowering his glass, Phillip turned to find Ian climbing the ladder onto the quarterdeck. He wore a red knit cap, pulled low over his ears to protect them from the wind, and a heavy pea jacket. His cheeks were raw, his nose nearly the color of his cap. "Actually, old man, you're only partially correct," Phillip responded. "I was thinking about how we were finally going to whip those British scum. 'Tis a good feeling."

The gold tooth glittered brightly in the sun as Ian returned Phillip's smile. "Aye, laddie. 'Twill no' be long now, and I'm itchin' tae get into the thick o' it."

"Call all hands to quarters. Have the lads man their battle stations. There's no telling what we'll encounter when we arrive, and I want to be prepared." His ship boasted fourteen gun ports, seven on each side of the vessel, carrying four-pounders. If they had to make a showing, it was damn well going to be a good one, Phillip decided.

"Aye, laddie." Ian saluted smartly. "And will there be anything else, Captain?"

Phillip grinned, tying his mask over his face. "Aye, old man. Tell Brewster to lower the black flag and raise the Continental colors. I want everyone to know whose side we're on. I don't want some trigger-happy Frenchman pummeling my sails with grapeshot."

"I hae no' been this excited since me weddin' night, laddie. 'Tis goin' tae be a glorious day," Ian said, rubbing his hands together in anticipation.

Chuckling, Phillip retorted, "I'll be sure to convey that sentiment to Charlotte upon my return, old man," and was amused by the look of horror Ian cast back over his shoulder.

"I'd rather face them bloody, red-coated devils then me Charlotte when she's in a temper."

"Then let's get with it, old man. 'Tis time to make haste."

With a stiff wind at their stern propelling them forward, the Phantom's ship arrived at Cape Henry off the York Town peninsula in record time to join De Grasse's fleet of thirty-six ships, which rode at anchor in the bay.

The French admiral seemed almost as excited to meet the infamous Phantom as Phillip was in participating in the siege.

"*Mon capitaine,* I am most honored to meet you," the comte de Grasse said in welcome as Phillip boarded the flagship *Ville de Paris.* "Your reputation has preceded you, my masked friend. But can you not discard your disguise? You are among friends and allies now."

Grabbing the hilt of his sword, Phillip bowed, flourishing his tricornered hat as he did so. "There is still a price on my head, Admiral, and many who desire to stretch my neck. I will remain masked for the time being." At the very least until Ellsworth was stretched out before him on the deck of his ship as dead as he deserved.

The Frenchman nodded in understanding, issuing an invitation for the Phantom to join him in his cabin for refreshment. Phillip obliged and was soon seated at the highly polished mahogany table, admiring the rich furnishings of the officer's cabin. He'd always thought his own ship handsomely appointed, but it certainly didn't come close to the opulence of De Grasse's cabin. Teak walls and red velvet hangings made for a comfortable abode.

Sipping wine from a cut-crystal goblet, Phillip listened as the comte de Grasse brought him up to date on the situation in York Town.

"As you know, *monsieur,* from the missive that was sent to you by my first officer, we vastly outnumber our British foe in both guns and manpower." He smiled, adding, "And brains, apparently. It seems that our impetuous earl has abandoned his outer line of defenses. Those abandoned works have been occupied by our forces and the digging of new earthworks has begun. The American forces are positioned on Cornwallis's left flank, my French brethren to his right."

Phillip's grin widened at the news. "It would seem everything is under control." Perhaps so much so that he would be able to sail home and enjoy a brief visit with Danielle.

"*Oui, mon capitaine;* Washington and Rochambeau have lured the British pig into the trap. Now all that is left is to bury him in it." The admiral took a sip of the red cabernet, savoring the aged oak flavor, then added, "General Washington has left word that he wishes to see you. You're to present yourself to him this evening, to be his guest for a light supper."

Phillip's blue eyes widened imperceptibly. Washington desired an audience with him? Why? he wondered. What had he done to deserve such an honor?

He was soon to find out a few hours later when the general's aide ushered him inside the large canvas tent that served as Washington's field headquarters. Outside, a steady rain fell, and the drops pitted noisily against the heavy, gray material.

The tent was dimly lit by several candles, and Washington's white head was bent over a battered camp desk as he studied the papers before him. His face was masked in concentration, prompting Phillip to clear his throat before announcing his arrival.

"You wished to see me, General?" Washington's head came up and Phillip saluted his commander in chief.

Unfolding his large frame from the wooden chair, the general returned the salute. At three inches over six feet, George Washington's head nearly touched the roof of the tent. "Don't stand on ceremony, Mr. Cameron. Please come in and be seated." He indicated the table that had been set with fine china and crystal. "I am forever indebted to you, sir, and I wish to honor you this evening as my guest."

"The honor is mine, General," Phillip said, removing his heavy pea coat and mask before lowering himself to sit at the table. There was no need to conceal

his identity from the general; it was Washington who
had procured the Phantom's letters of marque. "I am
doubly honored that at such a critical time, you
would turn your thoughts to a mere sailor."

Washington threw back his head and laughed, the
deep sound ricocheting off the canvas walls. "You
are much too modest, Mr. Cameron. You, who have
single-handedly destroyed many of His Majesty's
finest ships of the line. And, who saved my army
from certain starvation a while back. I am very much
in your debt."

Phillip felt uncomfortable with such lavish praise;
his motives for doing what he did weren't purely
unselfish and he let the general know. "I have my
own ax to grind, General Washington. Some of my
actions were self-serving and I am not deserving of
your gratitude or your praise."

"Come with me, Mr. Cameron. Let me show you
something."

The general led him outside to a small rise where
they could observe the activity going on in the distance. Like a human tide of moles burrowing in the
night, the soldiers dug—one row in the ditches, one
row standing guard—to fashion the earthworks that
would protect them during battle.

The sound of picks and shovels hummed an eerie
litany as the fifteen hundred soldiers dug diligently
into the soft, sandy soil. Thick bundles of twigs,
known as *fascines*, stood ready to fill the trenches;
and *gabions*, bottomless, wicker-type baskets filled
with soil, would form the breastworks of the new
fortifications.

As Phillip watched, visibly impressed with the
general's cleverness at constructing a parallel so close

to enemy lines, a shot rang out and then another, but the pickets posted to guard the digging troops reported no casualties.

"Take a good look, Mr. Cameron, for these men before you all have their own axes to grind, whether it be hatred of the nobility, resentment of unjust taxation, or love for this fledgling country of ours.

"It doesn't matter what propels you to undertake the course that you do; it only matters that you do it. We do not seek the burdens we undertake, but we do them, nevertheless. Follow your heart, Mr. Cameron, always and forever. It will never steer you wrong."

Later that night, as Phillip reclined on his bunk, listening to the waves splash against the hull of the ship, he recounted the general's words and knew what he must do.

His heart impelled him to return to Fredericksburg, if only for one night. He had to see Danielle again before entering the field of battle. He had to taste her lips, feel her soft flesh beneath his own, before he could rid himself of the demons that plagued him. Then perhaps he could put aside the Andrew Ellsworths of the world and live in peace.

He didn't know if he could, only that he had to try.

Danielle paced nervously across her bedchamber. The sun was melting quickly into the horizon and dark shadows replaced the light of moments before. She crossed to the nightstand to light a taper, knowing that it would soon be time to take her sister's bag to the stable.

Apprehension continued to assault her, not only because of her sister's foolhardy plan to elope, but

also because she hadn't heard from Phillip. A fortnight had passed, but it may as well have been two
months rather than two weeks. Phillip had not written;
there'd been no word as he had promised.

Her heart hammered loud in her chest as the clock
on the mantel stuck seven. It was time. She eased
open the door and stuck her head out, to make certain no one would see her departure. She hadn't told
Lottie about what she intended to do. Her friend
would only chastise her for being foolish, and
Danielle had castigated herself enough as it was
already.

Peering into the hallway, she breathed a sigh of
relief. No one was about. Lottie was probably in her
room feeding the baby, and Mrs. Dunstan would be
in the kitchen preparing supper. Now was the perfect
time to go. Grabbing her sister's portmanteau off the
bed, she exited her room, closing the door quietly
behind her, and tiptoed down the stairs.

The night air was brisk as she hurried toward the
tavern, and she wished she'd had the good sense to
don her cloak. The gingham gown she wore offered
little protection from the cool autumn wind.

The noise of the waterfront alerted her to the
fact that she was getting close. Spying the Golden
Pineapple up ahead, she veered off to her right, taking a path down by the river that would lead her to
the stables.

Fearing she would be spotted by the stableboy, she
waited inside the barn as Regina had instructed her
to do. Danielle cursed herself a thousand times a fool
for allowing herself to be talked into her sister's
scheme, but despite her reservations, she pulled open
the heavy door and entered.

Snorts and whinnies greeted her arrival. A lantern had been left burning, indicating that Billy would be back after he finished his supper. She felt herself growing a bit queasy as the odor of soiled hay and leather rose up to assault her senses. Taking a deep breath, she entered an empty horse stall and sat down on a hay bale to wait.

The door creaked open, alerting Danielle to the fact that she was no longer alone. "Regina, is that you?" she called out softly, hoping it wasn't Billy. He was as curious a lad as ever she'd seen and quite loyal to her parents.

"Yes. Where are you?" her sister's voice rang out, filling Danielle with relief. She wanted to get this whole miserable affair over with as quickly as possible.

"Over here, behind the stall, to your left."

Regina soon materialized, but her smug smile turned Danielle's feeling of comfort to consternation.

"I see you brought my bag, Danielle. Pity you did not bring one for yourself."

The dark brows drew together in confusion. "Why would I need one for myself? I am not the one eloping."

Regina smiled. "I fooled you, Danielle. Just like when we were children. You were always so gullible."

Apprehension tingled Danielle's spine as she gazed at her sister's spiteful expression. "Your childish games do not amuse me, Gina."

"'Tis not a game, Danielle. We are planning a very serious mission. One that you're going to help us with."

"You're not making any sense, Regina. I don't know what you're talking about."

"Of course you don't. It's a secret. One that only me and André are privileged to know."

"André?" At the mention of the Frenchman, Danielle's uneasiness grew and she rose to her feet. "What does he have to do with this mission of yours?"

Regina couldn't contain her excitement as she blurted, "André has found a way for us to become rich! Wealthy beyond our wildest dreams."

As usual, Regina's prattle didn't make any sense. "I thought you said André was wealthy. Why would he need more money?"

"You can never have too much money, sister dear. And once we capture the Phantom—"

Danielle gasped, her face whitening. "The Phantom!"

"Surely you know about the reward for his capture, Danielle."

Her sister's boastful manner annoyed her, and she sought to deflate her ambitions. "And just how do you propose to capture him? The British have been trying for years, without any success."

Regina's smile was malicious, sending warning signals flashing through Danielle's brain. "Why, you're going to help us, of course."

Danielle laughed. "How stupid you are, Regina. I would never help you capture the Phantom. Not for all the money in the world."

Regina's face reddened. "Yes, you will, Danielle. You're the only one that can help us claim the reward."

The purple orbs narrowed into thin slits as Danielle observed the greed written all over her sister's face. She should have known. Regina's avarice was an integral part of her personality. She brazened out, "Well, I guess you'll be disappointed then; the Phantom is gone, and you'll not be receiving any reward for his capture."

"Oh, but you're wrong, Mrs. Ashland."

The deep male voice sent chills down Danielle's spine. Fear, stark and vivid, glittered in her eyes as she took in the sight of the French army officer who emerged from the shadows. His features were sharp, almost pointed, reminding Danielle of a ferret. She shivered, chafing at the gooseflesh on her arms.

"Who are you? What do you want?"

"This is André, Danielle," Regina said. "My betrothed."

Danielle didn't miss André's flinch at the title bestowed upon him and knew Regina had been thoroughly fooled by this man. As thoroughly duped as she had been by her own sister's guile. Rage began to mount and she threw caution to the wind, saying, "If you think this man is going to wed you, Regina, you're stupider than I thought. He's only using you. Can't you see that?"

At the uncertainty marring Regina's features, the Frenchman snapped, "Cease your prattling, woman! We're not in need of your opinions, just your presence."

A large knot of fear lodged in Danielle's throat, tightening her stomach into a hard ball; her hand covered it protectively. "My presence? What are you talking about? I'm not going anywhere with you."

"Now who's being stupid, Mrs. Ashland? Of course you're going with us. You're the bait who is going to lure the Phantom from his hiding place."

The Frenchman's smile was full of self-confidence and Danielle knew she had to escape. The Phantom's life depended on it, as did her unborn child's. Slowly she edged toward the door, but before she could turn and run, her sister latched on to her arm.

"Oh, no you don't, Danielle. We need you to catch the Phantom. There's two thousand pounds sterling to be had from his capture."

"Let go of me, Regina," Danielle snapped, pulling her arm from her sister's embrace, but she was quickly subdued by the stronger arms of the Frenchman.

"You must cooperate with us, madame. Else you may suffer a similar fate as the Phantom's. He isn't worth dying for, is he?"

Danielle's struggles drew Ellsworth's attention to her breasts. Her fichu had fallen out, and he was afforded an enticing glimpse of her ample bosom. His eyes glittered as they traveled from her breasts, down her body, then back up to her face, which was burning in anger and embarrassment.

It wasn't difficult to see, after comparing the two sisters, who had the beauty and brains in the family, Ellsworth thought. Regina was a child compared to this curvaceous, spirited woman. What sweet revenge it would be to take the woman the Phantom fancied.

Noting the lascivious glint in the copper-colored eyes, Danielle shuddered, struggling harder to escape her captor's hold. "Let go of me, you vile, French bastard!"

Regina gasped. "You mustn't speak to André like that, Danielle. We're to be married. He's soon to be your brother-in-law."

The absurdity of Regina's comment brought vindictive laughter to Danielle's lips. Ignoring the shock on her sister's face and the anger on the Frenchman's, she spat out, "You two deserve each other. Do you know that, Regina? You're as wicked as your lover, maybe worse. How could you, Regina?"

Tears formed in Regina's eyes and she covered her ears to block out Danielle's taunts. André's grip tightened on Danielle's arms and he warned her to be quiet.

"I won't," she insisted, tilting her chin defiantly. "I intend to scream my head off." And she proceeded to do just that but was promptly silenced by a blow to the side of her head from Ellsworth's fist. She slumped to the ground at his feet.

"Stupid woman!" he remarked, angered that she had forced him to mar such perfection. Even now, an ugly bruise was forming on her cheek.

Horrified, Regina clamped her hand over her mouth and stared down at her sister's inert form, finally asking, "Is she dead? Have you killed my sister?"

"Shut up and help me get her to the horses. Our ship is waiting down the coast."

"But . . . what of Danielle? She might need a doctor."

"Do you want the money, Regina? Do you want to marry me when all this is through? If you do, I would suggest taking your cloak and placing it over your sister. We don't want to draw attention to ourselves."

Regina swallowed and it only took her a moment to make her decision. Removing her cloak, she covered Danielle with it.

Though she wanted no harm to come to Danielle,

she couldn't let her sister interfere with her plans again. Not this time. This time she would be the one to marry the rich man. She would be the one to live in the big, fancy house and wear the pretty clothes.

This time it must be Danielle who made the sacrifice.

25

Phillip knew something was wrong as soon as he entered the house. It was too quiet. The only sounds, other than the crackling of the fire in the parlor hearth, were Ian's labored breathing as he stood beside him in the entry hall. The old man had fairly flew up the hill in his eagerness to see his wife and daughter and was quite out of breath.

Gazing about the empty rooms, Phillip wondered where everyone had gone. He was as anxious as a randy schoolboy to see Danielle and couldn't understand why she wasn't waiting just as anxiously to see him. "What do you make of it, old man? I thought surely Danielle would be here to greet us. I sent Tim ahead with a note."

Before Ian could speculate, the back door banged shut and Lottie rushed forward from the rear of the house with Mrs. Dunstan and Timothy Luck following close on her heels. Both the housekeeper and cabin boy looked distraught, but it was the look of fear on Lottie's face that sent Phillip's stomach plummeting to the floor. *Something was terribly wrong.*

Unaware of Phillip's anxiety, Ian's face lit with pleasure as he observed his wife rushing toward him; he held out his arms to embrace her, but Lottie ignored him, heading straight for Phillip, bringing a frown to his lips.

"Praise the heavens; you've come!" she exclaimed. "Something terrible's happened."

Ian's face paled as he stared at Lottie, who was wringing her hands nervously; his first thought went to his child. "Is it the bairn, lass?"

She shook her head and Phillip tensed. "Nay, 'tisn't Grace; she's upstairs sleeping like a little angel." At Ian's sigh of relief, she patted his cheek, saying to Phillip, "It's Danny, Mr. Cameron. She's gone. Her bed was not slept in last night."

Phillip swallowed his fear and tried to think logically. There could be many reasons for Danielle's absence, he told himself. Perhaps Mrs. Washington had taken ill, or she was needed at an emergency meeting of the Daughters.

"Have you checked with the neighbors? With her friends? Perhaps she's gone visiting and decided to stay the night." Though those possibilities were reasonable, he knew deep down that there could only be one reason for Danielle's absence, and it was one he didn't want to face.

His worst fears were confirmed a moment later when Lottie reached into her pocket to withdraw a wrinkled piece of parchment.

"I thought that myself, at first. This was delivered by messenger early this morning." She handed it to him. "The lad said he'd been paid by a tall Frenchman to deliver it."

Phillip and Ian exchanged knowing looks, then Phillip's face turned stonelike; fear for Danielle's safety thundered in his chest, but he said nothing.

"'Twas Regina's lover no doubt. I knew that bitch was up to no good. She was here the other day to speak to Danielle."

A muscle quivered at Phillip's jaw, his blue eyes darkening to black in his anger as he read the missive. Danielle had been abducted aboard the British ship *Orion*. If the Phantom wanted to see her alive again, he was to surrender himself to the British authorities in York Town. Andrew Ellsworth of His Majesty's Royal Navy was named as the contact person.

Cold fury masked his features and he crumpled the note, raising his fist in the air as he bellowed his rage. "Goddamn that bloody bastard! I'll kill him. As God is my witness, he'll never draw another breath."

Mrs. Dunstan started to cry, as did Grace, who had awakened at all the commotion and was wailing loudly at the top of her lungs.

Phillip turned to face his cabin boy. "Tim, run down to the docks and tell Dunny to prepare the ship for sailing. We leave immediately for York Town." Thank God, Phillip thought, he'd had the presence of mind to sail the ship up the Rappahannock River, directly to Fredericksburg, rather than conceal it at Port Royal, as had been his usual practice. It rested only a few hundred yards from where they now stood.

Because of the siege at York Town, time was a precious commodity, and he'd known that his time with Danielle would be short. But now, because of that bastard Ellsworth, there would be no time at all. It had run out. He just hoped there would be enough to find Ellsworth and rescue Danielle.

The boy was off in a flash, and Lottie and Ian disappeared to have a few quiet moments together before the ship's departure, leaving Mrs. Dunstan alone with Phillip.

The older woman sniffed loudly, wiping her face with her apron. "I know it ain't my place to say this, Mr. Cameron, but I love that girl like she was my own daughter. You will be bringing her back?"

Phillip placed a comforting hand on his housekeeper's shoulder, patting the older woman gently, his gesture in direct contrast to his voice, which still rang harsh and cold.

"Never fear, Mrs. Dunstan. Danielle will be brought back alive. You've my word on it."

"And the Phantom's?" she asked, chills careening down her spine at the savageness of his smile.

"Aye, and the Phantom's."

Danielle awoke, not knowing how long she'd been unconscious. It was dark and dank where she'd been deposited like so much unnecessary ballast, and she smelled of pitch fumes, bilge water, and the filthy straw she rested upon. A rat scurried by her and she gasped, righting herself. Pulling her knees up under her chin, she curled her bare toes inward, not caring to offer any incentive to the hungry rodent.

Gazing about, she noticed iron manacles and leg shackles fastened to the timbers and shivered, thankful she'd not been restrained by the horrible devices. *The brig.* She was deep in the bowels of the ship, which accounted for the noxious odors and her own queasiness.

The ship pitched back and forth, and as it did, her

stomach followed suit. She was hungry and thirsty. But it was probably just as well they hadn't thought to feed her; she would have thrown it all back up.

She was wearing Regina's red fur-lined cloak; small comfort, but at least she wasn't freezing to death. Pulling the warm garment close about her, she buried her head in her lap, unable to believe her sister's treachery. "Traitor," she whispered, the word forming easily on her lips, even as her heart ached at her sister's perfidy.

How could Regina have been so stupid? How could *she*? For she'd been taken in by her sister's glib tongue and tearful appeals and now had put Phillip's life in danger.

They knew the Phantom would follow, and when he did, they would capture and hang him.

"Oh, God," she wailed, her eyes brimming with tears. She couldn't let that happen. Somehow, someway, she had to escape. But how? The door was at least a foot thick, made of solid oak. It was no doubt locked, but she pushed herself to her feet and tried to open it, just to make certain she couldn't. It didn't budge. Returning to her resting place, she slid dejectedly to the floor, covering her face as tears fell in rivulets down her cheeks. She was doomed; they all were.

The rain fell in torrents as the Phantom's ship pursued the British frigate *Orion*. Sheets of water poured from the sky, ripping at the sails, tossing the ship to and fro upon the turbulent waves as it sailed into the center of the storm.

"We should put into shore, laddie, until this storm

dies down. Ye'll do the lass no good if yer not alive tae save her," Ian shouted against the roar of the wind.

Phillip gripped the wheel tighter, ignoring the water that lashed his face and plastered his clothing to his body. With a shake of his head, he growled, "Nay, old man, I'll not stop.

"Ellsworth's just insane enough to remain afloat. I can't give him more of an advantage than he already has. We've got to catch up. His ship's larger and carrying more cannon; he won't be able to sail as swiftly as we can, especially in this weather. We must seize the edge. He won't be expecting us to take the risk."

"Risk!" Ian shouted, shaking his head in disbelief, grasping the rail just in time to prevent a wave from washing him overboard. Once the ship had righted and he had spit out a good portion of the seawater he'd swallowed, he spewed out a string of colorful epithets, adding, "Yer daft, laddie. We'll be shark bait before morn, mark me words."

Phillip's voice was chilling as he shouted back, "Mark mine, old man. Ellsworth is a dead man, and there's nothing or no one who's going to stop me from killing him."

"Danielle . . . Danielle, can you hear me?"

Regina's voice floated through the heavy oak door on a whisper, and Danielle scrambled to her feet, hanging on to the timbers as she made her way toward the sound. "I can hear you; what is it you want? Have you come to gloat?"

Regina's voice was choked with tears. "Danielle, I'm sorry. You were right; André doesn't love me. It was all a lie. He wasn't even French, but an Englishman by the name of Andrew Ellsworth; he's the captain of this ship.

"Oh, Danielle, please forgive me. I never would have helped him if I'd known what he was like; how horribly he would treat you."

Oh, Gina, Danielle thought, tears filling her eyes for her sister's naiveté before she swallowed and said, "You must help me get out of here, Regina. I am with child. I'm going to have a baby very soon." She heard her sister's shocked gasp. "You must find the key that unlocks this door. Together we can escape the clutches of this madman."

"I will. I'll go to André—Andrew's—cabin and find the key. I'll—"

Regina's loud piercing scream rent the air, followed by the sound of heavy boots in the hold area; Danielle's heart leapt into her throat.

"Get away from that door, you stupid slut." Andrew Ellsworth's voice was coldly furious as he screamed vile invectives at Regina. "Get back to the cabin; I'll deal with you later."

The panic in Regina's voice was easily discerned. "Please, Andrew, it isn't what you think. I was only trying to fool Danielle into thinking I would help her."

Danielle listened to the exchange and knew she was finished. A sharp roll of the ship sent her pitching forward, and she landed harshly on her hands and knees. Crawling slowly, she made her way back to the makeshift pallet.

A moment later the door flung open, emitting a shaft of light into the darkened area. It took a moment for her eyes to adjust to the change, and when they did, she discovered Captain Ellsworth standing in the doorway. He was garbed in a British naval officer's uniform.

Nostrils flaring, he glared down at her. "It won't work, you know. You'll not escape this ship, so I would advise you to quit trying to talk that stupid sister of yours into helping you. Though I sail with only a small contingent of my regular crew, I assure you, madam, it is enough to contain the likes of yourself."

Danielle's voice was venomous, filled with all the hatred she felt for Ellsworth. "I thought there was a code of conduct you British naval officers followed, Captain. Your harsh treatment of both me and my sister leads me to believe that you're a disgrace to that uniform you wear."

Ellsworth's face colored crimson, except for a line slashing white across his mouth where his lips thinned. "You'd be wise to hold your tongue, Mrs. Ashland. You know nothing of the present circumstances that led me to abandon chivalry in pursuit of your pirate lover.

"Does your husband know that you've taken a lover, Mrs. Ashland? Will he care if you take another?"

He stepped forward, and Danielle shrank back against the boards. "Don't you dare touch me, you filthy swine. I'd sooner die than bed an English dog like you."

The captain shook with impotent rage. "Why you—"

The sound of metal against wood made Ellsworth turn to find Regina standing in the doorway, dragging a heavy sword behind her.

Danielle gasped as she stared at her sister's pathetic form. There were tears streaming down her face, tears of anger, of betrayal, and the sword she held shook as she tried to lift it.

"Leave her alone, Andrew," Regina ordered. "You'll not vent your lust upon my sister's flesh."

Ellsworth's face became a mask of fury, and Danielle feared for Regina's safety; she called out, her voice unsteady, "Go back to your cabin, Regina. There's nothing you can do to help me."

Easing his hand onto the butt of the pistol at his waist, Ellsworth smiled maliciously. "You'd better listen to your big sister, Regina, and leave quickly. Don't worry, I'll still have plenty of energy to fuck you after I'm done with her."

Regina's crazed scream split the air as she rushed toward Ellsworth, brandishing the sword. Danielle watched in horror as Ellsworth pulled the pistol from his breeches and fired point blank at Regina's chest. "No!" Danielle screamed, grabbing on to his legs. "Noooo!"

Ellsworth brushed her efforts off as he pulled out of her grasp. Regina stared wide-eyed at the spreading crimson stain on her chest, mouthed Andrew's name, then slumped to the floor, a permanent expression of disbelief etched on her face.

Scrambling forward on all fours, Danielle hurried to her sister's side, pressing her fingers against Regina's neck to feel for a pulse. There was none. Anger and pain ripped through her as she gazed at her sister's lifeless form, then up at Ellsworth.

"How could you?" she screamed. "How could you do such a horrible thing?" Her tears fell freely to land on Regina's porcelain cheeks as she caressed the dead woman's face. "Gina, my God, Gina." Rocking back and forth, she clutched her sister to her breast. "Murderer! Murderer!"

"*Tsk, tsk,* Mrs. Ashland, your hysterics hardly become you. But to show you what a generous soul I am, I'll let you have a few moments alone with your sister, before I toss her body into the sea."

Before Danielle could respond, a loud roar rocked the ship, knocking Ellsworth to his knees. A measure of alarm entered his eyes, but he quickly composed himself.

"The storm worsens, Mrs. Ashland. You'd do well to brace yourself for the onslaught," he advised.

She countered icily, "You'd best follow your own advice, Captain; that wasn't thunder you heard but the roar of cannon. Your day of reckoning has arrived."

Another blast gave credence to Danielle's words, and Ellsworth scrambled to his feet, rushing toward the door. He paused momentarily to look back over his shoulder at her, and the fear in his eyes belied the confidence of his words.

"Prepare to take a new lover, Danielle. Your old one dies this day." Slamming the door behind him, Danielle heard the click of the lock as he turned the key.

Staring down at her sister's still face, she brushed the gold silk strands away from her face. "The Phantom has come, Gina," she whispered.

Suddenly, a sharp pain tore through her and she clutched at her belly, crying out. It was followed by another, even more intense, and she found herself drenched in sweat. Waves of nausea brought bile to her throat, and she covered her mouth to keep from retching.

Please, God, don't let anything happen to my child, she prayed. Then when the pain became too much for her to endure, she gave in to it and blacked out.

* * *

First Lieutenant Simon Pettigrew's mouth gaped open at the sight of the familiar black ship coming up fast on the *Orion*'s larboard side. 'Twas a nightmare come true, he thought, as cannon balls and grapeshot spewed forth to land with unerring accuracy, splintering the mainmast of the vessel and shredding the topgallant sails.

"Not again," he lamented, shouting out orders to his crew. "All hands to quarters! All hands to quarters! Man your gun ports." But even as he spoke, Pettigrew knew how grossly undermanned the *Orion* was. Ellsworth had sailed for York Town in such a hurry, there hadn't been time to secure the entire crew from their shore leave.

A four-pound shot blew the head off the figurehead, and the once-proud lion looked as disjointed as the English sailors who scrambled and screamed in their haste to avoid the enemy's firepower.

The multiclawed grappling irons landed with amazing accuracy, affixing themselves to the lower yardarms, forecastle, and gangways.

Where the hell was Captain Ellsworth? Pettigrew wondered, throwing up his hands at the destruction all around him.

As if conjured up by his thoughts, the *Orion*'s captain stepped out onto the main deck to find his ship had been boarded by the Phantom's crew. Everywhere he looked chaos abounded. Black smoke belched thickly as cannons exploded. The acrid stench of gunpowder and death surrounded him on all sides.

"My God, Pettigrew!" Ellsworth shouted. "Why haven't we returned fire?" As he spoke, several of his crewmen jumped into the chilly waters of the Chesapeake to take their chances with the elements rather than face the Phantom's wrath.

"Come back here, you cowards," Ellsworth screamed, raising his fist in the air. "I'll see you all strung from the yardarm."

"There wasn't time to return fire, Captain," the first officer tried to explain. "The enemy was upon us before we knew what was happening." Rage twisted Ellsworth's face, making it appear demonic, and Pettigrew cringed.

"I'll have you brought before the Admiralty for this, Pettigrew. You've lost control of the ship; you've lost the battle."

"'Tis you who have lost, Ellsworth," came the taunting voice that Ellsworth recognized immediately. He turned to find the Phantom standing only a few feet away, his sword drawn, his blue eyes as cold as the depths of the ocean.

"Where is Danielle, Ellsworth? If you've harmed a hair on her head, I'll cut out your heart and serve it up as fish bait."

Pettigrew blanched and backed away. He'd warned Ellsworth not to bring the two women aboard the ship. Women were bad luck on a sailing vessel. Very bad luck.

Ellsworth smiled maliciously. "Danielle was a ripe little piece, was she not? We spent many enjoyable hours together. But she served her usefulness. I'm afraid you've arrived too late."

With a fiendish yell, the Phantom's sword came up so swiftly, Ellsworth had no time to react; he swallowed with difficulty as the pointed tip pressed into his Adam's apple.

"I should stick you now like the pig you are, Ellsworth, but that would be too quick a death for you." Backing up a few paces, he lowered his blade. "Draw and fight for your life, Englishman. Your death will be swift and just."

Surprise, then satisfaction, touched the nobleman's face, and Ellsworth's rapier cleared its sheath. The conflagration between the two enemies had begun. A hush fell over the deck as crewmen from both sides stood by to watch the ensuing battle to the death.

Ian crossed himself several times, muttering a prayer under his breath, then placed his hand on the pistol at his belt . . . just in case.

Cold steel clanked against steel as each man thrust and parried his opponents' movements. Phillip had removed his cape, Ellsworth his jacket, and the two men were silhouetted against a darkening sky. Soon the rain began to fall in earnest, making the deck slippery and treacherous and their movements precarious.

Phillip attacked the British nobleman like a man possessed; he gave no quarter, just pushed and thrust until all Ellsworth could do was defend himself against the onslaught of the powerful blows. Phillip's footing slipped once and he dropped to his knee, giving Ellsworth a momentary advantage when the man thrust his sword into Phillip's left shoulder.

Ian cried out, as did several of the Phantom's crew, but though his shoulder pained him, Phillip faltered only momentarily.

Ellsworth smiled smugly as he surveyed the damage he'd inflicted. "Your blood has been drawn, pirate. Do you care to withdraw and surrender?"

Though blood seeped through the black silk of his

shirt, Phillip's only answer was continued assault as he thrust his sword at Ellsworth. The sword slashed through the air with a swishing sound; the rain was falling harder now, blurring his vision, but he kept on.

Back and forth they parried until the British captain, emboldened by his previous hit, lunged forward to stab at Phillip's midsection. But Phillip was faster, sidestepping the assault, and Ellsworth met the blade of Phillip's sword instead. Ellsworth's eyes widened in surprise as the blade entered his heart, then he fell to the deck, dead.

Without a moment's hesitation, Phillip sheathed his weapon and ran to the companionway. His thoughts were only for Danielle and her safety as he headed below decks.

He headed aft past the officers' quarters on the starboard side, reaching the captain's cabin at the rear of the ship. It was empty. He climbed back to the main deck, where Ian had already secured the enemy sailors for transport to York Town. Swiftly, he went below to the galley and crew's quarters to search, but as before there was no sign of Danielle.

Fear gnawed at his belly. Had Ellsworth's taunts been more truthful than he realized? Perhaps the crazed bastard had killed Danielle and thrown her body overboard; perhaps he had arrived too late to save her. "Danielle!" he screamed, his pained cry resembling a wounded animal's. "Danielle!"

But there was no answer. Only the sound of pounding footsteps from above as his men continued to clear the decks and the pelting rain, which continued to fall.

He opened the main hatch to enter the bowels of the ship, stepping over a dead seaman who'd been hit by a falling timber from the blast of cannon fire, and lowered himself into the hold.

Removing a lit lantern from a hook on the beam, he surveyed the area, noting the ship's stores of beef, potatoes and flour, ammunition of shot and cannon balls, and casks of drinking water and grog.

Moving forward he came to an enclosed area secured by a heavy oak door. He pounded on it, calling Danielle's name. *No answer.* Removing the flintlock from his belt, he aimed at the lock and fired; the shattered metal fell to the floor and he pushed open the door.

The sight that greeted him brought his heart to his throat. Stretched out before him on the rough-hewn planks lay the body of a woman cloaked in red, her identity obscured by the hood covering her head.

Tears blurred his vision and his hands grew cold and clammy in fear as he dropped to his knees beside her. "Danielle," he choked out, turning the body over to face him.

Relief and pity surged through him as Regina Sheridan's face, frozen hideously in death, stared up at him. Her skin was pasty white, her blue eyes, which once sparkled in mischief, were wide open but lifeless. Gently, he closed her lids and stood.

With the lantern raised above his head, he searched the remaining area. It was then he saw her, garbed in a pink gingham dress splattered with blood.

"Danielle!" he screamed, rushing toward her. He set the lantern beside him and felt for her pulse. She was still alive. "Thank you, Lord," he whispered. With quick efficiency, he undressed her to check the seriousness of her wounds. Placing his hands on the taut skin of her belly, he felt the movement of the baby and breathed a sigh of relief. He examined the rest of her, but he could find no sign of injury, save for an ugly bruise on her cheekbone. Puzzled, he gently rolled her over but found no sign of abuse there either.

"Danielle," he called out again, lifting her body against his chest. Her hands and arms were like ice, and he chafed at her extremities to try and get the blood flowing back into them. Her lips, dry and cracked, looked as frozen as the rest of her and he placed a soft kiss upon them. "Sweeting, can you hear me?" She appeared to be in a deep sleep, but not totally unconscious.

After a moment, her eyelids fluttered, then opened. "Phillip, is that you?" Danielle's voice was hoarse from lack of water.

"You're safe now, sweeting. Ellsworth is dead."

Her hands went to her stomach and her eyes widened in fright. "My baby?"

He caressed her cheek. "He's fine too."

Tears filled her eyes. "He killed Regina. He was going to kill you, too." It was then she noticed the blood on his shirt and she gasped. "You're hurt! You've been injured."

"'Tis naught but a scratch, sweeting." Though it hurt like the very devil. Cradling her, he brushed the hair from her forehead and placed a kiss there. "Ellsworth will never hurt anyone again. He's dead. I saw to it myself."

She smiled weakly then. "You mean the Phantom, don't you?"

"Aye. 'Twas a promise I made to Mrs. Dunstan and vowed to keep above all else."

"I love you, Phillip James Cameron—Ashland—Phantom and any other identities you've not told me about."

He smiled, placing a kiss on the tip of her nose, then carefully lifted her in his arms, carrying her from the room, leaving all the unpleasantness behind them. He would have Ian arrange for Regina's body to be transported to his ship immediately.

Once they were safely ensconced in the captain's cabin aboard the black schooner, and Danielle was tucked warmly in his bunk beneath a mountain of blankets, Phillip explained that they would be sailing on to York Town to assist Washington in his defeat of the British.

Danielle sighed at the news, unable to keep the disappointment out of her voice. "I'd hoped we'd be able to go home, Phillip. I'm heartily sick of war."

And she had to tell her parents of Regina's death, but she didn't want to face that responsibility just yet. Regina had died trying to protect her. With guilt and joy, she would remember that one unselfish act the rest of her days.

"I'll be all yours soon enough, sweeting," Phillip said, interrupting her thoughts. "But first we must sail to York Town to finish what we've started. We're close to victory, Danielle. This war is all but over."

Hearing the excitement in his voice, and noting the fervor in his eyes, Danielle squeezed the hand she held tightly in her own and asked, "Before we go off to do battle with the British, do you think we could eat first? I'm starving."

Phillip chuckled. "Me, too, sweeting, but for something other than food."

A look of mock horror crossed her face. "Does this mean you intend to ravish me? You are the Phantom, after all."

Pulling back the covers, Phillip surveyed her body from head to toe with a look so hot it warmed her far more effectively than the blankets, bringing a bright flush to her skin.

His smile was wicked, when he replied, "Most assuredly, madam. First we'll appease your appetite, then we'll see to mine."

Epilogue

July 4 1782
Fredericksburg, Virginia

Grace MacGregor giggled, running as fast as her chubby little legs would carry her across the lawn toward her mother, who sat on a patchwork quilt beneath a giant oak.

"Come to Mama, lovey," Lottie crooned, motioning the child forward. Her heart filled with love for the child who looked so much like her.

"Will ye look at that?" Ian boasted, gazing proudly at his daughter. "'Tis amazing. Not even a year old and already walking by herself. Me Grace is a clever lass."

"She's clever all right, Mr. MacGregor," Elsie Sheridan agreed. "But my Jamie is the real looker in the family. Why look at those black, curly locks, those big, blue eyes. He's going to be a heartbreaker one day."

Phillip and Danielle exchanged amused glances at the good-natured rivalry that continually occurred between the MacGregors and the Sheridans.

Luther didn't join in the repartee this time. Having opted for a nap, he was sound asleep, and not even the roar of cannonade, marking this country's independence, could rouse him from his slumber.

"Your father sleeps like the dead," Phillip remarked, reaching into the wicker basket to pull out another piece of fried chicken. His fourth, by Danielle's estimation. She watched his eating habits like a hawk. Knowing what he looked like with a paunch, she had no intention of letting him become like his alter ego James Ashland.

Danielle smiled happily, gazing at her extended family who were gathered together in the Cameron's rear yard for a picnic to celebrate Washington's recent victory at York Town over the British General Cornwallis.

The British had been soundly defeated and had surrendered shortly after Danielle and Phillip had arrived in York Town. They were there to witness the spectacle; and it was a sight that Danielle wasn't likely to ever forget.

The struggle for American independence was drawing to a close. It would only be a matter of time before a treaty of peace was signed, formally indicating Great Britain's recognition of its former colonies.

"I can hardly hear the cannon above the roar of your father's snoring," Phillip quipped, forcing Danielle's attention back.

"You'd better be happy he does sleep soundly, Phillip Cameron, or young James wouldn't be here now."

Young James presently crawled into his father's lap, much to Phillip's consternation, when he felt his legs grow wet. He held the child aloft, a pleading look on his face that brought a smile to Danielle's lips.

"Have mercy! The child is leaking like a sieve."

James thought the whole matter quite amusing and produced a toothless smile, melting his mother's heart. She reached out to take him, but he was snatched up by his grandmother.

"I'll do it, Danielle. You just sit down and rest. Jamie and Grandma will be back in a moment."

Danielle watched her mother depart, smiling contentedly. "Thank heavens for Jamie," she remarked, lowering herself to the blanket to sit beside her husband. "He's been a godsend to my mother. She was so distraught after Regina's death; the child has given her something to live for."

Phillip nodded, glancing over at Danielle's father, thinking of the time, shortly after they'd returned, when he'd entered the common room to find Luther weeping quietly over his dead daughter.

"Luther might keep things close to his chest, but he cares deeply. He's as proud as a peacock over his grandson."

"And his son-in-law. Why he's hung that mask of yours on his caged bar for everyone to see. He refers to the common room as the Phantom's Pub now."

"Aye," Phillip said, chuckling. "He offered me a job. Asked me if I wanted to sit and relate my adventures to the customers in the evenings."

"Do you miss it?" Danielle asked.

Phillip had retired his Phantom disguise after the recent victory at York Town and had become "a regular citizen" as Ian put it. Soon they would journey to

York Town to take up residence in Phillip's newly reconstructed house, which was nearly destroyed during the battle.

'Twould be good to put down permanent roots, Danielle thought, but she would miss Fredericksburg and her parents, though they promised to visit frequently. Luther had even talked about relocating to York Town, possibly buying another ordinary. There was a great deal of construction going on there, thanks to the accurate aim of British bombardiers. And, of course, Ian, Lottie, and Mrs. Dunstan would be going with them, which made their leaving easier.

Phillip pulled Danielle onto his lap, startling her out of her reverie. She laughed when he wiggled his eyebrows suggestively and replied to her question, "Do I miss being the Phantom? Only the part where I get to ravish innocent, young virgins."

She slapped him playfully on the arm. "I'm afraid there'll no more virgins for you, Phillip Cameron. You'll have to be content with an old married woman."

"And does this old married woman have a kiss for her husband?" Without waiting for her reply, he planted his lips firmly over hers, kissing her passionately.

Danielle's heart started to pound at the same moment the cannons exploded, but she ignored the noise, knowing with a certainty that the explosions she heard were coming from within.

It was always that way when the Phantom kissed her.

Dear Readers:

Though pavement now covers the cobblestones, the charm and historical significance of Fredericksburg, Virginia shines through.

Many of the houses and buildings depicted in Phantom Lover *still exist: Kenmore, the home of Fielding and Betty Lewis, has often been described as "the most beautiful home in America"; the Mary Washington House on Charles Street; St. George's Church; Hugh Mercer's Apothecary; and the tavern upon which the Golden Pineapple was patterned, the Rising Sun, once owned by Charles Washington, brother to our first president.*

I hope you'll be able to visit my historic community someday and stroll the streets as did George Washington, the marquis de Lafayette, James Monroe, and many other notable figures, including of course my hero and heroine, Phillip Cameron and Danielle Sheridan.

As our chamber of commerce is so fond of saying, "George Washington slept in many places, but he lived here in Fredericksburg."

COMING NEXT MONTH

DREAM TIME by Parris Afton Bonds
A passionate tale of a determined young woman who, because of a scandal, wound up in the untamed Australia of the early 1800s.

ALWAYS . . . by Jeane Renick
Marielle McCleary wants a baby, but her prospects look slim—until she meets handsome actor Tom Saxon. Too late, however, she finds out that Thomas isn't as perfect as he seems. Will she ever have the life she's always wanted?

THE BRIDEGROOM by Carol Jerina
A compelling historical romance set in Texas. Payne Trefarrow's family abandoned him, and he held his identical twin brother Prescott responsible. To exact revenge, Payne planned to take the things his brother loved most—his money and his fiancée.

THE WOMEN OF LIBERTY CREEK
by Marilyn Cunningham
From the author of *Seasons of the Heart*. A sweeping tale of three women's lives and loves and how they are bound together, over the generations, by a small town in Idaho.

LOST TREASURE by Catriona Flynt
A zany romantic adventure set in Northern California at the turn of the century. When her dramatic production went up in smoke, actress Moll Kennedy was forced to take a job to pay her debts—as a schoolteacher doubling as a spy. Then she fell in love with the ruggedly handsome Winslow Fortune, the very man she was spying on.

SAPPHIRE by Venita Helton
An intriguing historical tale of love divided by loyalty. When her clipper ship sank, New Orleans beauty Arienne Lloyd was rescued by handsome Yankee Joshua Langdon. At the very sight of him she was filled with longing, despite her own allegiances to the South. Would Arienne fight to win the heart of her beloved enemy—even if it meant risking everything in which she believed?

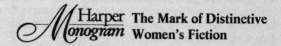 **Harper Monogram** The Mark of Distinctive Women's Fiction